Albert Henry Wratislaw

Sixty Folk-tales

From Exclusively Slavonic Sources

Albert Henry Wratislaw

Sixty Folk-tales
From Exclusively Slavonic Sources

ISBN/EAN: 9783744773416

Printed in Europe, USA, Canada, Australia, Japan

Cover: Foto ©Andreas Hilbeck / pixelio.de

More available books at **www.hansebooks.com**

FROM

EXCLUSIVELY SLAVONIC SOURCES.

Translated,
with Brief Introductions and Notes,

BY

A. H. WRATISLAW, M.A.,
Sometime Fellow and Tutor of Christ's College, Cambridge;
Late Head Master of Felsted and Bury St. Edmund's Schools;
Corresponding Member of the Royal Bohemian Society of Sciences.

LONDON:
ELLIOT STOCK, 62, PATERNOSTER ROW, E.C.
1889.

PREFACE.

So much interest has lately been awakened in, and centred round, Folk-lore, that it needs no apology to lay before the British reader additional information upon the subject. Interesting enough in itself, it has been rendered doubly interesting by the rise and progress of the new science of Comparative Mythology, which has already yielded considerable results, and promises to yield results of still greater magnitude, when all the data requisite for a full and complete induction have been brought under the ken of the inquirer. The stories of most European races have been laid under contribution, but those of the Slavonians have, as yet, been only partially examined. Circumstances have enabled me to make a considerable addition to what is as yet known of Slavonic Folk-lore, although I cannot make any pretence to having exhausted the mine, or, rather, the many mines, which the various Slavonic races and tribes possess, and which still, more or less, await the advent of competent explorers.

In offering to the public a selection of sixty folk-lcre stories translated from exclusively Slavonic sources, it is but fitting to give some account of the work from which I have derived them. In 1865, the late K. J. Erben, the celebrated Archivarius of the old town of Prague, published a 'Citanka,' or reading-book, intended to enable Bohemians to commence the study of all the numerous Slavonic dialects, containing 'one hundred simple national tales and stories, in their original dialects.' To this he appended a vocabulary, with explanations of words and forms strange to, or divergent from, the Bohemian, briefly given in the Bohemian language. This vocabulary is divided into two parts, one illustrating the tales of those Slavonians who make use of the Cyrillic characters, and belong to the Orthodox Greek Church; and the other, those of the Catholic and Protestant Slavonians, who employ alphabets founded on the Latin characters of the West of Europe. Pan Erben paid special attention to the preservation of the simple national forms of speech, as taken down from the lips of the people; and, besides laying printed collections under contribution, obtained several previously unpublished stories.

Beginning with his native tongue, the Bohemian language, he passes on to the closely-allied Moravian and Hungarian-Slovenish (Slovak) dialects, and then takes the Upper and Lower Lusatian, the former of which is related to the old Bohemian, while the latter inclines rather to the Polish language. He next goes on to the Kashubian, a rapidly-perishing sub-dialect of Polish, and then to the Polish tongue itself.

Next comes the White Russian, forming a transition from Polish to Great Russian, whereas the Little Russian in Galicia, the Ukraine, and South Russia, is more nearly allied to the Bohemian than to the White Russian. The ancient Russian language, which was also much allied to the Old Bohemian, is the basis of the present written Russian, and presents a transition to the Bulgarian, which, in the north-west, melts into the Serbian, which again, in its Croatian branch, near Varazdin, approaches most nearly to the Bohemian. The Illyrian-Slovenish of Carinthia, though, in locality, least distant from Bohemia, exhibits forms most removed from the Bohemian language, just as the Upper Lusatian is less allied to the Bohemian than is the locally-distant Kashubian.

I took up the book, originally, for the purpose for which it was compiled, viz., that of obtaining an acquaintance with the main features of all the Slavonic dialects, but found myself tempted, by the extreme beauty of some of the stories, to translate the major portion of them. That I do not present a still larger selection to the reader is due to the fact that so many of the Great Russian *skazkas* have been so admirably translated, edited, and illustrated by my friend —alas! that I must now term him my late friend—Mr. W. R. S. Ralston, that I have scarcely considered them as coming within the sphere of the present work.

For an essay on the singular mythical being, *Kurent*, occurring only in the Serbian tales from Carniola, and as yet unnoticed in any work on Slavonic mythology, I am indebted to Professor Gregor Krek, of Grätz, in Styria. This will be found prefixed to the stories which it illustrates.

I have also prefixed a short introduction, containing various matters of interest, to each set of tales, as they follow each other, according to their different languages, dialects, or sub-dialects.

The table of contents immediately following will give a general view of the stories and their respective sources, arranged under the three heads of: (*a*) The Western Slavonians, (*b*) the Eastern Slavonians, and (*c*) the Southern Slavonians.

CONTENTS.

(N.B.—*Ch* as *ch* in *church.*)

A.—WESTERN SLAVONIANS.

B.—EASTERN SLAVONIANS.

C.—SOUTHERN SLAVONIANS.

CROATIAN STORIES—*continued.*

WESTERN SLAVONIANS.

BOHEMIAN STORIES.

THESE stories are translated from the language of the Slavonic inhabitants of nearly three-fourths of Bohemia, the 'Czechs,' as the Poles write the word, or 'Chekhs,' if we adopt the nearest orthographical approximation to it that the English alphabet allows us to make. This nation had an early literary development, commencing before the foundation of the University of Prague (*Praha*) by the Emperor Charles IV. in 1348. For a long time after that epoch the Bohemians could justly claim the title of the best educated nation in Europe. They produced a prose writer —Thomas of Stitny, whose first original work was published in 1377—whose equal is not to be found in English literature till the age of Queen Elizabeth. In the Thirty Years' War (1620) the people and literature of Bohemia were crushed for more than two centuries, the population being reduced during that terrible war from over four millions to eight hundred thousand.

The Bohemian language itself is a very remarkable one. It possesses both accent and quantity independent of each other, like Latin and Greek. Thus it is difficult for a foreigner to read aloud or to speak, for, if he attends carefully to the accent, he is liable to neglect quantity, and if he attends to quantity, he is likely to slur over the proper accentuation of words. It, as well as Polish, employs a sibillated *r*, which in many words is difficult to pronounce. It also writes semi-vowels, especially *r*, without a vowel; so that many syllables appear as if there were no vowel in them. But this it is sufficient to notice once for all, as it causes no real difficulty in pronunciation.

The fairy-tales relating to the kindly or malevolent superhuman inhabitants of the woods are peculiar and striking. In No. 5 these imaginary beings are represented under the latter, and in No. 6 under the former aspect.

Two waters, one of death and the other of life, are found in the Bohemian stories, just as in the Russian ones—a point wherein the Slavonic tales regularly differ from those of Western Europe, which only acknowledge the water of life. As Mr. Ralston remarks ('Songs of the Russian People,' p. 97): 'When the "dead water" is applied to the wounds of a corpse, it heals them, but before the dead body can be brought to life, it is necessary to sprinkle it with the "living water."'

I.—LONG, BROAD, AND SHARPSIGHT.

THERE was a king, who was already old, and had but one son. Once upon a time he called this son to him, and said to him, 'My dear son! you know that old fruit falls to make room for other fruit. My head is already ripening, and maybe the sun will soon no longer shine upon it; but before you bury me, I should like to see your wife, my future daughter. My son, marry!' The prince said, 'I would gladly, father, do as you wish; but I have no bride, and don't know any.' The old king put his hand into his pocket, took out a golden key and showed it to his son, with the words, 'Go up into the tower, to the top story, look round there, and then tell me which you fancy.' The prince went without delay. Nobody within the memory of man had been up there, or had ever heard what was up there.

When he got up to the last story, he saw in the ceiling a little iron door like a trap-door. It was closed. He opened it with the golden key, lifted it, and went up above it. There there was a large circular room. The ceiling was blue like the sky on a clear night, and silver stars glittered on it; the floor was a carpet of green silk, and around in the wall were twelve high windows in golden frames, and in each window on crystal glass was a damsel painted with the colours of the rainbow, with a royal crown on her head, in each window a different one in a different dress, each handsomer than the other, and it was a wonder that the prince did not let his eyes dwell upon them. When he had gazed at them with astonishment, the damsels began to move as if they were alive, looked down upon him, smiled, and did everything but speak.

Now the prince observed that one of the twelve windows was covered with a white curtain; he drew the curtain to see what was behind it. There there was a damsel in a white dress, girt with a silver girdle, with a crown of pearls on her head; she was the most beautiful of all, but was sad and pale, as if she had risen from the grave. The prince stood long before the picture, as if he had made a discovery, and as he thus gazed, his heart pained him, and he cried, 'This one will I have, and no other.' As he said the words the damsel bowed her head, blushed like a rose, and that instant all the pictures disappeared.

When he went down and related to his father what he had seen and which damsel he had selected, the old king became sad, bethought himself, and said, 'You have done ill, my son, in uncovering what was curtained over, and have placed yourself in great danger on account of those words. That damsel is in the power of a wicked wizard, and kept captive in an iron castle; of all who have attempted to set her free, not one has hitherto returned. But what's done cannot be undone; the plighted word is a law. Go! try your luck, and return home safe and sound!'

The prince took leave of his father, mounted his horse, and rode away in search of his bride. It came to pass that he rode through a vast forest, and through the forest he rode on and on till he lost the road. And as he was wandering with his horse in thickets and amongst rocks and morasses, not knowing which way to turn, he heard somebody shout behind him, 'Hi! stop!' The prince looked round, and saw a tall man hastening after him. 'Stop and take me with you, and take me into your service, and you won't regret it!' 'Who are you,' said the prince, 'and what can you do?' 'My name is Long, and I can extend myself. Do you see a bird's nest in that pine yonder? I will bring you the nest down without having to climb up.'

Long then began to extend himself; his body grew rapidly till it was as tall as the pine; he then reached the nest, and in a moment contracted himself again and gave it to the prince. 'You know your business well, but what's the use of birds' nests to me, if you can't conduct me out of this forest?' 'Ahem! that's an easy matter,' said Long, and began to extend himself till he was thrice as high as the highest fir in the forest, looked round, and said: 'Here on this side we have the nearest way out of the forest.' He then contracted himself, took the horse by the bridle, and before the prince had any idea of it, they were beyond the forest. Before them was a long and wide plain, and beyond the plain tall gray rocks, like the walls of a large town, and mountains overgrown with forest trees.

'Yonder, sir, goes my comrade!' said Long, and pointed suddenly to the plain; 'you should take him also into your service; I believe he would serve you well.' 'Shout to him, and call him hither, that I may see what he is good for.' 'It is a little too far, sir,' said Long; 'he would hardly hear me, and it would take a long time before he came, because he has a great deal to carry. I'll jump after him instead.' Then Long again extended himself to such a height that his head plunged into the clouds, made two or three steps, took his comrade by the arm, and placed him before the prince. He was a short, thick-set fellow, with a paunch like a sixty-four gallon cask. 'Who are you?' demanded the prince, 'and what can you do?' 'My name, sir, is Broad; I can widen myself.' 'Give me a specimen.' 'Ride quick, sir, quick, back into the forest!' cried Broad, as he began to blow himself out.

The prince didn't understand why he was to ride away; but seeing that Long made all haste to get into the forest, he spurred his horse, and rode full gallop after him. It was high time that he did ride away, or else Broad would have squashed him, horse and all, as his paunch rapidly grew in all directions; it filled everything everywhere, just as if a mountain had rolled up. Broad then ceased to blow himself out, and took himself in again, raising such a wind that the trees in the forest bowed and bent, and became what he was at first. 'You've played me a nice trick,' said the prince, 'but I shan't find such a fellow every day; come with me.'

They proceeded further. When they approached the rocks, they met a man who had his eyes bandaged with a handkerchief. 'Sir, this is our third comrade,' said Long, 'you ought to take him also into your service. I'm sure he won't eat his victuals for naught.' 'Who are you?' the prince asked him, 'and why are your eyes bandaged? You don't see your way!' 'No, sir, quite the contrary! It is just because I see too well that I am obliged to bandage my eyes; I see with bandaged eyės just as well as others with unbandaged eyes; and if I unbandage them I look everything through and through, and when I gaze sharply at anything, it catches fire and bursts into flame, and what can't burn splits into pieces. For this reason my name is Sharpsight.' He then turned to a rock opposite, removed the bandage, and fixed his flaming eyes upon it; the rock began to crackle, pieces flew on every side, and in a very short time nothing of it remained but a heap of sand, on which something glittered like fire. Sharpsight went to fetch it, and brought it to the prince. It was pure gold.

'Heigho! you're a fellow that money can't purchase!' said the prince. 'He is a fool who wouldn't make use of your services, and if you have such good sight, look and tell me whether it is far to the iron castle, and what is now going on there?' 'If you rode by yourself, sir,' answered Sharpsight, 'maybe you wouldn't get there within a year; but with us you'll arrive to-day—they're just getting supper ready for us.' 'And what is my bride doing?'

'An iron lattice is before her,
In a tower that's high
She doth sit and sigh,
A wizard watch and ward keeps o'er her.'

The prince cried, 'Whoever is well disposed, help me to set her free!' They all promised to help him. They guided him among the gray rocks through the breach that Sharpsight had made in them with his eyes, and further and further on through rocks, through high mountains and deep forests, and wherever there was any obstacle in the road, forthwith it was removed by the three comrades. And when the sun was declining towards the west, the mountains began to become lower, the forests less dense, and the rocks concealed themselves amongst the heath; and when it was almost on the point of setting, the prince saw not far before him an iron castle; and when it was actually setting, he rode by an iron bridge to the gate, and as soon as it had set, up rose the iron bridge of itself, the gate closed with a single movement, and the prince and his companions were captives in the iron castle.

When they had looked round in the court, the prince put his horse up in the stable, where everything was ready for it, and then they went into the castle. In the court, in the stable, in the castle hall, and in the rooms, they saw in the twilight many richly-dressed people, gentlemen and servants, but not one of them stirred—they were all turned to stone. They went through several rooms, and came into the supper-room. This was brilliantly lighted up, and in the midst was a table, and on it plenty of good meats and drinks, and covers were laid for four persons. They waited and waited, thinking that someone would come; but when nobody came for a long time, they sat down and ate and drank what the palate fancied.

When they had done eating, they looked about to find where to sleep. Thereupon the door flew open unexpectedly all at once, and into the room came the wizard; a bent old man in a long black garb, with a bald head, a gray beard down to his knees, and three iron hoops instead of a girdle. By the hand he led a beautiful, very beautiful damsel, dressed in white; she had a silver girdle round her waist, and a crown of pearls on her head, but was pale and sad, as if she had risen from the grave. The prince recognised her at once, sprang forward, and went to meet her; but before he could utter a word the wizard addressed him: 'I know for what you have come; you want to take the princess away. Well, be it so! Take her, if you can keep her in sight for three nights, so that she doesn't vanish from you.

If she vanishes, you will be turned into stone as well as your three servants; like all who have come before you.' He then motioned the princess to a seat and departed.

The prince could not take his eyes off the princess, so beautiful was she. He began to talk to her, and asked her all manner of questions, but she neither answered nor smiled, nor looked at anyone any more than if she had been of marble. He sat down by her, and determined not to sleep all night long lest she should vanish from him, and, to make surer, Long extended himself like a strap, and wound himself round the whole room along the wall; Broad posted himself in the doorway, swelled himself up, and stopped it up so tight that not even a mouse could have slipped through; while Sharpsight placed himself against a pillar in the midst of the room on the look-out. But after a time they all began to nod, fell asleep, and slept the whole night, just as if the wizard had thrown them into the water.

In the morning, when it began to dawn, the prince was the first to wake, but—as if a knife had been thrust into his heart—the princess was gone! He forthwith awoke his servants, and asked what was to be done. 'Never mind, sir,' said Sharpsight, and looked sharply out through the window, 'I see her already. A hundred miles hence is a forest, in the midst of the forest an old oak, and on the top of the oak an acorn, and she is that acorn.' Long immediately took him on his shoulders, extended himself, and went ten miles at a step, while Sharpsight showed him the way.

No more time elapsed than would have been wanted to move once round a cottage before they were back again, and Long delivered the acorn to the prince. 'Sir, let it fall on the ground.' The prince let it fall, and that moment the princess stood beside him. And when the sun began to show itself beyond the mountains, the folding doors flew open with a crash, and the wizard entered the room and smiled spitefully; but when he saw the princess he frowned, growled, and bang! one of the iron hoops which he wore splintered and sprang off him. He then took the damsel by the hand and led her away.

The whole day after the prince had nothing to do but walk up and down the castle, and round about the castle, and look at the wonderful things that were there. It was everywhere as if life had been lost in a single moment. In one hall he saw a prince, who held in both hands a brandished sword, as if he intended to cleave somebody in twain; but the blow never fell: he had been turned into stone. In one chamber was a knight turned into stone, just as if he had been fleeing from some one in terror, and, stumbling on the threshold, had taken a downward direction, but not fallen. Under the chimney sat a servant, who held in one hand a piece of roast meat, and with the other lifted a mouthful towards his mouth, which never reached it; when it was just in front of his mouth, he had also been turned to stone. Many others he saw there turned to stone, each in the position in which he was when the wizard said, 'Be turned into stone.' He likewise saw many fine horses turned to stone, and in the castle and round the castle all was desolate and dead; there were trees, but without leaves; there were meadows, but without grass; there was a river, but it did not flow; nowhere was there even a singing bird, or a flower, the offspring of the ground, or a white fish in the water.

Morning, noon, and evening the prince and his companions found good and abundant entertainment in the castle; the viands came of themselves, the wine poured itself out. After supper the folding doors opened again, and the wizard brought in the princess for the prince to guard. And although they all determined to exert themselves with all their might not to fall asleep, yet it was of no use, fall asleep again they did. And when the prince awoke at dawn and saw the princess had vanished, he jumped up and pulled Sharpsight by the arm, 'Hey! get up, Sharpsight, do you know where the princess is?' He rubbed his eyes, looked, and said, 'I see her. There's a mountain 200 miles off, and in the mountain a rock, and in the rock a precious stone, and she's that precious stone. If Long carries me thither, we shall obtain her.'

Long took him at once on his shoulders, extended himself, and went twenty miles at a step. Sharpsight fixed his flaming eyes on the mountain, the mountain crumbled, and the rock in it split into a thousand pieces, and amongst them glittered the precious stone. They took it up and brought it to the prince, and when he let it fall on the ground, the princess again stood there. When afterwards the wizard came and saw her there, his eyes flashed with spite, and bang! again an iron hoop cracked upon him and flew off. He growled and led the princess out of the room.

That day all was again as it had been the day before. After supper the wizard brought the princess in again, looked the prince keenly in the face, and scornfully uttered the words, 'It will be seen who's a match for whom; whether you are victorious or I,' and with that he departed. This day they all exerted themselves still more to avoid going to sleep. They wouldn't even sit down, they wanted to walk about all night long, but all in vain; they were bewitched; one fell asleep after the other as he walked, and the princess vanished away from them.

In the morning the prince again awoke earliest, and when he didn't see the princess, woke Sharpsight. 'Hey! get up, Sharpsight! look where the princess is!' Sharpsight looked out for a long time. 'Oh sir,' says he, 'she is a long way off, a long way off! Three hundred miles off is a black sea, and in the midst of the sea a shell on the bottom, and in the shell is a gold ring, and she's the ring. But never mind! we shall obtain her, but to-day Long must take Broad with him as well; we shall want him.' Long took Sharpsight on one shoulder, and Broad on the other, and went thirty miles at a step. When they came to the black sea, Sharpsight showed him where he must reach into the water for the shell. Long extended his hand as far as he could, but could not reach the bottom.

'Wait, comrades! wait only a little and I'll help you,' said Broad, and swelled himself out as far as his paunch would stretch; he then lay down on the shore and drank. In a very short time the water fell so low that Long easily reached the bottom and took the shell out of the sea. Out of it he extracted the ring, took his comrades on his shoulders, and hastened back. But on the way he found it a little difficult to run with Broad, who had half a sea of water inside him, so he cast him from his shoulder on to the ground in a wide valley. Thump he went like a sack let fall from a tower, and in a moment the whole valley was under water like a vast lake. Broad himself barely crawled out of it.

Meanwhile the prince was in great trouble in the castle. The dawn began to display itself over the mountains, and his servants had not returned; the more brilliantly the rays ascended, the greater was his anxiety; a deadly perspiration came out upon his forehead. Soon the sun showed itself in the east like a thin strip of flame—and then with a loud crash the door flew open, and on the threshold stood the wizard. He looked round the room, and seeing the princess was not there, laughed a hateful laugh and entered the room. But just at that moment, pop! the window flew in pieces, the gold ring fell on the floor, and in an instant there stood the princess again. Sharpsight, seeing what was going on in the castle, and in what danger his master was, told Long. Long made a step, and threw the ring through the window into the room. The wizard roared with rage, till the castle quaked, and then bang! went the third iron hoop that was round his waist, and sprang off him; the wizard turned into a raven, and flew out and away through the shattered window.

Then, and not till then, did the beautiful damsel speak and thank the prince for setting her free, and blushed like a rose. In the castle and round the castle everything became alive again at once. He who was holding in the hall the outstretched sword, swung it into the air, which whistled again, and then returned it to its sheath; he who was stumbling on the threshold, fell on the ground, but immediately got up again and felt his nose to see whether it was still entire; he who was sitting under the chimney put the piece of meat into his mouth and went on eating; and thus everybody completed what he had begun doing, and at the point where he had left off. In the stables the horses merrily stamped and snorted, the trees round the castle became green like periwinkles, the meadows were full of variegated flowers, high in the air warbled the skylark, and abundance of small fishes appeared in the clear river. Everywhere was life, everywhere enjoyment.

Meanwhile a number of gentlemen assembled in the room where the prince was, and all thanked him for their liberation. But he said, 'You have nothing to thank me for; if it had not been for my trusty servants Long, Broad, and Sharpsight, I too should have been what you were.' He then immediately started on his way home to the old king, his father, with his bride and servants. On the way they met Broad and took him with them.

The old king wept for joy at the success of his son; he had thought he would return no more. Soon afterwards there was a grand wedding, the festivities of which lasted three weeks; all the gentlemen that the prince had liberated were invited. After the wedding Long, Broad, and Sharpsight announced to the young king that they were going again into the world to look for work. The young king tried to persuade them to stay with him. 'I will give you everything you want, as long as you live,' said he; 'you needn't work at all.' But they didn't like such an idle life, took leave of him, went away and have been ever since knocking about somewhere or other in the world.

This story appears to me to be the perfection of 'Natural Science in Allegory.' It is not a mere 'Natur-myth,' exhibiting the contests, victories, and defeats of the forces of Nature. In interpreting it we must distinguish between the mere machinery and the essential actors. The king's son does nothing himself, and the whole work is performed by the three men, whom he takes into his service. I understand by the king's son Man, who wishes to cultivate the earth, who is the princess imprisoned by the enchanter, the drought. She is released by the agency of the three phenomena that usher in the rainy season, the rainbow (Long), the cloud (Broad), and the lightning (Sharpsight). Man, by the aid of these three phenomena, is enabled to cultivate the earth. Such a story could only originate in a country of periodic rains. The rapid recovery of vegetation and almost instantaneous reappearance of fish in dried-up brooks in India are well known. The common story of the Sleeping Beauty is evidently a fragment from the myth which exhibits figuratively the speedy wake up of all things when released from the bondage of the drought.

It is possible also to consider the prince as the sun, who cannot marry the drought-enslaved earth, until he has taken into his service and obtained the aid of the same three phenomena. Those who had previously attempted to set the princess free would then be the suns immediately preceding the rainy season, which had not had the aid of Long, Broad, and Sharpsight.

II.—'THE THREE GOLDEN HAIRS OF GRANDFATHER ALLKNOW.'

THERE was once upon a time a king who delighted in hunting wild animals in forests. One day he chased a stag to a great distance and lost his way. He was all alone; night came on, and the king was only too glad to find a cottage in a clearing. A charcoal-burner lived there. The king asked him whether he would guide him out of the forest to the road, promising to pay him well for it. 'I would gladly go with you,' said the charcoal-burner, 'but, you see, my wife is expecting; I cannot go away. And whither would you go at this time of night? Lie down on some hay on the garret floor, and to-morrow morning I will be your guide.' Soon afterwards a baby boy was born to the charcoal-burner. The king was lying on the floor and couldn't sleep. At midnight he observed a kind of light in the keeping-room below. He peeped through a chink in the boarding and saw the charcoal-burner asleep, his wife lying in a dead faint, and three old hags, all in white, standing by the baby, each with a lighted taper in her hand. The first said: 'My gift to this boy is, that he shall come into great dangers.' The second said: 'My gift to him is, that he shall escape from them all and live long.' And the third said: 'And I give him to wife the baby daughter who has this day been born to that king who is lying upstairs on the hay.' Thereupon the hags put out their tapers, and all was still again. They were the Fates.

The king felt as if a sword had been thrust into his breast. He didn't sleep till morning, thinking over what to do, and how to do it, to prevent that coming to pass which he had heard. When day dawned the child began to cry. The charcoal-burner got up and saw that his wife had gone to sleep for ever. 'Oh, my poor little orphan!' whimpered he; 'what shall I do with you now?' 'Give me the baby,' said the king; 'I'll take care that it shall be well with it, and will give you so much money that you needn't burn charcoal as long as you live.' The charcoal-burner was delighted at this, and the king promised to send for the baby. When he arrived at his palace they told him, with great joy, that a beautiful baby-daughter had been born to him on such and such a night. It was the very night on which he saw the three Fates. The king frowned, called one of his servants, and told him: 'Go to such a place in the forest; a charcoal-burner lives there in a cottage. Give him this money, and he will give you a little child. Take the child and drown it on your way back. If you don't drown it, you shall drink water yourself.' The servant went, took the baby and put it into a basket, and when he came to a narrow foot-bridge, under which flowed a deep and broad river, he threw the basket and all into the water. 'Good-night, uninvited son-in-law!' said the king, when the servant told him what he had done.

The king thought that the baby was drowned, but it wasn't. It floated in the water in the basket as if it had been its cradle, and slept as if the river were singing to it, till it floated down to a fisherman's cottage. The fisherman was sitting by the bank mending his net. He saw something floating down the river, jumped into his boat, and went to catch it, and out of the water he drew the baby in the basket. He carried it to his wife, and said: 'You've always wanted a little son, and here you have one. The water has brought him to us.' The fisherman's wife was delighted, and brought up the child as her own. They named him 'Floatling' (*Plavączek*), because he had floated to them on the water.

The river flowed on and years passed on, and from a boy he became a handsome youth, the like of whom was not to be found far and wide. One day in the summer it came to pass that the king rode that way all alone. It was hot, and he was thirsty, and beckoned to the fisherman to give him a little fresh water. When Floatling brought it to him, the king looked at him with astonishment. 'You've a fine lad, fisherman!' said he; 'is he your son?' 'He is and he isn't,' replied the fisherman; 'just twenty years ago he floated, as a little baby, down the river in a basket, and we brought him up.' A mist came before the king's eyes; he became as pale as a whitewashed wall, perceiving that it was the child he had ordered to be drowned. But he soon recollected himself, sprang from his horse, and said: 'I want a messenger to my palace, and have nobody with me: can this youth go thither for me?' 'Your majesty has but to command and the lad will go,' said the fisherman. The king sat down and wrote a letter to his queen: 'Cause this young man whom I send you to be run through with a sword at once; he is a dangerous enemy of mine. Let it be done before I return. Such is my will.' He then folded the letter, fastened and sealed it with his signet.

Floatling started at once with the letter. He had to go through a great forest, but missed the road and lost his way. He went from thicket to thicket till it began to grow dark. Then he met an old hag, who said to him: 'Whither are you going, Floatling?' 'I am going with a letter to the king's palace, and have lost my way. Can't you tell me, mother, how to get into the right road?' 'Anyhow, you won't get there to-day,' said the hag; 'it's dark. Stay the night with me. You won't be with a stranger. I am your godmother.' The young man allowed himself to be persuaded, and they hadn't gone many paces when they saw before them a pretty little house, just as if it had grown all at once out of the ground. In the night, when the lad was asleep, the hag took the letter out of his pocket and put another in its place, in which it was written thus: 'Cause this young man whom I send you to be married to our daughter at once; he is my destined son-in-law. Let it be done before I return. Such is my will.'

When the queen read the letter, she immediately ordered arrangements to be made for the wedding, and neither she nor the young princess could gaze enough at the bridegroom, so delighted were they with him; and Floatling was similarly delighted with his royal bride. Some days after, the king came home, and when he found what had happened, he was violently enraged at his queen for what she had done. 'Anyhow, you ordered me yourself to have him married to our daughter before you returned,' answered the queen, and gave him the letter. The king took the letter and looked it through—writing, seal, paper, everything was his own. He had his son-in-law called, and questioned him about what had happened on his way to the palace.

Floatling related how he had started and had lost his way in the forest, and stayed the night with his old godmother. 'What did she look like?' 'So and so.' The king perceived from his statement that it was the same person that had, twenty years before, assigned his daughter to the charcoal-burner's son. He thought and thought, and then he said: 'What's done can't be altered; still, you can't be my son-in-law for nothing. If you want to have my daughter, you must bring me for a dowry three golden hairs of Grandfather Allknow.' He thought to himself that he should thus be quit of his distasteful son-in-law.

Floatling took leave of his bride and went—which way, and whither? I don't know; but, as a Fate was his godmother, it was easy for him to find the right road. He went far and wide, over hills and dales, over fords and rivers, till he came to a black sea. There he saw a boat, and in it a ferryman. 'God bless you, old ferryman!' 'God grant it, young pilgrim! Whither are you travelling?' 'To Grandfather Allknow, for three golden hairs.' 'Ho, ho! I have long been waiting for such a messenger. For twenty years I've been ferrying here, and nobody's come to set me free. If you promise me to ask Grandfather Allknow when the end of my work will be, I will ferry you over.' Floatling promised, and the ferryman ferried him across.

After this he came to a great city, but it was decayed and sad. In front of the city he met an old man, who had a staff in his hand, and could scarcely crawl. 'God bless you, aged grandfather!' 'God grant it, handsome youth! Whither are you going?' 'To Grandfather Allknow, for three golden hairs.' 'Ah! ah! we've long been waiting for some such messenger; I must at once conduct you to our lord the king.' When they got there the king said: 'I hear that you are going on an errand to Grandfather Allknow. We had an apple-tree here that bore youth-producing apples. If anybody ate one, though he were on the brink of the grave, he got young again, and became like a young man. But for the last twenty years our apple-tree has produced no fruit. If you promise me to ask Grandfather Allknow whether there is any help for us, I will requite you royally.' Floatling promised, and the king dismissed him graciously.

After that he came again to another great city, which was half ruined. Not far from the city a son was burying his deceased father, and tears, like peas, were rolling down his cheek. 'God bless you, mournful grave-digger!' said Floatling. 'God grant it, good pilgrim! Whither are you going?' 'I am going to Grandfather Allknow, for three golden hairs.' 'To Grandfather Allknow? It's a pity you didn't come sooner! But our king has long been waiting for some such messenger; I must conduct you to him.' When they got there, the king said: 'I hear that you are going on an errand to Grandfather Allknow. We had a well here, out of which sprang living water; if anybody drank it, even were he at the point of death, he would get well at once; nay, were he already a corpse, if this water were sprinkled upon him, he would immediately rise up and walk. But for the last twenty years the water has ceased to flow. If you promise me to ask Grandfather Allknow whether there is any help for us, I will give you a royal reward.' Floatling promised, and the king dismissed him graciously.

After this he went far and wide through a black forest, and in the midst of that forest espied a large green meadow, full of beautiful flowers, and in it a golden palace. This was Grandfather Allknow's palace; it glittered as if on fire. Floatling went into the palace, but found nobody there but an old hag sitting and spinning in a corner. 'Welcome, Floatling!' said she; 'I am delighted to see you again.' It was his godmother, at whose house he had spent the night when he was carrying the letter. 'What has brought you here?' 'The king would not allow me to be his son-in-law for nothing, so he sent me for three golden hairs of Grandfather Allknow.' The hag smiled, and said: 'Grandfather Allknow is my son, the bright Sun; in the morning he is a little lad, at noon a grown man, and in the evening an old grandfather. I will provide you with the three golden hairs from his golden head, that I too mayn't be your godmother for nothing. But, my boy! you can't remain as you are. My son is certainly a good soul, but when he comes home hungry in the evening, it might easily happen that he might roast and eat you for his supper. Yonder is an empty tub; I will cover you over with it.' Floatling begged her also to question Grandfather Allknow about the three things concerning which he had promised on the road to bring answers. 'I will,' said the hag, 'and do you give heed to what he says.'

All at once a wind arose outside and in flew the Sun, an old grandfather with a golden head, by the west window into the room. 'A smell, a smell of human flesh!' says he; 'have you anybody here, mother?' 'Star of the day! whom could I have here without your seeing him? But so it is; you're all day long flying over God's world, and your nose is filled with the scent of human flesh; so it's no wonder that you still smell it when you come home in the evening.' The old man said nothing in reply, and sat down to his supper.

After supper he laid his golden head on the hag's lap and began to slumber. As soon as she saw that he was sound asleep, she pulled out a golden hair and threw it on the ground. It rang like a harp-string. 'What do you want, mother?' said the old man. 'Nothing, sonny, nothing! I was asleep, and had a marvellous dream.' 'What did you dream about?' 'I dreamt about a city, where they had a spring of living water; when anybody was ill and drank of it, he got well again; and if he died and was sprinkled with this water, he came to life again. But for the last twenty years the water has ceased to flow; is there any help that it may flow again?' 'Quite easy; there's a toad sitting on the spring in the well that won't let the water flow. Let them kill the toad and clean out the well; the water will flow as before.' When the old man fell asleep again, the hag pulled out a second golden hair and threw it on the ground. 'What ails you again, mother?' 'Nothing, sonny, nothing; I was asleep, and again had a marvellous dream. I dreamt of a city where they had an apple-tree which bore youth-restoring apples; when anybody grew old and ate one he became young again. But for the last twenty years the apple-tree has borne no fruit; is there any help?' 'Quite easy; under the tree there lies a snake that exhausts its powers; let them kill the snake and transplant the apple-tree; it will bear fruit as before.' The old man then fell asleep again, and the hag pulled out a third golden hair. 'Why won't you let me sleep, mother?' said the old man crossly, and wanted to get up. 'Lie still, sonny, lie still! Don't be angry, I didn't want to wake you. But a heavy sleep fell upon me, and I had another marvellous dream. I dreamt of a ferry-man on a black sea; for twenty years he has been ferrying across it, and no one has come to set him free. When will his work have an end?' 'He's the son of a stupid mother. Let him give the oar into another person's hand and jump ashore himself; the other will be ferryman in his stead. But let me be quiet now; I must get up early to-morrow and go to dry the tears which the king's daughter sheds every night for her husband, the charcoal-burner's son, whom the king has sent for three golden hairs of mine.'

In the morning a wind again arose outside, and on the lap of its old mother awoke, instead of the old man, a beautiful golden-haired child, the divine Sun, who bade farewell to his mother and flew out by the east window. The hag turned up the tub and said to Floatling: 'There are the three golden hairs for you, and you also know what Grandfather Allknow has answered to those three things. Go; and good-bye! You will see me no more; there is no need of it.' Floatling thanked the hag gratefully, and departed.

When he came to the first city, the king asked him what news he brought him. 'Good news,' said Floatling. 'Have the well cleaned out, and kill the toad which sits on the spring, and the water will flow again as aforetime.' The king had this done without delay, and when he saw the water bubbling up with a full stream, he presented Floatling with twelve horses white as swans, and on them as much gold and silver as they could carry.

When he came to the second city the king asked him again what news he brought. 'Good news!' said Floatling. Have the apple-tree dug up; you will find a snake under the roots; kill it; then plant the apple-tree again, and it will bear fruit as aforetime.' The king had this done at once, and during the night the apple-tree was clothed with bloom, just as if it had been bestrewn with roses. The king was delighted, and presented Floatling with twelve horses as black as ravens, and on them as much riches as they could carry.

Floatling travelled on, and when he came to the black sea, the ferryman asked him whether he had learnt when he would be liberated. 'I have,' said Floatling. 'But ferry me over first, and then I will tell you.' The ferryman objected, but when he saw that there was nothing else to be done, he ferried him over with his four-and-twenty horses. 'Before you ferry anybody over again,' said Floatling, 'put the oar into his hand and jump ashore, and he will be ferryman in your stead.'

The king didn't believe his eyes when Floatling brought him the three golden hairs of Grandfather Allknow; and his daughter wept, not from sorrow, but from joy at his return. 'But where did you get these beautiful horses and this great wealth?' asked the king. 'I earned it,' said Floatling; and related how he had helped one king again to the youth-restoring apples, which make young people out of old ones; and another to the living water, which makes sick people well and dead people living. 'Youth - restoring apples! living water!' repeated the king quietly to himself. 'If I ate one I should become young again; and if I died I should be restored to life by that water.' Without delay he started on the road for the youth-restoring apples and the living water—and hasn't returned yet.

Thus the charcoal-burner's son became the king's son-in-law, as the Fate decreed; and as for the king, maybe he is still ferrying across the black sea.

This story is a variant of Grimm's 'Giant with the Three Golden Hairs.' But, whereas in Grimm there is nothing to indicate who the giant is, or whether he has three golden hairs and three only, in the Bohemian tale it is plain that 'Grandfather Allknow' is the Sun, and that the three golden hairs are three sunbeams.

III.—GOLDENHAIR.

THERE was a king who was so clever that he understood all animals, and knew what they said to each other. Hear how he learnt it. Once upon a time there came to him a little old woman, who brought him a snake in a basket, and told him to have it cooked for him; if he dined off it, he would understand what any animal in the air, on the earth, or in the water said. The king liked the idea of understanding what nobody else understood, paid the old woman well, and forthwith ordered his servant to cook the fish for dinner. 'But,' said he, 'be sure you don't take a morsel of it even on your tongue, else you shall pay for it with your head.'

George, the servant, thought it odd that the king forbade him so energetically to do this. 'In my life I never saw such a fish,' said he to himself; 'it looks just like a snake! And what sort of cook would that be who didn't take a taste of what he was cooking?' When it was cooked, he took a morsel on his tongue, and tasted it. Thereupon he heard something buzzing round his ears: 'Some for us, too!

some for us, too!' George looked round, and saw nothing but some flies that were flying about in the kitchen. Again somebody called with a hissing voice in the street outside: 'Where are you going? where are you going?' And shriller voices answered: 'To the miller's barley! to the miller's barley!' George peeped through the window, and saw a gander and a flock of geese. 'Aha!' said he; 'that's the kind of fish it is.' Now he knew what it was. He hastily thrust one more morsel into his mouth, and carried the snake to the king as if nothing had happened.

After dinner the king ordered George to saddle the horses and accompany him, as he wished to take a ride. The king rode in front and George behind. As they were riding over a green meadow, George's horse bounded and began to neigh. 'Ho! ho! brother. I feel so light that I should like to jump over mountains!' 'As for that,' said the other, 'I should like to jump about, too, but there's an old man on my back; if I were to skip, he'd tumble on the ground like a sack and break his neck.' 'Let him break it—what matter?' said George's horse; 'instead of an old man you'll carry a young one.' George laughed heartily at this conversation, but so quietly that the king knew nothing about it. But the king also understood perfectly well what the horses were saying to each other, looked round, and seeing a smile on George's face, asked him what he was laughing at. 'Nothing, your illustrious majesty,' said George in excuse; 'only something occurred to my mind.' Nevertheless, the old king already suspected him, neither did he feel confidence in the horses, so he turned and rode back home.

When they arrived at the palace, the king ordered George to pour him out a glass of wine. 'But your head for it,' said he, 'if you don't pour it full, or if you pour it so that it runs over.' George took the decanter and poured. Just then in flew two birds through the window; one was chasing the other, and the one that was trying to get away carried three golden hairs in its beak. 'Give them to me!' said the first; 'they are mine.' 'I shan't; they're mine; I took them up.' 'But I saw them fall, when the golden-haired maiden was combing her hair. At any rate, give me two.' 'Not one!' Hereupon the other bird made a rush, and seized the golden hairs. As they struggled for them on the wing, one remained in each bird's beak, and the third golden hair fell on the ground, where it rang again. At this moment George looked round at it, and then poured the wine over. 'You've forfeited your life!' shouted the king; 'but I'll deal mercifully with you if you obtain the golden-haired maiden, and bring her me to wife.'

What was George to do? If he wanted to save his life, he must go in search of the maiden, though he did not know where to look for her. He saddled his horse, and rode at random. He came to a black forest, and there, under the forest by the roadside, a bush was burning; some cowherd had set it on fire. Under the bush was an ant-hill; sparks were falling on it, and the ants were fleeing in all directions with their little white eggs. 'Help, George, help!' cried they mournfully; 'we're being burnt to death, as well as our young ones in the eggs.' He got down from his horse at once, cut away the bush, and put out the fire. 'When you are in trouble think of us, and we'll help you.'

He rode on through the forest, and came to a lofty pine. On the top of this pine was a raven's nest, and below, on the ground, were two young ravens crying and complaining: 'Our father and mother have flown away; we've got to seek food for ourselves, and we poor little birds can't fly yet. Help us, George, help us! Feed us, or we shall die of hunger!' George did not stop long to consider, but jumped down from his horse, and thrust his sword into its side, that the young ravens might have something to eat. 'When you are in need think of us, and we'll help you.'

After this, George had to go on on foot. He walked a long, long way through the forest, and when he at last got out of it, he saw before him a long and broad sea. On the shore of this sea two fishermen were quarrelling. They had caught a large golden fish in their net, and each wanted to have it for himself. 'The net is mine, and mine's the fish.' The other replied: 'Much good would your net have been, if it hadn't been for my boat and my help.' 'If we catch such another fish again, it will be yours.' 'Not so; wait you for the next, and give me this.' 'I'll set you at one,' said George. 'Sell me the fish—I'll pay you well for it—and you divide the money between you, share and share alike.' He gave them all the money that the king had given him for his journey, leaving nothing at all for himself. The fishermen were delighted, and George let the fish go again into the sea. It splashed merrily through the water, dived, and then, not far from the shore, put out its head: 'When you want me, George, think of me, and I'll requite you.' It then disappeared. 'Where are you going?' the fishermen asked George. 'I'm going for the golden-haired maiden to be the bride of the old king, my lord, and I don't even know where to look for her.' 'We can tell you all about her,' said the fishermen. 'It's Goldenhair, the king's daughter, of the Crystal Palace, on the island yonder. Every day at dawn she combs her golden hair, and the bright gleam therefrom goes over sky and over sea. If you wish it, we'll take you over to the island ourselves, as you set us at one again so nicely. But take care to bring away the right maiden; there are twelve maidens—the king's daughters—but only one has golden hair.'

When George was on the island, he went into the Crystal

Palace to entreat the king to give the king, his lord, his golden-haired daughter to wife. 'I will,' said the king, 'but you must earn her; you must in three days perform three tasks, which I shall impose upon you, each day one. Meanwhile, you can rest till to-morrow.' Next day, early, the king said to him: 'My Goldenhair had a necklace of costly pearls; the necklace broke, and the pearls were scattered in the long grass in the green meadow. You must collect all these pearls, without one being wanting.' George went into the meadow; it was long and broad; he knelt on the grass, and began to seek. He sought and sought from morn to noon, but never saw a pearl. 'Ah! if my ants were here, they might help me.' 'Here we are to help you,' said the ants, running in every direction, but always crowding round him. 'What do you want?' 'I have to collect pearls in this meadow, but I don't see one.' 'Only wait a bit, we'll collect them for you.' Before long they brought him a multitude of pearls out of the grass, and he had nothing to do but string them on the necklace. Afterwards, when he was going to fasten up the necklace, one more ant limped up—it was lame, its foot had been scorched when the fire was at the ant-hill—and cried out: 'Stop, George, don't fasten it up; I'm bringing you one more pearl.'

When George brought the pearls to the king, the king counted them over; not one was wanting. 'You have done your business well,' said he; 'to-morrow I shall give you another piece of work.' In the morning George came, and the king said to him: 'My Goldenhair was bathing in the sea, and lost there a gold ring; you must find and bring it.' George went to the sea, and walked sorrowfully along the shore. The sea was clear, but so deep that he couldn't even see the bottom, much less could he seek and find the ring there. 'Oh that my golden fish were here; it might be able to help me.' Whereupon something glittered in the sea, and up swam the golden fish from the deep to the surface of the water: 'Here I am to help you; what do you want?' 'I've got to find a gold ring in the sea, and I can't even see the bottom.' 'I just met a pike which was carrying a gold ring in its mouth. Only wait a bit, I'll bring it to you.' Ere long it returned from the deep water, and brought him the pike, ring and all.

The king commended George for doing his business well, and then next morning laid upon him the third task: 'If you wish me to give your king my Goldenhair to wife, you must bring her the waters of death and of life—she will require them.' George did not know whither to betake himself for these waters, and went at haphazard hither and thither, whither his feet carried him, till he came to a black forest: 'Ah, if my young ravens were here, perhaps they would help me.' Now there was a rustling over his head, and two young ravens appeared above him: 'Here we are to help you; what do you wish?' 'I've got to bring the waters of death and of life, and I don't know where to look for them.' 'Oh, we know them well; only wait a bit, we'll bring them to you.' After a short time they each brought George a bottle-gourd full of water; in the one gourd was the water of life, in the other the water of death. George was delighted with his good fortune, and hastened to the castle. At the edge of the forest he saw a cobweb extending from one pine-tree to another; in the midst of the cobweb sat a large spider sucking a fly. George took the bottle with the water of death, sprinkled the spider, and the spider dropped to the ground like a ripe cherry—he was dead. He then sprinkled the fly with the water of life out of the other bottle, and the fly began to move, extricated itself from the cobweb, and off into the air. 'Lucky for you, George, that you've brought me to life again,' it buzzed round his ears; 'without me you'd scarcely guess aright which of the twelve is Goldenhair.'

When the king saw that George had completed this matter also, he said he would give him his golden-haired daughter. 'But,' said he, 'you must select her yourself.' He then led him into a great hall, in the midst of which was a round table, and round the table sat twelve beautiful maidens, one like the other; but each had on her head a long kerchief reaching down to the ground, white as snow, so that it couldn't be seen what manner of hair any of them had. 'Here are my daughters,' said the king; 'if you guess which of them is Goldenhair, you have won her, and can take her away at once; but if you don't guess right, she is not adjudged to you, you must depart without her.' George was in the greatest anxiety; he didn't know what to do. Whereupon something whispered into his ear: 'Buzz! buzz! go round the table, I'll tell you which is the one.' It was the fly that George had restored to life with the water of life. 'It isn't this maiden—nor this—nor this; this is Goldenhair!' 'Give me this one of your daughters,' cried George; 'I have earned her for my lord.' 'You have guessed right,' said the king; and the maiden at once rose from the table, threw off her kerchief, and her golden hair flowed in streams from her head to the ground, and such a brightness came from them, even as when the sun rises in the morning, that George's eyes were dazzled.

Then the king gave his daughter all that was fitting for her journey, and George took her away to be his lord's bride. The old king's eyes sparkled, and he jumped for joy, when he saw Goldenhair, and gave orders at once for preparations to be made for the wedding. I intended to have you hanged for your disobedience, that the ravens might devour you,' said he to George; 'but you have served me so well, that I shall only have your head cut off with an axe, and then I shall have you honourably buried.' When George had been executed, Goldenhair begged the old king to grant her the body of his dead servant, and the king couldn't deny his golden-haired bride anything. She then fitted George's head to his body, and sprinkled him with the water of death, and the body and head grew together so that no mark of the wound remained. Then she sprinkled him with the water of life, and George rose up again, as if he had been born anew, as fresh as a stag, and youth beamed from his countenance. 'Oh, how heavily I have slept!' said George, and rubbed his eyes. 'Yes, indeed, you have slept heavily,' said Goldenhair; 'and if it hadn't been for me, you wouldn't have waked for ever and ever.' When the old king saw that George had come to life again, and that he was younger and handsomer than before, he wanted to be made young again also. He gave orders at once that his head should be cut off, and that he should be sprinkled with the water. They cut his head off and sprinkled him with the water of life, till they'd sprinkled it all away; but his head wouldn't grow on to the body. Then, and not till then, did they begin to sprinkle him with the water of death, and in an instant the head grew on to the body; but the king was dead all the same, because they had no more of the water of life to bring him to life again. And since the kingdom couldn't be without a king, and they'd no one so intelligent as to understand all animals like George, they made George king and Goldenhair queen.

This story is a variant, and a very beautiful variant, of Grimm's 'White Snake.' The two kinds of water, that of death and that of life, appear here, showing that it is a true Slavonic, and not a Teutonic story.

IV.—INTELLIGENCE AND LUCK.

ONCE upon a time Luck met Intelligence on a garden-seat. 'Make room for me!' said Luck. Intelligence was then as yet inexperienced, and didn't know who ought to make room for whom. He said: 'Why should I make room for you? you're no better than I am.' 'He's the better man,' answered Luck, 'who performs most. See you there yon peasant's son who's ploughing in the field? Enter into him, and if he gets on better through you than through me, I'll always submissively make way for you, whensoever and wheresoever we meet.' Intelligence agreed, and entered at once into the ploughboy's head. As soon as the ploughboy felt that he had intelligence in his head, he began to think: 'Why must I follow the plough to the day of my death? I can go somewhere else and make my fortune more easily.' He left off ploughing, put up the plough, and drove home. 'Daddy,' says he, 'I don't like this peasant's life; I'd rather learn to be a gardener.' His father said: 'What ails you, Vanek? have you lost your wits?' However, he bethought himself, and said: 'Well, if you will, learn, and God be with you! Your brother will be heir to the cottage after me.' Vanek lost the cottage, but he didn't care for that, but went and put himself apprentice to the king's gardener. For every little that the gardener showed him, Vanek comprehended ever so much more. Ere long he didn't even obey the gardener's orders as to how he ought to do anything, but did everything his own way. At first the gardener was angry, but, seeing everything thus getting on better, he was content. 'I see that you've more intelligence than I,' said he, and henceforth let Vanek garden as he thought fit. In no long space of time Vanek made the garden so beautiful, that the king took great delight in it, and frequently walked in it with the queen and with his only daughter.

The princess was a very beautiful damsel, but ever since she was twelve years old she had ceased speaking, and no one ever heard a single word from her. The king was much grieved, and caused proclamation to be made, that whoever should bring it to pass that she should speak again, should be her husband. Many young kings, princes and other great lords announced themselves one after the other, but all went away as they had come; no one succeeded in causing her to speak. 'Why shouldn't I too try my luck?' thought Vanek; 'who knows whether I mayn't succeed in bringing her to answer when I ask her a question?' He at once caused himself to be announced at the palace, and the king and his councillors conducted him into the room where the princess was. The king's daughter had a pretty little dog, and was very fond of him because he was so clever, understanding everything that she wanted. When Vanek went into the room with the king and his councillors, he made as if he didn't even see the princess, but turned to the dog and said: 'I have heard, doggie, that you are very clever, and I come to you for advice. We are three companions in travel, a sculptor, a tailor and myself. Once upon a time we were going through a forest and were obliged to pass the night in it. To be safe from wolves, we made a fire, and agreed to keep watch one after the other. The sculptor kept watch first, and for amusement to kill time took a log and carved a damsel out of it. When it was finished he woke the tailor to keep watch in his turn. The tailor, seeing the wooden damsel, asked what it meant. "As you see," said the sculptor, "I was weary, and didn't know what to do with myself, so I carved a damsel out of a log; if you find time hang heavy on your hands, you can dress her." The tailor at once took out his scissors, needle and thread, cut out the clothes, stitched away, and when they were ready, dressed the damsel in them. He then called me to come and keep watch. I, too, asked him what the meaning of all this was. "As you see," said the tailor, "the sculptor found time hang heavy on his hands and carved a damsel out of a log, and I for the same reason clothed her; and if you find time hanging on your hands, you can teach her to speak." And by morning dawn I had actually taught her to speak. But in the morning when my companions woke up, each wanted to possess the damsel. The sculptor said, "I made her;" the tailor, "I clothed her." I, too, maintained my right. Tell me, therefore, doggie, to which of us the damsel belongs?' The dog said nothing, but instead of the dog the princess replied: 'To whom can she belong but to yourself? What's the good of the sculptor's damsel without life? What's the good of the tailor's dressing without speech? You gave her the best gift, life and speech, and therefore she by right belongs to you.' 'You have passed your own sentence,' said Vanek; 'I have given you speech again and a new life, and you therefore by right belong to me.' Then said one of the king's councillors: 'His Royal Grace will give you a plenteous reward for succeeding in unloosing his daughter's tongue; but you cannot have her to wife, as you are of mean lineage.' The king said: 'You are of mean lineage; I will give you a plenteous reward instead of our daughter.' But Vanek wouldn't hear of any other reward, and said: 'The king promised without any exception, that whoever caused his daughter to speak again should be her husband. A king's word is a law; and if the king wants others to observe his laws, he must first keep them himself. Therefore the king *must* give me his daughter.' 'Seize and bind him!' shouted the councillor. 'Whoever says the king *must* do anything, offers an insult to his Majesty, and is worthy of death. May it please your Majesty to order this malefactor to be executed with the sword?' The king said: 'Let him be executed.' Vanek was immediately bound and led to execution. When they came to the place of execution Luck was there waiting for him, and said secretly to Intelligence, 'See how this man has got on through you, till he has to lose his head! Make way, and let me take your place!' As soon as Luck entered Vanek, the executioner's sword broke against the scaffold, just as if someone had snapped it; and before they brought him another, up rode a trumpeter on horseback from the city, galloping as swift as a bird, trumpeted merrily, and waved a white flag, and after him came the royal carriage for Vanek. This is what had happened: The princess had told her father at home that Vanek had but spoken the truth, and the king's word ought not to be broken. If Vanek were of mean lineage the king could easily make him a prince. The king said: 'You're right; let him be a prince!' The royal carriage was immediately sent for Vanek, and the councillor who had irritated the king against him was executed in his stead. Afterwards, when Vanek and the princess were going together in a carriage from the wedding, Intelligence happened to be somewhere on the road, and seeing that he couldn't help meeting Luck, bent his head and slipped on one side, just as if cold water had been thrown upon him. And from that time forth it is said that Intelligence has always given a wide berth to Luck whenever he has had to meet him.

V.—THE JEZINKAS.

THERE was a poor orphan lad who had neither father nor mother, and was compelled to go out to service to get his living. He travelled a long way without being able to obtain an engagement, till one day he came to a hovel all by itself under a wood. On the threshold sat an old man, who had dark caverns in his head instead of eyes. The goats were bleating in the stall, and the old man said: 'I wish I could take you, poor goats, to pasture, but I can't, I am blind; and I have nobody to send with you.' 'Daddy, send me,' answered the lad; 'I will pasture your goats, and also be glad to wait upon you.' 'Who are you? and what is your name?' The lad told him all, and that they called him Johnny. 'Well, Johnny, I will take you; but drive out the goats for me to pasture first of all. But don't lead them to yon hill in the forest; the Jezinkas will come to you, will put you to sleep, and will then tear out your eyes, as they have mine.' 'Never fear, Daddy, answered Johnny;' the Jezinkas won't tear out *my* eyes.' He then let the goats out of the stall, and drove them to pasture. The first and second day he pastured them under the forest, but the third day he said to himself: 'Why should I be afraid of the Jezinkas? I'll drive them where there is better pasture.' He then broke off three green shoots of bramble, put them into his hat, and drove the goats straight on to the hill in the forest. There the goats wandered about for pasture, and Johnny sat down on a stone in the cool. He had not sat long, when all of a sudden, how it came about he knew not, a beautiful damsel stood before him, all dressed in white, with her hair—raven-black—prettily dressed and flowing down her back, and eyes like sloes. 'God bless you, young goatherd!' said she. 'See what apples grow in our garden! Here's one for you; I'll give it you, that you may know how good they are.' She offered him a beautiful rosy apple. But Johnny knew that if he took the apple and ate it he would fall asleep, and she would afterwards tear out his eyes, so he said: 'I am much obliged to you, beautiful damsel! My master has an apple-tree in his garden, on which still handsomer apples grow; I have eaten my fill of them.' 'Well, if you'd rather not, I won't compel you,' said the damsel, and went away.

After a while came another, still prettier, damsel, with a beautiful red rose in her hand, and said: 'God bless you, young goatherd! See what a beautiful rose I've just plucked off the hedge. It smells so nice; smell it yourself.' 'I am much obliged to you, beautiful damsel. My master has still handsomer roses in his garden; I have smelt my fill of them.' 'Well, then, if you won't, let it alone!' said the damsel, quite enraged, turned round, and retired. After a while, a third damsel, the youngest and prettiest of them all, came up. 'God bless you, young goatherd!' 'Thank you, beautiful damsel!' 'Indeed, you're a fine lad,' said the damsel, 'but you'd be still handsomer if you had your hair nicely combed and dressed. Come, I'll comb it for you.' Johnny said nothing, but when the damsel came up to him to comb his hair, he took his hat from his head, drew out a bramble-shoot, and pop! struck her on both hands. The damsel screamed 'Help, help!' began to weep, but was unable to move from the place. Johnny cared naught for her weeping, and bound her hands together with the bramble. Then up ran the other two damsels, and, seeing their sister a captive, began to beg Johnny to unbind her and let her go. 'Unbind her yourselves,' said Johnny. 'Alas! we can't, we have tender hands, we should prick ourselves.' But when they saw that the lad would not do as they wished, they went to their sister and wanted to unfasten the bramble. Thereupon Johnny leapt up, and pop! pop! struck them too with a spray, and then bound both their hands together. 'See, I've got you, you wicked Jezinkas! Why did you tear out my master's eyes?' After this, he went home to his master, and said, 'Come, daddy, I've found somebody who will give you your eyes again.' When they came to the hill, he said to the first Jezinka, 'Now tell me where the old man's eyes are. If you don't tell me, I shall throw you at once into the water.' The Jezinka made excuse that she didn't know, and Johnny was going to throw her into the river, which flowed hard by under the hill. 'Don't, Johnny, don't!' entreated the Jezinka, 'and I'll give you the old man's eyes.' She conducted him into a cavern, where was a great heap of eyes, large and small, black, red, blue and green, and took two out of the heap. But when Johnny placed them in the old man's sockets, the poor man began to cry: 'Alas, alas! these are not my eyes. I see nothing but owls.' Johnny became exasperated, seized the Jezinka, and threw her into the water. He then said to the second: 'Tell me, you, where the old man's eyes are.' She, too, began to make excuses that she didn't know; but when the lad threatened to throw her, too, into the water, she led him again to the cavern, and took out two other eyes. But the old man cried again: 'Alas! these are not my eyes. I see nothing but wolves.' The same was done to the second Jezinka as to the first; the water closed over her. 'Tell me, you, where the old man's eyes are,' said Johnny to the third and youngest Jezinka. She, too, led him to the heap in the cavern, and took out two eyes for him. But when they were inserted, the old man cried out again that they were not his eyes. 'I see nothing but pike.' Johnny saw that she, too, was cheating him, and was going to drown her as well; but the Jezinka besought him with tears: 'Don't, Johnny, don't! I will give you the old man's proper eyes.' She took them from under the whole heap. And when Johnny inserted them into the old man's sockets, he cried out joyfully: 'These, these are my eyes! Praise be to God! now I see well again!' Afterwards Johnny and the old man lived together happily; Johnny pastured the goats, and the old man made cheeses at home, and they ate them together; but the Jezinka never showed herself again on that hill.

VI.—THE WOOD-LADY.

BETTY was a little girl; her mother was a widow, and had no more of her property left than a dilapidated cottage and two she-goats; but Betty was, nevertheless, always cheerful. From spring to autumn she pastured the goats in the birch-wood. Whenever she went from home, her mother always gave her in a basket a slice of bread and a spindle, with the injunction, 'Let it be full.' As she had no distaff, she used to twine the flax round her head. Betty took the basket, and skipped off singing merrily after the goats to the birch-wood. When she got there, the goats went after pasture, and Betty sat under a tree, drew the fibres from her head with her left hand, and let down the spindle with her right so that it just hummed over the ground, and therewith she sang till the wood echoed; the goats meanwhile pastured. When the sun indicated mid-day, she put aside her spindle, called the goats, and after giving them each a morsel of bread that they mightn't stray from her, bounded into the wood for a few strawberries or any other woodland fruit that might happen to be just then in season, that she might have dessert to her bread. When she had finished her meal, she sprang up, folded her hands, danced and sang. The sun smiled on her through the green foliage, and the goats, enjoying themselves among the grass, thought: 'What a merry shepherdess we have!' After her dance, she spun again industriously, and at even, when she drove the goats home, her mother never scolded her for bringing back her spindle empty.

Once, when according to custom, exactly at mid-day, after her scanty dinner, she was getting ready for a dance, all of a sudden—where she came, there she came—a very beautiful maiden stood before her. She had on a white dress as fine as gossamer, golden-coloured hair flowed from her head to her waist, and on her head she wore a garland of woodland flowers. Betty was struck dumb with astonishment. The maiden smiled at her, and said in an attractive voice, 'Betty, are you fond of dancing?' When the maiden spoke so prettily to her, Betty's terror quitted her, and she answered, 'Oh, I should like to dance all day long!' 'Come, then, let's dance together. I'll teach you!' So spoke the maiden, tucked her dress up on one side, took Betty by the waist, and began to dance with her. As they circled, such delightful music sounded over their heads, that Betty's heart skipped within her. The musicians sat on the branches of the birches in black, ash-coloured, brown, and variegated coats. It was a company of choice musicians that had come together at the beck of the beautiful maiden—nightingales, larks, linnets, goldfinches, greenfinches, thrushes, blackbirds, and a very skilful mocking-bird. Betty's cheek flamed, her eyes glittered, she forgot her task and her goats, and only gazed at her partner, who twirled before and round her with the most charming movements, and so lightly that the grass didn't even bend beneath her delicate foot. They danced from noon till eve, and Betty's feet were neither wearied nor painful. Then the beautiful maiden stopped, the music ceased, and as she came so she disappeared. Betty looked about her; the sun was setting behind the wood. She clapped her hands on the top of her head, and, feeling the unspun flax, remembered that her spindle, which was lying on the grass, was by no means full. She took the flax down from her head, and put it with the spindle into her basket, called the goats, and drove them home. She did not sing on the way, but bitterly reproached herself for letting the beautiful maiden delude her, and determined that if the maiden should come to her again, she would never listen to her any more. The goats, hearing no merry song behind them, looked round to see whether their own shepherdess was really following them. Her mother, too, wondered, and asked her daughter whether she was ill, as she didn't sing. 'No, mother dear, I'm not ill; but my throat is dry from very singing, and therefore I don't sing,' said Betty in excuse, and went to put away the spindle and the unspun flax. Knowing that her mother was not in the habit of reeling up the yarn at once, she intended to make up the next day what she had neglected to do the first day, and therefore did not say a word to her mother about the beautiful maiden.

The next day Betty again drove the goats as usual to the birch-wood, and sang to herself again merrily. On arriving at the birch-wood the goats began to pasture, and she sat under the tree and began to spin industriously, singing to herself all the time, for work comes better from the hand while one sings. The sun indicated mid-day. Betty gave each of the goats a morsel of bread, went off for strawberries, and after returning began to eat her dinner and chatter with the goats. 'Ah, my little goats, I mustn't dance to-day,' sighed she, when after dinner she collected the crumbs from her lap in her hand and placed them on a stone that the birds might take them away. 'And why mustn't you?' spoke a pleasing voice, and the beautiful maiden stood beside her, as if she had dropped from the clouds. Betty was still more frightened than the first time, and closed her eyes that she might not even see the maiden; but when the maiden repeated the question, she answered modestly: 'Excuse me, beautiful lady, I can't dance with you, because I should again fail to perform my task of spinning, and my mother would scold me. To-day, before the sun sets, I must make up what I left undone yesterday.' 'Only come and dance; before the sun sets help will be found for you,' said the maiden, tucked up her dress, took Betty round the waist, the musicians sitting on the birch branches struck up, and the two dancers began to whirl. The beautiful maiden danced still more enchantingly. Betty couldn't take her eyes off her, and forgot the goats and her task. At last the dancer stopped, the music ceased, the sun was on the verge of setting. Betty clapped her hand on the top of her head, where the unspun flax was twined, and began to cry. The beautiful maiden put her hand on her head, took off the flax, twined it round the stem of a slender birch, seized the spindle, and began to spin. The spindle just swung over the surface of the ground, grew fuller before her eyes, and before the sun set behind the wood all the yarn was spun, as well as that which Betty had not finished the day before. While giving the full spool into the girl's hand the beautiful maiden said: 'Reel, and grumble not—remember my words, "Reel, and grumble not!"' After these words she vanished, as if the ground had sunk in beneath her. Betty was content, and thought on her way, 'If she is so good and kind, I will dance with her again if she comes again.' She sang again that the goats might step on merrily. But her mother gave her no cheerful welcome. Wishing in the course of the day to reel the yarn, she saw that the spindle was not full, and was therefore out of humour. 'What were you doing yesterday that you didn't finish your task?' asked her mother reprovingly. 'Pardon, mother; I danced a little too long,' said Betty humbly, and, showing her mother the spindle, added: 'To-day it is more than full to make up for it.' Her mother said no more, but went to milk the goats, and Betty put the spindle away. She wished to tell her mother of her adventure, but bethought herself again, 'No, not unless she comes again, and then I will ask her what kind of person she is, and will tell my mother.' So she made up her mind and held her tongue.

The third morning, as usual, she drove the goats to the birch-wood. The goats began to pasture; Betty sat under the tree, and began to sing and spin. The sun indicated mid-day. Betty laid her spindle on the grass, gave each of the goats a morsel of bread, collected strawberries, ate her dinner, and while giving the crumbs to the birds, said: 'My little goats, I will dance to you to-day!' She jumped up, folded her hands, and was just going to try whether she could manage to dance as prettily as the beautiful maiden, when all at once she herself stood before her. 'Let's go together, together!' said she to Betty, seized her round the waist, and at the same moment the music struck up over their heads, and the maidens circled round with flying step. Betty forgot her spindle and her goats, saw nothing but the beautiful maiden, whose body bent in every direction like a willow-wand, and thought of nothing but the delightful music, in tune with which her feet bounded of their own accord. They danced from mid-day till even. Then the maiden stopped, and the music ceased. Betty looked round; the sun was behind the wood. With tears she clasped her hands on the top of her head, and turning in search of the half-empty spindle, lamented about what her mother would say to her. 'Give me your basket,' said the beautiful maiden. 'I will make up to you for what you have left undone to-day.' Betty handed her the basket, and the maiden disappeared for a moment, and afterwards handed Betty the basket again, saying, 'Not now; look at it at home,' and was gone, as if the wind had blown her away. Betty was afraid to peep into the basket immediately, but half-way home she couldn't restrain herself. The basket was as light as if there was just nothing in it. She couldn't help looking to see whether the maiden hadn't tricked her. And how frightened she was when she saw that the basket was full—of birch leaves! Then, and not till then, did she begin to weep and lament that she had been so credulous. In anger she threw out two handfuls of leaves, and was going to shake the basket out; but then she bethought herself, 'I will use them as litter for the goats,' and left some leaves in the basket. She was almost afraid to go home. The goats again could hardly recognise their shepherdess. Her mother was waiting for her on the threshold, full of anxiety. 'For Heaven's sake, girl! what sort of spool did you bring me home yesterday?' were her first words. 'Why?' asked Betty anxiously. 'When you went out in the morning, I went to reel; I reeled and reeled, and the spool still remained full. One skein, two, three skeins; the spool still full. "What evil spirit has spun it?" said I in a temper; and that instant the yarn vanished from the spindle, as if it were spirited away. Tell me what the meaning of this is!' Then Betty confessed, and began to tell about the beautiful maiden. 'That was a wood-lady!' cried her mother in astonishment; 'about mid-day and midnight the wood-ladies hold their dances. Lucky that you are not a boy, or you wouldn't have come out of her arms alive. She would have danced with you as long as there was breath in your body, or have tickled you to death. But they have compassion on girls, and often give them rich presents. It's a pity that you didn't tell me; if I hadn't spoken in a temper, I might have had a room full of yarn.' Then Betty bethought herself of the basket, and it occurred to her that perhaps, after all, there might have been something under those leaves. She took out the spindle and unspun flax from the top, and looked once more, and, 'See, mother!' she cried out. Her mother looked and clapped her hands. The birch-leaves were turned into gold! 'She ordered me: "Don't look now, but at home!" but I did not obey.' 'Lucky that you didn't empty out the whole basket,' thought her mother.

The next morning she went herself to look at the place where Betty had thrown out the two handfuls of leaves, but on the road there lay nothing but fresh birch-leaves. But the riches that Betty had brought home were large enough.

Her mother bought a small estate; they had many cattle. Betty had handsome clothes, and was not obliged to pasture goats; but whatever she had, however cheerful and happy she was, nothing ever gave her so great delight as the dance with the wood-lady. She often went to the birch-wood; she was attracted there. She hoped for the good fortune of seeing the beautiful maiden; but she never set eyes on her more.

VII.—GEORGE WITH THE GOAT.

THERE was a king who had a daughter who never could be induced to laugh; she was always sad. So the king proclaimed that she should be given to anyone who could cause her to laugh. There was also a shepherd who had a son named George. He said: 'Daddy! I, too, will go to see whether I can make her laugh. I want nothing from you but the goat.' His father said, 'Well, go.' The goat was of such a nature that, when her master wished, she detained everybody, and that person was obliged to stay by her.

So he took the goat and went, and met a man who had a foot on his shoulder. George said: 'Why have you a foot on your shoulder?' He replied: 'If I take it off, I leap a hundred miles.' 'Whither are you going?' 'I am going in search of service, to see if anyone will take me.' 'Well, come with us.'

They went on, and again met a man who had a bandage on his eyes. 'Why have you a bandage on your eyes?' He answered, 'If I remove the bandage, I see a hundred miles.' 'Whither are you going?' 'I am going in search of service, if you will take me?' 'Yes, I'll take you. Come also with me.'

They went on a bit further, and met another fellow, who

had a bottle under his arm, and, instead of a stopper, held his thumb in it. 'Why do you hold your thumb there?' 'If I pull it out, I squirt a hundred miles, and besprinkle everything that I choose. If you like, take me also into your service; it may be to your advantage and ours too.' George replied: 'Well, come too!'

Afterwards they came to the town where the king lived, and bought a silken riband for the goat. They came to an inn, and orders had already been given there beforehand, that when such people came, they were to give them what they liked to eat and drink—the king would pay for all. So they tied the goat with that very riband and placed it in the innkeeper's room to be taken care of, and he put it in the side room where his daughters slept. The innkeeper had three maiden daughters, who were not yet asleep. So Manka said: 'Oh! if I, too, could have such a riband! I will go and unfasten it from that goat.' The second, Dodla, said: 'Don't; he'll find it out in the morning.' But she went notwithstanding. And when Manka did not return for a long time, the third, Kate, said: 'Go, fetch her.' So Dodla went, and gave Manka a pat on the back. 'Come, leave it alone!' And now she too was unable to withdraw herself from her. So Kate said: 'Come, don't unfasten it!' Kate went and gave Dodla a pat on the petticoat; and now she, too, couldn't get away, but was obliged to stay by her.

In the morning George made haste and went for the goat, and led the whole set away—Kate, Dodla, and Manka. The innkeeper was still asleep. They went through the village, and the judge looked out of a window and said, 'Fie, Kate! what's this? what's this?' He went and took her by the hand, wishing to pull her away, but remained also by her. After this, a cowherd drove some cows through a narrow street, and the bull came rushing round; he stuck fast, and George led him, too, in the procession.

Thus they afterwards came in front of the castle, and the servants came out of doors; and when they saw such things, they went and told the king. 'O sire, we have such a spectacle here; we have already had all manner of masquerades, but this has never been here yet.' So they immediately led the king's daughter to the square in front of the castle, and she looked and laughed till the castle shook.

Now they asked him what sort of person he was. He said that he was a shepherd's son, and was named George. They said that it could not be done; for he was of mean lineage, and they could not give him the damsel; but he must accomplish something more for them. He said, 'What?' They replied that there was a spring yonder, a hundred miles off; if he brought a goblet of water from it in a minute, then he should obtain the damsel. So George said to the man who had the foot on his shoulder: 'You said that if you took the foot down, you could jump a hundred miles.' He replied: 'I'll easily do that.' He took the foot down, jumped, and was there. But after this there was only a very little time to spare, and by then he ought to have been back. So George said to the second: 'You said that if you removed the bandage from your eyes, you could see a hundred miles. Peep and see what is going on.' 'Ah, sir! Goodness gracious! he's fallen asleep!' 'That will be a bad job,' said George; 'the time will be up. You, third man, you said if you pulled your thumb out, you could squirt a hundred miles; be quick and squirt thither, that he may get up. And you, look whether he is moving, or what.' 'Oh, sir! he's getting up now; he's knocking the dust off; he's drawing the water.' He then gave a jump, and was there exactly in time.

After this they said that he must perform one task more; that yonder, in a rock, was a wild beast, a unicorn, of such a nature that he destroyed a great many of their people; if he cleared him out of the world he should obtain the damsel. So he took his people and went into the forest. They came to a firwood. There were three wild beasts, and three lairs had been formed by wallowing as they lay. Two did nothing; but the third destroyed people. So they took some stones and some pine-cones in their pockets, and climbed up into a tree; and when the beasts lay down, they dropped a stone down upon that one which was the unicorn. He said to the next: 'Be quiet; don't butt me.' It said: 'I'm not doing anything to you.' Again they let a stone fall from above upon the unicorn. 'Be quiet! you've already done it to me twice.' 'Indeed, I'm doing nothing to you.' So they attacked each other and fought together. The unicorn wanted to pierce the second beast through; but it jumped out of the way, and he rushed so violently after it, that he struck his horn into a tree, and couldn't pull it out quickly. So they sprang speedily down from the fir, and the other two beasts ran away and escaped, but they cut off the head of the third, the unicorn, took it up, and carried it to the castle.

Now those in the castle saw that George had again accomplished that task. 'What, prithee, shall we do? Perhaps we must after all give him the damsel!' 'No, sire,' said one of the attendants, 'that cannot be; he is too lowborn to obtain a king's daughter! On the contrary, we must clear him out of the world.' So the king ordered them to note his words, what he should say. There was a hired female servant there, and she said to him: 'George, it will be evil for you to-day; they're going to clear you out of the world.' He answered: 'Oh, I'm not afraid. When I was only just twelve years old, I killed twelve of them at one blow!' But this was the fact: when his mother was baking a flat-cake, a dozen flies settled upon her, and he killed them all at a single blow.

When they heard this, they said: 'Nothing else will do

but we must shoot him.' So they drew up the soldiers, and said they would hold a review in his honour, for they would celebrate the wedding in the square before the castle. Then they conducted him thither, and the soldiers were already going to let fly at him. But George said to the man who held his thumb in the bottle in place of a stopper: 'You said, if you pulled your thumb out, you could besprinkle everything. Pull it out—quick!' 'Oh, sir, I'll easily perform that.' So he pulled out his thumb and gave them all such a sprinkling, that they were all blind, and not one could see.

So, when they perceived that nothing else was to be done, they told him to go, for they would give him the damsel. Then they gave him a handsome royal robe, and the wedding took place. I, too, was at the wedding; they had music there, sang, ate, and drank; there was meat, there were cheesecakes, and baskets full of everything, and buckets full of strong waters. To-day I went, yesterday I came; I found an egg among the tree-stumps; I knocked it against somebody's head, and gave him a bald place, and he's got it still.

This story is related to Grimm's tale of the 'Golden Goose,' but it is much more rationally constructed, and much more interesting. The man who jumps one hundred miles appears to be the rainbow, the man with bandaged eyes the lightning, and the man with the bottle the cloud. The interpretation will be very similar to that of No. 1, but the allegory is by no means so clear or so well constructed. As to the nonsense at the end, it is a specimen of the manner in which the narrators of stories frequently finish them in all Slavonic languages.

MORAVIA is so named from the river Morava (in German the river March), of which, and its affluents, it is the basin. It falls into the Danube a little above Presburg. In very early times Moravia appears to have been more civilized and powerful than Bohemia; but later, Bohemia became a considerable kingdom, and Moravia a dependency of, and eventually a margravate under the Bohemian crown.

The Moravian stories differ but little in character from those of Bohemia. The country, unlike Bohemia, abounds in dialects, although the literary language is the Bohemian. On the east the Moravian melts into the Silesian, or 'Water-Polish.'

No. 8, 'Godmother Death,' is an interesting variant of the Teutonic 'Godfather Death,' which is given by Grimm. The reason why Death is represented as a Godmother, rather than a Godfather, in the Moravian story, is, that Death (*Smrt*) is feminine in all Slavonic dialects. The story constructed on this basis is more graceful and fuller of incident than the Teutonic tale, in which Death is masculine.

No. 9 is another story falling under the head of 'Natural Science in Allegory,' which is clearer and simpler in construction and interpretation than any variant of it that I am acquainted with.

VIII.—GODMOTHER DEATH.

THERE was a man, very poor in this world's goods, whose wife presented him with a baby boy. No one was willing to stand sponsor, because he was so very poor. The father said to himself: 'Dear Lord, I am so poor that no one is willing to be at my service in this matter; I'll take the baby, I'll go, and I'll ask the first person I meet to act as sponsor, and if I don't meet anybody, perhaps the sexton will help me.' He went and met Death, but didn't know what manner of person she was; she was a handsome woman, like any other woman. He asked her to be godmother. She didn't make any excuse, and immediately saluted him as parent of her godchild, took the baby in her arms, and carried him to church. The little lad was properly christened. When they came out of church, the child's father took the godmother to an inn, and wanted to give her a little treat as godmother. But she said to him, 'Gossip,* leave this alone, and come with me to my abode.' She took him with her to her apartment, which was very handsomely furnished. Afterwards she conducted him into great vaults, and through these vaults they went right into the under-world in the dark. There tapers were burning of three sizes—small, large, and middle-sized; and those which were not yet alight were very large. The godmother said to the godchild's father: 'Look, Gossip, here I have the duration of everybody's life.' The child's father gazed thereat, found there a tiny taper close to the very ground, and asked her: 'But, Gossip, I pray you, whose is this little taper close to the ground?' She said to him: 'That is yours! When any taper whatsoever

* The Slavonians are rich in terms, both masculine and feminine, expressing the various relationships between godparents and godchildren and their parents. We have only one form, 'gossip,' which thus has to do duty for both the godmother and the father of the godchild.

burns down, I must go for that man.' He said to her: 'Gossip, I pray you, give me somewhat additional.' She said to him: 'Gossip, I cannot do that!' Afterwards she went and lighted a large new taper for the baby boy whom they had had christened. Meanwhile, while the godmother was not looking, the child's father took for himself a large new taper, lit it, and placed it where his tiny taper was burning down.

The godmother looked round at him and said: 'Gossip, you ought not to have done that to me; but if you have given yourself additional lifetime, you have done so and possess it. Let us go hence, and we'll go to your wife.'

She took a present, and went with the child's father and the child to the mother. She arrived, and placed the boy on his mother's bed, and asked her how she was, and whether she had any pain anywhere. The mother confided her griefs to her, and the father sent for some beer, and wanted to entertain her in his cottage, as godmother, in order to gratify her and show his gratitude. They drank and feasted together. Afterwards the godmother said to her godchild's father: 'Gossip, you are so poor that no one but myself would be at your service in this matter; but never mind, you shall bear me in memory! I will go to the houses of various respectable people and make them ill, and you shall physic and cure them. I will tell you all the remedies. I possess them all, and everybody will be glad to recompense you well, only observe this: When I stand at anyone's feet, you can be of assistance to every such person; but if I stand at anybody's head, don't attempt to aid him.' It came to pass. The child's father went from patient to patient, where the godmother caused illness, and benefited every one. All at once he became a distinguished physician. A prince was dying—nay, he had breathed his last—nevertheless, they sent for the physician. He came, he began to anoint him with salves and give him his powders, and did him good. When he had restored him to health, they paid him well, without asking how much they were indebted. Again, a count was dying. They sent for the physician again. The physician came. Death was standing behind the bed at his head. The physician cried: 'It's a bad case, but we'll have a try.' He summoned the servants, and ordered them to turn the bed round with the patient's feet towards Death, and began to anoint him with salves and administer powders into his mouth, and did him good. The count paid him in return as much as he could carry away, without ever asking how much he was indebted; he was only too glad that he had restored him to health. When Death met the physician, she said to him: 'Gossip, if this occurs to you again, don't play me that trick any more. True, you have done him good, but only for a while; I must, none the less, take him off whither he is due.' The child's father went on in this way for some years; he was now very old. But at last he was wearied out, and asked Death herself to take him. Death was unable to take him, because he had given himself a long additional taper; she was obliged to wait till it burned out. One day he drove to a certain patient to restore him to health, and did so. Afterwards Death revealed herself to him, and rode with him in his carriage. She began to tickle and play with him, and tap him with a green twig under the throat; he threw himself into her lap, and went off into the last sleep. Death laid him in the carriage, and took herself off. They found the physician lying dead in his carriage, and conveyed him home. The whole town and all the villages lamented: 'That physician is much to be regretted. What a good doctor he was! He was of great assistance; there will never be his like again!' His son remained after him, but had not the same skill.

The son went one day into church, and his godmother met

him. She asked him: 'My dear son, how are you?' He said to her: 'Not all alike; so long as I have what my dad saved up for me, it is well with me, but after that the Lord God knows how it will be with me.' His godmother said: 'Well, my son, fear nought. I am your christening mamma; I helped your father to what he had, and will give you, too, a livelihood. You shall go to a physician as a pupil, and you shall be more skilful than he, only behave nicely.' After this she anointed him with salve over the ears, and conducted him to a physician. The physician didn't know what manner of lady it was, and what sort of son she brought him for instruction. The lady enjoined her son to behave nicely, and requested the physician to instruct him well, and bring him into a good position. Then she took leave of him and departed. The physician and the lad went together to gather herbs, and each herb cried out to the pupil what remedial virtue it had, and the pupil gathered it. The physician also gathered herbs, but knew not, with regard to any herb, what remedial virtue it possessed. The pupil's herbs were beneficial in every disease. The physician said to the pupil: 'You are cleverer than I, for I diagnose no one that comes to me; but you know herbs counter to every disease. Do you know what? Let us join partnership. I will give my doctor's diploma up to you, and will be your assistant, and am willing to be with you till death.' The lad was successful in doctoring and curing till his taper burned out in limbo.

IX.—THE FOUR BROTHERS.

THERE was, once upon a time, a huntsman who had four sons, and these sons wanted to go to gain experience in the world. When they were all over sixteen years old, they said to their father: 'We are going into the world, father; we pray you give us money for our journey.' The father gave them 100 florins and a horse apiece. They mounted their horses and rode to the mountains. On a mountain were four roads, and between them stood a beech-tree. At this beech-tree they halted, and the eldest said to the rest, 'Brothers, let us separate here, and go each by a different road to seek his fortune in the world. Let us each stick his knife into this beech-tree, and in a year and a day let us all meet together here. These knives will be tokens for us; if any one of the knives is rusty, the one of us to whom it belongs will be dead; and he whose knife is free from rust will be alive and well.' They separated, and went each his way, and when they came to suitable places they each learned a handicraft. The eldest learned to be a cobbler, the second to be a thief, the third to be an astrologer, and the fourth to be a huntsman. When the year and day arrived, they started on their return. The eldest came first to the beech-tree, pulled out his own knife and looked at the other knives. Seeing that they were all free from rust, he rejoiced, and said, 'Praise be to God! we are all alive and well.' He went home. When he came to his father, his father asked him, 'What manner of handicraft have you learnt?' The son replied, 'Daddy, it's no use telling you stories; I'm a cobbler.' The father said, 'Well, you've learned a nice gainful handicraft.' The son answered, 'But, daddy, I'm not a cobbler like other cobblers, but I'm this kind of cobbler: if anything is worn out, I only say, "Let it be mended up," and it is so at once.' The father had a coat worn out at the elbows, and told him to cobble it up. The son gave the command, 'Let it be mended up,' and in a moment the coat was mended up as if it were brand new, nor was it possible to know that it had been mended at all. Upon this the father said nothing more. The next day the second son came to the beech. He pulled out his own knife, and looked at the remaining two; the third was already gone. Seeing that they were both free from rust, he rejoiced, and said, 'Praise be to God! we are all alive and well; our eldest brother is at home already.' He also went home. When he came to his father, his father asked him, 'What manner of handicraft have you learned?' The son replied, 'Dear daddy, it's no use telling stories to you; I'm a thief.' The father said, 'Oh, you've learned a nice gainful trade! Shame on you!' The son said to him, 'But, daddy, I'm not a thief like a thief, but I'm such a thief that, if I think of anything, be it where it may, I have it with me at once.' Just then a hare came running on the hillside; it could be seen through the window; the father told him to fetch the hare. The son immediately said, 'Let yon hare be here,' and it was with them at once. After this the father said no more. The third day the third son came to the beech, pulled out his own knife and looked at the other knife, two not being there. Seeing that it was clear of rust, he said, 'Praise be to God! we are all alive and well; my two elder brothers are at home already.' He also went home. When he came to his father, his father asked him what manner of handicraft he had learned. The son replied, 'Dear daddy, it's no use to tell you stories; I'm an astrologer.' His father said to him that it was a nice pretty handicraft. The son answered, 'But, daddy, I am this kind of astrologer: if I look at the sky, I see at once where anything is in the whole earth.' On the fourth day the youngest son came to the beech and pulled out his knife, the other three being there no longer. He was glad, and said, 'My brothers are already all at home.' He also went home. When he came to his father, the father asked him what manner of handicraft he had learned. The son answered that he was a huntsman. The father said, 'Anyhow, you have not despised my craft; for that you're a good lad.' The son said, 'But, dear daddy, I'm not such a huntsman as you are, but one of this kind; if there is an unusually fine head of game, I say, 'Let it be shot,' and immediately shot it is.' There was a hare darting along the hillside; it was visible through the window. The father said, 'Shoot it!' The youngest son spoke the word, and the hare lay dead. The father said, 'I don't see whether it is lying dead.' The astrologer looked at the sky, and said, 'Yes, daddy, it's lying there behind the bushes.' The father said, 'Yes, it's lying there, but how are we to get it?' The brother who was a thief said, 'Let it be here,' and immediately there it was. But it had come through thorny bushes, and was all torn. The father said, 'The whole skin is torn; who'll buy it of us?' The brother who was a cobbler said, 'Let it be mended up,' and immediately mended up it was. The father said, 'Well, you'll all four maintain yourselves by your handicrafts.'

They lived for some time at home with their father, and maintained themselves well. Then a king lost the princess, his daughter, and made proclamation that whoever should find her, to that person he would give his daughter and the kingdom as well. The brothers said to one another, 'Let us go thither.' The father didn't give them leave to go, but go they did, and gave out that they were the people who would find the lost princess. The king immediately sent a carriage for them. When they came to the king, they said that they understood he had made proclamation that his daughter was lost, and that he would give her and the kingdom as well to whoever should find her. The king said that this was very truth, and immediately asked them to tell him where his daughter was. The astrologer replied that he could not tell him just then, but when evening came he would perceive in the sky where she was. About eight or nine o'clock they went out and gazed at the sky. The astrologer said that she had been taken captive by a dragon;

that the dragon had seized her as she was out walking, and was keeping her on an island beyond the Red Sea; that she was obliged to fondle him for two hours every day, and that the dragon then had his head placed on her lap. When day came, they assembled and drove in the carriage to the Red Sea. Then they got into a boat and rowed to the island where the princess was. When they arrived at the island, the princess was out walking, and the dragon wasn't at home; but the princess made signs to them that they were in evil case, for the dragon was just flying home. The thief-brother called out with speed, 'Let the princess be here!' She was with them in the boat at once, but cried out that they were in evil case, and would all perish. They rowed speedily away in the boat, but the dragon, full of wrath, roared and growled and rose in the air above them. The astrologer said to the huntsman, 'Brother, shoot him.' The huntsman-brother said, 'Let him be shot.' The dragon was shot, but fell on the boat and broke a hole in it, so that the water came in. They threw the dragon into the sea, and the huntsman-brother gave the word to the cobbler-brother, 'Mend the leak.' The cobbler-brother mended the leak, so that not a drop of water came into the boat to them. Thus they arrived safely with the princess at the sea-shore, landed on the beach, took their seats in the carriage with the princess, and drove off. But as they drove along in the carriage, they disputed to which of them the princess and the kingdom belonged. The astrologer said, 'The princess is mine. If it hadn't been for me, we shouldn't have known where the princess was.' The thief said, 'The princess is mine. If it hadn't been for me, we shouldn't have got the princess into the boat.' The huntsman said that the princess was his; if it hadn't been for him, they wouldn't have shot the dragon. The cobbler shouted that the princess was his; if it hadn't been for him, they would all have been drowned and have perished. When they came to the palace to the king, they asked him to decide to whom the princess belonged. The king said, 'Dear brothers, I will judge you righteously. It is true that you have all deserved her, but you cannot all obtain her. According to my promise, the astrologer-brother must obtain her, for I made proclamation that whoever should *find* the lost princess should obtain her and the kingdom with her; the astrologer found her, and told us where she was. But, that none of you may be unfairly dealt with, each shall receive a district of his own, and ye shall each be kings in your own districts.' They were all content. The astrologer, as soon as the wedding was over, sent home for his father. The father came, and was delighted that his sons had become monarchs each in his district. In the spring he lived with the cobbler, in the summer with the thief, in the autumn with the huntsman, and in winter with the astrologer, and enjoyed himself everywhere till death.

I think that this story is connected with the Ceres and Proserpine cycle, only the daughter is lost by a father instead of a mother. It will be seen, also, that at the conclusion of the story the order of the brothers is not the same as in the story itself. And I think the error is in the story, and that the astrologer ought to have been the youngest brother instead of the huntsman. The brothers are the four seasons of the year, which in ancient times began with spring, the cobbler, who mends up all things, and makes them new again; next comes summer, the thief, who gathers the products of the earth; third comes autumn, the huntsman, when the wild animals that have increased and multiplied during the year are destroyed and reduced within limits; last comes winter, the astrologer, when ploughing, sowing, and other agricultural operations that govern the whole year go on by calculation. Thus the princess herself, the earth or its fertility, is assigned to the representative of winter, while the other seasons are lords each in his own district.

This Moravian tale will bear an advantageous comparison with Grimm's tale of the 'Four Accomplished Brothers,' in which neither of the brothers is allowed to obtain the princess.

HUNGARIAN-SLOVENISH STORIES.

THE Slovenes or Slovaks of North Hungary speak a great number of dialects, their literary language being, however, the Bohemian. They seem to be the *débris* of a much larger nation or assemblage of nations, which was forced out of the plains of Pannonia into the mountains by the invasion of the Magyar or Hungarian horsemen, who, according to the Russian chronicler Nestor, marched past Kief in A.D. 898, on their way to establish themselves in their present abode.

Their stories are not very dissimilar to the Bohemian tales, although they do not resemble them so closely as the Moravian stories do. No. 10 is one of the tales that especially attracted my attention, and caused me to entertain the idea of translating a considerable selection out of the hundred given by Erben. No. 11 contains incidents which occur again in the White Russian story (No. 22), and in the great Russian tale of 'Ivan Popyalof,' given by Ralston, though in other respects the stories are very different. No. 22 is a superior variant of the German 'Rumpelstilskin' given by Grimm, and No. 13 is a specimen of an entirely different kind of story, illustrating 'The biter bitten.'

X.—THE THREE LEMONS.

THERE was once upon a time an old king who had an only son. This son he one day summoned before him, and spoke to him thus: 'My son, you see that my head has become white; ere long I shall close my eyes, and I do not yet know in what condition I shall leave you. Take a wife, my son! Let me bless you in good time, before I close my eyes.' The son made no reply, but became lost in thought; he would gladly with all his heart have fulfilled his father's wish, but there was no damsel in whom his heart could take delight.

Once upon a time, when he was sitting in the garden, and just considering what to do, all of a sudden an old woman appeared before him—where she came, there she came. 'Go to the glass hill, pluck the three lemons, and you will have a wife in whom your heart will take delight,' said she, and as she had appeared so she disappeared. Like a bright flash did these words dart through the prince's soul. At that moment he determined, come what might, to seek the glass hill and pluck the three lemons. He made known his determination to his father, and his father gave him for the journey a horse, arms and armour, and his fatherly blessing.

Through forest-covered mountains, through desert plains, went our prince on his pilgrimage, for a very, very great distance; but there was nothing to be seen, nothing to be heard of the glass hill and the three lemons. Once, quite wearied out with his long journey, he threw himself down under the cool shade of a broad lime-tree. As he threw himself down, his father's sword, which he wore at his side, clanged against the ground, and a dozen ravens began croaking at the top of the tree. Frightened by the clang of the sword, they rose on their wings, and flew into the air above the lofty tree. 'Hem! till now I haven't seen a living creature for a long while,' said the prince to himself, springing from the ground. 'I will go in the direction in which the ravens have flown; maybe some hope will disclose itself to me.'

He went on—he went on anew for three whole days and three nights, till at last a lofty castle displayed itself to him at a distance. 'Praise be to God! I shall now at any rate come to human beings,' cried he, and proceeded further.

The castle was of pure lead; round it flew the twelve ravens, and in front of it stood an old woman—it was Jezibaba*—leaning on a long leaden staff. 'Ah, my son! whither have you come? Here there is neither bird nor insect to be seen, much less a human being,' said Jezibaba to the prince. 'Flee, if life is dear to you; for, if my son comes, he will devour you.' 'Ah! not so, old mother, not so!' entreated the prince. 'I have come to you for counsel as to whether you cannot let me have some information about the glass hill and the three lemons.' 'I have never heard of the glass hill; but stay! when my son comes home, maybe he will be able to let you have the information. But I will now conceal you somewhat; you will hide yourself under the besom, and wait there concealed till I call you.'

The mountains echoed, the castle quaked, and Jezibaba whispered to the prince that her son was coming. 'Foh! foh! there is a smell of human flesh; I am going to eat it!' shouted Jezibaba's son, while still in the doorway, and thumped on the ground with a huge leaden club, so that the whole castle quaked. 'Ah, not so, my son, not so!' said Jezibaba, soothing him. 'There has come a handsome youth who wants to consult you about something.' 'Well, if he wants to consult me, let him come here.' 'Yes,

* Jezibaba is said to represent winter.

indeed, my son, he shall come, but only on condition that you promise to do nothing to him.' 'Well, I'll do nothing to him, only let him come.'

The prince was trembling like an aspen under the besom, for he saw before him through the twigs an ogre, up to whose knees he didn't reach. Happily his life was safeguarded, when Jezibaba bade him come out from under the besom. 'Well, you beetle, why are you afraid?' shouted the giant. 'Whence are you? What do you want?' 'What do I want?' replied the prince. 'I've long been wandering in these mountains, and can't find that which I am seeking. Now I've come to ask you whether you can't give me information about the glass hill and the three lemons.' Jezibaba's son wrinkled his brow, but, after a while, said in a somewhat gentler voice: 'There's nothing to be seen here of the glass hill; but go to my brother in the silver castle, maybe he'll be able to tell you something. But stay, I won't let you go away hungry. Mother, here with the dumplings!' Old Jezibaba set a large dish upon the table, and her gigantic son sat down to it. 'Come and eat!' shouted he to the prince. The prince took the first dumpling and began to eat, but two of his teeth broke, for they were dumplings of lead. 'Well, why don't you eat? maybe you don't like them?' inquired Jezibaba's son. 'Yes, they are good; but I don't want any just now.' 'Well, if you don't want any just now, pocket some, and go your way.' The good prince—would he, nould he—was obliged to put some of the leaden dumplings into his pocket. He then took leave and proceeded further.

On he went and on he went for three whole days and three nights, and the further he went, the deeper he wandered into a thickly wooded and gloomy range of mountains. Before him it was desolate, behind him it was desolate; there wasn't a single living creature to be seen. All wearied from his long journey, he threw himself on the ground. The clang of his silver-mounted sword spread far and wide. Above him four and twenty ravens, frightened by the clash of his sword, began to croak, and, rising on their wings, flew into the air. 'A good sign!' cried the prince. 'I will go in the direction in which the birds have flown.'

And on he went in that direction, on he went as fast as his feet could carry him, till all at once a lofty castle displayed itself to him! He was still far from the castle, and already its walls were glistening in his eyes, for the castle was of pure silver. In front of the castle stood an old woman bent with age, leaning on a long silver staff, and this was Jezibaba. 'Ah, my son! How is it that you have come here? Here there is neither bird nor insect, much less a human being!' cried Jezibaba to the prince; 'if life is dear to you, flee away, for if my son comes, he will devour you!' 'Nay, old mother, he will hardly eat me. I bring him a greeting from his brother in the leaden castle.' 'Well, if you bring a greeting from the leaden castle, then come into the parlour, my son, and tell me what you are seeking.' 'What I am seeking, old mother? For ever so long a time I've been seeking the glass hill and the three lemons, and cannot find them; now I've come to inquire whether you can't give me information about them.' 'I know nothing about the glass hill; but stay! when my son comes, maybe he will be able to give you the information. Hide yourself under the bed, and don't make yourself known unless I call you.'

The mountains echoed with a mighty voice, the castle quaked, and the prince knew that Jezibaba's son was coming home. 'Foh! foh! there's a smell of human flesh; I'm going to eat it!' roared a horrible ogre already in the doorway, and thumped upon the ground with a silver club, so that the whole castle quaked. 'Ah! not so, my son, not so; but a handsome youth has come and has brought you a greeting from your brother in the leaden castle.' 'Well, if he's been at my brother's, and if he has done nothing to him, let him have no fear of me either; let him come out.' The prince sprang out from under the bed, and went up to him, looking beside him as if he had placed himself under a very tall pine. 'Well, beetle, have you been at my brother's?' 'Indeed, I have; and here I've still the dumplings, which he gave me for the journey.' 'Well, I believe you; now tell me what it is you want.' 'What I want? I am come to ask you whether you can't give me information about the glass hill or the three lemons.' 'Hem! I've heard formerly about it, but I don't know how to direct you. Meanwhile, do you know what? Go to my brother in the golden castle, he will direct you. But stay, I won't let you go away hungry. Mother, here with the dumplings!' Jezibaba brought the dumplings on a large silver dish, and set them on the table. 'Eat!' shouted her son. The prince, seeing that they were silver dumplings, said that he didn't want to eat just then, but would take some for his journey, if he would give him them. 'Take as many as you like, and greet my brother and aunt.' The prince took the dumplings, thanked him courteously, and proceeded further.

Three days had already passed since he quitted the silver castle, wandering continuously through densely wooded mountains, not knowing which way to go, whether to the right hand or to the left. All wearied out, he threw himself down under a wide-spreading beech, to take a little breath. His silver-mounted sword clanged on the ground, and the sound spread far and wide. 'Krr, krr, krr!' croaked a flock of ravens over the traveller, scared by the clash of his sword, and flew into the air. 'Praise be to God! the golden castle won't be far off now,' cried the prince, and proceeded, encouraged, onwards in the direction in which the ravens showed him the road. Scarcely had he come out of the valley on to a small hill, when he saw a beautiful and wide meadow, and in the midst of the meadow stood a golden castle, just as if he were gazing at the sun; and before the gate of the castle stood an old bent Jezibaba, leaning on a golden staff. 'Ah! my son! what do you seek for here?' cried she to the prince. 'Here there is neither bird nor insect to be seen, much less a human being! If your life is dear to you, flee, for if my son comes, he will devour you!' 'Nay, old mother, he'll hardly eat me,' replied he. 'I bring him a greeting from his brother in the silver castle.' 'Well, if you bring him a greeting from the silver castle, come into the parlour and tell me what has brought you to us.' 'What has brought me to you, old mother? I have long been wandering in this mountain range, and haven't been able to find out where are the glass hill and the three lemons. I was directed to you, because haply you might be able to give me information about it.' 'Where is the glass hill? I cannot tell you that; but stay! when my son comes, he will counsel you which way you must go, and what you must do. Hide yourself under the table, and stay there till I call you.'

The mountains echoed, the castle quaked, and Jezibaba's son stepped into the parlour. 'Foh! foh! there's a smell of human flesh; I'm going to eat it!' shouted he, while still in the doorway, and thumped with a golden club upon the ground, so that the whole castle quaked. 'Gently, my son, gently!' said Jezibaba, soothing him; 'there is a handsome youth come, who brings you a greeting from your brother in the silver castle. If you will do nothing to him, I will call him at once.' 'Well, if my brother has done nothing to him, neither will I do anything to him.' The prince came out from under the table and placed himself beside him, looking, in comparison, as if he had placed himself beside a lofty tower, and showed him the silver dumplings in token that he had really been at the silver castle. 'Well, tell me, you beetle, what you want!' shouted the monstrous ogre; 'if I can counsel you, counsel you I will; don't fear!' Then the prince explained to him the aim of his long journey, and begged him to advise him which way to go to the glass hill, and what he must do to obtain the three lemons. 'Do you see that black knoll that looms yonder?' said he, pointing with his golden club; 'that is the glass hill; on the top of the hill stands a tree, and on the tree hang three lemons, whose scent spreads seven miles round. You will go up the glass hill, kneel under the tree, and hold up your hands; if the lemons are destined for you, they will fall off into your hands of themselves; but, if they are not destined for you, you will not pluck them, whatever you do. When you are on your return, and are hungry or thirsty, cut one of the lemons into halves, and you will eat and drink your fill. And now go, and God be with you! But stay, I won't let you go hungry. Mother, here with the dumplings!' Jezibaba set a large golden dish on the table. 'Eat!' said her son to the prince, 'or, if you don't want to do so now, put some into your pocket; you will eat them on the road.' The prince had no desire to eat, but put some into his pocket, saying that he would eat them on the road. He then thanked him courteously for his hospitality and counsel, and proceeded further.

Swiftly he paced from hill into dale, from dale on to a fresh hill, and never stopped till he was beneath the glass hill itself. There he stopped, as if turned to a stone. The hill was high and smooth; there wasn't a single crack in it. On the top spread the branches of a wondrous tree, and on the tree swung three lemons, whose scent was so powerful that the prince almost fainted. 'God help me! Now, as it shall be, so it will be. Now that I'm once here, I will at any rate make the attempt,' thought he to himself, and began to climb up the smooth glass; but scarcely had he ascended a few fathoms when his foot slipped, and he himself, pop! down the hill, so that he didn't know where he was, or what he was, till he found himself on the ground at the bottom. Wearied out, he began to throw away the dumplings, thinking that their weight was a hindrance to him. He threw away the first, and lo! the dumpling fixed itself on the glass hill. He threw a second and a third, and saw before him three steps, on which he could stand with safety. The prince was overjoyed. He kept throwing the dumplings before him, and in every case steps formed themselves from them for him. First he threw the leaden ones, then the silver, and then the golden ones. By the steps thus constructed he ascended higher and higher till he happily attained the topmost ridge of the glass hill. Here he knelt down under the tree and held up his hands. And lo! the three beautiful lemons flew down of themselves into the palms of his hands. The tree disappeared, the glass hill crashed and vanished, and when the prince came to himself, there was no tree, no hill, but a wide plain lay extended before him.

He commenced his return homeward with delight. He neither ate nor drank, nor saw nor heard, for very joy. But when the third day came, a vacuum began to make itself felt in his stomach. He was so hungry that he would gladly have then and there betaken himself to the leaden dumplings if his pocket hadn't been empty. His pocket was empty, and all around was just as bare as the palm of his hand. Then he took a lemon out of his pocket and cut it into halves; and what came to pass? Out of the lemon sprang a beautiful damsel, who made a reverence before him, and cried out: 'Have you made ready for me to eat? Have you made ready for me to drink? Have you made pretty dresses ready for me?' 'I have nothing, beautiful creature, for you to eat, nothing for you to drink, nothing for you to put on,' said the prince, in a sorrowful voice, and the beautiful damsel clapped her white hands thrice before him, made a reverence and vanished.

'Aha! now I know what sort of lemons these are,' said the prince; 'stay! I won't cut them up so lightly.' From the cut one he ate and drank to his satisfaction, and thus refreshed, proceeded onwards.

But on the third day a hunger three times worse than the preceding, assailed him. 'God help me!' said he; 'I have still one remaining over. I'll cut it up.' He then took out the second lemon, cut it in halves, and lo! a damsel still more beautiful than the preceding one placed herself before him. 'Have you made ready for me to eat? Have you made ready for me to drink? Have you made pretty dresses ready for me?' 'I have not, dear soul! I have not!' and the beautiful damsel clapped her hands thrice before him, made a reverence, and vanished.

Now he had only one lemon remaining; he took it in his hand and said: 'I will not cut you open save in my father's house,' and therewith proceeded onwards. On the third day he saw, after long absence, his native town. He didn't know himself how he got there, when he found himself at once in his father's castle. Tears of joy bedewed his old father's cheeks: 'Welcome, my son! welcome a hundred times!' he cried, and fell upon his neck. The prince related how it had gone with him on his journey, and the members of the household how anxiously they had waited for him.

On the next day a grand entertainment was prepared; lords and ladies were invited from all quarters; and beautiful dresses, embroidered with gold and studded with pearls were got ready. The lords and ladies assembled, took their seats at the tables, and waited expectantly to see what would happen. Then the prince took out the last lemon, cut it in halves, and out of the lemon sprang a lady thrice as beautiful as had been the preceding ones. 'Have you made ready for me to eat? Have you made ready for me to drink? Have you got pretty dresses ready for me?' 'I have, my dear soul, got everything ready for you,' answered the prince, and presented the handsome dresses to her. The beautiful damsel put on the beautiful clothes, and all rejoiced at her extraordinary beauty. Ere long the betrothal took place, and after the betrothal a magnificent wedding.

Now was fulfilled the old king's wish; he blessed his son, resigned the kingdom into his hands, and ere long died.

The first thing that occurred to the new king after his father's death was a war, which a neighbouring king excited against him. Now he was constrained for the first time to part from his hard-earned wife. Lest, therefore, anything should happen to her in his absence, he caused a throne to be erected for her in a garden beside a lake, which no one could ascend, save the person to whom she let down a silken cord, and drew that person up to her.

Not far from the royal castle lived an old woman, the same that had given the prince the counsel about the three lemons. She had a servant, a gipsy, whom she was in the habit of sending to the lake for water. She knew very well that the young king had obtained a wife, and it annoyed her excessively that he had not invited her to the wedding, nay, had not even thanked her for her good advice. One day she sent her maidservant to the lake for water. She went, drew water, and saw a beautiful image in the water. Under the impression that this was her own reflection, she banged her pitcher on the ground, so that it flew into a thousand pieces. 'Are you worthy,' said she, 'that so beautiful a person as myself should carry water for an old witch like you?' As she uttered this she looked up, and lo! it wasn't her own reflection that she saw in the water, but that of the beautiful queen. Ashamed, she picked up the pieces and returned home. The old woman, who knew beforehand what had occurred, went out to meet her with a fresh pitcher, and asked her servant, for appearance' sake, what had happened to her. The servant related all as it had occurred. 'Well, that's nothing!' said the old woman. 'But, do you know what? Go you once more to the lake, and ask the lady to let down the silken cord and draw you up, promising to comb and dress her hair. If she draws you up, you will comb her hair, and when she falls asleep, stick this pin into her head. Then dress yourself in her clothes and sit there as queen.'

It wasn't necessary to use much persuasion to the gipsy; she took the pin, took the pitcher, and returned to the lake. She drew water and looked at the beautiful queen. 'Dear me! how beautiful you are! Ah! you are beautiful!' she screamed, and looked with coaxing gestures into her eyes. 'Yes,' said she; 'but you would be a hundred times more beautiful if you would let me comb and dress your hair; in truth, I would so twine those golden locks that your lord could not help being delighted.' And thus she jabbered, thus she coaxed, till the queen let down the silken cord and drew her up.

The nasty gipsy combed, separated, and plaited the golden hair till the beautiful queen fell sound asleep. Then the gipsy drew out the pin, and stuck it into the sleeping queen's head. At that moment a beautiful white dove flew off the golden throne, and not a vestige remained of the lovely queen save her handsome clothes, in which the gipsy speedily dressed herself, took her seat in the place where the queen sat before, and gazed into the lake; but the beautiful reflection displayed itself no more in the lake, for even in the queen's clothes the gipsy nevertheless remained a gipsy.

The young king was successful in overcoming his enemies, and made peace with them. Scarcely had he returned to the town, when he went to the garden to seek his delight, and to see whether anything had happened to her. But who shall express his astonishment and horror, when, instead of his beautiful queen, he beheld a sorry gipsy. 'Ah, my dear, my very dear one, how you have altered!' sighed he, and tears bedewed his cheeks. 'I have altered, my beloved! I have altered; for anxiety for you has tortured me,' answered the gipsy, and wanted to fall upon his neck; but the king turned away from her and departed in anger. From that time forth he had no settled abode, no rest; he knew neither day nor night; but merely mourned over the lost beauty of his wife, and nothing could comfort him.

Thus agitated and melancholy, he was walking one day in the garden. Here, as he moved about at haphazard, a beautiful white dove flew on to his hand from a high tree, and looked with mournful gaze into his bloodshot eyes. 'Ah, my dove! why are you so sad? Has your mate been transformed like my beautiful wife?' said the young king, talking to it and caressingly stroking its head and back. But feeling a kind of protuberance on its head, he blew the feathers apart, and behold! the head of a pin! Touched with compassion, the king extracted the pin; that instant the beautiful mourning dove was changed into his beautiful wife. She narrated to him all that had happened to her, and how it had happened; how the gipsy had deluded her, and how she had stuck the pin into her head. The king immediately caused the gipsy and the old woman to be apprehended and burnt without further ado.

From that time forth nothing interfered with his happiness, neither the might of his enemies nor the spite of wicked people. He lived with his beautiful wife in peace and love; he reigned prosperously, and is reigning yet, if he be yet alive.

XI.—THE SUN-HORSE.

THERE was once upon a time a country, sad and gloomy as the grave, on which God's sun never shone. But there was a king there, and this king possessed a horse with a sun on his forehead; and this sun-horse of his the king caused to be led up and down the dark country, from one end to the other, that the people might be able to exist there; and light came from him on all sides wherever he was led, just as in the most beautiful day.

All at once the sun-horse disappeared. A darkness worse than that of night prevailed over the whole country, and nothing could disperse it. Unheard-of terror spread among the subjects; frightful misery began to afflict them, for they could neither manufacture anything nor earn anything, and such confusion arose among them that everything was turned topsy-turvy. The king, therefore, in order to liberate his realm and prevent universal destruction, made ready to seek the sun-horse with his whole army.

Through thick darkness he made his way as best he could to the frontier of his realm. Over dense mountains thousands of ages old God's light began now to break from another country, as if the sun were rising in the morning out of thick fogs. On such a mountain the king came with his army to a poor lonely cottage. He went in to inquire where he was, what it was, and how to get further. At a table sat a peasant, diligently reading in an open book. When the king bowed to him he raised his eyes, thanked him, and stood up. His whole person announced that he was not a man like another man, but a seer.

'I was just reading about you,' said he to the king, 'how that you are going to seek the sun-horse. Journey no further, for you will not obtain him; but rely on me: I will find him for you.' 'I promise you, good man, I will recompense you royally,' replied the king, 'if you bring him here to me.' 'I require no recompense; return home with your army—you're wanted there; only leave me one servant.'

The next day the seer set out with the servant. The way was far and long, for they passed through six countries, and had still further to go, till in the seventh country they stopped at the royal palace. In this seventh country ruled three own brothers, who had to wife three own sisters, whose mother was a witch. When they stopped in front of the palace, the seer said to his servant: 'Do you hear? you stay here, and I will go in to ascertain whether the kings are at home; for the horse with the sun is in their possession—the youngest rides upon him.' Therewith he transformed himself into a green bird, and, flying on the gable of the eldest queen's roof, flew up and down and pecked at it until she opened the window and let him into her chamber. And when she let him in he perched on her white hand, and the queen was as delighted with him as a little child. 'Ah, what a dear creature you are!' said she, as she played with him; 'if my husband were at home he would indeed be delighted with you; but he won't come till evening; he has gone to visit the third part of his country.'

All at once the old witch came into the room, and, seeing the bird, screamed to her daughter, 'Wring the accursed bird's neck, for it's making you bleed!' 'Well, what if it should make me bleed? it's such a dear; it's such an innocent dear!' answered the daughter. But the witch said: 'Dear innocent mischief! here with him! let me wring his neck!' and dashed at it. But the bird cunningly transformed itself into a man, and, pop! out through the door, and they didn't know whither he had betaken himself.

Afterwards he again transformed himself into a green bird, flew on the gable of the middle sister, and pecked at it till she opened the window for him. And when she let him in he flew on to her white hand, and fluttered from one hand to the other. 'Oh, what a dear creature you are!' cried the queen, smiling; 'my husband would indeed be delighted with you if he were at home; but he won't come till to-morrow evening; he has gone to visit two thirds of his kingdom.'

Thereupon the witch burst into the room. 'Wring the accursed bird's neck! wring its neck, for it's making you bleed!' cried she as soon as she espied it. 'Well, what if it should make me bleed? it's such a dear, such an innocent dear!' replied the daughter. But the witch said: 'Dear innocent mischief! here with it! let me wring its neck!' and was already trying to seize it. But at that moment the green bird changed itself into a man, ran out through the door, and disappeared, as it were, in the clap of a hand, so that they didn't know whither he had gone.

A little while afterwards he changed himself again into a green bird and flew on the gable of the youngest queen's roof, and flew up and down, and pecked at it until she opened the window to him. And when she had let him in he flew straight on to her white hand, and made himself so agreeable to her that she played with him with the delight of a child. 'Ah, what a dear creature you are!' said the queen; 'if my husband were at home he would certainly be delighted with you, but he won't come till the day after to-morrow at even; he has gone to visit all three parts of his kingdom.'

At that moment the old witch came into the room. 'Wring, wring the accursed bird's neck!' screamed she in the doorway, 'for it is making you bleed.' 'Well, what if it should make me bleed, mother? it is so beautiful, so innocent,' answered the daughter. The witch said, 'Beautiful innocent mischief! here with him! let me wring his neck!' But at that moment the bird changed itself into a man, and pop! out through the door, so that none of them saw him more.

Now the seer knew where the kings were, and when they would arrive. He went to his servant and ordered him to follow him out of the town. On they went with rapid step till they came to a bridge, over which the kings were obliged to pass.

Under this bridge they stayed waiting till the evening. When at even the sun was sinking behind the mountains, the clatter of a horse was heard near the bridge. It was the eldest king returning home. Close to the bridge his horse stumbled over a log of wood, which the seer had thrown across the bridge. 'Ha! what scoundrel was that who threw this log across the road?' exclaimed the king in anger. Thereat the seer sprang out from under the bridge and rushed upon the king for 'daring to call him a scoundrel,' and, drawing his sword, attacked him. The king, too, drew his sword to defend himself, but after a short combat fell dead from his horse. The seer bound the dead king on the horse, and gave the horse a lash with the whip to make him carry his dead master home. He then withdrew under the bridge, and they waited there till the next evening.

When day a second time declined towards evening, the middle king came to the bridge, and, seeing the ground sprinkled with blood, cried out, 'Somebody's been killed here! Who has dared to perpetrate such a crime in my kingdom?' At these words the seer sprang out from under the bridge and rushed upon the king with drawn sword, exclaiming, 'How dare you insult me? Defend yourself as best you can!' The king did defend himself, but after a brief struggle yielded up his life under the sword of the seer. The seer again fastened his corpse upon the horse, and gave the horse a lash with the whip to make him carry his dead master home. They then withdrew under the bridge and waited till the third evening came.

The third evening, at the very setting of the sun, up darted the youngest king on the sun-horse, darted up with speed, for he was somewhat late; but when he saw the red blood in front of the bridge, he stopped, and gazing at it exclaimed, 'It is an unheard-of villain who has dared to murder a man in my kingdom!' Scarcely had these words issued from his mouth when the seer placed himself before him with drawn sword, sternly bidding him defend himself, 'for he had wounded his honour.' 'I don't know how,' answered the king, 'unless it is you that are the villain.' But as his adversary attacked him with a sword, he, too, drew his, and defended himself manfully.

It had been mere play to the seer to overcome the first two kings, but it was not so with this one. Long time they fought, and broke their swords, yet victory didn't show itself either on the one side or on the other. 'We shall effect nothing with swords,' said the seer, 'but do you know what? Let us turn ourselves into wheels and start down from the hill; the wheel which breaks shall be the conquered.' 'Good!' said the king; 'I'll be a cart-wheel, and you shall be a lighter wheel.' 'Not so,' cunningly said the seer; 'you shall be the lighter wheel, and I will be the cart-wheel;' and the king agreed to it. Then they went up the hill, turned themselves into wheels, and started downwards. The cart-wheel flew to pieces, and bang! right into the lighter wheel, so that it all smashed up. Immediately the seer arose out of the cart-wheel and joyfully exclaimed, 'There you are, the victory is mine!' 'Not a bit of it, sir brother!' cried the king, placing himself in front of the seer; 'you have only broken my fingers. But do you know what? Let us make ourselves into flames, and the flame which burns up the other shall be the victor. I will make myself into a red flame, and do you make yourself into a bluish one.' 'Not so!' interrupted the seer; 'you make yourself into a bluish flame, and I will make myself into a red one.' The king agreed to this also. They went into the road to the bridge, and, changing themselves into flames, began to burn each other unmercifully. Long did they burn each other, but nothing came of it. Thereupon, by coincidence, up came an old beggar with a long gray beard, a bald head, a large scrip at his side, leaning upon a thick staff. 'Old father!' said the bluish flame, 'bring some water and quench this red flame; I'll give you a penny for it.' The red flame cunningly exclaimed, 'Old father! I'll give you a shilling if you'll pour the water on this bluish flame.' The old beggar liked the shilling better than the penny, brought water and quenched the bluish flame. Then it was all over with the king. The red flame turned itself into a man, took the sun-horse by the bridle, mounted on his back, called the servant, thanked the beggar for the service he had rendered, and went off.

In the royal palaces there was deep grief at the murder of the two kings; the entire palaces were draped with black cloth, and the people crowded into them from all quarters to gaze at the cut and slashed bodies of the two elder brothers, whose horses had brought them home. The old witch, exasperated at the death of her sons-in-law, devised a plan of vengeance on their murderer, the seer. She seated herself with speed on an iron rake, took her three daughters under her arms, and pop! off with them into the air.

The seer and his servant had already got through a good part of their journey, and were then crossing desert mountains, a treeless waste. Here a terrible hunger seized the servant, and there wasn't even a wild plum to assuage it. All of a sudden they came to an apple-tree. Apples were hanging on it; the branches were all but breaking under their weight; their scent was beautiful; they were delightfully ruddy, so that they almost offered themselves to be eaten. 'Praise be to God!' cried the delighted servant; 'I shall eat one of those apples with an excellent appetite.' 'Don't attempt to gather one of them!' cried the seer to him; 'wait, I'll gather some for you myself.' But instead of plucking an apple, he drew his sword and thrust it mightily into the apple-tree; red blood spouted out of it. 'There,' said he, 'you would have come to harm if you had eaten any of those apples, for the apple-tree was the eldest queen, whose mother placed her there to put us out of this world.'

After a time they came to a spring; water clear as crystal bubbled up in it, all but running over the brim and thus attracting wayfarers. 'Ah!' said the servant, 'if we can't get anything better, let us at any rate have a drink of this good water.' 'Don't venture to drink of it!' shouted the seer; 'but stay, I'll get you some of it.' Yet he didn't get him any water, but thrust his drawn sword into the midst of it; it was immediately discoloured with blood, which began to flow from it in mighty waves. 'That is the middle queen, whose mother placed her here to put us out of this world,' said the seer, and the servant thanked him for his warning, and went on, would he, nould he, in hunger and thirst, whithersoever the seer led him.

After a time they came to a rose-bush, which was red with delightful roses, and filled the air round about with their scent. 'Oh, what beautiful roses!' said the servant; 'I never saw such beauties in all my life. I'll go and gather a few of them; I will at any rate comfort myself with them if I can't assuage my hunger and thirst.' 'Don't venture to gather one of them!' cried the seer; 'I will gather them for you.' With that he cut into the bush with his sword; red blood spurted out, as if he had cut the vein of a human being. 'That is the youngest queen,' said the seer to his servant, 'whom her mother, the witch, placed here with the intention of taking vengeance upon us for the death of her sons-in-law.' They then went on.

When they crossed the frontier of the dark realm, flashes flew in all directions from the horse's forehead, and everything came to life again, beautiful regions rejoiced and blossomed with the flowers of spring. The king didn't know how to thank the seer sufficiently, and offered him the half of his kingdom as a reward, but he declined it. 'You are king,' said he; 'rule over the whole realm, and I will return to my cottage in peace.' He took leave and departed.

XII.—THE GOLDEN SPINSTER.

FAR away somewhere beyond the Red Sea, there was a certain young lord. When he had grown up in body and mind, he bethought himself that indeed it would not be a bad thing to look round him in the world and seek out a nice wife for himself, and a good mistress for his household. Well, as he determined, so he did. He went out into the world, but could not find such a one as he would have liked. At last he went somehow into the house of a widow, who had three daughters, all maidens. The two elder were as active as wasps for work, but the youngest, who was named Hanka, was like a leaden bird for everything that wanted doing. When the young lord came to them at spinning time he was astounded. 'How is it,' thought he, 'that Hanka can be sleeping in the chimney-corner, while the other spinsters are hard at work at their tasks?' He said to their mother: 'But, old lady, tell me, why don't you make that one, too, take a distaff? She is quite a grown-up girl, and would amuse herself by work.' 'Ah!

young sir,' replied the mother, 'I would allow her to spin with all my heart; I would fill her distaff myself; but what then? She is such a spinster, that by herself she would by morning spin up not only all our spinning materials, but all the thatch from the roof, and that into golden threads; nay, at last she would betake herself to my gray hairs; I am obliged, therefore, to give her a holiday.' 'If this be so,' said the delighted suitor, 'and if it is God's will, you can give her to me to wife. You see, I have a nice establishment—flax, hemp, whole heaps of the finer and commoner kinds of tow; she could spin away to her heart's content.' At such language the old woman did not take long for consideration, and Hanka woke from her slumbers. They brought the bridegroom expectant a handsome olive-coloured handkerchief out of the clothes-chest, adorned him with periwinkles, and performed the marriage ceremony that very evening. The other spinsters were somewhat mortified at Hanka's good fortune, but finally were content at it, hoping that they, too, would get rings on their fingers,* now that the idle hand, as they nicknamed Hanka, had obtained a husband. The next day our young bridegroom ordered his horses to be harnessed, and when all was ready, placed the tearful bride beside him in a handsome carriage, gave his hand to his mother-in-law, called out 'Farewell!' to the bride's sisters, and they left the village at a gallop.

For better or worse! Poor Hanka sat by her youthful husband mournful and tearful, just as if the chickens had eaten up all her bread. He talked to her enough, but Hanka was as mute as a fish. 'What's the matter with you?' said he. 'Don't be frightened. At my house, indeed, there will be no going to sleep for you. I shall give you all that your heart desires. You will have flax, hemp, fine and coarse tow enough for the whole winter, and I

* Literally, 'Would come under the garland.'

have got in a store of apples for spittle.' But our Hanka became more sorrowful the further they went. Thus they arrived in the evening at the young lord's castle, got down from the carriage, and, after supper, the future lady was conducted into a large room, in which, from top to bottom, lay nothing but spinning materials. 'Well,' said he, 'here you have distaff, spindle, and spindle-ring, and rosy apples and a few peas for spittle—spin away! If you spin all this, by morning, into golden threads, we shall be man and wife at once; if not, I shall cause you to be put to death without further ado.' Thereupon the young lord went out and left the spinster to spin. When Hanka was left alone, she didn't seat herself under the distaff, for she didn't even know how to twirl the threads, but began sorrowfully to exclaim: 'Oh God! God! here I am come out to vile disgrace! Why did not my mother teach me to work and spin like my two sisters? I might then have reposed in peace at home; but, as it is, sinful creature that I am, I must perish miserably.' As she was thus expressing her feelings, the wall suddenly opened, and a little mannikin stood before the terrified Hanka, with a red cap on his head and an apron girt round his waist; before him he pushed a little golden hand-cart. 'Why have you your eyes so tearful?' inquired he of Hanka. 'What has happened to you?' 'As if, sinful soul that I am, I should not weep,' said she; 'only think, they have ordered me to spin all these spinning materials into golden threads by morning, and if I don't do so, they will have me put to death without any ceremony. Oh God! God! what shall I do, forlorn in this strange world?' 'If that is all,' said the mannikin, 'don't be frightened. I will teach you to spin golden threads cleverly; but only on this condition, that I find you this time next year in this very place. Then, if you do not guess my honourable name, you will become my wife, and I shall convey you away in this cart. But, if you guess it, I shall leave you in peace. But this I tell you: if you choose to hide yourself anywhere this time next year, and if you fly ever so far beneath the sky, I shall find you, and will wring your neck. Well, have you agreed to this?' It was not, sooth to say, very satisfactory to Hanka; but what could the poor thing do? At length she bethought herself: 'Let it be left to God, whether I perish this way or that! I agree.' The mannikin, on hearing this, made three circuits round her with his golden cart, seated himself under the distaff, and repeating:

'Thus, Haniczka, thus!
Thus, Haniczka, thus!
Thus, Haniczka, thus!'

taught and instructed her to spin golden threads. After this, as he came, so he departed, and the wall closed up of itself behind him. Our damsel, from that time forth a real golden spinster, sat under the distaff, and seeing how the spinning materials decreased and the golden threads increased, spun and spun away, and by morning had not only spun up all, but had had a good sleep into the bargain. In the morning, as soon as the young lord awoke, he dressed himself and went to visit the golden spinster. When he entered the room he was all but blinded by the glitter, and wouldn't even believe his eyes, that it was all gold. But when he had satisfied himself that so it was, he began to embrace the golden spinster, and declared her his true and lawful wife. Thus they lived in the fear of God, and if our young lord had previously loved his Haniczka for the golden spinning, he then loved her a thousand times more for the beautiful son that she in the meantime bore him.

But what? There's no footpath without an end, neither could the joy of our wedded pair endure for ever. Day passed after day, till finally the appointed time approached within a span. Now our Hanka began to be more sorrowful from moment to moment; her eyes were as red as if they were baked, and she did nothing but creep like a shadow from room to room. And, indeed, it was a serious thing for a young mother to have to lose all at once her good husband and her beautiful son! Hitherto her poor husband knew nought about anything, and comforted his wife as well as he could; but she would not be comforted. When she bethought herself what a nasty dwarf she was going to obtain instead of her shapely husband, she all but dashed herself against the walls from excessive agony. At last she managed to overcome herself, and revealed everything to her husband as it had occurred to her on that first night. He became, from horror, as pale as a whitewashed wall, and caused proclamation to be made throughout the whole district that, if anyone knew of such a dwarf, and should make known his real name, he would give him a piece of gold as large as his head. 'Ah! what a windfall such a piece of gold as that would be!' whispered neighbour to neighbour, and they dispersed on all sides, examined all corners, all but looked into the mouseholes, searched and searched as for a needle, but, after all, couldn't find anything out. Nobody knew and nobody had seen the dwarf, and as for his name, no living soul could guess it. Under such circumstances the last day arrived; nothing had been seen or heard of the mannikin, and our Hanka, with her boy at her breast, was wringing her hands at the prospect of losing her husband. Her unhappy husband, whose eyes were almost exhausted from weeping, in order, at any rate, to escape from beholding the agony of his wife, took his gun on his shoulder, fastened his faithful hounds in a leash, and went out hunting. After hunting time—it was about the hour of afternoon luncheon—it began to lighten on all sides and in all directions, rain poured so that it would have been a shame to turn a dog out into the roads, and in this tempest all our young lord's servants sought shelter where they could, and got so lost that he remained with only one on a densely wooded unknown hill, and that as soaked and dripping as a rat. Where were they to seek shelter before the ever-increasing storm? where to dry themselves? where to obtain harbour for the night? The unlucky pair, master and servant, looked round on all sides to see whether they couldn't espy a shepherd's hut or a cattle-shed; but where nothing is, there is nothing. Finally, when they had almost strained their eyes out of the sockets, they saw where, out of the hole of the side shaft of a mine, puffs of smoke were rolling, as from a limekiln. 'Go, lad,' said the young lord to the servant, 'look whence this smoke issues; there must be people there. Ask them whether they will give us lodging for the night.' The servant went off and returned in a jiffy with the intelligence that neither door, nor shed, nor people were there. 'Fie, you're only a duffer!' said the lord to his servant with chattering teeth. 'I'll go myself; you, for a punishment, shall drip and freeze.' Well, the noble lord took the job in hand, but neither could he espy anything, save that in one place smoke kept continually issuing out of the side shaft. At last in disgust he said: 'Whatever devil on devil may bring, know I must whence all this smoke comes.' So he went to the hole itself, knelt beside it and peeped in. As he was thus peeping, he espied, somewhere under ground, where food was cooking in a kitchen, and covers were laid for two on a stone table. Round this table ran a little mannikin in a red cap with a golden hand-cart before him, and from time to time, after making the circuit, he sang:

'I've manufactured a golden spinster for the young lord,
She will try to guess my name to night;
If she guesses my name aright, I shall leave her;

If she guesses it not, I shall take her:
My name is Martynko Klyngas.'

And again he ran like mad round the table and shouted:

'I'm preparing nine dishes for supper,
I'll place her in a silken bed;
If she guesses,' etc.

The young lord wanted nothing more; he ran as fast as his legs could carry him to his servant, and, as it now cleared up a little, they were fortunate enough to find a path, by which they hastened home. He found his wife at home in agony, in misery, streaming with tears; for she thought she would not be able even to take leave of her husband, as he was so long away. 'Don't afflict yourself, my wife,' were the young lord's first words when he entered the room. 'I know what you require; his name is Martynko Klyngas.' And then he, without delay, recounted to her everything, where he had gone and what had happened to him. Hanka could scarcely keep on her feet for joy, embraced and kissed her husband, and betook herself joyfully into the room, in which she had spent the first night, to finish spinning the golden threads. At midnight the wall opened, and the mannikin with the red cap came in, as he had done that time last year, and running round her with the golden cart shouted with the utmost power of his lungs:

'If you guess my name, I leave you;
If you guess it not, I take you;
Only guess, guess away!'

'I'll have a try to guess,' said Hanka; 'your name is Martynko Klyngas.' As soon as she had uttered this, the little dwarf seized his cart, threw his cap on the ground, and departed as he had come; the wall closed, and Hanka breathed in peace. From that time forth she spun no more gold, and, indeed, neither was it necessary for her so to do, for they were rich enough. She and her husband lived happily together, their boy grew like a young tree by the water's side; and they bought a cow, and on the cow a bell, and here's an end to the tale I tell.'

[This story may be compared with 'Rumpelstiltskin' in Grimm. The principle is the same; but, I think, the variation in the details is much in favour of the Slavonic tale.]

XIII.—ARE YOU ANGRY?

WHERE it was, there it was, a certain village there was, in which lived a father with three sons. One of them was silly, and always sat in the chimney corner,* but the other two were considered clever. One of these went out to service in a village not far off. His mother put on his back a wallet full of cakes baked under the ashes. He went into a house and made an engagement with the master upon the terms that whichever got angry first was to have his nose cut off. The servant went to thresh. He was not called by his master either to breakfast or to dinner. His master asked him: 'Well, Mishek, are you angry?' 'What have I to be angry for?' Evening came, and supper was cooked; again they did not ask Mishek. His master asked him: 'Well, Mishek, are you angry?' 'What have I to be angry for?' He wasn't angry, for the cakes from home still held out. But during the second and third day the wallet was emptied, and again he wasn't summoned to dinner. His master asked him: 'Mishek, are you not angry?' 'Wouldn't even the devil be angry, when you are thus killing me with hunger?' Then his master pulled out a knife and cut off Mishek's nose. He hastened home noseless, and complained to his father and brothers of his wicked master. 'You

* Literally, 'Behind the stove.'

simpleton!' said the next brother, Pavko. 'Stay, I'll go! Hey, mother, bake some cakes under the ashes!' Pavko started off and went straight to the same village and to the same house, and made an engagement with the same master, on the terms that whichever was the first to become angry was to have his nose cut off. They set him, too, to thresh for three days, but neither on the first, nor on the second, nor on the third day, did they call him to take a meal. 'Pavko, are you not angry?' 'Wouldn't even devils be angry with you? My belly has already grown to my backbone.' Thereupon his master pulled out a knife and cut off Pavko's nose. Pavko went home noseless, and said to his elder brother: 'That's a cruel house of entertainment; the devil's got my nose.' Then Adam, the youngest, shouted from the chimney-corner: 'You are idiots! I'll go, and you'll see that I shall make a good job of it.' He went with cakes baked under the ashes in his wallet, and hit right upon the same village in which his brothers had been, and engaged himself with the same master upon the terms that whichever got angry first should have his nose cut off. But Adam knew how to proceed intelligently. When his master didn't call him to dinner, he went to the public-house with what he had threshed and pawned it all. His master came and didn't see a grain of corn. Adam then asked him: 'Master, are you angry?' 'Why should I be angry?' This occurred several times, and his master always said that he wasn't angry, for fear of losing his nose. Once there came a day on which the master and mistress were obliged to be from home, and they ordered Adam by their return to kill the first sheep that looked at him when he entered the stable, to dress it and boil it in a caldron, putting parsley with it. Adam went into the stable with great banging and noise, so that all the sheep looked at him at once, whereupon he slaughtered them all. One he dressed and put in the caldron, but instead of parsley he threw in a dog called by that name. His master and mistress came and asked Adam whether he had done everything properly? He said: 'I've slaughtered the sheep and thrown Parsley into the caldron till I' saw his feet. Now, master, are you angry?' 'What have I to be angry about?' he replied, for he preferred keeping his nose. On Christmas Eve, when they had to go to church, it was very dark. Adam's master said to him: 'It would be a good thing if somebody would light us as far as the church.' 'Go! go! I'll light you.' He took fire and set the roof on fire, till the whole house was in flames. The master hurried up, and Adam said to him: 'Master, are you angry?' 'Why should I be angry?' said he; for his nose was dearer to him than his house. But what was he to do without a house, without everything? They went into the world, master, mistress, and servant. They wanted to put him to death; and planned together, that when he was asleep his master should throw him into the water. But Adam was up to this; he didn't lie down on the side nearest the water, but got up in the night and threw his mistress, who was on that side, into the water. His master woke, and saw that his wife was gone; and began to cry out. But Adám asked him: 'Well, master, are you angry?' 'Wouldn't even the devil be angry, now that you've done me out of everything?' Adam took a knife and cut off his master's nose. He then took to his heels, went home, and said to his brothers: 'Now you see, you wiseacres, that I've earned the nose.'

UPPER AND LOWER LUSATIAN STORIES.

THE Upper Lusatian language is spoken in a district which may be marked by the towns of Löbau, Bautzen, and Muskau, while the Lower Lusatians dwell round the towns of Spremberg and Kottbus. Of the Upper Lusatians the larger portion live in Saxony and the smaller in Prussian territory; the Lower Lusatians are all Prussian subjects.

The Upper Lusatian story illustrates, in folklore style, a moral principle of great value. The Lower Lusatian tale is a variant of our own 'Little Red Ridinghood.' But it completes the story in such a manner as to explain the allegorical meaning of the narrative in the sense in which I am inclined to interpret it, as will be shown at the conclusion of the story.

But the Slavonic remnant in Lusatia is so surrounded by German territory, that most of its folklore has already been pressed into the service of the Germans.

A remarkable point in the Lusatian language is the completeness of the dual number in both nouns, adjectives, and verbs.

XIV.—RIGHT ALWAYS REMAINS RIGHT.

THERE was once upon a time a huntsman, who had a son, who was also a huntsman. He sent his son into a foreign land, to look about him and learn something additional. Here he went into a tavern, where he found a stranger, with whom he entered into conversation. They told each other all the news, till they also began to talk about right and wrong. The stranger asserted that the greatest wrong could be made right for money. But the huntsman opined that right always remained right, and offered to bet three hundred dollars upon it, if the stranger would do the same.* The stranger was content therewith, and they agreed to ask three advocates the question at once. They went to the first advocate, and he said that it was possible to make wrong right for money. They then went to another. He also asserted that wrong could be made right for money. Finally, they went to a third. He also told them that wrong could be made right for money. They then went back again, and as they had been going about the whole day, it wasn't till late in the evening that they got to their tavern. The stranger then asked the huntsman whether he still disbelieved that the greatest wrong could be made right for money, and the huntsman replied that he should soon be obliged to believe it on the assertion of the three advocates, although he was very unwilling to do so. The stranger was willing to grant him his life if he consented to pay three hundred dollars; but as they were talking about it, in came a man who overpersuaded the stranger that he must needs abide by what they had previously agreed upon. He did not, however, do this, but only, with a red-hot iron, took his eyesight from him, and told him at the same time, that he would then and then only believe that right remained right in the world, when the huntsman regained his sight.

The huntsman entreated the host of the tavern to put

* This surely ought, from what transpires later in the story, to have run thus: 'To stake his life against three hundred dollars to be staked by the stranger.'

him on the right road to the town. He put him on the road to the gallows, and went his way. When the huntsman had gone a little further, there was the end of the road, and he heard it strike eleven. He couldn't go any further, and remained lying where he was in hope that perhaps somebody would come there in the morning. After a short time he heard a clatter, and soon somebody came up; nor was it long before a second and a third arrived. These were three evil spirits, who quitted their bodies in the night time, and perpetrated all manner of villainy in the world. They began to talk together, and one said: 'To-day it is a year and a day since we were here together and related the good deeds that we had done during the year before. A year has again elapsed, and it is therefore time that we should ascertain which of us has done the best action during the past year.' The first spoke, and said: 'I have deprived the inhabitants of the city of Ramul of their water supply; they can only be helped if somebody finds out what it is that stops up the spring.' 'What's that?' said the second; and the first replied: 'I have placed a great toad on the spring out of which the water at other times flowed; if that be removed, the water will spring up again as before.' The second said: 'I have caused the beauty of the princess of Sarahawsky to disappear, and herself to fade away to skin and bones; she cannot be helped until the silver nail, which hangs above her bed, be pulled out.' The third said: 'Yesterday I caused a person to be deprived of his eyesight with a red hot iron; he can only be helped by washing his eyes with the water that is in the well not far from this gallows.' It then struck twelve in the town, and the three disappeared at once, but the huntsman remembered all that he had heard, and rejoiced that it was in his power to regain his eyesight.

Early on the morrow he heard somebody passing by, and

begged him to send him people from the town, to tell where the healing spring was. Then all manner of people came to him, but no one could show him the spring, save at length one old woman. He caused himself to be led thither, and as soon as he had washed his eyes in it, he immediately obtained his eyesight again.

He now asked the way to the city of Ramul, and went thither. As soon as he arrived, he told the town council that he would restore them their water. But plenty of people had been there already, and the city had spent a great deal of money upon them, yet no one had effected aught, so, as it had been all in vain, they intended to have nothing more to do with the matter. Well, he said that he would do it all for nothing, only they must give him some labourers to help him. It was done. When they had dug as far as the place where the pipes, through which the water used to flow, were laid into the spring, he sent all the workmen away and dug a little further himself, and behold! a toad, like a boiler, was sitting on the spring. He removed it, and immediately the water began to flow, and ere long all the fountains were filled with water. The citizens got up a grand banquet in his honour, and paid him a large sum of money for what he had done.

He then went on and came to Sarahawsky. Then in a short time he learnt that the princess was ill, just as he had heard, and that no physician was able to help her; moreover that the king had promised that the person who could cure her malady should obtain her to wife. He therefore equipped himself very handsomely, went to the king's palace, and there declared that he had come from a far country, and would cure the princess. The king replied to him that he had scarce any hope left, but would nevertheless make the experiment with him. The huntsman said that he would fetch his medicine. He went out and bought all manner of sweet comfits, and then went to the princess. He gave her a first dose, and looked about to see in what part of her bed's head the silver nail was sticking. Early on the second day he came again, gave her again some of his medicine, took the opportunity of laying hold of the nail, and pulled it till it began to move. In the afternoon the princess felt that she was better. The third day he came again, and while the princess was taking the medicine, pulled again at the bed's head, pulled the nail clean out, and put it secretly into his pocket. At noon the princess was so far recovered, that she wanted to have her dinner, and the king invited the huntsman to a grand banquet. They settled when the wedding was to take place, but the huntsman considered that he must first go home.

And when he had got home, he went again to the tavern where he had lost the sight of his eyes, and the stranger was there also. They began to tell each other all the news, and the huntsman related what he had heard under the gallows; how he had discovered the water, and finally how he had regained the sight of his eyes, and said that the stranger must now believe that in the world right always remained right. The stranger marvelled exceedingly, and said that he would believe it.

After this the huntsman went on and came to his princess, and they had a grand wedding festival, which lasted a whole week. The stranger bethought himself that he, too, would go under the gallows; peradventure he might also hear some such things as the huntsman had heard, and might in consequence also obtain a princess to wife. And when the year had elapsed, he also went there. He heard it strike one, and in a short time he heard a clatter; then up came somebody again, and it wasn't long before a second and third arrived. They began to talk together, and one said: 'It cannot but be, that some one overheard us last year, and through that everything that we have done is ruined. Let us, therefore, make a careful search before we again recount to each other what we have done.' They immediately began to search, and found the stranger. They tore him into three pieces and hung them up on the three corners of the gallows.

When the old king died they took the huntsman for king, and if he has not died, he is reigning still at the present day, and firmly believes that in his realm right will always remain right.

XV.—LITTLE RED HOOD.

ONCE upon a time, there was a little darling damsel, whom everybody loved that looked upon her, but her old granny loved her best of all, and didn't know what to give the dear child for love. Once she made her a hood of red samite, and since that became her so well, and she, too, would wear nothing else on her head, people gave her the name of 'Red Hood.' Once her mother said to Red Hood, 'Go; here is a slice of cake and a bottle of wine; carry them to old granny. She is ill and weak, and they will refresh her. But be pretty behaved, and don't peep about in all corners when you come into her room, and don't forget to say "Good-day." Walk, too, prettily, and don't go out of the road, otherwise you will fall and break the bottle, and then poor granny will have nothing.' Red Hood said, 'I will observe everything well that you have told me,' and gave her mother her hand upon it.

But granny lived out in a forest, half an hour's walk from the village. When Red Hood went into the forest, she met a wolf. But she did not know what a wicked beast he was, and was not afraid of him. 'God help you, Red Hood!' said he. 'God bless you, wolf!' replied she. 'Whither so early, Red Hood?' 'To granny.' 'What have you there under your mantle?' 'Cake and wine. We baked yesterday; old granny must have a good meal for once, and strengthen herself therewith.' 'Where does your granny live, Red Hood?' 'A good quarter of an hour's walk further in the forest, under yon three large oaks. There stands her house; further beneath are the nut-trees, which you will see there,' said Red Hood. The wolf thought within himself, 'This nice young damsel is a rich morsel. She will taste better than the old woman; but you must trick her cleverly, that you may catch both.' For a time he went by Red Hood's side. Then said he, 'Red Hood! just look! there are such pretty flowers here! Why don't you look round at them all? Methinks you don't even hear how delightfully the birds are singing! You are as dull as if you were going to school, and yet it is so cheerful in the forest!' Little Red Hood lifted up her eyes, and when she saw how the sun's rays glistened through the tops of the trees, and every place was full of flowers, she bethought herself, 'If I bring with me a sweet smelling nosegay to granny, it will cheer her. It is still so early, that I shall come to her in plenty of time,' and therewith she skipped into the forest and looked for flowers. And when she had plucked one, she fancied that another further off was nicer, and ran there, and went always deeper and deeper into the forest. But the wolf went by the straight road to old granny's, and knocked at the door. 'Who's there?' 'Little Red Hood, who has brought cake and wine. Open!' 'Only press the latch,' cried granny; 'I am so weak that I cannot stand.' The wolf pressed the latch, walked in, and went without saying a word straight to granny's bed and ate her up. Then he took her clothes, dressed himself in them, put her cap on his head, lay down in her bed and drew the curtains.

Meanwhile little Red Hood was running after flowers, and when she had so many that she could not carry any more, she bethought her of her granny, and started on the way to her. It seemed strange to her that the door was wide open, and when she entered the room everything seemed to her so peculiar, that she thought, 'Ah! my God! how strange I feel to-day, and yet at other times I am so glad to be with granny!' She said, 'Good-day!' but received no answer. Thereupon she went to the bed and undrew the curtains. There lay granny, with her cap drawn down to her eyes, and looking so queer! 'Ah, granny! why have you such long ears?' 'The better to hear you.' 'Ah, granny! why have you such large eyes?' 'The better to see you.' 'Ah, granny! why have you such large hands?' 'The better to take hold of you.' 'But, granny! why have you such a terribly large mouth?' 'The better to eat you up!' And therewith the wolf sprang out of bed at once on poor little Red Hood, and ate her up.

When the wolf had satisfied his appetite, he lay down again in the bed, and began to snore tremendously. A huntsman came past, and bethought himself, 'How can an old woman snore like that? I'll just have a look to see what it is.' He went into the room, and looked into the bed; there lay the wolf. 'Have I found you now, old rascal?' said he. 'I've long been looking for you.' He was just going to take aim with his gun, when he bethought himself, 'Perhaps the wolf has only swallowed granny, and she may yet be released;' therefore he did not shoot, but took a knife and began to cut open the sleeping wolf's maw. When he had made several cuts, he saw a red hood gleam, and after one or two more cuts out skipped Red Hood, and cried, 'Oh, how frightened I have been; it was so dark in the wolf's maw!' Afterwards out came old granny, still alive, but scarcely able to breathe. But Red Hood made haste and fetched large stones, with which they filled the wolf's maw, and when he woke he wanted to jump up and run away, but the stones were so heavy that he fell on the ground and beat himself to death. Now, they were all

7—2

three merry. The huntsman took off the wolf's skin; granny ate the cake and drank the wine which little Red Hood had brought, and became strong and well again; and little Red Hood thought to herself, 'As long as I live, I won't go out of the road into the forest, when mother has forbidden me.'

[Little Red Hood, like many folklore tales, is a singular mixture of myth and morality. In Cox's 'Comparative Mythology,' vol. ii., p. 831, note, Little Redcap, or Little Red Riding Hood, is interpreted as 'the evening with her scarlet robe of twilight,' who is swallowed up by the wolf of darkness, the Fenris of the Edda. It appears to me that this explanation may suit the colour of her cap or hood, but is at variance with the other incidents of the story. I am inclined to look upon the tale as a lunar legend, although the moon is only actually red during one portion of the year, at the harvest moon in the autumn. Red Hood is represented as wandering, like Io, who is undoubtedly the moon, through trees, the clouds, and flowers, the stars, before she reaches the place where she is intercepted by the wolf. An eclipse to untutored minds would naturally suggest the notion that some evil beast was endeavouring to devour the moon, who is afterwards rescued by the sun, the archer of the heavens, whose bow and arrow are by a common anachronism represented in the story by a gun. Though the moon is masculine in Slavonic, as in German, yet she is a lady, 'my lady Luna,' in the Croatian legend No. 53, below. In the Norse mythology, when Loki is let loose at the end of the world, he is to 'hurry in the form of a wolf to swallow the moon' (Cox ii., p. 200). The present masculine Slavonic word for moon, which is also that for month, 'mesic,' or 'mesec,' is a secondary formation, the original word having perished. In Greek and Latin the moon is always feminine.]

KASHUBIAN STORY.

THE Kashubians inhabit a small district in the North-east of Pomerania, 'the province upon the sea,' from *po*, upon, and *more*, the sea. The limits of the district may be roughly marked by the towns of Leba, Lauenburg and Bütow or Bytom.

The story contains many of the circumstances of the German story of 'The Table, the Ass and the Stick' in Grimm's collection. The Kashubian tales again would naturally be pressed into the service of the surrounding Germans. Bitter complaints have been made by Slavonic literati, that their Folklore tales have been appropriated by the Germans. Of course there is a vast amount of common ground in Folklore, and incidents belonging to one tale will sometimes start up at a distance in another apparently entirely unconnected with it. But I believe that there is considerable ground for the complaint.

XVI.—CUDGEL, BESTIR YOURSELF!

A COBBLER was busying himself on Saturday with mending old shoes, that he might be able to go to church on Sunday. He worked till late in the evening, and, having finished his work, early in the morning dressed himself, and took his book to service. In church he heard this doctrine, that if any one dedicates his property to the church, God will recompense him a hundredfold in another form. And as he was poor, he therefore determined to sell his cottage and goods and take the whole price to the priest at the church. He went home and told his wife of his intentions; and in a few days the money was in the hands of the parson.* But day passed after day, and nothing was to be seen of a recompense. At last, when hunger sorely tried the cobbler, he dressed himself like an old beggar and went to seek for the Lord God, After wandering a couple of days he met with an old shepherd, who was pasturing a large flock of lambs. And as he was very hungry, he made up his mind to go up to the old shepherd, and ask him to give him a little to eat out of his dinner-basket.† During the meal he related all that he had done, and how it was then going with him. The old shepherd compassionated the poor cobbler, and gave him a lamb, which scattered ducats at every call: 'Lamb, shake yourself!' but gave it him under the condition, that in one village, through which he was obliged to pass, he was not to enter the house of his old gossip. He laid the lamb on his shoulder with great joy, thanked the old man for it, and started with speed on his way home to rejoice his wife and children. When he got behind the hill, he began to distrust the words of the old shepherd, for he could not get it into his head that an ordinary lamb would scatter ducats. Wishing, therefore, to assure himself of their truth, he placed the lamb on the ground and uttered the old man's words: 'Lamb, shake yourself!' and when at the selfsame moment he espied ducats round the lamb's feet, he con-

* *Plebanus*, the priest of a church in which baptisms are celebrated.

† Or dinner-pot: two earthenware pots united together, used by shepherds and others to carry their dinners in.

sidered himself the most fortunate man in the whole world. Without delay he put the lamb on his back, and went on towards home. But when he went past his gossip's tavern, she besought him to pay her a visit, for they had not seen each other for a very long time. The cobbler at first hesitated a little, but wishing to show that he had ducats in his pocket, and that he had met with such good fortune, he went into the tavern; and, after first giving into her charge his present from the old man, with these words, 'But don't say to him, "Lamb, shake yourself!"' went to the table and drank off a noggin of brandy. But his gossip, a knavish old woman, bethought herself at once that there must be some secret lying in these words. She, therefore, took the lamb into another room, and when she was there by herself, said to the lamb: 'Lamb, shake yourself!' when she saw that he scattered ducats she began to consider how to cheat her gossip. After a short time she determined to make the cobbler drunk, to detain him all night at her house, and next day, early, to give him instead of his lamb another like it out of her own flock; which was effected according to her intention. Well, early in the morning the cobbler took the lamb on his shoulder and now hastened straight to his wife and children, and tossed them, as they wept, a couple of ducats, that his wife might get a good meal ready. His wife could not wonder enough whence her little husband had got so much money, but she did not venture to question him. After the meal the cobbler put the lamb on the table, called his children, that they might enjoy with him the rolling ducats, and shouted: 'Lamb, shake yourself!' But the lamb stood as if he were made of wood, and never even moved his head. The children, who had eaten their fill, began to laugh, and the wife thought that her husband was not quite right in his head. The cobbler, angry that his wish had not come to pass, repeated once more the old man's words, but this time, too, without effect, therefore he pushed the lamb off the table. So long as the ducats held out, there was content in the home; but as soon as they began to run short in the cottage, his wife began to reproach her husband for doing no work, and not troubling himself about a livelihood. So nothing again remained for the cobbler but, stick in hand, to go to look for the old man. He knew very well what a bad welcome he would receive from him, but what was to be done? However, the old man had compassion on the poor family, and this time gave him a tablecloth, which at every summons: 'Tablecloth, spread yourself!' spread itself of its own accord, and on it stood most excellent food and drink; but under the condition that he didn't go into his gossip's house. The cobbler, well content with the present, thanked the old man and moved towards home. In a short time he was behind the hill, sat down upon the ground, and, not from curiosity but from hunger, gave the word of command to the tablecloth to spread itself, for his inside was croaking. When, after eating his fill, he went past the tavern, his old gossip was waiting for him in front of the door; she begged him in the kindest terms not to pass her tavern, adding the proverb: 'Whoever passes a tavern sprains his foot.' The cobbler wavered long, but at last went in and entrusted her with the tablecloth with these words: 'Dear gossip, don't say, "Tablecloth, spread yourself!" The crafty woman gave him brandy in welcome, not for money; therefore, her gossip tossed off noggin after noggin, till there came a dizziness in his head. Then his gossip did the same with the tablecloth as with the lamb. The cobbler came to his wife and children, placed the tablecloth on the table and cried: 'Tablecloth, spread yourself!' But the tablecloth didn't stir, and the cobbler began to despair and to revile the old woman, his gossip. He returned again to the old man, begged pardon of him on his knees for not fulfilling the condition that time also, and prayed him, nevertheless, to have compassion on him and to be his preserver once more. The old man for a long time refused, but at last gave him a cudgel with a silver mounting set with precious stones, and ordered him this time to visit his gossip, and take note of these words: 'Cudgel, bestir yourself!' The cobbler, seized with new joy, thanked the old man a hundred times, and made the more haste towards his wife and children. Still, when behind the hill, he was curious to know what the cudgel meant, and wishing to satisfy himself, said: 'Cudgel, bestir yourself!' In a moment there stood before him a couple of stout fellows, who began to thrash him mercilessly. The cobbler, seized by cruel terror, did not know how to order them to cease beating him; at last, when already well beaten, he cried out: 'Cudgel, leave off!' Instantly the fellows disappeared and the cudgel stood before him. 'You're good, you're good!' said the cobbler, getting up from the ground, 'you'll help me to those former gifts.' When he arrived at the village, where his gossip lived, he stepped into her house and made himself at home as with an old acquaintance. She was very glad to see him, for she thought she would again make a good profit, entertained him well, and afterwards began to inquire whether he hadn't something for her to take charge of. Then the cobbler gave up to her his cudgel with the request not to say: 'Cudgel, bestir yourself!' The old woman laughed in her sleeve at the simpleton, thinking to herself, 'He wouldn't tell me without cause what I'm not to say!' She went at once with the cudgel into the other room, and scarcely had she crossed the threshold, when she cried out impatiently: 'Cudgel, bestir yourself!' Immediately the two fellows with cudgels began to beat her, and she lost all self-possession. At her piercing shrieks the host darted up to help her, when, hey ho! he got it too. The cobbler all the time kept calling out: 'Go it, cudgel! go it! till they give me back my lamb and my tablecloth!' Then nothing remained to his gossip but to give up his property to him. She ordered the lamb and tablecloth to be brought. As soon as the cobbler had satisfied himself that this was really done, he shouted 'Cudgel, leave off!' and went with the three gifts as quick as he could to his wife and children. Then there was great joy, for they had money and victuals in abundance; and did not withal forget God and other people, but assisted every poor person.

POLISH STORIES.

THE Polish language is one of great beauty and flexibility, but it is disfigured by an orthography which causes English readers to imagine that it is very difficult to pronounce, which is by no means the case. The letter *z* in Polish performs the office frequently assigned to *h* in English, viz., that of softening the preceding consonant without possessing any further power of its own. Thus *cz* is the exact equivalent in Polish of our *ch*, and *sz* exactly represents our *sh*. The other grand peculiarities of the Polish language are the sibillated *r*, written *rz*, the retention of the nasal sounds of long *a* (as *on*) and long *e* (as *en* in French), and the dull *ł*, represented by a curved stroke through the letter *l*, which has the sound of our final *ll* in 'bull,' but is somewhat difficult to pronounce at the beginning or in the middle of a word.

Poland, or rather Lithuania, the aristocracy of which is Polish, has produced a really great poet, Mickiewicz, whose poems are so beautiful, that it would be worth while for a literary person of leisure to study the language for the mere purpose of reading them. See Morfill's 'Russia' (Sampson Low, 1880), pp. 207-212. One of the most celebrated of Mickiewicz's poems, 'Pan Taddeus,' has lately been translated by Miss M. A. Biggs (Trübner and Co.).

In the Polish story, No. 17, we make acquaintance with 'Kostchey the Deathless,' who plays a great part in Russian stories, but is entirely unknown by name among the southern and most of the western Slavonians. His place is with them taken by dragons and evil shapes of various kinds. His name is probably derived from *kost*, a 'bone,' and I have ventured to Anglicize it accordingly. He is generally supposed to symbolize winter, and certainly deciduous trees and bushes then exhibit a very skeleton-like appearance. In a story from the government of Perm, given by Mr. Ralston, the secret of his immortality is discovered, and he is put to death accordingly. But I cannot help inferring that his death is of annual occurrence, and that he resumes his reign annually at the proper season, to be again put to death towards spring. With No. 18 several Russian tales given by Mr. Ralston (pp. 185-193) may be compared. No. 19 is a singular story of a more Oriental than European cast, and No. 20 reads as much like a dream dreamed after the consumption of a considerable quantity of *vodka*, as a genuine Folklore story. Such is also the case with several of Crofton Croker's Legends of the south of Ireland.

Tale No. 17 has already appeared in the 'Folklore Journal' for January, 1884. For mere beauty of construction and narration I doubt whether its equal can be found in any language.

XVII.—PRINCE UNEXPECTED.

There was a king and queen who had been married for three years, but had no children, at which they were both much distressed. Once upon a time the king found himself obliged to make a visit of inspection round his dominions; he took leave of his queen, set off and was not at home for eight months. Towards the end of the ninth month the king returned from his progress through his country, and was already hard by his capital city, when, as he journeyed over an uninhabited plain during the most scorching heat of summer, he felt such excessive thirst that he sent his servants round about to see if they could find water anywhere and let him know of it at once. The servants dispersed in various directions, sought in vain for a whole hour, and returned without success to the king. The thirst-tormented king proceeded to traverse the whole plain far and wide himself, not believing that there was not a spring somewhere or other; on he rode, and on a level spot, on which there had not previously been any water, he espied a well with a new wooden fence round it, full to the brim with spring water, in the midst of which floated a silver cup with a golden handle. The king sprang from his horse and reached after the cup with his right hand; but the cup, just as if it were alive and had eyes, darted quickly on one side and floated again by itself. The king knelt down and began to try to catch it, now with his right hand, now with his left, but it moved and dodged away in such a manner that, not being able to seize it with one hand, he tried to catch it with both. But scarcely had he reached out with both hands when the cup dived like a fish, and floated again on the surface. 'Hang it!' thought the king, 'I can't help myself with the cup, I'll manage without it.' He then bent down to the water, which was as clear as crystal and as cold as ice, and began in his thirst to drink. Meanwhile his long beard, which reached down to his girdle, dipped into the water. When he had quenched his thirst, he wanted to get up again—something was holding his beard and wouldn't let it go. He pulled once and again, but it was of no use; he cried out therefore in anger, 'Who's there? let go!' 'It's I, the subterranean king, immortal Bony, and I shall not let go till you give me that which you left unknowingly at home, and which you do not expect to find on your return.' The king looked into the depth of the well, and there was a huge head like a tub, with green eyes and a mouth from ear to ear, which was holding the king by the beard with extended claws like those of a crab, and was laughing mischievously. The king thought that a thing of which he had not known before starting, and which he did not expect on his return, could not be of great value, so he said to the apparition, 'I give it.' The apparition burst with laughter and vanished with a flash of fire, and with it vanished also the well, the water, the wooden fence, and the cup; and the king was again on a hillock by a little wood kneeling on dry sand, and there was nothing more. The king got up, crossed himself, sprang on his horse, hastened to his attendants, and rode on.

In a week or maybe a fortnight the king arrived at his capital; the people came out in crowds to meet him; he went in procession to the great court of the palace and entered the corridor. In the corridor stood the queen awaiting him, and holding close to her bosom a cushion, on which lay a child, beautiful as the moon, kicking in swaddling clothes. The king recollected himself, sighed painfully, and said within himself: 'This is what I left without knowing and found without expecting!' And bitterly, bitterly did he weep. All marvelled, but nobody dared to ask the cause. The king took his son, without saying a word, in his arms, gazed long on his innocent face; carried him into the palace himself, laid him in the cradle, and, suppressing his sorrow, devoted himself to the government of his realm, but was never again cheerful as formerly, since he was perpetually tormented by the thought that some day Bony would claim his son.

Meanwhile weeks, months, and years flowed on, and no one came for his son. The prince, named 'Unexpected,' grew and developed, and eventually became a handsome youth. The king also in course of time regained his usual cheerfulness; and forgot what had taken place, but alas! everybody did not forget so easily.

Once the prince, while hunting in a forest, became separated from his suite and found himself in a savage wilderness. Suddenly there appeared before him a hideous old man with green eyes, who said: 'How do you do, Prince Unexpected? You have made me wait for you a long time.' 'Who are you?' 'That you will find out hereafter, but now, when you return to your father, greet him from me, and tell him that I should be glad if he would close accounts with me, for if he doesn't soon get out of my debt of himself, he will repent it bitterly.' After saying this the hideous old man disappeared, and the prince in amazement turned his horse, rode home and told the king his adventure. The king turned as pale as a sheet, and revealed the frightful secret to his son. 'Don't cry, father!' replied the prince, 'it isn't a great misfortune! I shall manage to force Bony to renounce the right over me, which he tricked you out of in so underhand a manner, and if in the course of a year I do not return, it will be a token that we shall see each other no more.' The prince prepared for his journey, the king gave him a suit of steel armour, a sword, and a horse, and the queen hung round his neck a cross of pure gold. At leave-taking they embraced affectionately, wept heartily, and the prince rode off.

On he rode one day, two days, three days, and at the end of the fourth day at the setting of the sun he came to the shore of the sea, and in the self-same bay espied twelve dresses, white as snow, though in the water, as far as the eye could reach, there was no living soul to be seen; only twelve white geese were swimming at a distance from the shore. Curious to know to whom they belonged, he took one of the dresses, let his horse loose in a meadow, concealed himself in a neighbouring thicket, and waited to see what would come to pass. Thereupon the geese, after disporting themselves on the sea, swam to the shore; eleven of them went to the dresses, each threw herself on the ground and became a beautiful damsel, dressed herself with speed, and flew away into the plain. The twelfth goose, the last and prettiest of all, did not venture to come out on the shore, but only wistfully stretched out her neck, looking on all sides. On seeing the prince she called out with a human voice: 'Prince Unexpected, give me my dress; I will be grateful to you in return.' The prince hearkened to her, placed the dress on the grass, and modestly turned away in another direction. The goose came out on the grass, changed herself into a damsel, dressed herself hastily, and stood before the prince; she was young and more beautiful than eye had seen or ear heard of. Blushing, she gave him her white hand, and, casting her eyes down, said with a pleasing voice: 'I thank you, good prince, for hearkening to me: I am the youngest daughter of immortal Bony; he has twelve young daughters, and rules in the subterranean realm. My father, prince, has long been expecting you and is very angry; however, don't grieve, and don't be frightened, but do as I tell you. As soon as you see King Bony, fall at once on your knees, and, paying no regard to his outcry, upbraiding, and threats, approach him boldly. What will happen afterwards you will learn, but now we must part.' On saying this the princess stamped on the ground with her little foot; the ground sprang open at once, and they descended into the subterranean realm, right into Bony's palace, which shone all underground brighter than our sun. The prince stepped boldly into the reception-room. Bony was sitting on a golden throne with a glittering crown on his head; his eyes gleamed like two saucers of green glass and his hands were like the nippers of a crab. As soon as he espied him at a distance, the prince fell on his knees, and Bony yelled so horribly that the vaults of the subterranean dominion quaked; but the prince boldly moved on his knees towards the throne, and, when he was only a few paces from it, the king smiled and said: 'Thou hast marvellous luck in succeeding in making me smile; remain in our subterranean realm, but before thou becomest a true citizen thereof thou art bound to execute three commands of mine; but because it is late to-day, we will begin to-morrow; meanwhile go to thy room.'

The prince slept comfortably in the room assigned to him, and early on the morrow Bony summoned him and said: 'We will see, prince, what thou canst do. In the course of the following night build me a palace of pure marble; let the windows be of crystal, the roof of gold, an elegant garden round about it, and in the garden seats and fountains; if thou buildest it, thou wilt gain thyself my love; if not, I shall command thy head to be cut off.' The prince heard it, returned to his apartment, and was sitting mournfully thinking of the death that threatened him, when outside at the window a bee came buzzing and said: 'Let me in!' He opened the lattice, in flew the bee, and the princess, Bony's youngest daughter, appeared before the wondering prince. 'What are you thus thinking about, Prince Unexpected?' 'Alas! I am thinking that your father wishes to deprive me of life.' 'Don't be afraid! lie down to sleep, and when you get up to-morrow morning your palace will be ready.'

So, too, it came to pass. At dawn the prince came out of his room and espied a more beautiful palace than he had ever seen, and Bony, when he saw it, wondered, and wouldn't believe his own eyes. 'Well! thou hast won this time, and now thou hast my second command. I shall place my twelve daughters before thee to-morrow; if thou dost not guess which of them is the youngest, thou wilt place thy head beneath the axe.' 'I unable to recognise the youngest princess!' said the prince in his room; 'what difficulty can there be in that?' 'This,' answered the princess, flying into the room in the shape of a bee, 'that if I don't help you, you won't recognise me, for we are all so alike that even our father only distinguishes us by our dress.' 'What am I to do?' 'What, indeed! That will be the youngest over whose right eye you espy a ladycow; only look well. Adieu!' On the morrow King Bony again summoned Prince Unexpected. The princesses stood in a row side by side, all dressed alike and with eyes cast down. The prince looked and marvelled how alike all the princesses were; he went past them once, twice—he did not find the appointed token; the third time he saw a ladycow over the eyebrow of one, and cried out: 'This is the youngest princess!' 'How the deuce have you guessed it?' said Bony angrily. 'There must be some trickery here. I must deal with your lordship differently. In three hours you will come here again, and will show your cleverness in my presence. I shall light a straw, and you will stitch a pair of boots before it goes out, and if you don't do it you will perish.'

The prince returned desponding and found the bee already in his apartment. 'Why pensive again, prince?' 'How shouldn't I be pensive, when your father wants me to stitch him a pair of boots, for what sort of cobbler am I?' 'What else will you do?' 'What am I to do? I shan't stitch the boots, and I'm not afraid of death—one can but die once!' 'No, prince, you shall not die! I will endeavour to rescue you, and we will either escape together or perish together! We must flee—there's nothing else to be done.' Saying this, the princess spat on one of the window-panes, and the spittle immediately froze. She then went out of the room with the prince, locked the door after her, and threw the key far away; then, taking each other by the hands, they ascended rapidly, and in a moment found themselves on the very spot whence they had descended into the subterranean realm; there was the self-same sea, the self-same shore overgrown with rushes and thornbushes, the self-same fresh meadow, and in the meadow cantered the prince's well-fed horse, who, as soon as he descried his rider, came galloping straight to him. The prince didn't stop long to think, but sprang on his horse, the princess seated herself behind him, and off they set as swift as an arrow.

King Bony at the appointed hour did not wait for Prince Unexpected, but sent to ask him why he did not appear. Finding the door locked, the servants knocked at it vigorously, and the spittle answered them from the middle of the room in the prince's voice, 'Anon!' The servants carried this answer to the king; he waited, waited, no prince; he therefore again sent the same servants, who heard the same answer: 'Anon!' and carried what they had heard to the king. 'What's this? Does he mean to make fun of me?' shouted the king in wrath: 'Go at once, break the door open and conduct him to me!' The servants hurried off, broke open the door, and rushed in. What, indeed? there was nobody there, and the spittle on the pane of glass was splitting with laughter at them. Bony all but burst with rage, and ordered them all to start off in pursuit of the prince, threatening them with death if they returned empty-handed. They sprang on horseback and hastened away after the prince and princess.

Meanwhile Prince Unexpected and the princess, Bony's daughter, were hurrying away on their spirited horse, and amidst their rapid flight heard 'tramp, tramp,' behind them. The prince sprang from the horse, put his ear to the ground and said, 'They are pursuing us.' 'Then,' said the princess, 'we have no time to lose.' Instantly she transformed herself into a river, changed the prince into a bridge, the horse into a raven, and the grand highway beyond the bridge divided into three roads. Swiftly on the fresh track hastened the pursuers, came on to the bridge, and stood stupefied; they saw the track up to the bridge, but beyond it disappeared, and the highway divided into three roads. There was nothing to be done but to return, and they came with nought. Bony shouted with rage, and cried out: 'A bridge and a river! It was they. How was it that ye did not guess it? Back, and don't return without them!' The pursuers recommenced the pursuit.

'I hear "tramp, tramp!"' whispered the princess, Bony's daughter, affrightedly to Prince Unexpected, who sprang from the saddle, put his ear to the ground, and replied: 'They are making haste, and are not far off.' That instant the princess and prince, and with them also their horse, became a gloomy forest, in which were roads, by-roads, and footpaths without number, and on one of them it seemed that two riders were hastening on a horse. Following the fresh track, the pursuers came up to the forest, and when they espied the fugitives in it, they hastened speedily after them. On and on hurried the pursuers, seeing continually before them a thick forest, a wide road and the fugitives on it; now, now they thought to overtake them, when the fugitives and the thick forest suddenly vanished, and they found themselves at the self-same place whence they had started in pursuit. They returned, therefore, again to Bony empty-handed. 'A horse, a horse! I'll go myself! they won't escape out of *my* hands!' yelled Bony, foaming at the mouth, and started in pursuit.

Again the princess said to Prince Unexpected: 'Methinks they are pursuing us, and this time it is Bony, my father, himself, but the first church is the boundary of his dominion, and he won't be able to pursue us further. Give me your golden cross.' The prince took off his affectionate mother's gift and gave it to the princess, and in a moment she was transformed into a church, he into the priest, and the horse into the bell; and that instant up came Bony. 'Monk!' Bony asked the priest, 'hast thou not seen some travellers on horseback?' 'Only just now Prince Unexpected rode this way with the princess, Bony's daughter. They came into the church, performed their devotions, gave money for a mass for your good health, and ordered me to present their respects to you if you should ride this way.' Bony, too, returned empty-handed. But Prince Unexpected rode on with the princess, Bony's daughter, in no further fear of pursuit.

They rode gently on, when they saw before them a beautiful town, into which the prince felt an irresistible longing to go. 'Prince,' said the princess, 'don't go; my heart forebodes misfortune there.' 'I'll only ride there for a short time, and look round the town, and we'll then proceed on our journey.' 'It's easy enough to ride thither, but will it be as easy to return? Nevertheless, as you absolutely desire it, go, and I will remain here in the form of a white stone till you return; be circumspect, my beloved; the king, the queen, and the princess, their daughter, will come out to meet you, and with them will be a beautiful little boy—don't kiss him, for, if you do, you will forget me at once, and will never set eyes on me more in the world—I shall die of despair. I will wait for you here on the road for three days, and if on the third day you don't return, remember that I perish, and perish all through you.' The prince took leave and rode to the town, and the princess transformed herself into a white stone, and remained on the road.

One day passed, a second passed, the third also passed, and nothing was seen of the prince. Poor princess! He had not obeyed her counsel; in the town, the king, the queen, and the princess their daughter, had come out to meet him, and with them walked a little boy, a curly-headed chatterbox, with eyes as bright as stars. The child rushed straight into the prince's arms, who was so captivated by the beauty of the lad that he forgot everything, and kissed the child affectionately. That moment his memory was darkened, and he utterly forgot the princess, Bony's daughter.

The princess lay as a white stone by the wayside, one day, two days, and when the third day passed and the prince did not return from the town, she transformed herself into a cornflower, and sprang in among the rye by the roadside. 'Here I shall stay by the roadside; maybe some passer-by will pull me up or trample me into the ground,' said she, and tears like dew-drops glittered on the azure petals. Just then an old man came along the road, espied the cornflower in the rye by the wayside, was captivated by its beauty, extracted it carefully from the ground, carried it into his dwelling, set it in a flower-pot, watered it, and began to tend it attentively. But—O marvel!—ever since the time that the cornflower was brought into his dwelling, all kind of wonders began to happen in it. Scarcely was the old man awake, when everything in the house was already set in order, nowhere was the least atom of dust remaining. At noon he came home—dinner was all ready, the table set; he had but to sit down and eat as much as he wanted. The old man wondered and wondered, till at last terror took possession of him, and he betook himself for advice to an old witch of his acquaintance in the neighbourhood. 'Do this,' the witch advised him: 'get up before the first morning dawn, before the cocks crow to announce daylight, and notice diligently what begins to stir first in the house, and that which does stir, cover with this napkin: what will happen further, you will see.'

The old man didn't close his eyes the whole night, and as soon as the first gleam appeared and things began to be visible in the house, he saw how the cornflower suddenly moved in the flower-pot, sprang out, and began to stir about the room; when simultaneously everything began to put itself in its place; the dust began to sweep itself clean away, and the fire kindled itself in the stove. The old man sprang cleverly out of his bed and placed the cloth on the flower as it endeavoured to escape, when lo! the flower became a beautiful damsel—the princess, Bony's daughter. 'What have you done?' cried the princess. 'Why have you brought life back again to me? My betrothed, Prince Unexpected, has forgotten me, and, therefore, life has become distasteful to me.' 'Your betrothed, Prince Unexpected, is going to be married to-day; the wedding feast is ready, and the guests are beginning to assemble.'

The princess wept, but after awhile dried her tears, dressed herself in frieze, and went into the town like a village girl. She came to the royal kitchen, where there was great noise and bustle. She went up to the clerk of the kitchen with humble and attractive grace, and said in a sweet voice: 'Dear sir, do me one favour; allow me to make a wedding-cake for Prince Unexpected.' Occupied with work, the first impulse of the clerk of the kitchen was to give the girl a rebuff, but when he looked at her, the words died on his lips, and he answered kindly: 'Ah, my beauty of beauties! do what you will; I will hand the prince your cake myself.' The cake was soon baked, and all the invited guests were sitting at table. The clerk of the kitchen himself placed a huge cake on a silver dish before the prince; but scarce had the prince made a cut in the side of it, when lo! an unheard-of marvel displayed itself in the presence of all. A gray tom-pigeon and a white hen-pigeon came out of the cake; the tom-pigeon walked along the table, and the hen-pigeon walked after him, cooing:

'Stay, stay, my pigeonet, oh stay!
Don't from thy true love flee away;
My faithless lover I pursue,
Prince Unexpected like unto,
Who Bony's daughter did betray.'

Scarcely had Prince Unexpected heard this cooing of the pigeon, when he regained his lost recollection, bounced from the table, rushed to the door, and behind the door the princess, Bony's daughter, took him by the hand; they went together down the corridor, and before them stood a horse saddled and bridled.

Why delay? Prince Unexpected and the princess, Bony's daughter, sprang on the horse, started on the road, and at last arrived happily in the realm of Prince Unexpected's father. The king and queen received them with joy and merriment, and didn't wait long before they prepared them a magnificent wedding, the like of which eye never saw and ear never heard of.

With the above story should be compared that of 'The Water King, and Vasilissa the Wise' (Ralston, p. 120). A large number of tales that may also be compared with it are mentioned by Mr. Ralston in pp. 132-133 of his Russian Folk-tales. As to the interpretation of 'Prince Unexpected,' it is very tempting to look upon Kostchey's twelve daughters as representing the twelve months. And, as the year anciently began with spring, Kostchey's youngest daughter would be the month which forms the transition from winter to spring. The interruption of their progress by Prince Unexpected's temporary forgetfulness may be explained as the temporary cessation of warm weather and return of a kind of secondary winter, which often occurs in early spring. Prince Unexpected himself may, perhaps, be considered as representing the sun, who has been held in captivity by the winter and has escaped with the last month of the year. Vasilissa the Wise is the *eldest* daughter of the Water King, and would thus represent the first month of the new year.

XVIII.—THE SPIRIT OF A BURIED MAN.

A POOR scholar was going by the highway into a town, and found under the walls of the gate the body of a dead man, unburied, trodden by the feet of the passers-by. He had not much in his purse, but willingly gave enough to bury him, that he might not be spat upon and have sticks thrown at him. He performed his devotions over the fresh heaped-up grave, and went on into the world to wander. In an oak wood sleep overpowered him, and when he awoke, he espied with wonderment a bag full of gold. He thanked the unseen beneficent hand, and came to the bank of a large river, where it was necessary to be ferried over. The two ferrymen, observing the bag full of gold, took him into the boat, and just at an eddy took from him the gold and threw him into the water. As the waves carried him away insensible, he by accident clutched a plank, and by its aid floated successfully to the shore. It was not a plank, but the spirit of the buried man, who addressed him in these words: 'You honoured my remains by burial; I thank you for it. In token of gratitude I will teach you how you can transform yourself into a crow, into a hare, and into a deer.' Then he taught him the spell. The scholar, when acquainted with the spell, could with ease transform himself into a crow, into a hare, and into a deer. He wandered far, he wandered wide, till he wandered to the court of a mighty king, where he remained as an archer in attendance at the court. This king had a beautiful daughter, but she dwelt on an inaccessible island, surrounded on all sides by the sea. She dwelt in a castle of copper, and possessed a sword such that he who brandished it could conquer the largest army. Enemies had invaded the territory of the king; he needed and desired the victorious sword. But how to obtain it, when nobody had up to that time succeeded in getting on to the lonely island? He therefore made proclamation that whoever should bring the victorious sword from the princess should obtain her hand, and, moreover, should sit upon the throne after him. No one was venturesome enough to attempt it, till the wandering scholar, then an archer attached to the court, stood before the king announcing his readiness to go, and requesting a letter, that on receipt of that token the princess might give up the weapon to him. All men were astonished, and the king entrusted him with a letter to his daughter. He went into the forest, without knowing in the least that another archer attached to the court was dogging his steps. He first transformed himself into a hare, then into a deer, and darted off with haste and speed; he traversed no small distance, till he stood on the shore of the sea. He then transformed himself into a crow, flew across the water of the sea, and didn't rest till he was on the island. He went into the castle of copper, delivered to the beautiful princess the letter from her father, and requested her to give him the victorious sword. The beautiful princess looked at the archer. He captured her heart at once. She asked inquisitively how he had been able to get to her castle, which was on all sides surrounded by water and knew no human footsteps. Thereupon the archer replied that he knew secret spells by which he could transform himself into a deer, a hare, and a crow. The beautiful princess, therefore, requested the archer to transform himself into a deer before her eyes. When he made himself into a graceful deer, and began to fawn and bound, the princess secretly pulled a tuft of fur from his back. When he transformed himself again into a hare, and bounded with pricked up ears, the princess secretly pulled a little fur off his back. When he changed himself into a crow and began to fly about in the room, the princess secretly pulled a few feathers from the bird's wings. She immediately wrote a letter to her father and delivered up the victorious sword. The young scholar flew across the sea in the form of a crow, then ran a great distance in that of a deer, till in the neighbourhood of the wood he bounded as a hare. The treacherous archer was already there in ambush, saw when he changed himself into a hare, and recognised him at once. He drew his bow, let fly the arrow, and killed the hare. He took from him the letter and carried off the sword, went to the castle, delivered to the king the letter and the sword of victory, and demanded at once the fulfilment of the promise that had been made. The king, transported with joy, promised him immediately his daughter's hand, mounted his horse, and rode boldly against his enemies with the sword. Scarcely had he espied their standards, when he brandished the sword mightily several times, and that towards the four quarters of the world. At every wave of the sword large masses of enemies fell dead on the spot, and others, seized with panic, fled like hares. The king returned joyful with victory, and sent for his beautiful daughter, to give her to wife to the archer who brought the sword. A banquet was prepared. The musicians were already striking up, the whole castle was brilliantly lighted; but the princess sat sorrowful beside the assassin-archer. She knew at once that he was in nowise the man whom she saw in the castle on the island, but she dared not ask her father where the other handsome archer was; she only wept much and secretly: her heart beat for the other.

The poor scholar, in the hare's skin, lay slain under the oak, lay there a whole year, till one night he felt himself awakened from a mighty sleep, and before him stood the well-known spirit, whose body he had buried. He told him what had happened to him, brought him back to life, and said: 'To-morrow is the princess's wedding; hasten, therefore, to the castle without a moment's delay; she will recognise you; the archer, too, who killed you treacherously, will recognise you.' The young man sprang up promptly, went to the castle with throbbing heart, and entered the grand saloon, where numerous guests were eating and drinking. The beautiful princess recognised him at once, shrieked with joy, and fainted; and the assassin-archer, the moment he set eyes on him, turned pale and green from fear. Then the young man related the treason and murderous act of the archer, and in order to prove his words, turned himself in presence of all the assembled company into a graceful deer, and began to fawn upon the princess. She placed the tuft of fur pulled off him in the castle on the back of the deer, and the fur immediately grew into its place. Again he transformed himself into a hare, and similarly the piece of fur pulled off, which the princess had kept, grew into its place immediately on contact. All looked on in astonishment till the young man changed himself into a crow. The princess brought out the feathers which she had pulled from its wings in the castle, and the feathers immediately grew into their places. Then the old king commanded the assassin-archer to be put to death. Four horses were led out, all wild and unbroken. He was bound to them by his hands and feet, the horses were started off by the whip, and at one bound they tore the assassin-archer to pieces. The young man obtained the hand of the young and charming princess. The whole castle was in a brilliant blaze of light, they drank, they ate with mirth; and the princess did not weep, for she possessed the husband that she wished for.

XIX.—THE PALE MAIDEN.

A PEASANT farmer in reduced circumstances had a beautiful daughter, whom an old knight, the proprietor of the village, wanted to marry, and that even by compulsion. But the damsel disliked him, and her parents also refused to consent to the marriage. So the proprietor persecuted them in every way in his power, and so oppressed them with forced labour and ordered them to be beaten on the slightest occasion, that the poor farmer could hold out no longer, but determined to remove from the village with his whole family. In the cottage in which the farmer dwelt there was something continually grating behind the stove, but though they searched several times, and turned the seat constructed at the side of the stove upside down, yet were they unable to discover aught. But when, on the day of their departure, they were removing the rest of their goods, they heard a more and more articulate grating, and whilst they were impatiently listening, as the grating and scraping went on, out of the stove sprang a thin pale form, like a buried maiden. 'What the devil is this?' cried the father. 'For heaven's sake!' screamed the mother, and all the children after her. 'I am no devil,' said the thin pale maiden, 'but I am your Poverty. You are now taking yourselves off hence, and you are bound to take me with you to your new abode.' The poor householder was no fool; he bethought himself a little, and neither seized nor throttled his Poverty, for she was so slight that he could have done nothing of any consequence to her, but he made the lowest possible reverence to her, and said: 'Well, your gracious ladyship, if you are so well satisfied amongst us, then come with us; but, as you see, we are removing everything for ourselves, so help us to carry something, and we shall get off the quicker.' Poverty agreed to this, and wanted to take a couple of small vessels out of the house, but the householder distributed the small vessels among his children to remove, and said that there was still a block of wood in the yard which must also be taken away. Going out into the yard, he made a cut in the block from above with his axe. He then called Poverty, and politely requested her to help him remove the block. Poverty did not see on which side to lift the block, till, when the farmer pointed out the cleft to her, she put her long thin fingers in the chink. The farmer, pretending to lift the block on the other side, suddenly pulled his axe out of the cleft, and Poverty's long thin fingers remained squeezed in the block, so that, being utterly unable to pull them out, she shrieked out immediately in what pain she was. But all in vain. The farmer removed all his goods as well as his children, quitted the cottage completely, and returned to the place no more.

When the farmer settled in another village, things went with him so prosperously that ere long he was the richest man in the whole village; he married his daughter to a respectable and wealthy farmer's son, twenty years old, and the whole family prospered. On the other hand, the proprietor of the first village, the oppressor of these poor people, having to assign vacant cottages to fresh tenants, came to inspect the cottage left vacant by the reduced farmer, who had refused to give him his daughter. Seeing Poverty beside the block complaining of the pain of her fingers, he took pity on the pale maiden, took her fingers out by means of a wedge, and set her completely free.

From the time of her liberation the pale maiden never quitted the side of her liberator, and when, moreover, the devil lit a fire in the old stove, and the proprietor went dotty with love in his old age, he spent and spent, and ran through everything that he had.

XX.—THE PLAGUE-SWARM.

A RUTHENIAN, having lost his wife and children by the plague, fled into the forest from his desolate cottage and sought safety there. He wandered about all day long; towards evening he constructed a booth of branches, lit a little fire, and fell asleep, wearied out. It was already after midnight when a mighty noise awoke him. He rose to his feet, listened, and heard a kind of songs in the distance, and accompanying the songs a sound of tambourines and fifes. He listened, in no small astonishment, that, when death was raging around, people were rejoicing there so merrily. The noise that he heard kept continually approaching, and the terrified Podolian* espied a swarming multitude advancing along a wide road. It was a troop of strange-looking spectres that circled round a carriage; the carriage was black and elevated, and in it sat the Plague. At every step the frightful company kept increasing; for on the road almost everything was transformed into a spectre.

Feebly burned his little fire; a tolerably large firebrand was still smoking a little. Scarcely had the plague-swarm drawn near when the firebrand stood upon feet, extended two arms—the burning part began to glitter with two glaring eyes—it began to sing in concert with the others. The villager was stupefied; in speechless terror he seized his axe and was on the point of striking the nearest spectre, but the axe flew out of his hands, transformed itself into a

* A Ruthenian by nationality, a Podolian by locality.

tall woman with raven-black tresses, and, singing, vanished before his eyes. The plague-swarm proceeded onwards ; and the Podolian saw how the trees, the bushes, the owls, the screech-owls, assuming tall shapes, increased the multitude, the terrible harbinger of a frightful death. He fell down powerless, and when in the morning the warmth of the sun awoke him, the vessels that he had brought with him were smashed and broken, the clothes torn to rags, the provisions spoilt. He perceived that no one but the plague-swarm had done him all this mischief, and, thanking God that he had at any rate escaped with life, proceeded further to seek shelter and food.

EASTERN SLAVONIANS.

WHITE RUSSIAN STORIES.

WE now come to the first set of stories belonging to those Slavonians who make use of the Cyrillic instead of the Latin characters. The White Russians occupy the whole of the Governments of Minsk and Mogilef, and great part of those of Vitebsk and Grodno. In these stories we first met with the distinction between the Western and Eastern Slavonic terms for monarch. The Western Slavonians employ the terms *kral*, *krul*, or *korol*, for a monarch, which are believed to originate from the name of the mighty Frankish monarch, KARL the Great, whom we generally know by his French title, Charlemagne. The Eastern Slavonians usually make use of the term TZAR, 'Emperor,' which is a corruption of the Latin 'Cæsar,' the title of the emperors of Constantinople, and later of the Russian emperors. Thus in the following stories we shall find emperors and empresses generally, though not invariably, replacing kings and queens, till we return again to the West.

The White Russian language possesses but little literature, but was employed for diplomatic purposes by the once powerful state of Lithuania (Morfill's 'Slavonic Literature,' S.P.C.K., p. 113).

The heroes 'Overturn-hill' (*Vertogor*) and 'Overturn-oak'

(*Vertodub*), who appear in No. 22, occur also in a story from the Ukraine, given by Mr. Ralston (pp. 170-175). Several circumstances in No. 22 are also similar to incidents in the Russian tale of 'Ivan Popyalof' (Ralston, p. 66), but in spite of these similarities the stories are truly distinct.

XXI.—THE FROST, THE SUN, AND THE WIND.

ONCE upon a time a man went out alone, and met on the road the Sun, the Frost, and the Wind. Well, on meeting them, he gave them a salutation: 'Praised' [be the Lord Jesus Christ]! To which did he present the salutation? The Sun said: 'To me, that I might not burn him.' The Frost said: 'To me, and not to you, for he is not so much afraid of you as of me.' 'Story-tellers! it's false!' said, lastly, the Wind; 'that man presented the salutation not to you two, but to me.' They began to jangle and quarrel together, and all but pulled the mantles off each other's backs. 'Well, if it's so, let's ask him to whom he presented the salutation, to me or to you?' They overtook the man and asked him; then he said: 'To the Wind.' 'Didn't I say that it was to me?' 'Stop you! I'll give you a baking, you rascal!' said the Sun; 'you shall remember me.' Then said the Wind: 'Never fear, he won't bake you; I shall blow and cool him.' 'So will I freeze you up, you scoundrel!' said the Frost. 'Don't be frightened, poor fellow! then I shan't blow, and he'll do nothing to you; he doesn't freeze you up without a wind.'

XXII.—LITTLE ROLLING-PEA.

IN a certain empire and a certain province, on the ocean sea, on the island of Bujan, stood a green oak, and under the oak a roasted ox, and by its side a whetted knife; suddenly the knife was seized. Be so good as to eat! This isn't a story (*kazka*), but only a preface to a story (*prikazka*): whoever shall listen to my story, may he have a sableskin cloak, and a horseskin cloak, and a very beautiful damsel, a hundred roubles for the wedding, and fifty for a jollification!

There was a husband and wife. The wife went for water, took a bucket, and after drawing water, went home, and all at once she saw a pea rolling along. She thought to herself: 'This is the gift of God.' She took it up and ate it, and in course of time became the mother of a baby boy, who grew not by years, but by hours, like millet dough when leavened. They nursed and petted him in a way that couldn't be improved upon, and put him to school. What others learnt in three or four years he understood in a single year, and the book was not sufficient for him. He came from the school to his father and mother: 'Now, then, daddy and mammy, thank my teachers, for already many come to school to me. Thank God, I know more than they.' Well, he went into the street to amuse himself, and found a pin, which he brought to his father and mother. He said to his father: 'Here's this piece of iron; take it to a smith, and let him make me a mace of seven poods weight.' His father didn't say a single word to him, but only thought in his own mind: 'The Lord has given me a child different from other people; I think he has a middling understanding, but he is now making a fool of me. Can it possibly be that a seven-pood* mace can be made out of a pin?' His father, having a considerable sum of money in gold, silver, and paper, drove to the town, bought seven poods of iron, and gave them to a smith to make a mace of. They made him a seven-pood mace, and he brought it home. Little Rolling-pea came out from the attic, took his seven-pood mace, and, hearing a

* A pood is 40 Russian, 36 English, pounds.

storm in the sky, threw it into the clouds. He went up into his attic: 'Mother, look in my head before I start; a nasty thing is biting me, for I am a young lad.' . . . Well, rising from his mother's knees, he went out into the yard and saw the clouds. He fell down with his right ear to the broad ground, and on rising up called his father: 'Father, come here: see what is whizzing and humming; my mace is coming to the ground.' He placed his knee in the way of his mace; the mace struck him on the knee and broke in halves. He became angry with his father: 'Well, father, why did you not have a mace made for me out of the iron that I gave you? If you had done so, it would not have broken, but only bent. Here is the same iron for you, go and get it made; don't add any of your own.' The smiths put the iron in the fire and began to beat it with hammers and pull it, and made a seven-pood mace.

Little Rolling-pea took his seven-pood mace and got ready to go on a journey, a long journey; he went and went, and Overturn-hill met him. 'I salute you, brother Little Rolling-pea! whither are you going? whither are you journeying?' Little Rolling-pea also asked him a question: 'Who are you?' 'I am the mighty hero Overturn-hill.' 'Will you be my comrade?' said Little Rolling-pea. He replied: 'Possibly I will be at your service.' They went on together. They went and went, and the mighty hero Overturn-oak met them. 'God bless you, brothers! Good health to you! What manner of men are you?' inquired Overturn-oak. 'Little Rolling-pea and Overturn-hill.' 'Whither are you going?' 'To such a city. A dragon devours people there, so we are going to smite him.' 'Is it not possible for me to join your company?' 'It is possible,' said Little Rolling-pea. They went to the city, and made themselves known to the emperor. 'What manner of men are you?' 'We are mighty heroes!' 'Is it in your power to deliver this city? A dragon is ravenous and destroys much people. He must be slain.' 'Why do we call ourselves mighty heroes, if we do not slay him?' Midnight came, and they went up to a bridge of guelder-rose-wood over a river of fire. Lo! up came a six-headed dragon, and posted himself upon the bridge, and immediately his horse neighed, his falcon chattered, and his hound howled. He gave his horse a blow on the head: 'Don't neigh, devil's carrion!* Don't chatter, falcon! And you, hound, don't howl! For here is Little Rolling-pea. Well now,' said he, 'come forth, Little Rolling-pea! shall we fight or shall we try our strength?' Little Rolling-pea answered: 'Not to try their strength do good youths travel, but only to fight.' They began the combat. Little Rolling-pea and his comrades struck the dragon three blows at a time on three heads. The dragon, seeing that he could not escape destruction, said: 'Well, brothers, it is only little Rolling-pea that troubles me. I'd settle matters with you two.' They began to fight again, smashed the dragon's remaining heads, took the dragon's horse to the stable, his falcon to the mews, and his hound to the kennel; and Little Rolling-pea cut out the tongues from all six heads, took and placed them in his knapsack, and the headless trunk they cast into the river of fire. They came to the emperor, and brought him the tongues as certain proof. The emperor thanked them. 'I see that you are mighty heroes and deliverers of the city, and all the people. If you wish to drink and eat, take all manner of beverages and eatables without money and without tax.' And from joy he issued a proclamation throughout the whole town, that all the eating-houses, inns, and small public-houses were to be open for the mighty heroes. Well, they went everywhere, drank, amused themselves, refreshed themselves, and enjoyed various honours.

* An insulting nickname.

Night came, and exactly at midnight they went under the guelder-rose bridge to the river of fire, and speedily up came a seven-headed dragon. Immediately his horse neighed, his falcon chattered, and his hound howled. The dragon immediately struck his horse on the head. 'Neigh not, devil's carrion! chatter not, falcon! howl not, hound! for here is Little Rolling-pea. Now then,' said he, 'come forth, Little Rolling-pea! Shall we fight or try our strength?' 'Good youths travel not to try their strength, but only to fight.' And they began the combat, and the heroes beat off six of the dragon's heads; the seventh remained. The dragon said: 'Give me breathing time!' But Little Rolling-pea said: 'Don't expect me to give you breathing time.' They began the combat again. He beat off the last head also, cut out the tongues, and placed them in his knapsack, but threw the trunk into the river of fire. They came to the emperor, and brought the tongues for certain proof.

The third time they went at midnight to the bridge of guelder-rose and the river of fire; speedily up came to them a nine-headed dragon. Immediately his horse neighed, his falcon chattered, and his hound howled. The dragon struck his horse on the head. 'Neigh not, devil's carrion! falcon, chatter not! hound, howl not! for here is Little Rolling-pea. And now come forth, Little Rolling-pea! Shall we fight or try our strength?' Little Rolling-pea said: 'Not to try their strength do good youths travel, but only to fight.' They began the combat, and the heroes beat off eight heads; the ninth remained. Little Rolling-pea said: 'Give us breathing time, unclean power!' It answered: 'Take breathing time or not, you will not overcome me; you slew my brothers by craft, not by strength.' Little Rolling-pea not only fought, but thought how to delude the dragon. All at once he thought of a plan, and said: 'Yes, there's still much of your brother behind—I'll take you all.' Hastily the dragon looked round, and he cut off the ninth head also, cut out the tongues, put them into his knapsack, and threw the trunk into the river of fire. They went to the emperor. The emperor said: 'I thank you, mighty heroes! live with God, and with joy and courage, and take as much gold, silver, and paper money as you want.'

After this the wives of the three dragons met together and took counsel together. 'Whence did those men come who slew our husbands? Well, we *shall* be women if we don't get rid of them out of the world.' The youngest said: 'Now then, sisters! let us go by the highroad, where they will go. I will make myself into a very beautiful wayside seat, and if, when wearied, they sit down upon it, it will be death to them all.' The second said to her: 'If you do nothing to them, I will make myself into an apple-tree beside the highroad, and when they begin to come up to me, the agreeable odour will attract them; and if they taste the apples, it will be death to them all.' Well, the heroes came up to the beautiful wayside seat. Little Rolling-pea thrust his sword into it up to the hilt—blood poured forth! They went on to the apple-tree. 'Brother Little Rolling-pea,' said the heroes, 'let us each eat an apple.' But he said: 'If it is possible, let us eat; if it is not possible, let us go on further. He drew his sword and thrust it into the apple-tree up to the hilt, and blood poured forth immediately. The third she-dragon hastened after them, and extended her jaws from the earth to the sky. Little Rolling-pea saw that there was not room for them to pass by. How were they to save themselves? He looked about and saw that she specially aimed at him, and threw the three horses into her mouth. The she-dragon flew off to the blue sea to drink water, and they proceeded further. She pursued them again. He saw that she was near, and threw the three falcons into her mouth. Again the she-dragon flew to the blue sea to drink water, and they proceeded further. Little Rolling-pea looked round; the she-dragon was again pursuing him, and seeing his danger, he took and threw the three hounds into her mouth. Again she flew off to the blue sea to drink water; while she drank her fill, they proceeded still further. He looked round and saw that she was catching them up again. Little Rolling-pea took his two comrades and threw them into her mouth. The she-dragon flew to the blue sea to drink water, and he went on. Again she overtook him; he looked round, saw that she was not far off, and said: 'Lord, protect me and save my soul!' He saw before him an iron workshop, and fled into the smithy. The smith said to him: 'Why, stranger, are you so cowardly?' 'Honourable gentlemen! protect me from an unclean power, and save my soul!' They took and shut the smithy completely up. 'Give up to me what is mine!' said the she-dragon. Then the smiths said to her: 'Lick the iron door through, and we will place him on your tongue.' She licked the door through, and placed her tongue in the centre. The smiths seized her tongue three at a time with red-hot pincers, and said: 'Come, stranger, do with her what you will!' He went out into the yard, and began to pound the she-dragon, and pounded her skin to the bones, and her bones to the marrow; then took her with her whole carcase and buried her seven fathoms deep. Then, and not till then, did he live and eat morsels; but we ate bread, for he had none. I was there, too, and drank honey-wine; it flowed over my beard, but didn't get into my mouth.

XXIII.—THE WONDERFUL BOYS.

A FATHER had three daughters; they went to the river to wash the linen. The king's son rode up. One said: 'Well, if the king's son were to marry me, I would hem the whole palace round with a single needle.' The second said: 'If the king's son were to marry me, I would feed the whole palace with a single roll.' But the third said: 'If the king's son were to marry me, I would bring him two sons, each with a moon on his head and a star on the nape of his neck.' The king rode up to the one that said: 'I would bring him two sons;' they lived one year, two years, and she was expecting to become a mother. The king came and gave orders to her mother: 'Whatever God gives my wife, let it be reared.' He rode away twenty miles off, and God gave his wife children; she brought him two sons, each with a moon on his head and a star on the nape of his neck. His wife wrote a letter, that God had given them two sons, each with a moon on his head and a star on the nape of his neck. A servant carried the letter to him, and went in to stop the night at the house of the queen's sister, without knowing that it was her sister. He lay down to sleep; then she took and opened the letter, erased that which was written in it—'Each with a moon on his head and a star on the nape of his neck'—and wrote instead, that it was not a snake nor a lizard—it was nobody knew what, that she had become the mother of. The man went to the king and delivered the letter. He read it through: 'What God has given her, let it not be destroyed without my orders.' He went back and again stopped at the same place to pass the night; she took the letter again, opened it, erased what the king had written, and wrote instead, that before he returned, she was to bury her sons. When he arrived, the king's wife read it through, and began to weep; she was grieved to bury those beautiful sons. She dug two graves in the yard and buried them; out of them grew two maples, a golden stem and a silver one. The king came to the house and put her away because she had buried them without his orders.

He rode off and married his wife's second sister. They lived together, and after a time she said: 'My most illustrious husband! let us cut down those maples and make ourselves a bed.'—'Ah! my most illustrious husband! let us cut up that bed and burn it, and sprinkle the ashes on the road.' A shepherd was driving sheep that way; a ewe strayed and swallowed some of the ashes; she bore two he-lambs; on the head of each was a moon, on the back of the neck a star. Then she disliked those lambs, ordered them to be slaughtered, and the entrails to be thrown out into the street. The first wife came out, collected the entrails, cooked and ate them, and became the mother of two sons; each had a moon on his head and a star on the nape of his neck. The two sons grew and grew, and never took off their caps. Then the king had a desire that somebody should come to tell him stories. People said that there were two brothers there who could tell stories. They came to tell stories.

They began to tell a story. 'There was a king who had a queen; the queen become the mother of two sons; on the head of each was a moon, on the nape of the neck a star. Afterwards the king went hunting; the queen wrote a letter and sent it. The man went to her sister's for the night; she took the letter, opened it, and wrote that it was not a snake nor a lizard—it was nobody knew what, that the queen had been the mother of. The king read it through, and replied that it was to be reared, whether it were a snake or a lizard. The man went homewards, and again rested at the house where he had passed the night. She opened the letter, and wrote that she was to bury it '*by my arrival.*' Then she dug two holes—graves—and buried them; and two maples grew out, a golden stem and a silver one. The new queen contrived that they should be cut down and a bed made of them, and began to sleep on it, and began to be uncomfortable: she ordered the bed to be cut up and burnt, and the ashes to be thrown out into the yard. A shepherd was driving sheep; a ewe swallowed some of the ashes and bore two he-lambs; each had a moon on the head and a star on the back of the neck. The queen ordered the lambs to be slaughtered, and their entrails to be thrown out into the street. Her divorced sister went out into the street, collected the entrails, took them to her house, cooked and ate them, and became the mother of two sons; each had a moon on his head and a star on the nape of his neck.' The boys bowed and took off their caps, thus illuminating the whole room. The second wife was placed on an iron harrow, and torn to pieces, but the king took his first wife, and they began to live happily.

LITTLE RUSSIAN STORIES.

(FROM GALICIA.)

MR. RALSTON does not seem to have been directly acquainted with these tales; at any rate, none of them are given in either his book of Russian folk-tales or in that of Russian songs. It is, therefore, the more necessary for me to supplement his admirable work by giving all the Galician stories in Erben's collection.

The Little Russians, or Ruthenians, form the bulk of the population in the Austrian province of Galicia, formerly the principality of Halicz, and also designated 'Red Russia.' The capital is Lemberg (contracted from Löwenberg), or Lvóv. They are also found in the adjoining parts of the north of Hungary, and in the Bukovina.

I think that the present selection is the first introduction of the literature of the Austrian Russians to the notice of the British reader.

The prophet Elijah (*Ilya*) is a very important and powerful personage in Russian folklore, and we find him accordingly in No. 27 holding a prominent position in the heavenly hierarchy, even before the creation of man! He seems to have taken the place of Perun, the god of thunder, among the heathen Slavonians.

I must also draw attention to the extreme stupidity of the

'devils' of Slavonic folklore. They are still less intelligent than their Teutonic brethren, and do not appear to have any connection with the Arch-Enemy, but to be, as Mr. Ralston says (p. 370), rather 'the lubber fiends of heathen mythology, beings endowed with supernatural might, but scantily provided with mental power.' No. 26 gives a specimen of their average intelligence.

XXIV.—GOD KNOWS HOW TO PUNISH MAN.

THERE was a wealthy, a very wealthy proprietor; he had buildings enough; there was where and wherewith for every purpose. Once upon a time he had guests at his house, and said to them: 'If my buildings were to be burnt down, I should know where and how to rebuild them.' He said, and it came to pass. While he was conversing thus with his guests, somebody went out into the courtyard, but returned still quicker and said: 'You're on fire!' But the proprietor said: 'Never mind; I wish it to be so.' He neither attempted to extinguish the fire himself nor allowed others to do so, and thus all was reduced to ashes; only the site was left. But he didn't trouble himself a bit, but went and lived by the waterside, and kept his money in a willow-tree, being thus a source of danger to himself. Unexpectedly a heavy rain fell, and before he could look about him the water had already undermined the willow and carried it away. He then became poor, so that it became his lot to serve others. He was obliged to carry letters for gentlemen.

Well, it came to pass once that he was going with a letter, and night overtook him on the way; what was he now to do? He begged a night's lodging at a certain man's house; this man was rich and kindly, so he said: 'Good! you shall not pass my house.' Meanwhile the mistress prepared supper, and after supping they prayed to God, but before they lay down to sleep they conversed together about this and that. The traveller began to relate how he had himself been wealthy, how he had been burnt out, and had come to poverty. 'I had,' said he, 'still a little money, and kept it in a willow-tree, but great floods came, undermined the willow, and carried my money away with the water! Thus I remained with nothing, and now it has been my lot more than once to beg for bread.'

Scarcely had his host heard this when he looked at his wife, for the willow had floated to shore under their barn, and when they began to cut it up, the money tumbled out a little at a time. They both went out into a room, and began to consult how to return the money to him without his knowing whence it came. They consulted. Then said the host: 'Well, what shall we do? Let us cut off the under part of a loaf, take out the crumb, put the money inside, then cover it again with the crust; and when he is on the point of departing let us give it him, as if it were provision for his journey.' And so they did. The next day when he was starting to proceed on his way, they gave him the loaf of bread, and said: 'Here's for you; it will be of use on the road.' He took it, made his bow, and went on his way. On the road there met him some merchants—pardon me, some drovers—purchasing swine, who had formerly visited him more than once, and they asked him: 'Of course you know what we're after?' and he replied: 'Formerly it was at my house; misfortune has come upon me; I've been burnt out, and now I serve others.' When he had spoken these words he all at once gave his knapsack a tap, and said: 'Come! buy some bread.' (He took it out.) 'Somehow I'm not hungry, and it's heavy to carry; some money would be more advantageous on my journey.' Bargain and sale. They came to an agreement. The merchants took the bread and he the money, and they parted.

The merchants came to that very same village, and went to the house of that very same proprietor, from whom the bread came, and began to make inquiries of him respecting their business. 'Not I, but God!' said he; 'sit down, meanwhile, and rest;' and he sent for a snack for them. But they said to him that he needn't trouble himself. 'On the road we bought a loaf of excellent bread from a man who was going with a letter.' They (the host and his wife) felt a quaking at the heart; they had a suspicion; but the merchants soon took it out and placed it on the table, the very same loaf, which they had given to the traveller. The proprietor looked at his wife, and said to their guests: 'Before anything is done, let us go and have a look round; maybe you will make a purchase.' 'Let us go!' and they went out of the house, but he winked to his wife, and she knew at once what he wanted. When they went out on their business, the mistress brought out another loaf and placed it on the table, but removed the first one. They returned, breakfasted, either did or didn't come to terms, and went away.

After some time the man came again with a letter, and turned in again at the proprietor's, just as at an old acquaintance's, for the night. They received him and were glad, for they thought they might now be successful in returning the money somehow or other. They waited; they passed the night, and when he had gone out of the house, they wrapped the money in a cloth, put it in his knapsack, gave him breakfast, and dismissed him. He went off, and as he went by a footpath through the orchard, he bethought himself: 'Ah! what beautiful apples! Come! let me pluck a few for my journey.' He took off his knapsack and hung it on a tree, that it mightn't embarrass him, and began himself to reach after the apples. Just then up came his host, the proprietor. He saw him, and took flight so much the quicker, leaving his knapsack on the tree. The proprietor espied the knapsack hanging on a branch, began to think, and afterwards also said: 'The poor fellow was frightened, and has forgotten his knapsack.' He took down the knapsack, and said: 'His road goes to the foot-bridge; he ran away through the bushes that he mightn't see me. I'll put it on the bridge, and then he'll be sure to take it up.' Even so he did. He ran round sideways, placed the money on the bridge, and went himself behind a bush not very far off, to keep a look-out and see what would happen.

Suddenly the traveller came up to the bridge, and looking downwards thought, and afterwards said: 'It's good that I still have some sight, at any rate, and can go on my way and earn something to get my bread. What should I do if I were to go blind? How should I get across this bridge? Come, I'll see whether I could do it successfully.' Then, closing his eyes, tap, tap, with his stick over the bridge, he went straight forwards, stepped over the money, and went his way. The proprietor, recovering from his astonishment, said aloud: 'He has angered God!'

XXV.—THE GOOD CHILDREN.

THE Lord was angered at mankind, and for three years there was a great famine over all the world; nowhere in the world was even a grain of corn produced, and what people sowed failed to come up from a drought so great, that for three years there was not a drop of rain or dew. For one year more people managed to live somehow or other, thrashing up what old corn there was; the rich made money, for corn rose very high. Autumn came. Where anybody had or purchased old seed, they sowed it; and entreated the Lord, hoped in the love of God, if God would give fertility, 'if God would forgive our sins.' But it was not so. They did not obtain the love of God. When they cast the seed into the holy earth, that was the last they saw of it; if it germinated somewhat, if it sent up shoots, it withered away close to the ground. Woe! and abundance of it! God's world went on, sorrowed and wept, for now it was manifest that death by hunger was approaching. They somehow got miserably through the winter. Spring came. Where anybody had still any grain, they sowed it. What would come to pass? No blessing was poured forth, for the drought began with wind. Moreover, there was but little snow in the winter, and everything dried up so that the black earth remained as it was. It now came to this—all the world began to perish! The people died; the cattle perished; as misery carried them, so did the people proceed.

There was at that time a powerful emperor in a certain empire; as the young ordinarily cleave to the young, so would he associate only with young men. Whether in council or in office or in the army, there were none but young men; no old man had access to anything anywhere. Well, as young men, unripe in understanding, were the counsellors, so was their counsel also unripe. One year passed, a second passed; then, in the third year, they saw that misery was already on every side, that it was already coming to this, that all the world would perish. The young emperor assembled his young council, and they began to advise after their fashion; they advised, they advised, and ah! the resolutions they came to were such that it is a sin even to give an account of their resolutions! Well, the emperor made proclamation after their advice, that all old people were to be drowned, in order that, said he, bread might not be wasted in vain, but there might be a supply of bread for the young; and that no one should venture, on pain of death, to maintain or harbour any old man. Well, heralds went about throughout the whole country, and promulgated the emperor's command everywhere—yea, brigands seized old people where they chose, and drowned them without mercy.

There were then in a certain place three own brothers, who had an aged father. When they heard of this edict, they told their father; and their father said: 'My sons, such is the will of God and the will of the emperor; take me, let me perish at once, only that you, my children, may live on. I am already with one foot in the grave.' 'No, our own daddy! we will die, but we will not give you up,' cried the good sons with one voice, and fell upon his neck; 'we will keep you; we will take from our own mouths, and will nourish you.'

The three brothers took their aged father, conducted him into their cottage, dug under the raised portion of the floor, made up a bed with sheets and frieze-coats, for straw was scarce, and placed the old man there, brought him a loaf of bread as black as the holy earth, and covered him over with the floor. There the old man abode for two or three months, and his sons brought him clandestinely all that they had. The summer passed without harvest, without mowing. September passed too. Autumn passed without joy. Winter passed too. Now came spring; the sun became warm. It was now time to sow, but there was no seed. The world was large, but there was no seed-corn. When one kind was used up, the people sowed others, hoping that there would be a crop; but when they cast it into the holy earth, it rotted there. It seemed as if the end of the world were come.

Then the three sons went to their father, and asked him: 'Daddy, what shall we do? It's time to sow. God is now sending showers of rain; the earth is warmed and is crumbling like grits; but of seed there is not a blessed grain.' 'Take, my sons, and strip the old roof off the house, and thresh the bundles and sow the chaff.' The lads stripped the house and barn (anyhow, there was nothing in it), and threshed away till the sweat ran from their brows, so that they crushed the bundles as small as poppy-seeds. When they sowed, God gave a blessing; so in a week's time it became green like rue; in a month's time, in two months' time, there was corn, ever so much—ever so much, and all manner of seed was found there: there was rye, there was wheat and barley; yea, maybe, there was also a plant or two of buckwheat and millet. Wherever you went throughout the world there was no corn to be seen; all the plain was overgrown with grasses, steppe-grasses, and thistles, but with *them* was corn like a forest. How people wondered and were astounded! The fame thereof went over the whole world, and the news reached the emperor himself, that in such and such a place there were three own brothers, and with them corn had sprung up for all the world, and so beautiful, never was the like beheld! The emperor ordered the three brothers to appear in the imperial presence.

The brothers heard of it, and smacked the tops of their heads with their hands. 'Now it will be amen with us!' They went again to their father. 'Daddy! they tell us to appear before the emperor. Advise us, daddy, what to do!' 'Go, my sons—what will be, will be; and tell the pure truth before the emperor.' The brothers started off and went to the emperor. The emperor inquired menacingly: 'Why, villains, did ye hoard up corn, when there was such a famine that so many people died of hunger? Tell the truth; if not, I shall order you to be tortured and racked even unto death.' The brothers related all as it had been, from the beginning to the end. 'Now, most gracious emperor, give us over to any torture whatever, or let thy kindness have compassion on us!' The emperor's brow became smooth, his eyes became serene. He then ordered the old father to be brought before him at once, and made him sit beside him close to his throne, and hearkened to his counsel till death, and his sons he rewarded handsomely. He ordered the corn to be collected ear by ear, and to be rubbed out in men's hands; and sent it about for seed-corn in all empires, and from it was produced holy corn for all the world.

XXVI.—THE DEVIL AND THE GIPSY.

An old gipsy went to engage himself as servant to a devil; the devil said: 'I will give you what you wish to bring me firewood and water regularly, and to put fire under the kettle.' 'Good!' The devil gave him a pail and said: 'Go yonder to the well and draw some water.'

Our gipsy went off, got some water into the pail, and drew it up with a hook; but, being old, he couldn't draw it out, and was obliged to pour the water out, in order not to lose the pail in the well. But what was he now to return home with? Well, our gipsy took some stakes out of a fence, and grubbed round about the well, as if he were digging. The devil waited and waited, and as the gipsy didn't appear himself, of course he didn't appear with the water. After awhile he went himself to meet the gipsy, and without thinking inquired: 'But why do you loiter so? Why haven't you brought water by this time?' 'Well, what? I want to dig out the whole well, and bring it to you!' 'But you would have wasted time, if you had purposed anything of the sort; then you wouldn't have brought the pail in time, that the quantity of fire-wood might not be diminished.' And he drew out the water and carried it himself. 'Eh! if I had but known, I should have brought it long ago.'

The devil sent him once to the wood for fire-wood. The gipsy started off, but rain assailed him in the wood and wetted him through; the old fellow caught cold and couldn't stoop after the sticks. What was he to do? Well, he took and pulled bast; he pulled several heaps, went round the wood, and tied one tree to another with strips of the bast. The devil waited, waited on, and was out of his wits on account of the gipsy. He went himself, and when he saw what was going on: 'What are you doing, loiterer?' said he. 'What am I doing? I want to bring you wood. I'm tying the whole forest into one bundle, in order not to do useless work.' The devil saw that he was having a bad time of it with the gipsy, took up the fire-wood, and went home.

After settling his affairs at home, he went to an older devil to ask his advice: 'I've hired a gipsy, but he's quite a nuisance; *we're* tolerably 'cute,' says he, 'but he's still stronger and 'cuter than we. Unless I kill him——' 'Good, when he lies down to sleep, kill him, that he mayn't lead us by the nose any more.' The time came to go home; they lay down to sleep; but the gipsy evidently noticed something, for he placed his fur-coat on the bench where he usually slept, and crept himself into a corner under the bench. When the time came, the devil thought that the gipsy was now in a dead sleep, took up an iron club, and beat the fur-coat till the sound went on all sides. He then lay down to sleep, thinking: 'Oho! it's now amen for the gipsy!' But the gipsy grunted: 'Oh!' and made a rustling in the corner. 'What ails you?' 'Oh, a flea bit me.'

The devil went again to the older one for advice: 'But where to kill him?' said he. 'When I smashed him with a club, he only made a rustling and said: "A flea bit me."' 'Then pay him up now,' said the elder devil, 'as much as he wants, and pack him off about his business.' The gipsy chose a bag with ducats and went off. Then the devil was sorry about the money, and consulted the older one again. 'Overtake the gipsy, and say that the one of you that kicks a stone best, so that the sound goes three miles, shall have the money.' The devil overtook him: 'Stay, gipsy! I've something to say to you.' 'What are you after, son of the enemy?' 'Oh, stay, let us kick; the one that kicks loudest against a stone, let his be the money.' 'Now then, kick away,' said the gipsy. The devil kicked once, twice, till it resounded in their ears; but the gipsy meanwhile poured some water on it: 'Eh! what's that, you fool?' 'When I kick a dry stone, water spurts out.' 'Ah! when he kicks, tremble! water has spurted out of the stone.'

The devil went again for advice. The elder one said: 'Let the one who throws the club highest have the money.' The gipsy had now got some miles on his way; he looked round; the devil was behind him: 'Stop! wait, gipsy!' 'What do you want, son of the enemy?' 'The one of us that throws the club highest, let his be the money.' 'Well, let us throw now. I've two brothers up yonder in heaven, both smiths, and it will just suit them either for a hammer or for tongs.' The devil threw, so that it whizzed, and was scarcely visible. The gipsy took it by the end, scarcely held it up, and shouted: 'Hold out your hands there, brothers —hey!' But the devil seized him by the hand: 'Ah, stop! don't throw; it would be a pity to lose it.'

The elder devil advised him again: 'Overtake him once more, and say, "The one that runs fastest to a certain point, let him have the money."' The devil overtook him; the gipsy said: 'Do you know what? I shan't contend with you any more, for you don't deserve it; but I've a young son, Hare, who's only just three days old; if you overtake him, you shall measure yourself with me.' The gipsy espied a hare in a firwood: 'There he is! little Hare!

now, then, Hare! Catch him up!' When the hare started he went hither and thither in bounds, only a line of dust rose behind him. 'Bah!' said the devil, 'he doesn't run straight.' 'In my family no one ever did run straight. He runs as he pleases.'

The elder devil advised him to wrestle; the stronger was to have the money. 'Eh!' said the gipsy; 'you hear the terms for me to wrestle with you: I have a father, he is so old that for the last seven years I have carried him food into a cave; if you floor him, then you shall wrestle with me.' But the gipsy knew of a bear, and led the devil to his cave. 'Go,' said he, 'in there; wake him up, and wrestle with him.' The devil went in and said: 'Get up, long-beard! let us have a wrestle.' Alas! when the bear began to hug him, when he began to claw him, he beat him out, he turned him out, and threw him down on the floor of the cave.

The elder devil advised that the one who whistled best, so that it could be heard for three miles, should have the money. The devil whistled so that it resounded and whizzed again. But the gipsy said: 'Do you know what? When I whistle you will go blind and deaf; bind up your eyes and ears.' He did so. The gipsy took a mallet for splitting logs, and banged it once and twice against his ears. 'Oh, stop! Oh! don't whistle, or you'll kill me! May ill luck smite you with your money! Go where you will never be heard of again!' That's all.

XXVII.—GOD AND THE DEVIL.

ONCE upon a time there was nothing; there was only the heaven above, and water beneath. Then God journeyed [in a boat] upon the water and saw a vast, vast crust of hard foam, on which sat the devil. God asked him: 'What art thou?' 'I will not converse with thee,' replied the wicked one, 'unless thou takest me into thy boat.' God promised, and heard in reply: 'I'm the devil.' They both journeyed on without conversing together at all, till the devil began: 'How very nice and beautiful it would be, if there were firm land in the world!' 'There shall be,' answered God; 'go down into the depth of the sea and bring up a handful of sand; I will make the land from it. When thou descendest, and art about to take the sand, say these words: "I take thee in the name of God."' The devil didn't wait long, but was immediately under the water. On the bottom he reached after the sand with both hands with these words: 'I take thee in my own name.' When he came up to the top he looked with curiosity at his closed fists, and was astonished at seeing that they were empty. But God, observing what had happened to him, consoled him, and told him to go down to the bottom once more. He did so, and as soon as he began to grub into the sand in the deep, he said: 'I take thee in his name.' However, he brought up only as much sand, as could get under his nails; God took a little of the sand and firm land formed itself, but only as much as was required for a bed. When night came, God and the devil lay down side by side on the firm land to pass the night. As soon as our Lord God fell asleep, the devil pushed him towards the east, in order that he might fall into the water and perish. In the direction in which he pushed him, there did it become land for a long way. The devil tried pushing him towards the west, and on that side the land extended far. A similar circumstance helped to form land also on the other sides of the world.

As soon as God had made the land, he ascended to heaven. The devil, not liking to stay without him, followed in his track. Now he heard how the angels praised God in hymns, and began to feel annoyed, that he had no one to rejoice at his arrival. He went up to God and whispered in his ear: 'What must I do, that I may have such a multitude?' God answered him: 'Wash thy hands and face, and sprinkle the water behind thee.' He did so, and there came into existence such a multitude of devils that the angels and saints no more had sufficient room in heaven. God observed what an injury there was from this to his own. He summoned St. Ilya, and ordered him to let off a storm of thunder and lightning. Ilya was glad at this; he roared, thundered, and lightened with a tempest, and poured rain for forty days and nights, and along with the great rain the devils also fell from heaven on to the earth. At last there were no more wicked ones, and angels also began to fall. Then God ordered Ilya to stop, and wherever any devil struck the ground at the time that he fell, there he remained. From that time to this bright little fires have darted about in heaven, and only now fall upon the earth.

LITTLE RUSSIAN STORIES

(FROM SOUTH RUSSIA).

HERE again Mr. Ralston informs us in his preface that he 'has been able to use but little the South Russian collections of Kulish and Rudchenko, there being no complete dictionary available of the dialect, or rather language, in which they are written.' He has, however, given a long and interesting story from the Ukraine, which I find also in Erben, the 'Norka.' One of Erben's South Russian stories is too closely identical with a pretty tale from the government of Voronezh, given by Ralston (p. 63), for me to give it a place here. All the other South Russian stories in Erben's collection I have translated, and only wish they had been more numerous.

The tales of Snake Husbands always appear to have an evil end, though the two that I have translated do not conclude so touchingly as the beautiful Great Russian story, 'The Watersnake' (Ralston, p. 116). Certainly the science of comparative mythology cannot be considered as having its data complete, until Slavonic folklore has been thoroughly investigated and analyzed.

In No. 28 an old friend will be discovered in a very rustic dress.

XXVIII.—THE BEAUTIFUL DAMSEL AND THE WICKED OLD WOMAN.

In the woods stood a cottage. In it lived a man and his wife, but they had no children. Well, they went on a pilgrimage to beseech God to give them a child. God gave them a daughter. She grew and prospered. The prince about that time rode up to the place, as he was out hunting, and sent his attendant, saying: 'Be so good as to go and ask for a draught of water at yon cottage.' The attendant went to ask for the water just when the child was weeping, and pearls were rolling down from her eyes. Her mother pacified her; she began to smile; all manner of flowers bloomed. The servant went out and said: 'Prince, I have seen a little girl; when she weeps, pearls roll down; and when she smiles, all manner of flowers bloom.' The prince went into the cottage, and began to tease the child to make her cry. She cried, and pearls rolled down. He then begged her mother to pacify her. When she smiled, the prince saw that all manner of flowers bloomed.

The girl continued to grow, and the prince always rode round that way when he went hunting. Well, she grew up. The prince said: 'Old man, give me your daughter to wife.' She now embroidered handkerchiefs with eagles. But the emperor said: 'Where are your wits gone to, my son, that you want to take a peasant girl to wife?' Then the prince took one of the handkerchiefs that she had embroidered, and carried it to the emperor, whereat the emperor clapped his hands. 'Marry,' said he, 'my son, marry!' Then he conducted her homeward, but in his suite was an old woman who had her daughter with her. Well, as they were on their way, the prince stopped to shoot something, and the old woman took everything from the damsel, scooped out her eyes, and thrust her into a cavern in the ground, and dressed her daughter in her apparel; so the prince took her to wife without recognising her.

But round the cavern there grew a multitude of bushes. An old man came to gather brushwood. The girl, the damsel, was sitting in the cavern, and in front of her a heap of pearls, which she had wept as she sat; but she had no eyes. 'Take me,' said she, 'kind old man, and pick up this jewellery here.' Well, the old man took her, collected the jewellery, and led her home. At the old man's there were no children, but there was an old woman. She, the damsel, said: 'Collect the jewellery in a bag, and carry it to the town for sale; and if a certain old woman meets you, then don't sell to her, but say: "Give what you have about you."' Well, he carried it to the town and met the old woman. The old woman said: 'Sell me the jewellery!' 'Purchase.' 'How much for it?' 'Give what you have about you?' She gave him an eye. Then the damsel began with one eye to embroider a handkerchief. Again the old man carried jewellery to the town. The old woman again said: 'Old man, sell me the jewellery!' 'Purchase.' 'How much for it?' 'Give what you have about you?' She gave him the other eye. The damsel then began to embroider still more beautifully. The old man said: 'There's a dinner at the emperor's.' The damsel said to him: 'Go, kind old man, to the dinner and take a jug, that you may beg some soup for me.' She also tied a handkerchief of her own sewing on the old man's neck. When the prince espied the handkerchief on the old man's neck, he cried: 'Whence come you, old man?' 'From the farm yonder, prince; and there is also a damsel living at my house, so be so kind as to give her something in this jug.' 'But, old man, where did you get that handkerchief?' 'I found a damsel in a cavern in the ground, and she embroidered it.' The prince at once recognised it by the embroidery. "'Tis she! 'tis she!' But the old woman's daughter he packed off to tend swine. That's all.

XXIX.—THE SNAKE AND THE PRINCESS.

THERE was an emperor and empress who had three daughters. The emperor fell ill, and sent his eldest daughter for water. She went to fetch it, when a snake said: 'Come! will you marry me?' The princess replied: 'No, I won't.' 'Then,' said he, 'I won't give you any water.' Then the second daughter said: 'I'll go; he'll give me some.' She went; the snake said to her: 'Come! will you marry me?' 'No,' she said, 'I won't.' He gave her no water. She returned and said: 'He gave me no water. He said: "If you will marry me I will give it."' The youngest said: 'I will go; he will give me some.' She went, and the snake said to her: 'Come! will you marry me?' 'I will,' she said. Then he drew her water from the very bottom, cold and fresh. She brought it home, gave it her father to drink, and her father recovered. Then on Sunday a carriage came, and those with it said:

'Open the door,
Princess!
Why did the dear one love?
Why draw water from the ford,
Princess?'

She was terrified, wept, and went and opened the door. Then they said again:

'Open the rooms,
Princess!
Why did the dear one love?
Why draw water from the ford,
Princess?'

Then they came into the house and placed the snake in a plate on the table. There he lay, just as if he were of gold! They went out of the house, and said:

'Sit in the carriage,
Princess!
Why did the dear one love?
Why draw water from the ford,
Princess?'

They drove off with her to the snake's abode. There they lived, and had a daughter born to them. They also took a godmother to live with them, but she was a wicked woman. The child soon died, and the mother died soon after it. The godmother went in the night to the place where she was buried, and cut off her hands. Then she came home, and heated water-gruel, scalded the hands, and took off the gold rings. Then the princess—such was the ordinance of God—came to her for the hands, and said:

'The fowls are asleep, the geese are asleep,
Only my godmother does not sleep.
She scalds white hands in water-gruel,
She takes off golden rings.'

The godmother concealed herself under the stove. She said again:

'The fowls are asleep, the geese are asleep,
Only my godmother does not sleep.
She scalds white hands in water-gruel,
She takes off golden rings.'

The next day they came and found the godmother dead under the stove. They didn't give her proper burial, but threw her into a hole.

XXX.—TRANSFORMATION INTO A NIGHTINGALE AND A CUCKOO.

A DAMSEL fell in love with a snake, and was also beloved by him. He took her to wife. His dwelling was of pure glass, all crystal. This dwelling was situated underground, in a kind of mound, or something of the sort. Well, it is said that her old mother at first grieved over her. How could she help doing so? Well, when the time came, the snake's wife became the mother of twins, a boy and a girl; they looked, as they lay by their mother, as if they were made of wax. And she was herself as beautiful as a flower. Well, God having given her children, she said: 'Now, then, since they have been born as human beings, let us christen them among human beings.' She took her seat in a golden carriage, laid the children on her knees, and drove off to the village to the pope.* The carriage had not got into the open country, when sadness was brought to the mother. The old woman had made an outcry in the whole village, seized a sickle, and rushed into the country. She saw she had manifest death before her, when she called to her children, and went on to say: 'Fly, my children, as birds about the world: you, my little son, as a nightingale, and you, my daughter, as a cuckoo.' Out flew a nightingale from the carriage by the right-hand, and a cuckoo by the left-hand window. What became of the carriage and horses and all nobody knows. Nor did their mistress remain, only a dead nettle sprang up by the roadside.

XXXI.—TRANSMIGRATION OF THE SOUL.

A CERTAIN woman had a kind of adventure. When she went out into the field to cut grass, or to fetch hemp, and placed food in the stove, then somebody took the victuals out of the stove, and ate them all clean up. She thought, what might such a thing as this signify? Nohow could she guess it. She came, the door was shut, and there was only remaining in the house a baby—maybe half a year old—in the cradle. Well, she betook herself to a wise woman. She entreated her and paid her to come, and she came. She

* The orthodox Greek priests are always designated 'popes.'

looked about, she snuffed about—I mean the wise woman. All at once she heard something indefinite. 'Go you,' she said, 'into the field, and I'll hide myself and we'll see what this is.' The woman went into the field, and the wise woman hid herself in a corner, and kept a look-out. Then, pop! the baby jumped out of the cradle! She looked, and it was no more a baby, but an old man. He was quite dwarfish, and his beard was long. In a moment he was after the eatables, pulled the victuals out of the stove, then gave a screech, and began to gobble up the food. When he had devoured all, then he became a baby again; but now he didn't crawl into the cradle, but lay down, and screeched till the whole house rang. Then the wise woman was after him: she placed him on a block of wood, and began to chop the block under his feet. He screeched and she chopped: he screeched and she chopped. Then she saw how, taking an opportunity, he became an old man again, and said: 'Old woman, I have transformed myself not once nor twice only: I was first a fish, then I became a bird, an ant, and a quadruped, and now I have once more made trial of being a hûman being. It isn't better thus than being among the ants; but among human beings—it isn't worse!'

XXXII.—THE WIZARD.

THERE was here once in our village a certain Avstriyat, who was such a wizard that he could cause rain or hail to pass away when he chose. It happened that we were cutting corn in the country; a cloud came up. We began to hurry off the sheaves, but he took no notice, cut and cut away by himself, smoked his pipe, and said: 'Don't be frightened—there'll be no rain.' Lo and behold, there was no rain. Once—all this I saw with my own eyes—we were cutting rye, when the sky became black, the wind rose: it began to whistle at first afar off, then over our very heads. There was thunder, lightning, whirlwind—such a tempest, that—O God! Thy will be done! We went after our sheaves, but he—'Don't be frightened, there'll be no rain.' 'Where won't it be?' We didn't hearken to him. But he smoked his pipe out, and cut away quietly by himself. Up came a man on a black horse, and all black himself: he darted straight up to Avstriyat: 'Hey! give permission!' said he. Avstriyat replied: 'No, I won't!' 'Give permission; be merciful!' 'I won't. It would be impossible to get such a quantity in.' The black horseman bowed to the man, and hastened off over the country.

Then the black cloud became gray and whitened. Our elders feared that there would be hail. But Avstriyat took no notice. He cut the corn by himself and smoked his pipe. But again a horseman came up; he hastened over the country still quicker than the first. But this one was all in white, and on a white horse. 'Give permission!' he shouted to Avstriyat. 'I won't!' 'Give permission, for God's sake!' 'I won't. It wouldn't be possible to get such a quantity in.' 'Hey! give permission; I can't hold out! Then, and not till then, did Avstriyat relent. 'Well, then, go now, but only into the glen, which is beyond the plain.' Scarcely had he spoken, when the horseman disappeared, and hail poured down as out of a basket. In the course of a short hour it filled the glen brimful, level with the banks.

HERE I have but little to remark that has not already been noticed by Mr. Ralston. In No. 33 I have given a pretty variant of Grimm's 'Fisherman's Wife.' In this story, which is from the Government of Moscow, there is a curious confusion between 'king' (*korol*), and 'emperor' (*tzar*). The peasant asks to be made *korol* 'king,' but is answered that an 'emperor' (*tzar*) is chosen by God. The King of Poland was formerly the mighty potentate west of Moscow, which emerged from Tartar bondage under a grand-duke, or grand-prince. This confusion may possibly imply that the story was crystallized in its present form not long after the assumption of the imperial dignity by the ruler of Muscovy.

As to No. 34, Mr. Ralston, in his 'Songs of the Russian People,' gives an account of the manner in which Ilya of Murom obtained a vast accession of strength from the still mightier hero Svyatozor (pp. 58-63). By his exploits, however, in the story which I have given, Ilya appears to have already possessed strength enough for most purposes.

XXXIII.—THE LIME-TREE.

ONE evening Vanyusha (Johnny) was sitting with his grandfather, and asked his grandfather: 'Whence comes it that bears' paws are like our hands and feet?' His grandfather replied: 'Listen, Johnny. I will tell you what I have myself heard from ancient people. Ancient people said bears were like human beings, like us orthodox Christians. In a certain village there lived a poor cottager. His cottage was wretched; he had no pony; a cow he never even thought of; he had no firewood. Winter came, and it was cold in his unwarmed room. The cottager took his axe, and went with it into the wood. An enchanted tree—a lime-tree—presented itself to his sight. He struck it with his axe, and now to cut it down; but the lime-tree addressed him in human speech: "I will give you all that you want. If you have no riches, if you have no wife, I will give you all." The peasant said: "Very good, mother, if you make me richer than any of the peasants. But I have no pony, no cow, and my cottage is wretched." The lime-tree said: "Go home; all shall be yours." The peasant went. A new house was his: fences of stout boards, horses that were ready to fly, and store-rooms full of corn. The cottager was not satisfied, because his wife was not handsomer. What was to be done? "I'll go off quick to Mother Lime-tree." He took his axe, and went off into the wood.

'He went into the wood to the lime-tree, and struck it with his axe. "What do you want?" "Mother Lime-tree, among mankind there are wives and wives, but mine is such a disagreeable one. Do me a service: give me a handsome wife." The lime-tree said: "Go home." The peasant went. His wife came to meet him—such a beauty—blood and milk, and store-rooms full of everything good. Well, the cottager began to live comfortably with his young wife, and thought: "It is a fine thing for us to live possessed of riches, but we're under a superior authority. Is it impossible for me to be the superior authority myself?" He thought it over with his wife. He went again to the enchanted lime-tree.

'He went into the wood, he struck it with his axe. "What do you want, peasant?" "What, indeed, Mother Lime-tree! It's a fine thing for us to live in possession of riches; but we're under a superior authority. Is it impossible for me to be head-borough myself?" "Very well: go home; all shall be yours." No sooner had the cottager got home, when a letter came for him—"The cottager was to be head-borough." The cottager got used to living as head-borough, and thought to himself: "It's a fine thing to be head-borough, but all is under the control of the lord of the manor. Is it impossible for me to be the lord myself?" He considered the matter with his wife, they consulted together, and he went off again to the lime-tree.

'He went up to it, and struck it with his axe. The tree asked him: "What do you want?" "Thanks to you, mother, for all; but how not to doff my cap before the lord, to become the lord myself?" "What is to be done with you? Go home; it shall all be yours." Scarcely had he got home, when up drove the lord-lieutenant, and brought him a letter from the king, that "he was to be a gentleman." It was advantageous to be a gentleman. He began to give entertainments and banquets. "It's a fine thing to be a gentleman, but without an official position! Was it impossible for him to become an official?" They thought and talked it over. He went off to the lime-tree and struck it with his axe. "What do you want, peasant?" "I thank you, mother, for all; but is it impossible for me to be an official?" "Well, then, go home!" No sooner had he got home, when a royal letter arrived—he was invested with orders. "It's a fine thing to be decorated, but all is under the control of the lord-lieutenant. Is it impossible for me to be lord-lieutenant myself?" He thought it over with his wife, went off into the wood to the enchanted tree, the lime-tree.

'He came to the lime-tree and struck it with his axe. It said: "What do you want, peasant? With what are you discontented?" "I thank you, mother, for everything; but is it impossible for me to be lord-lieutenant myself, and to have a rich patrimony?" "It is difficult to effect this. But what is to be done with you? Go home!" The cottager had scarcely got home, when a letter arrived—the cottager was to be lord-lieutenant, and was presented with an estate of inheritance. The cottager became used to living as lord-lieutenant—indeed, by descent, he was not a peasant. "It's a fine thing for me to live as lord-lieutenant, but all is under the control of the king." He considered; he went off into the wood to the enchanted tree, the lime-tree.

'He came to it, and struck it with his axe. The tree inquired: "What do you want?" "All is excellent; I thank you for all; but is it impossible for me to be king myself?" The lime-tree began to try to persuade him. "Foolish man, for what are you asking? Consider what you were, and what you have become. From a cottager you have become a man of high rank and everything; but an emperor* is chosen by God." The lime-tree endeavoured to persuade him with all manner of arguments that he had better not make the request, but all in vain. The cottager would not budge, but insisted that it should make him emperor. The lime-tree said to him: "It is impossible to effect this, and it will not be done; you will lose, too, what you have already obtained!" But the cottager still insisted. The lime-tree said: "Become a bear, and your wife a she-bear!" And he became a bear, and she a she-bear. They went off bears.'

The grandson inquired: 'Grandfather, can this be a true story?' 'In reality 'tis a fable. Do not desire what is impossible; be content with a little. If you desire much, you will lose what you have obtained.'

XXXIV.—ILYA OF MUROM AND NIGHTINGALE THE ROBBER.

In the famous city of Murom, in the village of Karatcharof, lived a peasant, Ivan Timofeewitch. He had an

* Note the transition from king (*korol*) to emperor (*tzar*).

only child, Ilya Murometz. He sat as children do for thirty years, and when thirty years had passed, he began to walk firmly on his feet, became conscious of vast strength, made himself a warrior's equipment and a steel spear, and saddled a good horse, worthy of a hero. He went to his father and mother, and begged their blessing. 'My honoured father and mother, let me go to the famous city of Kief to perform my devotions to God, and to kneel to the Prince of Kief.' His father and mother gave him their blessing, laid upon him serious injunctions, and spoke to this effect: 'Ride straight to the city of Kief, straight to the city of Chernigof, and on your road do no injury, shed no Christian blood causelessly.' Ivan Murometz received the blessing of his father and mother, prayed to God, took leave of his father and mother, and started on his journey.

He travelled far on into the gloomy forest, until he came to a robbers' camp. The robbers espied Ilya Murometz, and their robber hearts burned for his heroic horse, and they began to talk together about taking his horse from him, for they were not wont to see such horses anywhere, and now an unknown man was riding on so good a horse. And they arose to assail Ilya Murometz by tens and twenties. Ilya Murometz halted his heroic horse, and took out of his quiver an arrow of guelder-rosewood, and placed it on his tough bow. He shot the arrow of guelder-rosewood along the ground, and it penetrated to the distance of a fathom slanting. Seeing this, the robbers were terrified, collected into an orb, fell on their knees, and said: 'You are our lord and father, valiant and good youth! We are guilty before you; take for such a fault as ours as much as you please of coloured raiment and herds of horses.' Ilya smiled and said: 'I've nowhere to put it; but if you wish to live, don't venture any further!' and rode on his way to the famous city of Kief.

He rode on to the city of Chernigof, and under that city

of Chernigof were standing armies of heathen innumerable, and they were besieging the city of Chernigof, and wanted to destroy it and ravage the churches of God therein, and to take into captivity the Prince and Duke of Chernigof himself. Ilya Murometz was terrified at this great force; nevertheless, he committed himself to the Lord God, his Creator, and determined to risk his head for the Christian faith. Ilya Murometz began to slaughter the heathen forces with his steel spear, and defeated all the pagan power, and took captive the heathen prince, and led him into the city of Chernigof. The citizens came out of the city of Chernigof to meet him with honour; the Prince and Duke of Chernigof came himself. They received the good youth with honour, and gave thanks to the Lord God, because the Lord unexpectedly sent deliverance to the city, and caused them not all to perish in vain at the hands of such a heathen host. They received him into their houses, made him a great entertainment, and let him proceed on his journey.

Ilya Murometz rode off towards the city of Kief by the direct road from Chernigof, which had been beset for full thirty years by Nightingale the robber, who allowed neither horseman nor foot-traveller to pass, and slew them not by any weapon, but by his robber whistling. Out rode Ilya Murometz into the open country, and espied the tracks of horses, and rode on upon them, and arrived at the Branskian forest, at the muddy swamps, at the bridges of guelder-rosewood, and at the river Smorodinka. Nightingale the robber forboded his end and a great misfortune, and before Ilya Murometz approached within twenty versts, began to whistle vigorously with his robber whistling; but the hero's heart was not terrified. Then, before he approached within ten versts, he began to whistle still more violently, and from this whistling Ilya Murometz's horse tottered under him. Ilya Murometz rode up to the nest itself, which was constructed upon twelve oaks. Nightingale the robber espied the hero of Holy Russia, whistled with all his might, and wanted to smite Ilya Murometz to death.

Ilya Murometz took down his tough bow, placed on it an arrow of guelder-rosewood, shot it at Nightingale's nest, struck his right eye and knocked it out. Nightingale the robber tumbled down like a sack of oats. Ilya Murometz took Nightingale the robber, bound him fast to his steel stirrup, and rode on towards the famous city of Kief. On the way stood a mansion belonging to Nightingale the robber, and when Ilya Murometz came opposite the robber's mansion, the windows thereof were open, and at these windows the robber's three daughters were looking out. The youngest daughter saw him, and cried to her sisters: 'There's our father outside coming with booty, and leading to us a man bound to his steel stirrup.' But the eldest daughter looked, and began to weep bitterly. 'That isn't our father coming: it's an unknown man coming, and leading our father.' They began to scream to their husbands: 'Our dear husbands! ride and meet the man, and take our father from him; do not let our family be put to such contempt.' Their husbands, strong heroes, rode against the hero of Holy Russia; their horses were good, their spears were sharp, and they were about to receive Ilya on their spears. Nightingale the robber espied this, and said to them: 'My dear sons-in-law, do not cause yourselves to be put to shame, and do not provoke so mighty a hero; rather with humility entreat him to drink a cup of green wine in my house.' At the request of the sons-in-law, Ilya turned into the house, not knowing their villainy. The eldest daughter raised on chains an iron slab, which was placed over the door, in order to crush him. But Ilya observed her at the door, struck her with his spear, and smote her to death.

When Ilya Murometz arrived at Kief city, he rode straight to the prince's palace, and entered the house, which was of white stone, prayed to God, and knelt to the prince. The Prince of Kief asked him: 'Tell me, good youth, how men name you, and of what city you are a native?' Ilya Murometz made reply: 'My lord, men call me Little Ilya, but by my father's family I am an Ivanof; a native of the city of Murom, of the village of Karatcharof.' The prince inquired: 'By what road did you ride from Murom?' 'By that of Chernigof, and under the walls of Chernigof I defeated an innumerable heathen host, and delivered the city of Chernigof. Thence I proceeded by the direct road, and took captive the mighty hero, Nightingale the robber, and led him hither with me bound to my steel stirrup.' The prince, becoming angry, said: 'What a lie you are telling!' When the heroes, Alesha Popovitch and Dobrynya Nikititch, heard this, they flew to look, and assured the prince that it really was so. The prince ordered a cup of green wine to be brought to the good youth. The prince had a wish to listen to the robber's whistling. Ilya enveloped the prince and princess in a sable mantle, placed them beneath his arms, summoned Nightingale, and commanded him to give the Nightingale whistle with half strength. But Nightingale the robber whistled with his full robber whistle, and deafened the heroes, so that they fell on the floor. For this Ilya Murometz slew him.

Ilya Murometz made a brotherhood with Dobrynya Nikititch. They saddled their good steeds, and rode into the open country to seek adventures; and they rode full three months without finding any adversary. But they rode on in the open country; there came a wandering beggar: the ragged dress upon his back weighed fifty poods, his hat nine poods, his staff was ten fathoms long. Ilya Murometz began to urge his horse toward him, and was about to match his heroic strength with him. The wandering beggar recognised Ilya Murometz, and said: 'Oh! you are Ilya Murometz. If you remember, we learnt to read and write together at one school, and now you are urging your horse against a poor cripple like me, as against an enemy. But this you don't know, that in the famous city of Kief a great misfortune has happened. An infidel, a mighty hero, the unclean Idolishtcha, has arrived. His head is as big as a beer caldron, his shoulders are a fathom broad, the distance between his eyebrows is a span, that between his ears is an arrow of guelder-rosewood; he eats an ox at a time, and drinks a caldron at a draught; and the Prince of Kief is very grieved about you, because you have left him in such perplexity.' Clothing himself in the beggar's dress, Ilya Murometz went straight to the prince's court, and cried with heroic voice: 'Oh, is it you, Prince of Kief? Send me an alms, wandering beggar that I am.' The prince saw him, and spake as follows: 'Come into the palace to me, beggar; I will give you your fill of food and drink, and gold for your journey.' And the beggar entered the palace and stood by the stove; he looked on at what was occurring. Idolishtcha asked for something to eat. They brought him a whole ox roasted, and he ate it up, bones and all. Idolishtcha asked for something to drink. They brought him a caldron of beer, carried by twenty men; he took it up by the handles, and drank it all up. Ilya Murometz said: 'My father had a greedy mare; she over-ate herself and died.' Idolishtcha didn't stand that, and said: 'Oh, it's you, wandering beggar! Why do you insult me? It's nothing to me to take you up in my hands. Nay, what are you? If such an one as Ilya Murometz was among you, I'd make a fight of it even with him.' 'Then here's such an one as he,' said Ilya Murometz, and, taking off his hat, struck him gently on the head with it.—But he broke through the wall of the house, took the corpse of Idolishtcha, and threw it out by the rent. For this the prince honoured Ilya Murometz with great commendations, and placed him on the list of mighty heroes.

SOUTHERN SLAVONIANS.

BULGARIAN STORIES.

THE Bulgarians do not derive their name from a Slavonic origin, but from a small and warlike nation of horsemen, which in A.D. 679 crossed the Danube under a chief named Isperich, conquered the disunited Slavonic tribes that had settled in Mœsia, and consolidated them into a powerful realm. The conquerors melted into the conquered, and lost their language, but gave their name to the state and country. The Slavonic language of the people does not appear to have been affected by that of their Ugrian conquerors, but rather by the old Thracian language, which, conjointly with Latin, has produced the present Roumanian. The peculiarities of the present Bulgarian language are: (1) the loss of case-inflexions in nouns and adjectives, while the verbal system is most complete and complex; (2) the expression of the genitive and dative cases by prefixing the preposition *na*; (3) the post-positive article, which is also borrowed from the old Thracian language, which was akin to the Illyrian now spoken by the present Albanians and Epirots; (4) the loss of the infinitive mood, which is replaced by *da* with the finite verb. Baron Wenceslas Wratislaw, in describing his journey through Bulgaria in 1591, says of the people: 'They use a Slavonic language, so that we Bohemians can converse with them.'

The Bulgarian tales themselves are curious, and some of them very beautiful, as are also the songs, to which considerable space is devoted by Mr. Morfill in his 'Slavonic Literature' (pp. 125-144). There are old traditions as to the world and its inhabitants, apparently of heathen origin (No. 35); a singular fusion of the history of Abraham and Isaac with some other, probably heathen, tradition (No. 36); a version of 'Cinderella' (No. 37), which, involving as it does the transmigration of souls, clearly exhibits an Indian origin; a beautiful story (No. 38), the latter part of which is a variant of the latter part of the Russian tale of 'Marya Morevna' (Ralston, p. 85), and No. 39, in the latter part of which many people will recognise a variant of an old acquaintance.

XXXV.—THE LORD GOD AS AN OLD MAN.

In the beginning, when man began to plough, when he had cut a furrow from one end to the other, he lifted his plough on to his shoulder, and when he had carried it back to the same end that he had begun from, he began again to plough thence. The Lord, in the form of an old man, passed by and said to him, 'Not thus, my son, but when you make a furrow, turn your plough round at the same place to which you have cut the furrow, and plough back to the end from which you began.' And thus the ploughman learnt to plough aright, as people plough at this day.

Thence the Lord went away in the form of an old man, and saw a woman who was weaving at a loom, and putting the thread, three threads at a time, into her mouth; she bit the thread off at one end, and began again at the same side. The Lord said to her, 'Not thus, daughter; but put the thread hither and thither with two hands without biting the thread off.' And she learnt to weave as people weave at this day.

The next day the Lord again passed alongside of the ploughman in a different guise, and asked him: 'Who taught you, my son, to plough thus?' He replied to him: 'The Lord God, in the form of an old man.' The Lord blessed him, and said: 'A day to plough and a year to eat!' Afterwards he passed by the woman and asked her: 'Who taught you, daughter, to weave thus?' She replied: 'Myself, my very own self, quickly, quite quickly.' Then the Lord said to her: 'A year to weave, that you may carry it under the arm!'

They say, moreover, that at that time men had command not only over all animals, but also over inanimate things; but later, they say, it was altered when men became wicked. For instance, when a man had cut logs of wood and piled them in a heap, he struck them with a stick, and they went of themselves whither they were required to go. But a certain woman having cut logs and struck them to make them go, they started; but she, being tired of walking beside them on foot, seated herself at top, and the logs resisted. She struck them on one side, she struck them on the other, but they didn't move any whither. Then she unfastened her girdle, and put them on her back. On the way God showed himself to her, and said to her: 'Since you are wicked, instead of your riding on them, let them ride on you.'

When the Lord walked about the earth and blessed it, he went first to a herdsman. He was lying on his back under a tree, a pear-tree; his pitcher, in which he fetched water for himself, stood by empty. The Lord, in the form of an old man, asked him: 'My son, is there any water in the pitcher?' He said to him: 'No.' The Lord said to him: 'Go, my son, to fetch me a little water, that the old man may drink.' The herdsman made a sign to him with his foot: 'There is where the spring is; if you're thirsty, go, drink.' The Lord then gave the word that all the herd should run off as if assailed by the gadfly; then, when they began all to run in one direction, the herdsman took his hat in his hand and started off, and as he ran after them thought: 'How I have sinned against God!'

Then the Lord went to a shepherd. The shepherd also had a pitcher. The Lord asked him: 'My son, have you any water?' He replied to him: 'There is water, old man, but I cannot go to fetch it myself, or the sheep will disperse.' Then said the Lord: 'Go, my son; I will watch them.' When the shepherd went off for the water, the Lord took the shepherd's staff, and when he had stuck it into the ground, placed the shepherd's cloak upon it, and blessed the sheep. They became quiet and tranquil in the shade. During the shepherd's absence up came a wolf to obtain the appointed tribute which he received every day from the shepherd. The Lord gave him a lamb of little value. The wolf, discontented, did not choose to take it, but darted forward and seized another, which he liked. Then the Lord took the shepherd's trumpet, and struck him on the loins—on the spine. From this it has remained a property of the wolf that his loins are just as weak as his neck is strong. But he carried off the lamb which he had seized. The Lord took two little stones, threw them after the wolf and blessed them; they became two dogs, ran after the wolf, and took away the lamb which the wolf had seized. The shepherd came up bringing the Lord cold water, and saw the sheep quiet, for they were standing in the shade and the two dogs were frolicking round them. The shepherd then asked the old man: 'Well, old man, now when the sheep are standing quiet, and are like blocks of wood, how shall I drive them to pasture?' The Lord said to him: 'My son, take a copper trumpet, and blow it to them; they will start off in the direction from which the wind blows gently.' From that time forth down to the present day people drive their sheep to pasture blowing trumpets.

XXXVI.—BULGARIAN HOSPITALITY.

ONCE upon a time, when the Lord had formed the world, he wished to see how his people lived; he came down from heaven first of all on the Balkan Mountains, took the form of a man with a long white beard and white clothes; took a staff in his hand, and went about the world in the Bulgarian land; he travelled much, a whole day long, over desolate mountains. In the evening he came to a village to pass the night. He went into the first house at the end of the village and sat down on the threshold, said nothing, but meditated by himself. The mistress was in her house doing some work, and did not see him. But now her husband came from the field, from his plough, espied the old man, was delighted, and said to him: 'Old man, you are very tired; you are a weary traveller. Come into the house; rest yourself, if it is but a poor one. I will entertain you with all that the Lord has given me—only say the word.' The old man regarded him with cheerful eyes, went into the house and sat down. The man and his wife quickly rose up and prepared a hospitable meal according to what they possessed, and as nicely and as handsomely as they could, and placed it on the table. The couple ate of their homely meal, but the old man would not; he only smelt the homely banquet, said nothing, but watched how the two persons enjoyed themselves, and rejoiced. They urged him, they begged him. 'Old man, why don't you eat? You will remain hungry. Take, and taste, and try what you please. What we have is all here before you.' The old man only said this: 'Eat you—eat; I am thinking of something.'

When they had eaten their fill, they rose. The mistress went out to feed the child because it was crying. Then said the old man to her husband: 'Do you know what, master, if you wish to entertain me? I cannot eat everything, but I wish for baked human flesh. Kill your little son, wash him nicely, and place him whole on the frying-pan in the oven; only look out that your wife does not see you, for she will weep.' He replied: 'Is this all that you want, old man? Why did you not tell me long before, that you might not have sat a hungry guest in the house? Did I not tell you that all was yours that the Lord had given me? Indeed, I love you exceedingly, old man; my heart tells me that you are good and worthy, and now you shall see; only have a little patience, till I get ready that which you desire.' The man went out of doors, and his wife had begun to do some work, and had left her child to play by itself in the moonlight till it fell asleep, without knowing what was about to take place. Her husband stole the child, killed it with all haste, put it entire in the frying-pan, and shut it up in the oven, that its mother might not see it till it was cooked; he then went to the old man, sat down by him and conversed cheerfully with him. They had not talked long, when the old man became silent, sniffed with his nose, and said to the servant lad: 'Go, look at the baked meat; it smells nicely; perhaps it is cooked.'

The lad rose, went out, opened the oven to look at and take out the baked meat. But what did he see? He was amazed and frightened at the wonder; all the oven and all the house was glittering with the brightness of the child. The frying-pan and the child had become gold, and shone like the sun. The child was sitting in the frying-pan like a big boy—handsome, cheerful, bright, and well. On his head was a crown of pearls and precious stones; on the girdle at his waist was a sword. In his right hand he held a book of blessing; in his left hand he had a wheatsheaf full of ears; and all this was shining more than fire, because it had all become gold. He returned to tell the old man what a wonder had taken place, and to ask what was to be done; but the old man was no longer there; he had gone out in front of the house, and said to them: 'Fare ye well, and live as ye have done till now, honourably and contentedly. Your good hearts will have good from field and cattle, and blessing and peace upon your children and children's children from the Lord. He will receive you and entertain you in his heavenly house.' He then went away alone under cover of the night, no one knows whither.

XXXVII.—CINDERELLA.

ONCE upon a time, a number of girls were assembled spinning round a deep rift or chasm in the ground. As they spun they chattered together and told stories to each other. Up came a white-bearded old man, who said to them: 'Girls! as you spin and chatter, be circumspect round this rift; or, if any of you drops her spindle into it, her mother will be turned into a cow.' Thus saying he departed. The girls were astonished at his words, and crowded round the rift to look into it. Unfortunately, one of them, the most beautiful of all, dropped her spindle into it. Towards evening, when she went home, she espied a cow—her mother—in front of the gate, and drove her out with the other cattle to pasture. After some time the father of the girl married a widow, who brought a daughter with her into the house. The second wife had a spite at the man's first daughter, especially because she was more beautiful and more industrious than her own, and she allowed her neither to wash herself, nor to comb her hair, nor to change her clothes. One day she sent her out with the cattle, gave her a bag full of tow, and told her: 'If you don't spin this tow into yarn to-day, or if you don't wind it into a ball, you had better not come home at eventide—I shall kill you.' It was sad for the poor girl, as she went after the cattle, endeavouring as well as she could to keep them together. In the afternoon, when the cattle lay down to chew the cud, she began to look at the bag to see how to perform her task upon it; but when she saw that she could not make out what to do with it, she began to cry. When the cow which was her mother saw her crying, she asked her why she was crying. She told her how it was, and what it was. Then said the cow to her: 'Don't be afraid; I will help you. I will take all the tow into my mouth, and will chew it, and yarn will come up into my ear. You must take it and reel it into a ball, and you will finish it in good time.' As she said, so it was. She began to chew the tow, piece after piece; yarn came up into her ear, and the girl wound and reeled it, and finished the task. In the evening she departed and went to her stepmother, who was amazed at seeing so much work completed. The next time she gave her as much tow again. The girl spun till noon, and then in the afternoon, when the cattle lay down to chew the cud, the cow came up to her and began to chew the tow; yarn came up into her ear, and the girl wound and reeled it, and finished in good time. In the evening she went home and delivered to her stepmother all the tow spun and wound. She was astonished at seeing so much work completed. The third time she gave her still more tow, and sent her own daughter to see who helped her. The daughter went and concealed herself apart, and saw how it was and what it was, that the girl completed so much work in the day; she saw how the cow took the tow into her mouth, how yarn came up into her ear, and how the girl wound and reeled it. She went home to tell her mother. When she heard this from her daughter, she urged her husband to kill the cow. He endeavoured in every way to persuade her not to kill the cow, but could not over-persuade her. At last, when he saw that there was no escape, he promised to kill it on a certain day. When the girl heard that they were going to kill the cow she began to cry, and told the cow secretly that they were going to kill her. She said to the girl: 'Be quiet—don't cry! If they kill me, you must not eat any of my flesh, but must collect the bones and bury them behind the cottage. Then if need come to you, you must go to the grave, and help will come to you thence.' On hearing this she went away.

One day they killed the cow and boiled her flesh, brought it into the parlour, and began to eat. The girl alone did not eat of it, according to the instructions she had received; but collected the bones, and then, without anybody seeing her, took them and buried them behind the cottage, where the cow (her mother) had ordered her so to do. The girl was named Mary; but at length, when they had put all the work in the cottage upon her—that is to say, to sweep, to fetch water, to cook, to wash up the plates—she had become dirty and begrimed with ashes and cinders from excessive work at the fireplace; and therefore her stepmother nick-named her Cinderella (Pepelezka), and this remained her name afterwards.

One Sunday her stepmother got ready to go to church with her daughter, but, before starting, took a wooden dish of millet, scattered it on the ground in the cottage, and said to Cinderella: 'Here you, Cinderella! if you don't pick up this millet, and if you don't get dinner ready by the time that I return from church, don't come before my eyes, or I shall put you to death.' Then they went away. Poor Cinderella, when she looked at all the millet, cried out weeping and wailing: 'I will cook, I will sweep, I will attend to everything, but what poor girl can pick up all this millet?'

When she had wept and spoken, immediately there came into her mind what the cow had told her, to go to the grave, and there help would be given her in trouble. Cinderella went off to the grave. When there, what did she see? On the grave stood an open box, filled with all manner of rich clothes, and on the lid were two pigeons, white as snow. They said to her: 'Mary! take the clothes out, put them on, and go to church, and we will pick up the millet and get the dinner ready.' She put out her hands and took the upper ones, which were of pure silk and satin, put them on, and went to church. In the church people great and small marvelled at her beauty and her dress, especially because no one recognised her or knew who or what she was. Most of all did the emperor's son marvel at her, and never took his eyes off her. When service was ended, she stole away and ran quickly home, undressed immediately, and put the clothes in the box, and the box immediately vanished from sight. She went to the fireplace, and what did she see there? The millet picked up, dinner ready—in one word, everything attended to! Soon afterwards, lo! her stepmother came with her daughter from church, saw everything in proper order, and was astounded.

Next Sunday, when she was about to go to church, taking a larger dish of millet and scattering it on the ground, she threatened Cinderella that she would kill her if she didn't pick it up and get dinner ready. The stepmother went off with her daughter to church, and Cinderella betook herself to the grave of the cow. On the grave she found the two pigeons and the box with the dresses in it open. They told her to dress herself and go to church, and they would pick up the millet and get dinner ready. Taking a dress of pure silver, she dressed herself and went off to church. Now everybody, small and great, marvelled at her more than before, and the emperor's son did not take his eyes off her for a moment. Service ended, she stole off amidst the multitude and got away home. There she undressed, and put the clothes in the box, and the box disappeared from sight. Soon afterwards, lo! her stepmother came and looked about; the millet was picked up, dinner was ready, and Cinderella was at the fireplace. She was astonished at seeing so much work completed.

The third time her stepmother got ready to go to church, and before she started, taking a dish of millet thrice as large, and scattering it on the ground, she said to Cinderella: 'Cinderella, if you don't pick up all this millet before we return from church, and if you don't get dinner ready, go and hide yourself; don't come before my eyes—I shall kill you.' Then she went off to church. After this Cinderella went to the grave of the cow, and found there the box open and the two pigeons upon it. They told her to dress herself and go to church; they would pick up the millet and get the dinner ready. Taking a dress of pure gold, she dressed herself and went to church. There, when the people saw her, they marvelled, but no one knew who or what she was. The emperor's son never took his eyes off her, and planned, when service was over, to follow her closely, to see whither she betook herself. Service ended, she stole off amidst the crowd, hastening to get away before her stepmother; but as she was pushing through the crowd, she lost one of her shoes, and the emperor's son took it up. She escaped from among them with one shoe, undressed very quickly, put the clothes in the box, and the box vanished. She went home and looked in the cottage; the millet was picked up, dinner was ready, and everything attended to. She sat down at the fireplace, and, lo! her stepmother came and looked about the cottage; everything was in order, the millet picked up, dinner ready; she had nothing to find fault with her or scold her about.

The emperor's son left the people, disguised himself, took the shoe, and went from cottage to cottage to try it on, to find out whose it was; and wherever he went he made inquiries, and tried it on the foot of every girl, but it did not fit one. For some it was too large, and for others too small; for some too narrow, for others too broad. At last he came to Cinderella's cottage. As soon as her stepmother saw him, she concealed Cinderella under a trough. He asked whether there was any girl in the house. She replied that there was, and brought her daughter to him. He tried the shoe on her, but it wouldn't even allow her toes to go in. He then asked whether there wasn't another girl there, and she told him that there wasn't. The cock had flown on to the trough, and when she told the emperor's son that there was no other girl there, he crowed: 'Cock-a-doodle-doo! pretty girl under trough!' The stepmother shrieked out: 'Shoo! eagles have brought you!'* But the emperor's son, on hearing the cock say this, went up and took the trough off; and there was, indeed, the girl that he had seen in the church with those beautiful dresses, only on one foot she had no shoe. He tried the shoe on her; it went on, and was exactly the same as that on the other foot. Then the emperor's son took her by the hand, conducted her to his court, married her, and punished her stepmother for her evil heart.

XXXVIII.—THE GOLDEN APPLES AND THE NINE PEAHENS.

THERE was once upon a time an emperor who had three sons, and in his yard a golden apple-tree, which flowered and ripened every night; but somebody robbed it, and the emperor was utterly unable to discover who the robber was.

* Eagles are frequently supernatural messengers in Bulgarian tales. One might have expected, 'Eagles take you!' but it is as I have given it.

Once he was conversing with his sons, and said to them: 'I do not know whither goes the fruit from our apple-tree.' Then the eldest son answered him: 'I will go to-night to see who takes it.' When it became dark, the eldest son did as he had said: went out, and lay down under it. Well, when the apples began to ripen in the course of the night, slumber overtook him, and he fell asleep; and when he awoke at dawn he looked—but where were the apples? Taken away! When he saw this, he went and related all to his father just as it really happened. The second son said to his father: 'I will go to-night to watch, that I may see who takes it.' But he, too, watched it even as the first one. About the time when the apples began to ripen, he fell asleep. When he woke up in the morning, where were the apples? Taken away! Now came the turn of the third and youngest brother. He went out at eventide under the apple-tree, placed a sofa there, lay down, and went to sleep. About midnight, when the apples began to ripen, he woke up and looked at the apple-tree. It had just begun to ripen, and illuminated all the yard from the brightness of its fruit. Just then up flew nine peahens, eight of which settled upon the apple-tree, and the ninth on the ground beside his sofa, and, as soon as she had alighted, became a damsel, who shone with beauty like a bright sun. They conversed together while the other eight were rifling the tree, and when dawn came, she thanked him for the apples, and he begged her to leave just one behind her. She gave him two—one for himself, and one to take to his father—transformed herself into a peahen, and flew away, followed by the other eight. In the morning the prince rose up, and took one apple to his father, who did not know what to do for joy, and commended him without ceasing. The next evening the youngest prince went out again to watch the apple-tree, and as soon as he had gone out, lay down as before, and watched it that night also. In the morning he again brought his father an apple. This went on for a few days, when his brothers began to envy him, because they could not watch it, whereas he watched it successfully. They could not make out how to discover the manner in which he watched the apple-tree. So they sought out an old witch, who promised them to find out how their young brother watched the apple-tree. At the approach of evening, when the youngest prince was about to go out to watch the apple-tree, the accursed witch stole out and went off before him, lay down under his sofa, and there concealed herself. The prince came, lay down without knowing that the old woman was under his sofa, and went to sleep as previously. About midnight, when the prince had just woke up, the nine peahens arrived; eight of them settled on the tree, and the other on the ground beside his sofa, transformed herself into a damsel, and they began to converse together. While these were talking to each other, the accursed old witch softly raised herself up, and cut off a piece of the damsel's long hair. As soon as she felt this, the damsel sprang on one side, transformed herself into a peahen, and flew away, with the other eight behind her. The prince, on seeing this, sprang off his sofa, and shouted: 'What is this?' He erelong espied the old woman under the sofa, seized and hauled her from under it, and, when morning came, ordered her to be fastened to the tails of two horses and torn asunder. The peahens came no more to the apple-tree, and the prince was much grieved on this account, and wept and mourned day after day. At last he determined to go to seek them all over the world, and went and told his father what his intention was, and his father endeavoured to comfort him, and said: 'Stay, my son! I will find you another damsel in my empire, such an one as you wish for.' But in vain; he would not follow his father's advice, and made preparations to go; took with him one of his servants, and went into the world to find the peahen. When he had travelled a long time, he came to a lake, in the midst of which was a rich palace, and in the palace an aged empress, who had one daughter. The prince, on coming to the old empress, asked her to tell him about the nine peahens, if she knew about them; and the old woman replied that she did, and that the nine peahens came daily to bathe in the lake. On telling him this, she began to try to over-persuade him with these words: 'Never mind those nine peahens, my son. I have a handsome damsel, and abundance of wealth—it will all remain yours.' But as soon as the prince heard where the peahens were, he would not listen to her talk, but in the morning ordered his servant to get the horses ready to go to the lake. Before they started for the lake, the old woman called his servant, bribed him, and gave him a little whistle, saying to him: 'When the time approaches for the peahens to come to the lake, do you secretly look out, and blow the whistle behind your master's neck; he will immediately fall asleep, and will not see them.' The accursed servant hearkened to her, took the whistle, and did as the old woman told him. When they arrived at the shore of the lake, he calculated the time when the peahens would arrive, blew the whistle behind his master's neck, and he immediately fell as sound asleep as if he were dead. Scarcely had he fallen asleep, when the peahens arrived; eight of them settled on the lake, and the ninth perched upon his horse, and began to try to awaken him: 'Arise, my birdie! arise, my lamb! arise, my dove!' But he heard nothing, but slept on as if dead. When the peahens had finished bathing, they all flew away, and he awoke, and asked his servant: 'What is it? Did they come?' The servant replied: 'They did come,' and told him how eight of them settled on the lake, and the ninth on his horse, and that she tried to wake him. When the unhappy prince heard this from his servant, he was ready to kill himself from pain and anger. The next morning they visited the shore of the lake again, but his accursed servant calculated the time to blow the whistle behind his neck, and he immediately fell asleep as if he were dead. Scarcely had he fallen asleep, when the nine peahens arrived; eight settled on the lake, and the ninth on his horse, and began to try to awake him: 'Arise, my birdie! arise, my lamb! arise, my dove!' But he slept on as if he were dead, hearing nothing. When the peahen failed to wake him, and they were about to fly away again, the one which had been trying to wake him turned and said to his servant: 'When your master wakes, tell him that to-morrow it will once more be possible for him to see us, but after that, never more.' On saying this she took flight, and the others from the lake after her. Scarcely had they flown away, when the prince awoke, and asked his servant: 'Did they come?' He told him: 'They did come, and eight of them settled on the lake, and the ninth on your horse, and tried to wake you, but you slept soundly. As she departed, she told me to tell you that you will see her here once again to-morrow, and never more.' When the prince heard this, he was ready to kill himself in his unhappiness, and did not know what to do for sorrow. On the third day he got ready to go to the lake, mounted his horse, went to the shore, and, in order not to fall asleep, kept his horse continually in motion. But his wicked servant, as he followed him, calculated the time, and blew the whistle behind his neck, and he immediately leant forward on his horse and fell asleep. As soon as he fell asleep, the nine peahens flew up; eight settled on the lake, and the ninth on his horse, and endeavoured to wake him: 'Arise, my birdie! arise, my lamb! arise, my dove!' But he slept as if he were dead, and heard nothing. Then, when they were about to fly away again, the one which had perched on his horse turned round, and said to his servant: 'When your master wakes up, tell him to roll the under peg on the upper, and then he will find me.'* Then she flew off, and those from the lake after her. When they had flown away, he awoke again, and asked his servant: 'Did they come?' He replied: 'They did; and the one that had perched on your horse told me to tell you to roll the upper peg on the under one, and then you would find her. When the prince heard this, he drew his sword, and cut off his servant's head. When he had done this, he started to travel on alone. When he had travelled a long time, he came at dusk to the cottage of a hermit, and lodged there for the night. In the evening the prince asked the hermit: 'Grandfather, have you heard of nine golden peahens?' The hermit answered: 'Yes, my son; you are fortunate in having come to me to ask about them. They are not far hence; it is not more than half a day's journey to them from here.' In the morning, when the prince departed to seek them, the hermit came out to accompany him, and said to him: 'Go to the right, and you will find a large gate. When you enter that gate, turn to the right, and then you will go right into their town, and in that town is their palace. He went on his way according to the hermit's words, and went on till he came to that gate; then turned to the right, and descried the town upon a hill. When he saw the town he was much rejoiced. When he entered the town he inquired where the palace of the nine peahens was. It was pointed out to him. At the gate a watchman stopped him, and inquired whence and who he was. The prince told him all, whence he was and who he was. After this the watchman went off to announce him to the empress. When she heard it, she ran breathless, and stood in the form of a damsel before him,

* I do not understand this expression. It is afterwards inverted by the servant. But it has no further bearing on the story.

took him by the hand, and led him upstairs. Then the two rejoiced together, and in a day or two were wedded.

When a few days had elapsed after their marriage, the empress departed to go on a journey, and the prince remained alone. When she was about to start, she took out and gave him the keys of twelve cellars, and said to him: 'Open all the cellars, but do not have any nonsense with the twelfth.' She went away. When the prince remained alone in the palace, he bethought himself: 'What does this mean, that I am to open all the cellars, but not to open the twelfth? Glory to the Lord God! what can there be in it?' He then began to open them one after the other. He came to the twelfth, and at first would not open it; but as he had no occupation, he began to brood and to say to himself: 'How can it be in this cellar that she told me not to open it?' At last he opened it too, and found standing in the midst of it a cask bound with iron hoops, and a voice out of it was heard, saying: 'I pray you, brother—I am athirst for water—give me a cup of water.' On hearing this voice, the prince took a cup of water, and sprinkled it on the bung; and as soon as he had sprinkled it, one of the hoops of the cask burst. The voice then cried: 'Give me one more cup of water; I am athirst.' He took a cup of water and sprinkled it on the bung; and as soon as he had done so, another hoop burst on the cask. The voice then cried: 'I am athirst; give me, brother, one more cup of water.' The prince took another cup of water and poured it on the bung; but as soon as he had finished pouring it, the third hoop of the cask burst, the cask split asunder, and out of it flew a dragon, found the empress on her way, and carried her off. Thus it happened, and the attendants came and told their master that a dragon had carried the empress away. Finally he set off to seek her in the world. When he had travelled a long time, he came to a marsh, and in that marsh espied a little fish, which was endeavouring to jump into the water, but was unable to do so. This little fish, on seeing the prince, addressed itself to him: 'I pray you, brother, do a good action: throw me into the water; I shall some time be of use to you; only take a scale from me, and when you are in want of me, rub it between your fingers.' On hearing this he took a scale off it, threw the fish into the water, put the scale into a handkerchief, and went on his way. When he had gone a little further, he espied a fox caught in a trap. When the fox saw him, it called out: 'I pray you, brother, let me out of this trap; I shall some day be of use to you; only take one or two hairs from my fur, and when I am wanted for you, rub them between your fingers.' He let it out of the trap, took one or two hairs from it, and went on his way. Thus he proceeded onwards, till, as he went, he came to a hill, and found a crow caught in a trap just like the fox before. As soon as the crow saw him, it cried out: 'I pray you, be a brother to me, traveller; let me out of this trap; I shall some day be of use to you; only take a feather or two from me, and when you are in want of me, rub them between your fingers.' The prince took one or two feathers from the crow, let it out of the trap, and then went on his way. As he went on to find the empress, he met a man, and asked him: 'I pray you, brother, do you not know where is the palace of the dragon emperor?' The man showed him the way, and also told him at what time he was at home, that he might find him. The prince thanked him, and said: 'Farewell.' He then went on, and gradually came to the palace of the dragon emperor. On his arrival there he found his beloved, and when she saw him and he saw her, they were both full of joy. Now they began to plan together how to escape. Finally they agreed to saddle their horses and take to flight. They saddled them, mounted, and off. When they had

13

ridden off, the dragon arrived and looked about, but the empress was not to be found. 'Now what shall we do?' said the dragon to his horse. 'Shall we eat and drink, or pursue them?' The horse replied to him: 'Don't trouble yourself; eat and drink.' When he had dined, the dragon mounted his horse and galloped after them, and in course of time overtook them, and took the empress away, but said to the prince: 'Go in safety; this time you are forgiven, because you gave me water in the cellar; but do not come a second time if your life is dear to you.' The poor prince remained as if thunderstricken, then started and proceeded a little way; but as he could not overcome his heart, he returned to the dragon's palace. There he found the empress weeping. When they saw each other and met, they began to consult how to get away so as to escape. Then said the prince to the empress: 'When the dragon comes, ask him from whom he bought that horse, and tell me, that I may obtain such another, that we may escape.' After saying this to her he went out, that the dragon might not find him on his arrival. When the dragon came, the empress began to coax him and make herself agreeable to him, and said to him: 'What a swift horse yours is! From whom did you buy him? Tell me, I pray you.' He answered: 'Where I bought him nobody can make a purchase. On a certain hill lives an old woman who has twelve horses in her stable, such that you don't know which is better than another. One of them is in the corner, and this one looks skinny; but he is the best of all, and is brother of mine: this one could fly to the sky. Whoever seeks to obtain a horse from the old woman must serve her three days. The old woman has a mare with a foal; whoever watches the mare successfully for three days, to him the old woman gives the choice of whichever horse he wishes. Whoever engages himself to watch the mare, and fails to watch her successfully for three days and three nights, loses his life.' On the morrow the dragon went away, and the prince came in. The empress told him what the dragon had said. Then the prince started off and went to the hill where the old woman was to be found. When he entered her house, he said to her: 'Good-day, old woman!' The old woman replied: 'The Lord give you prosperity, my son!' She said to him: 'What brings you here, my son?' He replied: 'I should like to take service with you.' The old woman said to him: 'Very good, my son. I have a mare with a foal. If you watch her successfully for three days, I will give you one of these twelve horses of mine to take away, whichever you choose; but if you fail to watch her successfully, I shall take off your head.' Then she took him into the yard. In the yard post after post was fixed in the ground, and on each was stuck a human head; only one remained vacant, and this cried out continually: 'Old woman, give me a head!' When the old woman had shown him all, she said: 'Know that all these engaged to watch the mare and the foal, but were unable to watch her successfully.' But the prince was in no wise terrified thereby. In the afternoon he mounted the mare and galloped uphill and downhill, and the foal galloped after her. Thus till midnight, and then, would he nould he, sleep crept over him, and he fell asleep. When he woke up at dawn his arms were round a stump instead of the mare, but he held the halter in his hand. When he perceived this, the poor fellow became dizzy from terror, and started off to look for her; and while he was looking for her, came to a sheet of water, and when he came to the water, he remembered the little fish, unfolded the handkerchief, and took out the scale and rubbed it between his fingers. Up sprang the little fish out of the water, and lay before him. 'What is the matter, adopted brother?' said the fish. He replied: 'The old woman's mare has escaped from me, and I don't know where she is.' The fish said to him: 'Here she is amongst us; she has transformed herself into a fish, and her foal into a little fish; but do you flap the halter on the water, and call out: "Coop! coop! old woman's mare!"' He flapped the water with the halter, and called out: 'Coop! coop! old woman's mare!' and immediately she transformed herself again into a mare, and, pop! there she was on the brink of the water before him! He put the halter on her and mounted her, and trot! trot! and at the old woman's. When he brought her in, the old woman gave him his dinner, but led the mare into the stable, scolded her, and said: 'Among the fish, good-for-nothing rogue?' The mare replied: 'I was among the fish, but they told of me, because they are his friends.' The old woman said to her: 'Go among the foxes.' The second day he mounted the mare, and galloped uphill and downhill, and the foal galloped after. Thus till midnight. When it was about midnight sleep overcame him, and he fell asleep upon the mare's back. At dawn, when he awoke, his arms were round a stump, but he held the halter in his hand. When he perceived this, he sprang off again to seek her. As he was seeking her, it came at once into his head what the old woman had said to the mare when she was leading it into the stable. Then he unwrapped the fox's hairs out of the handkerchief, rubbed them between his fingers, and the fox immediately jumped out before him. 'What is it, adopted brother?' He replied: 'The old woman's mare has run away.' The fox said to him: 'Here she is amongst us; she has become a fox, and the foal a fox-cub. But do you flap the ground with the halter, and call out: "Coop! coop! old woman's mare!"' He flapped and called, and the mare leaped out before him. Then he caught her and put the halter on her, mounted her, and rode to the old woman's.

When he brought her home, the old woman gave him his dinner, led the mare off to the stable, and said: 'Among the foxes, good-for-nothing rogue?' The mare replied: 'I was among them, but they are his friends, and told of me.' The old woman said to her: 'Be among the crows.' The third day the prince again mounted the mare, and galloped her uphill and downhill, and the foal galloped after. Thus till midnight. About midnight he became sleepy, and fell asleep, and woke up at dawn; but his arms were round a stump, and he held the halter in his hand. As soon as he perceived this, he darted off again to seek the mare, and as he was seeking her, it came into his head what the old woman had said the day before when scolding the mare. He took out the handkerchief and unwrapped the crow's feathers, rubbed them between his fingers, and, pop! the crow was before him. 'What is it, adopted brother?' The prince replied: 'The old woman's mare has run away, and I don't know where she is.' The crow answered: 'Here she is amongst us; she has become a crow, and the foal a young crow. But flap the halter in the air, and cry: "Coop! coop! old woman's mare!"' He flapped the halter in the air, and cried: 'Coop! coop! old woman's mare!' and the mare transformed herself from a crow into a mare, just as she had been, and came before him. Then he put the halter on her, and mounted her, and galloped off, the foal following behind, to the old woman's. The old woman gave him his dinner, caught the mare, led her into the stable, and said to her: 'Among the crows, good-for-nothing rogue?' The mare replied: 'I was among them, but they are his friends, and told of me.' Then when the old woman came out, the prince said to her: 'Well, old woman, I have served you honestly; now I ask you to give me that which we agreed upon.' The old woman replied: 'My son, what is agreed upon must be given. Here are twelve horses—choose whichever you please.' He replied: 'Why shall I pick and choose? Give me that one where he is in the corner; there is none better in my eyes.' Then the old woman began to dissuade him: 'Why chose that skinny one when there are so many good ones?' He then insisted once for all: 'Give me the one which I ask, for such was our agreement.' The old woman twisted, turned, and without more ado gave him the one which he asked for. Then he mounted it, and 'Farewell, old woman!' 'Good-bye, my son!' When he took it to a wood and groomed it, it glittered like gold. Afterwards, when he mounted it and gave it its head, it flew, flew like a bird, and in a jiffy arrived at the dragon's palace. As soon as he entered the courtyard, he bade the empress to get ready for flight. She was not long in getting ready; they both mounted the horse and set off. They had not long started in flight when the dragon arrived—looked about. No empress. Then he said to his horse: 'Shall we eat and drink, or shall we pursue?' 'Eat or not, drink or not, pursue or not, you won't catch him.' When the dragon heard this, he immediately mounted his horse, and started to pursue them. When the prince and empress perceived that he was pursuing them, they were terrified, and urged their horse to go quickly, but the horse answered them: 'Never fear; there's no need to hurry.' The dragon came trot, trot, and the horse he rode called to that which bore the prince and the empress: 'Bless you, brother, wait! for I shall break my wind from pursuing you.' The other replied: 'Whose fault is it, if you're such a fool as to carry that spectre on your back? Buck, and throw him on the ground, and then follow me.' When the dragon's horse heard this, up with his head, a jump with his hind-quarters, and bang went the dragon against a stone. The dragon was smashed to pieces, and his horse followed the prince and empress. Then the empress caught and mounted it, and they arrived safe and sound in the empress's dominions, and reigned honourably as long as they lived.

XXXIX.—THE LANGUAGE OF ANIMALS.

A CERTAIN man had a shepherd, who served him faithfully and honestly for many years. This shepherd, when he was once upon a time following the sheep, heard a whistling on the hill, and, not knowing what it was, went off to see. When he got to the place, there was a conflagration, and in the middle of it a serpent was squeaking. When he saw this, he waited to see how the serpent would act, for all around it was burning, and the fire had almost come close to it. When the serpent saw him, it screamed: 'Dear shepherd, do a good action: take me out of this fire.' The shepherd took pity on its words, and reached it his crook, and it crawled out upon it. When it had crawled out, it coiled itself round his neck. When the shepherd saw this, he was frightened, and said: 'Indeed you are a wretch! Is that the way you are going to thank me for rescuing you? So runs the proverb: "Do good, and find evil."' The serpent answered him: 'Don't fear: I shall do you no harm; only carry me to my father; my father is the emperor of the serpents.' The shepherd begged pardon, and excused himself: 'I can't carry you to your father, because I have no one to leave in charge of my sheep.' The serpent said to him: 'Don't fear for your sheep; nothing will happen to them; only carry me to my father, and go quickly.' Then there was no help for it, so he started with it over the hill. When he came to a door, which was formed of nothing but serpents intertwined, and went up to it, the serpent which was coiled round his neck gave a whistle, and the serpents, which had twined themselves into the form of a door, immediately untwined, and made way for them to enter. As the shepherd and the serpent entered the palace, the serpent called to the shepherd: 'Stop! let me tell you something: when you come into my father's palace, he will promise you what you desire, silver and gold; but don't you accept anything, only ask him to give you such a tongue that you will be able to understand all animals. He will not give you this readily, but at last grant it you he will.' The shepherd went with it into its father's palace, and its father, on seeing it, shed tears, and asked it: 'Hey, my son, where have you been till now?' It replied, and told him everything in order: what had taken place, and how it had taken place, and how the shepherd had rescued it. Then the emperor of the serpents turned to the shepherd, and said to him: 'Come, my son, what do you wish me to give you in recompense for rescuing my child?' The shepherd replied to him: 'Nothing else, only give me such a tongue that I can understand all animals.' The emperor of the serpents said to him: 'That is not a proper gift for you, my son, because, if I give you anything of the kind, you will betray yourself in somebody's presence by boasting of it, and then you will die immediately; ask something else.' The shepherd replied to him: 'I wish for nothing else. If you will give it me, give it; if not, farewell!' He turned to go; but the emperor of the serpents cried out: 'Stay! Return! If you ask this, come, that I may give it you. Open your mouth.' The shepherd opened his mouth, and the emperor of the serpents spat into it, and told him to spit also into his mouth. And thus they spat thrice into each other's mouths. When this was done, the emperor of the serpents said to the shepherd: 'Now you have the tongue which you desired; go, and farewell! But it is not permitted you to tell anybody, because, if you do, you will die. I am telling you the truth.' The shepherd then departed. As he went over the hill, he understood the conversation of the birds, and, so to speak, of everything in the world. When he came to his sheep, he found them correct in number, and sat down to rest. But scarcely had he lain down, when two crows flew up, perched on a tree hard by him, and began to converse in their language: 'If that shepherd knew that just where that black lamb lies a vault full of silver and gold is buried in the ground, he would take its contents.' When he heard this, he went and told his master, and he brought a cart, and they broke open the door of the vault, and took out its valuable contents. His master was a righteous man, and said to him: 'Well, my son, this is all yours; the Lord has given it you. Go, provide a house, get married, and live comfortably.' The shepherd took the property, went away, provided a house, got married, and lived very comfortably. This shepherd, after a little time, became so rich and prosperous that there was nobody richer than he in his own or the neighbouring villages. He had shepherds, cowherds, swineherds, grooms, and everything on a handsome scale. Once upon a time this shepherd ordered his wife on New Year's Eve to provide wine, brandy, and everything requisite, and to go the next morning to his cattle, to take the provisions to the herdsmen, that they, too, might enjoy themselves. His wife obeyed him, and did as her husband ordered her.

The next day they got up, got ready, and went. When they arrived where the cattle were, the master said to his shepherds: 'Lads, assemble together, and sit down to eat and drink your fill, and I will watch the cattle to-night.' This was done; they assembled together, and he went out to sleep by the cattle. In the course of the night, after some time, the wolves began to howl and speak in their language, and the dogs to bark and speak in theirs. The wolves said: 'Can we capture any young cattle?' The dogs answered in their language: 'Come in, that we, too, may eat our fill of flesh.' But among the dogs there was one old dog, who had only two teeth left. This dog spoke and answered the wolves: 'In faith, as long as these two teeth of mine last, you shan't come near to do harm to my master.' In the morning, when it dawned, the master called the herdsmen, and told them to kill all the dogs except that old one. His servants began to implore him: 'Don't, master! Why? It's a sin.' But he said to them: 'Do just as I ordered you, and not otherwise.'

Then he and his wife mounted their horses and went off. His wife rode a mare, and he a horse. As they went, the master's horse outstripped the wife's mare, and began to say to her in their language: 'Go quicker; why do you hang back?' The mare's reply in defence of her lagging pace was so amusing that the man laughed out loud, turned his head, and looked behind him with a smile. His wife observed him smiling, whipped her mare to catch him up, and then asked him to tell her why he smiled. He said to her: 'Well, suppose I did? Something came into my head.' This answer did not satisfy her, but she began to worry him to tell her why he smiled. He said this and that to her to get out of it, but the more he said to get out of it, the more did she worry him. At length he said to her that, if he told her, he would die immediately. But she had no dread of her husband's dying, and went on worrying him: 'There is no alternative, but tell me you must.' When they got home, they dismounted from their horses, and as soon as they had done so, her husband ordered a grave to be dug for him. It was dug, and he lay down in it, and said to his wife: 'Did you not press me to tell you why I smiled? Come now, that I may tell you; but I shall die immediately.' On saying this, he gave one more look round him, and observed that the old dog had come from the cattle. Seeing this, he told his wife to give him a piece of bread. She gave it him, but the dog would not even look at it, but shed tears and wept; but the cock, seeing it, ran up and began to peck it. The dog was angry, and said: 'As if *you'd* die hungry! Don't you see that our master is going to die?' 'What a fool he is! Let him die! Whose fault is it? I have a hundred wives. When I find a grain of millet, I call them all to me, and finally eat it myself. If one of them gets cross at this, I give her one or two pecks, and she lowers her tail; but this man isn't equal to keeping one in order.' When the man heard the cock say this, he jumped up at once out of the grave, seized a stick, chased his wife over hill and dale, and at last settled her completely, so that it never entered her head any more to ask him why he smiled.

SERBIAN STORIES.

THE Serbian is the most widely spread of the South Slavonic dialects, being spoken not only in Serbia proper, but also in Bosnia, Herzegovina, Croatia, Carniola, and a great part of South Hungary. It has, like the Bulgarian, been affected by the old Thracian language, but not to the same extent. The infinitive is very frequently represented by *da* with the finite verb. Szafarzik includes the whole of the South Slavonic dialects, except the Bulgarian, under the common name 'Illyrian,' and subdivides them into the three divisions of Serbian, Croatian, and Carinthian-Slovenish.

The Serbian stories are generally good, particularly No. 40, which may be compared with a very inferior variant in Grimm, 'The Golden Bird.' No. 40 is one of the stories, the beauty of which set me to work upon the present series of translations. In it is to be noticed the *pobratimstvo*, or adoptive brotherhood, which plays so important a part in Serbian life, and of which we have just had a glimpse in the Bulgarian story, No. 38. No. 43 is a very good story, containing novel and interesting incidents. In No. 44 it must be observed that 'Fate' is represented as a man, for the converse reason to that for which Death is represented as a woman in the Moravian story, No 8.

Usud (Fate) is masculine, while *Smrt* (Death) is feminine in Slavonic.

The Serbs possess actual epic poetry, of which an account is given by Mr. Morfill ('Slavonic Literature,' pp. 154-162).

XL.—THE LAME FOX.

THERE was a man who had three sons—two intelligent, and one a simpleton. This man's right eye was always laughing, while his left eye was weeping and shedding tears. This man's sons agreed to go to him one by one, and ask him why his right eye laughed and his left eye shed tears.

Accordingly the eldest went to his father by himself, and asked him: 'Father, tell me truly what I am going to ask you. Why does your right eye always laugh and your left eye weep?' His father gave him no answer, but flew into a rage, seized a knife, and at him, and he fled out of doors, and the knife stuck in the door. The other two were outside, anxiously expecting their brother, and when he came out, asked him what his father had said to him. But he answered them: 'If you're not wiser than another, go, and you will hear.'

Then the middle brother went to his father by himself, and asked him: 'Father, tell me truly what I am going to ask you. Why does your right eye always laugh and your left weep?' His father gave him no answer, but flew into a rage, seized a knife, and at him, and he fled out of doors, and the knife stuck in the door. When he came out to his brothers, his brothers asked him: 'Tell us, brother—so may health and prosperity attend you!—what our father has said to you.' He answered them: 'If you're not wiser than another, go, and you will hear.' But this he said to his elder brother on account of the simpleton, that he, too, might go to his father to hear and see.

Then the simpleton, too, went by himself to his father, and asked him: 'Father, my two brothers won't tell me what you have said to them; tell me why your right eye always laughs and your left eye weeps?' His father immediately flew into a rage, seized a knife, and brandished the knife to pierce him through; but as he was standing, so he remained standing where he was, and wasn't frightened in the least. When his father saw that, he came to him, and said: 'Well, you're my true son, I will tell you; but those two are cowards. The reason why my right eye laughs is, that I rejoice and am glad because you children obey and serve me well. And why my left eye weeps, it weeps on this account: I had in my garden a vine, which poured forth a bucket of wine every hour, thus producing me twenty-four buckets of wine every day and night. This vine has been stolen from me, and I have not been able to find it, nor do I know who has taken it or where it is. And for this reason my left eye weeps, and will weep till I die, unless I find it.' When the simpleton came out of doors, his brothers asked him what his father had said, and he told them all in order.

Then they prepared a drinking bout for their father and the domestics, and set out on their journey. On the journey they came to a cross-road, and three ways lay before them. The two elder consulted together, and said to their youngest brother, the simpleton: 'Come, brother, let us each choose a road, and let each go by himself and seek his fortune.' 'Yes, brothers,' answered the simpleton; 'you choose each a road; I will take that which remains to me.' The two elder took two roads which ran into each other, started on their way, and afterwards met, came out into the road, and said: 'Praise be to God that we're quit of that fool! They then sat down to take their dinner. Scarcely had they sat down to eat, when up came a lame she-fox on three legs, which approached them, fawning and begging to obtain something to eat. But as soon as they saw the fox: 'Here's a fox,' said they; 'come, let us kill it.' Then, stick in hand, and after it. The fox limped away in the best fashion it could, and barely escaped from them. Meanwhile, shepherd-dogs came to their wallet and ate up everything that they had. When they returned to the wallet they had a sight to see.

The simpleton took the third road right on, and went forward till be began to feel hungry. Then he sat down on the grass under a pear-tree, and took bread and bacon out of his wallet to eat. Scarcely had he sat down to eat, when, lo! that very same lame fox which his two brothers had seen began to approach him, and to fawn and beg, limping on three feet. He had compassion on it because it was so lame, and said: 'Come, fox, I know that you are hungry, and that it is hard lines for you that you have not a fourth foot.' He gave it bread and bacon to eat, a portion for himself, and a portion for the fox. When they had refreshed themselves a little, the fox said to him: 'But, brother, tell me the truth: whither are you going?' He said: 'Thus and thus: I have a father and us three brothers; and one of my father's eyes always laughs, because we serve him well, and the other eye weeps, because there has been stolen from him a vine belonging to him, which poured forth a bucket of wine every hour; and now I am going to ask people all over the world whether someone cannot inform me about this vine, that I may obtain it for my father, that his eye may not weep any longer.'

The fox said: 'Well, I know where the vine is; follow me.' He followed the fox, and they came to a large garden. Then the fox said: 'There is the vine of which you are in search; but it is difficult to get to it. Do you now mark well what I am going to say to you. In the garden, before the vine is reached, it is necessary to pass twelve watches, and in each watch twelve warders. When the warders are looking, you can pass them freely, because they sleep with their eyes open. If they have their eyes closed, go not, for they are awake, not sleeping, with their eyes closed. When you come into the garden, there under the vine stand two shovels—one of wood, and the other of gold. But mind you don't take the golden shovel to dig up the vine, for the shovel will ring, and will wake up the watch; the watch will seize you, and you may fare badly. But take the wooden shovel, and with it dig up the vine, and, when the watch is looking, come quietly to me outside, and you will have obtained the vine.'

He went into the garden, arrived at the first watch; the warders directed their eyes towards him; one would have thought they would have looked him to powder. But he went past them as past a stone, came to the second, third, and all the watches in succession, and arrived in the garden at the vine itself. The vine poured forth a bucket of wine every hour. He was too lazy to dig with the wooden shovel, but took the golden one, and as soon as he struck it into the ground, the shovel rang and woke the watch; the watch assembled, seized him, and delivered him to their lord.

The lord asked the simpleton: 'How did you dare to pass so many watches, and come into the garden to take my vine away?' The simpleton said: 'It is not your vine, but my father's; and my father's left eye weeps, and will weep till I obtain him the vine, and I must do it; and if you don't give me my father's vine, I shall come again, and the second time I shall take it away.' The lord said: 'I cannot give you the vine. But if you procure me the golden apple-tree which blooms, ripens, and bears golden fruit every twenty-four hours, I will give it you.'

He went out to the fox, and the fox asked him: 'Well,

how is it?' He answered: 'No how. I went past the watch, and began to dig up the vine with the wooden shovel; but it was too long a job, and I took the golden shovel; the shovel rang and woke the watch; the watch seized me, and delivered me to their lord, and the lord promised to give me the vine, if I procured him the golden apple-tree which, every twenty-four hours, blooms, ripens, and bears golden fruit.' The fox said: 'But why did you not obey me? You see how nice it would have been to go to your father with the vine.' He shook his head: 'I see that I have done wrong; but I will do so no more.' The fox said: 'Come! now let us go to the golden apple-tree.' The fox led him to a far handsomer garden than the first one, and told him that he must pass similarly through twelve similar watches. 'And when you come in the garden,' said she, 'to where the golden apple-tree is, two very long poles stand there—one of gold, and the other of wood. Don't take the golden one to beat the golden apple-tree, for the golden branch will emit a whistling sound, and will wake the watch, and you will fare ill; but take the wooden pole to beat the golden apple-tree, and then mind you come out immediately to me. If you do not obey me, I will not help you further.' He said: 'I will, fox, only that it may be mine to acquire the golden apple-tree to purchase the vine; I am impatient to go to my father.' He went into the garden, and the fox stayed waiting for him outside. He passed the twelve watches, and also arrived at the apple-tree. But when he saw the apple-tree, and the golden apples on the apple-tree, he forgot for joy where he was, and hastily took the golden pole to beat the golden apple-tree. As soon as he had stripped a golden branch with the pole, the golden branch emitted a whistling sound, and woke the watch; the watch hastened up, seized and delivered him to the lord of the golden apple-tree.

14

The lord asked the simpleton: 'How did you dare, and how were you able, to go into my garden in face of so many watches of mine, to beat the golden apple-trees?' The simpleton said: 'Thus and thus: my father's left eye weeps because a vine has been stolen from him, which poured forth a bucket of wine every hour. That vine is kept in such and such a garden, and the lord of the garden and the vine said to me: "If you procure me the golden apple-tree which, every twenty-four hours, blooms, ripens, and produces golden fruit, I will give you the vine." And, therefore, I have come to beat the golden apple-tree, to give the apple-tree for the vine, and to carry the vine to my father, that his left eye may not weep. And if you do not give me the golden apple-tree now, I shall come again to steal it.'

The lord said: 'It is good, if it is so. Go you and procure me the golden horse which, in twenty-four hours, goes over the world, and I will give you the golden apple-tree; give the apple-tree for the vine, and take the vine to your father, that he may weep no more.'

Then he went outside, and the fox, awaiting him, said: 'Now, then; how is it?' 'Not very well. The golden apple-trees are so beautiful that you can't look at them for beauty. I forgot myself, and couldn't take the wooden pole, as you told me, but took the golden pole to beat the golden apple-tree; the branch emitted a whistling sound, and woke the watch; the watch seized me, and delivered me to their lord, and the lord told me, if I procured him the golden horse which goes over the world in twenty-four hours, he would give me the golden apple-tree, that I may give the apple-tree for the vine to take to my father, that he may weep no more.'

Again the fox began to scold and reproach him: 'Why did you not obey me? You see that you would have been by now at your father's. And thus you torment both yourself and me.' He said to the fox: 'Only procure me the horse, fox, and I will always henceforth obey you.'

The fox led him to a large and horrible forest, and in the forest they found a farmyard. In this farmyard twelve watches, as in the case of the vine and the apple-tree, guarded the golden horse. The fox said: 'Now you will pass the watches as before; go if they are looking; do not go if they have their eyes shut. When you enter the stable, there stands the golden horse, equipped with golden trappings. By the horse are two bridles—one of gold, and the other plaited of tow. Mind you don't take the golden bridle, but the one of tow; if you bridle him with the golden bridle, the horse will neigh and will wake the watch; the watch will seize you, and who will be worse off than you? Don't come into my sight without the horse!' 'I won't, fox,' said he, and went. He passed all the watches, and entered the stable where the horse was. When he was there, golden horse! golden wings! so beautiful, good heavens! that you couldn't look at them for beauty! He saw the golden bridle; it was beautiful and ornamented; he saw also that of tow; it was dirty, and couldn't be worse. Now he thought long what to do and how to do. 'I can't put that nasty thing' (the tow bridle)—'it's so nasty!—on that beauty; I had rather not have him at all than put such a horse to shame.' He took the golden bridle, bridled the golden horse, and mounted him. But the horse neighed, and woke the watch; the watch seized him and delivered him to their lord.

Then the lord said: 'How did you have resolution to pass my numerous warders into my stable to take away my golden horse?' The simpleton replied: 'Need drove me; I have a father at home, and his left eye continually weeps, and will weep till I obtain for him a vine which in a day and night poured forth twenty-four buckets of wine; this vine has been stolen from him. Well, I have found it, and it has been told me that I shall obtain the vine if I procure the golden apple-tree for the lord of the vine. And the lord of the golden apple-tree said if I procured him the golden horse, he would give me the golden apple-tree. And I came from him to take away the golden horse, that I might give the golden horse for the golden apple-tree, and the golden apple-tree for the vine, to take it home and give it my father, that he may weep no more.' The lord said: 'Good; if it is so, I will give you my golden horse, if you procure me the golden damsel in her cradle, who has never yet seen either the sun or the moon, so that her face is not tanned.' And the simpleton said: 'I will procure you the golden damsel, but you must give me your golden horse, on which to seek the golden damsel and bring her to you. And a golden horse properly appertains to a golden damsel.' The lord: 'And how will you guarantee that you will return to me again?' The simpleton: 'Behold, I swear to you by my father's eyesight, that I will return to you again, and either bring the horse, if I do not find the damsel, or give you the damsel, if I find her, for the horse.' To this the lord agreed, and gave him the golden horse; he bridled it with the golden bridle, and came outside to the fox. The fox was impatiently expecting him, to know what had happened.

The fox: 'Well, have you obtained the horse?' The simpleton: 'I have, but on condition that I procure for him the golden damsel in her cradle, who has never yet seen the sun or the moon, so that her face is not tanned. But if you know what need is, good friend, in the world, say whether she is anywhere, and whether you know of such a damsel.' The fox said: 'I know where the damsel is; only follow me.' He followed, and they came to a large cavern. Now the fox said: 'There the damsel is. You will go into that cavern, deep into the earth. You will pass the watches as before. In the last chamber lies the golden damsel in a golden cradle. By the damsel stands a huge spectre, which says: "No! No! No!" Now, don't be at all afraid; it cannot do anything to you in any wise; but her wicked mother has placed it beside her daughter, that no one may venture to approach her to take her away. And the damsel is impatiently waiting to be released and freed from her mother's cruelty. When you come back with the damsel in the cradle, push all the doors to behind you, that they may be shut, that the watch may not be able to come out after you in pursuit.' He did so. He passed all the watches, entered the last chamber, and in the chamber was the damsel, rocking herself in a golden cradle, and on the way to the cradle stood a huge spectre, which said: 'No! No! No!' But he paid no attention to it. He took the cradle in his hands, seated himself with the cradle on the horse, and proceeded, pushed the doors to, and the doors closed from the first to the last, and out he flew with the damsel in the cradle before the fox. The fox was anxiously expecting him.

Now the fox said to him: 'Are you not sorry to give so beautiful a damsel for the golden horse? But you will not otherwise be able to acquire the golden horse, because you have sworn by your father's eyesight. But come! let me try whether I can't be the golden damsel.' She bounded hither and thither, and transformed herself into a golden damsel; everything about her was damsel-like, only her eyes were shaped like a fox's eyes. He put her into the golden cradle, and left the real damsel under a tree to take charge of the golden horse. He went, he took away the golden cradle, and in the cradle the fox-damsel, delivered her to the lord of the golden horse, and absolved himself from the oath by his father's eyesight. He returned to the horse and the damsel. Now that same lord of the golden horse, full of joy at acquiring the golden damsel, assembled all his lordship, prepared a grand banquet for their entertainment, and showed them what he had acquired in exchange for his golden horse. While the guests were gazing at the damsel, one of them scrutinized her attentively, and said: 'All is damsel-like, and she is very beautiful, but her eyes are shaped like a fox's eyes.' No sooner had he said this, when up sprang the fox and ran away. The lord and the guests were enraged that he had said 'fox's eyes,' and put him to death.

The fox ran to the simpleton, and on they went to give the golden horse for the golden apple-tree. They arrived at the place. Here again the fox said: 'Now, you see, you have got possession of the golden damsel, but the golden horse properly appertains to the golden damsel. Are you sorry to give the golden horse?' 'Yes, fox; but though I am sorry, yet I wish my father not to weep.' The fox: 'But stay; let me try whether I can be the golden horse.' She bounded hither and thither, and transformed herself into a golden horse, only she had a fox's tail. Then she said: 'Now lead me; let them give you the golden apple-tree, and I know when I shall come to you.'

He led off the fox-horse, delivered it to the lord of the golden apple-tree, and obtained the golden apple-tree. Now, the lord of the golden apple-tree was delighted at having acquired so beautiful a horse, and invited his whole lordship to a feast, to boast to them what a horse he had acquired. The guests began to gaze at the horse, and to wonder how beautiful he was. All at once one scrutinized his tail attentively, and said: 'All is beautiful and all pleases me, only I should say that it is a fox's tail!' The moment he said that, the fox jumped up and ran away. But the guests were enraged at him for using the expression 'fox's tail,' and put him to death. The fox came to the simpleton, and proceeded with the golden damsel, the horse, and the golden apple-tree to the vine.

Now again the fox said: 'You see, now you have acquired the golden apple-tree. But the golden damsel is not appropriate without the golden horse, or the golden horse without the golden apple-tree. Are you sorry to give the golden apple-tree?' The simpleton: 'Yes, fox; but I must, to obtain the vine, that my father may not weep. I had rather that my father did not weep than all that I have.' The fox said: 'Stay! I will try whether I can be the golden apple-tree.' She bounded hither and thither, and transformed herself into a golden apple-tree, and told him to take it away and give it for the vine. He took off the golden fox-apple-tree, and gave it to the lord of the vine, obtained the vine, and went away.

The lord for joy assembled his whole lordship, and prepared a grand feast, to display what a golden apple-tree he had acquired. The guests assembled and began to gaze at the apple-tree. But one scrutinized it attentively, and said: 'All is beautiful, and cannot be more beautiful, only the fruit is in shape a fox's head, and not like other apples.' No sooner had he said this when up jumped the fox and ran away. But they were enraged at him and slew him, because he had said 'fox's head.'

Now the simpleton took leave of the fox and went home, having with him the golden damsel, the golden horse, the golden apple-tree, and the vine. When he arrived at the cross-road, where he had parted from his brothers when he went from home to seek the vine, he saw a multitude of people assembled, and he, too, went thither to see what was the matter. When he got there, his two brothers were standing condemned, and the people were going to hang them. He told the damsel that they were his brothers, and that he would like to ransom them. The damsel took a large quantity of treasure out of her bosom, and he ransomed his brothers, the malefactors, who had thought to acquire the vine by slaying, burning, and plundering. They envied him, but could not help themselves. They proceeded home. The simpleton planted the vine in the garden where it had been; the vine began to pour forth wine, and his father's left eye ceased to weep and began to laugh. The apple-tree began to blossom, the golden horse to neigh, the damsel to sing, and there was love and beauty at the farmhouse. Everything was merry, everything was rejoicing and making progress.

All at once the father sent his sons to bring him from the country three ears of rye, that he might see what manner of season it would be. When they came to a well in the country, they told their simpleton brother to get them some water to drink. He stooped over the well to reach the water for them; they pushed him into the water and he was drowned. Immediately the vine ceased to pour forth wine, the father's eye began to weep, the apple-tree drooped, the horse ceased to neigh, the damsel began to weep, and everything lost its cheerful appearance. Thereupon that selfsame lame fox came up, got down into the well, gently drew her adopted brother out, poured the water out of him, placed him on the fresh grass, and he revived. As soon as he revived the fox was transformed into a very beautiful damsel. Then she related to him how her mother had cursed her because she had rescued her greatest enemy from death. She was cursed, and was transformed into a cunning fox, and limped on three feet until she should rescue her benefactor from a watery death. 'And, lo! I have rescued you, my adopted brother. Now, adieu!' She went her way, and the simpleton his way to his father, and when he arrived at the farmhouse the vine began again to pour forth wine, his father's eye to laugh [the golden apple-tree to bloom], the golden horse to neigh, and the golden damsel to sing. He told his father what his brothers had done to him on the way, and how a damsel had rescued him and freed herself from a curse. When his father heard this he drove the two villains into the world. But he married the simpleton to the golden damsel, with whom he lived long in happiness and content.

XLI.—THE SONS' OATH TO THEIR DYING FATHER.

THERE was an old man who had three sons and one daughter. When the time came for the old man to die, he summoned all his three sons, and made them promise under oath to give their sister to the first who came to ask for her, whoever he might be. When some time had elapsed after the father's death, an old man arrived in a two-wheeler, and asked for the maiden in marriage. The two elder brothers would not give her to him immediately, because he was old and poor; but the youngest insisted that they should give her to him, rèminding them of the oath they had sworn to their father. And so they gave her in marriage to the old man, and the old man took her away to his home. After some time, the elder brother went on a visit to his sister. When he got there, it was a large house, and couldn't be better. The sister was greatly delighted when she saw her brother, and when he inquired of her how she was getting on, she replied: 'Excellently; it can't be better.' When the brother arrived at his sister's, the old man was not at home, but soon afterwards arrived, and was very pleased when he saw his wife's brother, and said to him: 'We will feast and be merry; but first you shall go on my horse to fetch him some grass, but you must cut it where the horse paws with his foot, and not where you please.' His wife's brother said to him: 'Good! brother-in-law, I will.' He then mounted the horse and went off. As on he went, he came to a silver bridge. When he espied the bridge and saw that it was all of silver, he became covetous, dismounted, and pulled off a silver plate, saying: 'I may benefit myself.' Afterwards he cut grass where he pleased, without waiting till the horse pawed with his foot, mounted the horse again, and returned back. On arriving at the house, he put the horse in the stable, placed the grass before him, and went off into the house. When he arrived in the house, the old man asked him whether he had satisfied the horse, and whether the horse was eating the grass. He replied, 'Yes,' and that the horse was eating. The old man said: 'It is good that I also look.' He then went into the stable. When he got there, the horse had not touched it. The old man understood that the grass had not been cut where he had told him; he therefore at once sent off his brother-in-law supperless, to go back whence he had come. On reaching home, he didn't tell his brothers how he had fared at his brother-in-law's, but said to the middle brother: 'Our brother-in-law salutes you, and wishes you to go to be his guest.' After some time, the middle brother went on a visit to his sister; but he, too, fared even as the first one. His sister's husband sent him, too, for grass, and when he got to the silver bridge, he, too, became covetous, like the first, pulled off a silver plate, and did not cut the grass as his brother-in-law told him, but where he thought fit. When he came back to his brother-in-law's house, his brother-in-law caught him, too, out in a lie, and sent him home supperless, like the first one. When he got home, he told nobody how he had fared at his brother-in-law's, but said to the youngest brother: 'Our brother-in-law salutes you, and wishes you to go to visit him.'

After some time, the youngest brother, too, went off.

When his sister espied him, she said to him: 'Only, brother, be sure not to do as our two brothers have done.' He didn't know what they had done, and his sister would not tell him anything more. When his sister's husband came home, he, too, was delighted with his wife's brother, and said to him: 'We will feast and be merry, only go first on my horse and fetch him some grass; but you will cut it there where the horse paws with his foot, and not where you please.' He mounted the horse and went off for the grass. When he arrived at the bridge, he was astonished at its beauty, but was quite sorry that it hadn't those two plates; and when he came to the middle, he looked on one side and the other, and saw under it, where water was bubbling in a huge caldron, and human heads boiling in it, and eagles pecking them from above. Afterwards, having passed over the bridge, he came to a village, and, as he passed through it, saw that there everything was sad and sorrowful, and wondered thereat, and asked a man: 'How is this, brother, that all is so sorrowful with you?' He replied: 'How should it not be sorrowful, when hail smites us every hour, and we have nothing.' When he came out of the village, he found two pigs on the road, and they were fighting without ceasing. He tried to part them, but in vain, and, being unable to part them, went on further. Thus proceeding, he came to another village, and, as he went through, heard on all sides singing and merriment, and said to someone: 'I went through one village and found everything sorrowful, and why is all so merry with you?' The villager answered him: 'Why should it not be so, when every hour is productive to us, and we have all in abundance?' Finally, the horse carried him to a very beautiful meadow. When they were in the middle of the meadow, the horse stood still and pawed with his foot, and he dismounted and cut grass, and returned back to the house.

When he got to the house, he led the horse into the stable, laid the grass before him, and the horse immediately began to eat. When his sister's husband saw that he had satisfied the horse, he was very pleased, and said to him: 'You are my true brother-in-law; now let us be merry and feast.' Then they sat down to table and began to sup. At supper the old man said to him: 'Now, tell me what you have seen.' He answered him: 'Oh, my brother-in-law! what I have seen cannot be expressed. First I saw a very beautiful silver bridge, but it was disfigured where it wanted a pair of plates. Whoever took these away, the living God hath slain him!' The old man thereupon told him: 'Your two brothers stole them. As they have done, so have they fared. But tell me what you saw next.' His wife's brother replied: 'At the middle under the bridge I saw a huge caldron, where it was bubbling, and in it the heads of dead people, and eagles were pecking them from above.' Thereupon his sister's husband said: 'Those are the eternal torments in that world. What did you see more?' His wife's brother continued: 'I saw a village, and in it everything miserable.' The old man said to him: 'There there is no union and no truth, nor knowledge of God. What did you see further?' His wife's brother said to him further: 'I saw two pigs fighting without ceasing.' His sister's husband replied: 'Those are two brothers who do not live in concord. What did you see further?' 'I saw another village, and in it all was cheerful.' His sister's husband said to that: 'Those are people after God's will; they gladly welcome and entertain everybody, and do not drive the poor empty-handed from before their houses. Tell me what you saw further.' His wife's brother said to him: 'I saw a very beautiful meadow. I would stay there three days to view such beauty.' His sister's husband replied: 'That is the paradise of that world, but it is difficult to attain to it.' After this they enjoyed each other's society for many days. Finally, the wife's brother declared that he must go home, and his sister's husband presented him with a large gift, and told him that he recognised him immediately for an honourable man, because he had insisted that his father's directions, which he had sworn to observe, should be carried out, and that he would be prosperous, and his two brothers unprosperous.

N.B.—There are two words for 'brother-in-law' in Servian: *shura*, the wife's brother, and *zet*, the sister's husband. This makes the tale read better in Servian than in English.

XLII.—THE WONDERFUL HAIR.

THERE was a man who was very poor, but so well supplied with children that he was utterly unable to maintain them, and one morning more than once prepared to kill them, in order not to see their misery in dying from hunger, but his wife prevented him. One night a child came to him in his sleep, and said to him: 'Man! I see that you are making up your mind to destroy and to kill your poor little children, and I know that you are distressed thereat; but in the morning you will find under your pillow a mirror, a red kerchief, and an embroidered pocket-handkerchief; take all three secretly and tell nobody; then go to such a hill; by it you will find a stream; go along it till you come to its fountain-head; there you will find a damsel as bright as the sun, with her hair hanging down over her back, and without a scrap of clothing. Be on your guard, that the ferocious she-dragon do not coil round you; do not converse with her if she speaks; for if you converse with her, she will poison you, and turn you into a fish, or something else, and will then devour you; but if she bids you examine her head, examine it, and as you turn over her hair, look, and you will find one hair as red as blood; pull it out and run back again; then, if she suspects and begins to run after you, throw her first the embroidered pocket-handkerchief, then the kerchief, and, lastly, the mirror; then she will find occupation for herself. And sell that hair to some rich man; but don't let them cheat you, for that hair is worth countless wealth; and you will thus enrich yourself and maintain your children.'

When the poor man awoke, he found everything under his pillow, just as the child had told him in his sleep; and then he went to the hill. When there, he found the stream, went on and on alongside of it, till he came to the fountain-head. Having looked about him to see where the damsel was, he espied her above a piece of water, like sunbeams threaded on a needle, and she was embroidering at a frame on stuff, the threads of which were young men's hair. As soon as he saw her, he made a reverence to her, and she stood on her feet and questioned him: 'Whence are you, unknown young man?' But he held his tongue. She questioned him again: 'Who are you? Why have you come?' and much else of all sorts; but he was as mute as a stone, making signs with his hands, as if he were deaf and wanted help. Then she told him to sit down on her skirt. He did not wait for any more orders, but sat down, and she bent down her head to him, that he might examine it. Turning over the hair of her head, as if to examine it, he was not long in finding that red hair, and separated it from the other hair, pulled it out, jumped off her skirt and ran away back as he best could. She noticed it, and ran at his heels full speed after him. He looked round, and seeing that she was about to overtake him, threw, as he was told, the embroidered pocket-handkerchief on the way, and when she saw the pocket-handkerchief, she stooped and began to overhaul it in every direction, admiring the embroidery, till he had got a good way off. Then the damsel placed the pocket-handkerchief in her bosom, and ran after him again. When he saw that she was about to overtake him, he threw the red kerchief, and she again occupied herself, admiring and gazing, till the poor man had again got a good way off. Then the damsel became exasperated, and threw both the pocket-handkerchief and the kerchief on the way, and ran after him in pursuit. Again, when he saw that she was about to overtake him, he threw the mirror. When the damsel came to the mirror, the like of which she had never seen before, she lifted it up, and when she saw herself in it, not knowing that it was herself, but thinking that it was somebody else, she, as it were, fell in love with herself in the mirror, and the man got so far off that she was no longer able to overtake him. When she saw that she could not catch him, she turned back, and the man reached his home safe and sound. After arriving at his home, he showed his wife the hair, and told her all that had happened to him, but she began to jeer and laugh at him. But he paid no attention to her, and went to a town to sell the hair. A crowd of all sorts of people and merchants collected round him; one offered a sequin, another two, and so on, higher and higher, till they came to a hundred gold sequins. Just then the emperor heard of the hair, summoned the man into his presence, and said to him that he would give him a thousand sequins for it, and he sold it to him. What was the hair? The emperor split it in two from top to bottom, and found registered in it in writing many remarkable things, which had happened in the olden time since the beginning of the world. Thus the man became rich and lived on with his wife and children. And that child, that came to him in his sleep, was an angel sent by the Lord God, whose will it was to aid the poor man, and to reveal secrets which had not been revealed till then.

XLIII.—THE DRAGON AND THE PRINCE.

THERE was an emperor who had three sons. One day the eldest son went out hunting, and when he got outside the town, up sprang a hare out of a bush, and he after it, and hither and thither, till the hare fled into a water-mill, and the prince after it. But it was not a hare, but a dragon, and it waited for the prince and devoured him. When several days had elapsed and the prince did not return home, people began to wonder why it was that he was not to be found. Then the middle son went hunting, and as he issued from the town, a hare sprang out of a bush, and the prince after it, and hither and thither, till the hare fled into the water-mill and the prince after it; but it was not a hare, but a dragon, which waited for and devoured him. When some days had elapsed and the princes did not return, either of them, the whole court was in sorrow. Then the third son went hunting, to see whether he could not find his brothers. When he issued from the town, again up sprang a hare out of a bush, and the prince after it, and hither and thither, till the hare fled into the water-mill. But the prince did not choose to follow it, but went to find other game, saying to himself: 'When I return I shall find you.' After this he went for a long time up and down the hill, but found nothing, and then returned to the water-mill; but when he got there, there was only an old woman in the mill. The prince invoked God in addressing her: 'God help you, old woman!' The old woman replied: 'God help you, my son!' Then the prince asked her: 'Where, old woman, is my hare?' She replied: 'My son, that was not a hare, but a dragon. It kills and throttles many people.' Hearing this, the prince was somewhat disturbed, and said to the old woman: 'What shall we do now? Doubtless my two brothers also have perished here.' The old woman answered: 'They have indeed; but there's no help for it. Go home, my son, lest you follow them.' Then he said to her: 'Dear old woman, do you know what? I know that you will be glad to liberate yourself from that pest.' The old woman interrupted him: 'How should I not? It captured me, too, in this way, but now I have no means of escape.' Then he proceeded: 'Listen well to what I am going to say to you. Ask it whither it goes and where its strength is; then kiss all that place where it tells you its strength is, as if from love, till you ascertain it, and afterwards tell me when I come.' Then the prince went off to the palace, and the old woman remained in the water-mill. When the dragon came in, the old woman began to question it: 'Where in God's name have you been? Whither do you go so far? You will never tell me whither you go.' The dragon replied: 'Well, my dear old woman, I do go far.' Then the old woman began to coax it: 'And why do you go so far? Tell me where your strength is. If I knew where your strength is, I don't know what I should do for love; I would kiss all that place.' Thereupon the dragon smiled and said to her: 'Yonder is my strength, in that fireplace.' Then the old woman began to fondle and kiss the fireplace, and the dragon on seeing it burst into a laugh, and said to her: 'Silly old woman, my strength isn't there; my strength is in that tree-fungus in front of the house.' Then the old woman began again to fondle and kiss the tree, and the dragon again laughed, and said to her: 'Away, old woman! my strength isn't there.' Then the old woman inquired: 'Where is it?' The dragon began to give an account in detail: 'My strength is a long way off, and you cannot go thither. Far in another empire under the emperor's city is a lake, in that lake is a dragon, and in the dragon a boar, and in the boar a pigeon, and in that is my strength.' The next morning when the dragon went away from the mill, the prince came to the old woman, and the old woman told him all that she had heard from the dragon. Then he left his home, and disguised himself; he put shepherd's boots on his feet, took a shepherd's staff in his hand, and went into the world. As he went on thus from village to village, and from town to town, at last he came into another empire and into the imperial city, in a lake under which the dragon was. On going into the town, he began to inquire who wanted a shepherd. The citizens told him that the emperor did. Then he went straight to the emperor. After he announced himself, the emperor admitted him into his presence, and asked him: 'Do you wish to keep sheep?' He replied: 'I do, illustrious crown!' Then the emperor engaged him, and began to inform and instruct him: 'There is here a lake, and alongside of the lake very beautiful pasture, and when you call the sheep out, they go thither at once, and spread themselves round the lake; but whatever shepherd goes off there, that shepherd returns back no more. Therefore, my son, I tell you, don't let the sheep have their own way and go where *they* will, but keep them where *you* will.' The prince thanked the emperor, got himself ready, and called out the sheep, taking with him, moreover, two hounds that could catch a boar in the open country, and a falcon that could capture any bird, and carrying also a pair of bagpipes. When he called out the sheep he let them go at once to the lake, and when the sheep arrived at the lake, they immediately spread round it, and the prince placed the falcon on a stump, and the hounds and bagpipes under the stump, then tucked up his hose and sleeves, waded into the lake, and began to shout 'Dragon! dragon! come out to single combat with me to-day that we may measure ourselves together, unless you're a woman.'* The dragon called out in reply, 'I will

* This is intended as an insult. 'Azhdaja,' a dragon, is feminine in Servian.

do so now, prince—now!' Erelong, behold the dragon! it is large, it is terrible, it is disgusting! When the dragon came out, it seized him by the waist, and they wrestled a summer day till afternoon. But when the heat of afternoon came on, the dragon said: 'Let me go, prince, that I may moisten my parched head in the lake, and toss you to the sky.' But the prince replied: 'Come, dragon, don't talk nonsense; if I had the emperor's daughter to kiss me on the forehead, I would toss you still higher.' Thereupon the dragon suddenly let go of him, and went off into the lake. On the approach of evening, he washed and got himself up nicely, placed the falcon on his arm, the hounds behind him, and the bagpipes under his arm, then drove the sheep and went into the town playing on the bagpipes. When he arrived at the town, the whole town assembled as to see a wondrous sight because he had come, whereas previously no shepherd had been able to come from the lake. The next day the prince got ready again, and went with his sheep straight to the lake. But the emperor sent two grooms after him to go stealthily and see what he did, and they placed themselves on a high hill whence they could have a good view. When the shepherd arrived, he put the hounds and bagpipes under the stump and the falcon upon it, then tucked up his hose and sleeves, waded into the lake and shouted: 'Dragon, dragon! come out to single combat with me, that we may measure ourselves once more together, unless you are a woman!' The dragon replied: 'I will do so, prince; now, now!' Erelong, behold the dragon! it was large, it was terrible, it was disgusting! And it seized him by the waist and wrestled with him a summer's day till afternoon. But when the afternoon heat came on, the dragon said: 'Let me go, prince, that I may moisten my parched head in the lake, and may toss you to the sky.' The prince replied: 'Come, dragon, don't talk nonsense;

if I had the emperor's daughter to kiss me on the forehead, I would toss you still higher.' Thereupon the dragon suddenly left hold of him, and went off into the lake. When night approached the prince drove the sheep as before, and went home playing the bagpipes. When he arrived at the town, the whole town was astir and began to wonder because the shepherd came home every evening, which no one had been able to do before. Those two grooms had already arrived at the palace before the prince, and related to the emperor in order everything that they had heard and seen. Now when the emperor saw that the shepherd returned home, he immediately summoned his daughter into his presence and told her all, what it was and how it was. 'But,' said he, 'to-morrow you must go with the shepherd to the lake and kiss him on the forehead.' When she heard this she burst into tears and began to entreat her father. 'You have no one but me, and I am your only daughter, and you don't care about me if I perish.' Then the emperor began to persuade and encourage her: 'Don't fear, my daughter; you see, we have had so many changes of shepherds, and of all that went out to the lake not one has returned; but *he* has been contending with the dragon for two whole days and it has done him no hurt. I assure you, in God's name, that he is able to overcome the dragon, only go to-morrow with him to see whether he will free us from this mischief which has destroyed so many people.'

When, on the morrow, the day dawned, the day dawned and the sun came forth, up rose the shepherd, up rose the maiden too, to begin to prepare for going to the lake. The shepherd was cheerful, more cheerful than ever, but the emperor's daughter was sad, and shed tears. The shepherd comforted her: 'Lady sister, I pray you, do not weep, but do what I tell you. When it is time, run up and kiss me, and fear not.' As he went and drove the sheep, the shepherd was thoroughly cheery, and played a merry tune on his bagpipes; but the damsel did nothing but weep as she went beside him, and he several times left off playing and turned towards her: 'Weep not, golden one; fear nought.' When they arrived at the lake, the sheep immediately spread round it, and the prince placed the falcon on the stump, and the hounds and bagpipes under it, then tucked up his hose and sleeves, waded into the water, and shouted: 'Dragon! dragon! Come out to single combat with me; let us measure ourselves once more, unless you're a woman!' The dragon replied: 'I will, prince; now, now!' Erelong, there was the dragon! it was huge, it was terrible, it was disgusting! When it came out, they seized each other by the middle, and wrestled a summer's day till afternoon. But when the afternoon heat came on, the dragon said: 'Let me go, prince, that I may moisten my parched head in the lake, and toss you to the skies.' The prince replied: 'Come, dragon, don't talk nonsense; if I had the emperor's daughter to kiss me on the forehead, I would toss you much higher.' When he said this, the emperor's daughter ran up and kissed him on the face, on the eye, and on the forehead. Then he swung the dragon, and tossed it high into the air, and when it fell to the ground it burst into pieces. But as it burst into pieces, out of it sprang a wild boar, and started to run away. But the prince shouted to his shepherd dogs: 'Hold it! don't let it go!' and the dogs sprang up and after it, caught it, and soon tore it to pieces. But out of the boar flew a pigeon, and the prince loosed the falcon, and the falcon caught the pigeon and brought it into the prince's hands. The prince said to it: 'Tell me now, where are my brothers?' The pigeon replied: 'I will; only do me no harm. Immediately behind your father's town is a water-mill, and in the water-mill are three wands that have sprouted up. Cut these three wands up from below, and strike with them upon their root; an iron door will immediately open into a large vault. In that vault are many people, old and young, rich and poor, small and great, wives and maidens, so that you could settle a populous empire; there, too, are your brothers.' When the pigeon had told him all this, the prince immediately wrung its neck.

The emperor had gone out in person, and posted himself on the hill from which the grooms had viewed the shepherd, and he, too, was a spectator of all that had taken place. After the shepherd had thus obtained the dragon's head, twilight began to approach. He washed himself nicely, took the falcon on his shoulder, the hounds behind him, and the bagpipes under his arm, played as he went, drove the sheep, and proceeded to the emperor's palace, with the damsel at his side still in terror. When they came to the town, all the town assembled as to see a wonder. The emperor, who had seen all his heroism from the hill, called him into his presence, and gave him his daughter, went immediately to church, had them married, and held a wedding festival for a week. After this the prince told him who and whence he was, and the emperor and the whole town rejoiced still more. Then, as the prince was urgent to go to his own home, the emperor gave him a large escort, and equipped him for the journey. When they were in the neighbourhood of the water-mill, the prince halted his attendants, went inside, cut up the three wands, and struck the root with them, and the iron door opened at once. In the vault was a vast multitude of people. The prince ordered them to come out one by one, and go whither each would, and stood himself at the door. They came out thus one after another, and lo! there were his brothers also, whom he embraced and kissed. When the whole multitude had come out, they thanked him for releasing and delivering them, and went each to his own home. But he went to his father's house with his brothers and bride, and there lived and reigned to the end of his days.

XLIV.—FATE.

There were two brothers living together in a house, one of whom did all the work, while the other did nothing but idle, and eat and drink what was ready at hand. And God gave them prosperity in everything—in cattle, in horses, in sheep, in swine, in bees, and in everything else. The one that worked one day began to think to himself: 'Why should I work for that lazybones as well? It is better that we should separate, and that I should work for myself, and he do as he likes.' So one day he said to his brother: 'Brother, it isn't right. I do all the work, and you don't help in anything, but merely eat and drink what's ready. I have made up my mind that we separate.' The other began to dissuade him: 'Don't, brother; it is good for us to be tenants in common; you have everything in your hands, both your own and mine, and I am content whatever you do.' But the first abode by his determination, so the second gave way, and said to him: 'If it is so, take your own course; make the division yourself, as you know how.' Then he divided everything in order, and took everything that was his before him. The do-nothing engaged a herdsman for his cattle, a horsekeeper for his horses, a shepherd for his sheep, a goatherd for his goats, a swineherd for his swine, a beeman for his bees, and said to them: 'I leave all my property in your hands and God's,' and began to live at home as before. The first took pains about his property himself as before, watched and overlooked, but saw no prosperity, but all loss. From day to day everything went worse, till he became so poverty-stricken, that he hadn't shoes to his feet, but went barefoot. Then said he to himself: 'I will go to my brother, and see how it is with him.' He did so, and as he went came to a flock of sheep in a meadow, and with the sheep there was no shepherd, but a very beautiful damsel was sitting there spinning golden thread. He addressed her: 'God help you!' and inquired whose the sheep were. She replied: 'The sheep belong to the person to whom I belong.' He asked her further: 'To whom do you belong?' She answered: 'I am your brother's luck.' He was put out, and said to her: 'And where is my luck?' The damsel answered him: 'Your luck is far from you.' 'But can I find it?' inquired he, and she replied: 'You can; go, seek for it.' When he heard this, and saw that his brother's sheep were good—so good, that they could not be better, he didn't care about going further to see other cattle, but went off straight to his brother. When his brother saw him, he had compassion on him, and began to weep: 'Where have you been so long a time?' Then, seeing him barehead and barefoot, he gave him at once a pair of boots and some money. Afterwards, when they had enjoyed each other's company for some days, the visitor rose up to go to his own house. When he got home, he took a wallet on his back, some bread in it, and a staff in his hand, and went into the world to look for his luck. As he travelled, he came to a large wood, and as he went through it, he saw a gray-haired old maid asleep under a bush, and reached out his staff to give her a push. She barely raised herself up, and, hardly opening her eyes for the rheum, addressed him: 'Thank God that I fell asleep, for, if I had been awake, you wouldn't have obtained even that pair of boots.' Then he said to her: 'Who are you, that I shouldn't even have obtained this pair of boots?' She replied: 'I am your luck.' When he heard this, he began to beat his breast: 'If you are my luck, God slay you! Who gave you to me?' She quickly rejoined: 'Fate gave me to you.' He then inquired: 'And where is this Fate?' She answered: 'Go and look for him.' And that instant she disappeared. Then the man went on to look for Fate. As he journeyed, he came to a village, and saw in the village a large farmhouse, and in it a large fire, and said to himself: 'Here there is surely some merry-making or festival,' and went in. When he went in, on the fire was a large caldron, in which supper was cooking, and in front of the fire sat the master of the house. The traveller, on going into the house, addressed the master: 'Good-evening!' The master replied: 'God give you prosperity!' and bade him sit down with him, and then began to ask him whence he came, and whither he was going. He related to him everything: how he had been a master, how he had become impoverished, and how he was now going to Fate to ask him why he was so poor. Then he inquired of the master of the house why he was preparing so large a quantity of food, and the master said to him: 'Well, my brother, I am master here, and have enough of everything, but I cannot anyhow satisfy my people; it is quite as if a dragon were in their stomachs. You'll see, when we begin to sup, what they will do.' When they sat down to sup, everybody snatched and grabbed from everybody else, and that large caldron of food was empty in no time. After supper, a maidservant came in, put all the bones in a heap, and threw them behind the stove; and he began to wonder why the young woman threw the bones behind the stove, till all at once out came two old poverty-stricken spectres, as dry as ghosts, and began to suck the bones. Then he asked the master of the house: 'What's this, brother, behind the stove?' He replied: 'Those, brother, are my father and mother; just as if they were fettered to this world, they wil not quit it.' The next day, at his departure, the master of the house said to him: 'Brother, remember me, too, if anywhere you find Fate, and ask him what manner of misfortune it is that I cannot satisfy my people, and why my father and mother do not die.' He promised to ask him the question, took leave of him, and went on to look for Fate. As on he went, he came, after a long time, to another village, and begged at a certain house that they would take him in for a night's lodging. They did so, and asked him whither he was going; and he told them all in order, what it was, and how it was. Then they began to say to him: 'In God's name, brother, when you get there, ask him with regard to us too, why our cattle are not productive, but the contrary.' He promised them to ask Fate the question, and the next day went on. As he went, he came to a stream of water, and began to shout: 'Water! water! carry me across.' The water asked him: 'Whither are you going?' He told it whither he was going. Then the water carried him across, and said to him: 'I pray you, brother, ask Fate why I have no offspring.' He promised the stream to ask the question, and then went on. He went on for a long time, and at last came to a wood, where he found a hermit, whom he asked whether he could tell him anything about Fate. The hermit answered: 'Go over the hill yonder, and you will come right in front of his abode; but when you come into Fate's presence, do not say a word, but do exactly what he does, until he questions you himself.' The man thanked the hermit, and went over the hill. When he came to Fate's abode, there was something for him to see. It was just as if it were an emperor's palace; there were men-servants and maid-servants there; everything was in good order, and Fate himself was sitting at a golden dinner-table at supper, When the man saw this, he, too, sat down to table, and began to sup. After supper, Fate lay down to sleep, and he lay down too. About midnight a terrible noise arose, and out of the noise a voice was heard: 'Fate! Fate! so many souls have been born to-day; assign them what you will.' Then Fate arose, and opened a chest with money in it, and began to throw nothing but ducats behind him, saying: 'As to me to-day, so to them for life!' When on the morrow day dawned, that large palace was no more, but instead of it a moderate-sized house; but in it again there was enough of everything.

At the approach of evening Fate sat down to supper; and he, too, sat down with him, but neither spoke a single word. After supper they lay down to sleep. About midnight a terrible noise began, and out of the noise was heard a voice: 'Fate! Fate! so many souls have been born to-day; assign them what you will.' Then Fate arose, and opened the money-chest; but there were not ducats in it, but silver coins, with an occasional ducat. Fate began to scatter the coins behind him, saying: 'As to me to-day, so to them for life.' When, on the morrow, day dawned, that house was no more, but instead of it there stood a smaller one. Thus did Fate every night, and his house became smaller every morning, till, finally, nothing remained of it but a little cottage. Fate took a mattock, and began to dig; the man, too, took a mattock and began to dig, and thus they dug all day. When it was eventide, Fate took a piece of bread, broke off half of it, and gave it to him. Thus they supped, and, after supper, lay down to sleep. About midnight, again, a terrible noise began, and out of the noise was heard a voice: 'Fate! Fate! so many souls have been born to-day; assign them what you will.' Then Fate arose, opened the chest, and began to scatter behind him nothing but bits of rag, and here and there a day-labourer's wage-penny,* shouting: 'As to me to-day, so to them for life.' When he

* A 'marjush,' a small coin with the image of the Virgin Mary on it.

arose on the morrow, the cottage was transformed into a large palace, like that which had been there the first day. Then Fate asked him: 'Why have you come?' He detailed to him all his distress, and said that he had come to ask him why he gave him evil luck. Fate then said to him: 'You saw how the first night I scattered ducats, and what took place afterwards. As it was to me the night when anyone was born, so will it be to him for life. You were born on an unlucky night, you will be poor for life; but your brother was born on a lucky night, and he will be lucky for life. But, as you have been so resolute, and have taken so much trouble, I will tell you how you may help yourself. Your brother has a daughter, Militza, who is lucky, just as her father is; adopt her, and, whatever you acquire, say that it is all hers.' Then he thanked Fate, and said to him again: 'In such a village there is a wealthy peasant, who has enough of everything; but he is unlucky in this, that his people can never be satisfied: they eat up a caldron full of food at a single meal, and even that is too little for them. And this peasant's father and mother are, as it were, fettered to this world; they are old and discoloured, and dried up like ghosts, but cannot die. He begged me, Fate, when I lodged with him for the night, to ask you why that was the case.' Then Fate replied: 'All that is because he does not honour his father and mother, throwing their food behind the stove; but, if he puts them in the best place at table, and if he gives them the first cup of brandy, and the first cup of wine, his servants would not eat half so much, and his parents' souls would be set at liberty.' After this he again questioned Fate: 'In such a village, when I spent the night in a house, the householder complained to me that his cattle were not productive, but the contrary, and he begged me to ask you why this was the case.' Fate replied: 'That is because on the festival of his name-day he slaughters the worst animals; but if he slaughtered the best he has, his cattle would all become productive.' Then he asked him the question about the stream of water: 'Why should it be that that stream of water has no offspring?' Fate replied: 'Because it has never drowned a human being; but don't have any nonsense; don't tell it till it carries you across, for if you tell it, it will immediately drown you.' Then he thanked Fate, and went home. When he came to the water, the water asked him: 'What is the news from Fate?' He replied: 'Carry me over, and then I will tell you.' When the water had carried him over, he ran on a little, and, when he had got a little way off, turned and shouted to the water: 'Water! Water! you have never drowned a human being, therefore you have no offspring.' When the water heard that, it overflowed its banks, and after him; but he ran, and barely escaped. When he came to the man whose cattle were unproductive, he was impatiently waiting for him. 'What news, brother, in God's name? Have you asked Fate the question?' He replied: 'I have; and Fate says when you celebrate the festival of your name-day, you slaughter the worst animals; but if you slaughter the best you have, all your cattle will be productive.' When he heard this, he said to him: 'Stay, brother, with us; it isn't three days to my name-day, and, if it is really true, I will give you an apple.'* He stayed till the name-day. When the name-day arrived, the householder slaughtered his best ox, and from that time forth his cattle became productive. After this, the householder presented him with five head of cattle. He thanked him, and proceeded on his way. When he came to the village of the householder who had the insatiable servants, the householder was impatiently expecting him. 'How is it, brother, in God's name? What says Fate?' He replied: 'Fate says you do not

* *I.e.*, a good present.

honour your father and mother, but throw their food behind the stove for them to eat; if you put them in the best place at table, and give them the first cup of brandy, and the first cup of wine, your people will not eat half as much, and your father and mother will be content.' When the householder heard this, he told his wife, and she immediately washed and combed her father and mother in law, and put nice shoes on their feet; and, when evening came, the householder put them in the best place at table, and gave them the first cup of brandy and the first cup of wine. From that time forth the household could not eat half what they did before, and on the morrow both the father and the mother departed this life. Then the householder gave him two oxen; he thanked him, and went home. When he came to his place of abode, his acquaintances began to congratulate him, and ask him: 'Whose are these cattle?' He replied to everybody: 'Brother, they are my niece Militza's.' When he got home he immediately went off to his brother, and began to beg and pray him: 'Give me, brother, your daughter Militza to be my daughter. You see that I have no one.' His brother replied: 'It is good, brother; Militza is yours.' He took Militza, and conducted her home, and afterwards acquired much, but said, with regard to everything, that it was Militza's. Once he went out into the field to go round some rye; the rye was beautiful; it could not be better. Thereupon a traveller happened to come up, and asked him: 'Whose is this rye?' He forgot himself, and said: 'Mine.' The moment he said that, the rye caught fire and began to burn. When he saw this, he ran after the man: 'Stop, brother! it is not mine; it belongs to Militza, my niece.' Then the fire in the rye went out, and he remained lucky with Militza.

SERBIAN STORIES FROM BOSNIA.

THE Bosnian stories are not written in the Cyrillic, but in the Latin character. This indicates that the Christian inhabitants of Bosnia belong to the Latin rather than to the Greek Church. The Serbians of the Kingdom of Serbia would, no doubt, gladly absorb Bosnia, but it is very doubtful whether the Bosnians would be equally glad to be absorbed by them. In Bosnia the landed proprietors are extensively Mahometans, and neither they nor the Latin Christians would be very willing to place themselves under the domination of the Orthodox Greek Church, without much stronger guarantees than the Serbians of the kingdom, as at present constituted, are likely to be able or willing to give them.

XLV.—THE BIRDCATCHER.

NEAR Constantinople there lived a man who knew no other occupation but that of catching birds; his neighbours called him the birdcatcher. Some he used to sell, others served him for food, and thus he maintained himself. One day he caught a crow, and wanted to let it go, but then he had nothing to take home. 'If I can't catch anything to-day, I'll take my children the crow, that they may amuse themselves; and they have no other birds at hand.' So he intended, and so he did. His wife, on seeing the crow, said: 'What mischief have you brought me? Wring the worthless thing's neck!' The crow, on hearing that sentence, besought the birdcatcher to let her go, and promised to be always at his service. 'I will bring birds to you; through me you will become prosperous.' 'Even if you're lying, it's no great loss,' said the birdcatcher to himself, and set the crow at liberty.

On the morrow the birdcatcher went out birdcatching as usual, and the crow kept her word; she brought him two nightingales; he caught them both, and took them home. The nightingales were not long with the birdcatcher, for the grand vizier heard of them, sent for the birdcatcher, took the two nightingales from him, and placed them in the new mosque. The nightingales were able to sing sweetly and agreeably; the people collected in front of the mosque and listened to their beautiful singing; and the wonder came to the ears of the emperor. The emperor summoned the grand vizier, took the birds from him, and inquired whence he had got them. When the emperor had thought the matter over, he sent his cavasses, and they summoned the birdcatcher. 'It's no joke to go before the emperor! I know why he summons me; no half torture will be mine. I am guilty of nothing, I owe nothing; but the emperor's will, that's my crime!' said the birdcatcher, and went into the emperor's presence all pale with fear. 'Birdcatcher, sirrah! are you the catcher of those nightingales which were at the new mosque.' 'Padishah! both father and mother! where your slipper is, there is my face!—I am.' 'Sirrah!' again said the emperor, 'I wish you to find their mother; doubtless your reward will be forthcoming. But do you hear? You may be quite sure of it; if you don't, there will be no head on your shoulders. I'm not joking.' Now the poor fellow went out of the emperor's presence, and how he got home he didn't know; a good two hours afterwards he came to himself and began to lament. 'I'm a fool! I thought my trade led no-whither, and not to misfortune for me; but now see! To find the mother of the birds—none but a fool could imagine it—and to catch her!' To this lamentation there was neither limit nor end. It was getting dark, and his wife summoned him to supper; just then the crow was at the window: 'What's this?' the crow asked. 'What are these lamentations? What's the distress?' 'Let me alone; don't add to my torture; I'm done for owing to you!' said the birdcatcher, and told her all, what it was and how it was. 'That's easy,' answered she; 'go to the emperor to-morrow, and ask for a thousand loads of wheat; then pile up the corn in one heap, and I will inform the birds that the emperor gives them a feast; they will all assemble; *their* mother, too, will doubtless come; the one with regard to which I give you a sign is she; bring a cage, put the two nightingales in it; the mother, seeing her two young birds, will fly up; let your snare be ready, and then we shall find and catch her.' As the crow instructed him, so he did. The emperor gave him the corn; he feasted the birds, caught the mother of the nightingales, and took her to the emperor. He received a handsome reward, but he would gladly have gone without such reward when he remembered how many tears he had shed. The crow, too, received a reward, for she persuaded the birdcatcher to give his wife a good beating, which he did, to the satisfaction of the crow, in her presence.

Time after time, behold some of the emperor's cavasses! 'Come, the emperor summons you!' sounded from the door. 'A new misfortune! a new sorrow!' thought the birdcatcher in his heart, and went before the emperor. 'Do you hear, sirrah? Just now I paid you a good recom-

16

pense, now a greater one awaits you. I wish you to seek the mistress of those birds, otherwise, valah! bilah! your head will be in danger! Do you understand me?' At these words of the emperor the birdcatcher either could not or dared not utter a word; he shrugged his shoulders and went out of his presence. As he went home he talked to himself weeping: 'I see that he is determined to destroy me, and some devil has put it into his head to torture me first.' On arriving at home he found his crow at the window: 'Has some misfortune again occurred to you?' 'Don't ask,' replied the birdcatcher; 'one still blacker and more miserable!' and told her all in detail, what it was and how it was. 'Don't trouble your head much about that,' said the crow. 'Be quick; ask the emperor for a boat full of all manner of wares. Then we will push off on the deep sea; when people hear that the emperor's agent is bringing wares, the people will assemble, and that lady is sure to come; the one on which I perch is she; up anchor and off with the boat!' This the birdcatcher remembered well. What he asked of the emperor, that he gave him, and he pushed the boat over the sea; his bringing wares for sale went from mouth to mouth; people came and purchased the wares. At last came the mistress of the birds also, and began to examine the wares; the crow perched on her shoulder; the anchor was raised, and in a short time the birdcatcher brought the boat to under the emperor's quay. When the birdcatcher brought her before the emperor, the emperor was astounded. He didn't know which to admire most, the birdcatcher's cleverness or her beauty. Her beauty overpowered the emperor's mind; he rewarded the birdcatcher handsomely, and placed the sultana in his house. 'You are the dearest to me of all,' said the emperor several times to her; 'if I were to banish all the sultanas, you should never go out of my seraglio.'

The birdcatcher was again in evil case. The new sultana was in a perpetual state of irritation, for it was poor luck to be obliged to be affectionate to an elderly longbeard. The emperor comforted her, and asked her what failed her, when she had everything in abundance with him. A woman's revenge is worse than a cat's. Not daring to tell the emperor the truth, she wanted to revenge herself on the poor birdcatcher. 'Dear Padishah, I had a valuable ring on my hand when that birdcatcher deluded me into the boat, and pushed it from the shore. I began to wring my hands in distress, the ring broke, and one half fell into the sea, just where it was my hap to be. But, dear sultan, if I am a little dear to you, send that birdcatcher, let him seek that half for me, that I may unite it to this one.' 'All shall be done,' said the emperor; and the cavasses soon brought the birdcatcher. 'My son,' said the emperor, 'if you do not intend to lose my love and favour, hearken to me once more. At the place where you captured that lady, she broke a ring; it fell into the sea. I know that you can do so—find her that half; your reward will not fail; otherwise, you know . . . .' When the poor fellow got home, a fit of laughter seized him from distress. 'I knew that the devil was teaching him how to torment and torture me before he put me to death. If hell were to open, all the devils wouldn't find it!' 'What's the matter, friend?' said the crow. 'Till now you were weeping and complaining, and now in a rage you are laughing.' He told her all—what it was, and how it was. 'Don't fret yourself,' continued the crow. 'Have you given your wife a good thrashing? I wish you to give her a good hiding again, when we go down to the sea. And now come, ask the emperor for a thousand barrels of oil.' The emperor had stores of oil and felt; he gave him as much as he required. Everybody thought that he was going to trade with the oil. When he arrived at the place where he captured the young lady, the crow gave the word of command, and they poured out all the oil into the sea. The sea became violently agitated, the crow darted in, and found the missing fragment of the ring. The bird-catcher took the boat back thence under the emperor's palace, and delivered the ring to the emperor, he passed it on to the lady, and she fitted it to the other half. Both she and the emperor were astonished at the birdcatcher's cleverness, commended him, and sent him home with a present.

The emperor wished by every means to induce the young lady to marry him, and to have a formal wedding. She for a long time declined, but at last said: 'If it is your will, I consent, but only on condition that before our wedding you destroy that birdcatcher.' The emperor now found himself between two fires. It was agony to destroy his benefactor, it was worse agony not to be able to withstand his heart, and to give up the love of the young lady. Love is eternal, and is often stronger even than truth. He summoned the birdcatcher, commended him for having so often fulfilled his will, and told him that he deserved to sit in the grand vizier's seat. . . . 'But there is nothing else for it, but you must go home, take leave of your wife, children, and friends, of whom I will undertake the care; in the afternoon come; you must of necessity jump into the fire.' He went home, and the crow came to meet him. He told her all that was to be done with him in the afternoon, and said to her: 'If you do not help me as usual now, I am done for, not through my fault, nor through the emperor's, but owing to you.' The crow informed him what to do, but before he went, he was to give his wife a thoroughly good beating. His wife departed this life from so many blows. A fire was flaming before the great mosque, the Turks came out of the mosque, the emperor came, the people swarmed round the fire The birdcatcher came cheerfully before the emperor.

Everyone deemed him a malefactor. 'Fortunate Padishah, it is your pleasure to burn me to death. I am happy to be able to be a sacrifice for you. It has occurred to my mind, I am anxious to have a ride on a good horse: permit me so to do before I jump into the fire.' The emperor smiled, and ordered his best horse to be brought for him. He mounted, and made the horse gallop well; when the horse sweated, he dismounted, anointed himself with the horse's foam, remounted, darted up to the fire, then dismounted, and darted into the fire. The people looked on; five times, six times did he cross the flames, sprang out of the fire, and stood before the emperor as a youth of twenty years of age, sound, young, goodly, and handsome. The people cried: 'Mercy, emperor! He has fulfilled his penalty.' And the emperor graciously pardoned him. The emperor now longed to become young and handsome also. He made the birdcatcher grand vizier, merely that he might tell him the secret. He said to him: 'My lord, it is easy. Take a good horse, gallop about an hour as I did, dismount when the horse sweats, anoint yourself with his perspiration, jump into the fire, and you will come out such as I am.' Friday dawned; the emperor's best horse was saddled for him; everybody thought that he was going to the mosque. A fire was burning furiously in front of the mosque. The people said: 'There's somebody going to jump in again,' and they were under no delusion. The emperor darted up to the fire all alone, the people looked on to see what was going to happen. The emperor dismounted with great speed, and sprang into the fire. . . . The people crowded to rescue the emperor—'twas all in vain. The emperor was burned to death. 'He was crazy!' shouted the chief men and soldiers. They conducted the birdcatcher into the mosque, and girt him with the emperor's sword. Then the birdcatcher became emperor, the damsel he selected sultana, and the crow the chief lady at court.

XLVI.—THE TWO BROTHERS.

THERE was a man who had a wife but no sons, a female hound but no puppies, and a mare but no foal. 'What in the world shall I do?' said he to himself. 'Come, let me go away from home to seek my fortune in the world, as I haven't any at home.' As he thought, so he did, and went out by himself into the white world as a bee from flower to flower. One day, when it was about dinner-time, he came to a spring, took down his knapsack, took out his provisions for the journey, and began to eat his dinner. Just then a traveller appeared in front of him, and sat down beside the spring to rest; he invited him to sit down by him that they might eat together. When they had inquired after each other's health and shaken hands, then the second comer asked the first on what business he was travelling about the world. He said to him: 'I have no luck at home, therefore I am going from home; my wife has no children, my hound has no puppies, and my mare has never had a foal; I am going about the white world as a bee from flower to flower.' When they had had a good dinner, and got up to travel further, then the one who had arrived last thanked the first for his dinner, and offered him an apple, saying: 'Here is this apple for you'—if I am not mistaken it was a Frederic pippin—'and return home at once; peel the apple and give the peel to your hound and mare; cut the apple in two, give half to your wife to eat, and eat the other half yourself. What has hitherto been unproductive will henceforth be productive. And as for the two pips which you will find in the apple, plant them on the top of your house.' The man thanked him for the apple; they rose up and parted, the one going onwards and the other back to his house. He peeled the apple and did everything as the other had instructed him. As time went on his wife became the mother of two sons, his hound of two puppies, and his mare of two foals, and, moreover, out of the house grew two apple-trees. While the two brothers were growing up, the young horses grew up, and the hounds became fit for hunting. After a short time the father and mother died, and the two sons, being now left alone like a tree cut down on a hill, agreed to go out into the world to seek their fortune. Even so they did: each brother took a horse and a hound, they cut down the two apple-trees, and made themselves a spear apiece, and went out into the wide world. I can't tell you for certain how many days they travelled together; this I do know, that at the first parting of the road they separated. Here they saw it written up: 'If you go by the upper road you will not see the world for five years; if you go by the lower road, you will not see the world for three years.' Here they parted, one going by the upper and the other by the lower road. The one that went by the lower road, after three years of travelling through another world, came to a lake, beside which there was written on a post: 'If you go in, you will repent it; if you don't go in, you will repent it.' 'If it is so,' thought he to himself, 'let me take whatever God gives,' and swam across the lake. And lo! a wonder! he, his horse, and his hound were all gilded with gold. After this he speedily arrived at a very large and spacious city. He went up to the emperor's palace and inquired for an inn where he might pass the night. They told him, up there, yon large tower, that was an inn. In front of this tower he dismounted; servants came out and welcomed him, and conducted him into the presence of their master in the courtyard. But it was not an innkeeper, but the king of the province himself. The king welcomed and entertained him handsomely. The next day he began to prepare to set forth on his journey. The evening before, the king's only daughter, when she saw him go in front of her apartments, had observed him well, and fixed her eyes upon him. This she did because such a golden traveller had never before arrived, and consequently she was unable to close her eyes the whole night. Her heart thumped, as it were; and it was fortunate that the summer night was brief, for if it had been a winter one, she could hardly have waited for the dawn. It all seemed to her and whirled in her brain as if the king was calling her to receive a ring and an apple; the poor thing would fly to the door, but it was shut and there was nobody at hand. Although the night was a short one, it seemed to her that three had passed one after another. When she observed in the morning that the traveller was getting ready to go, she flew to her father, implored him not to let that traveller quit his court, but to detain him and to give her to him in marriage. The king was good-natured, and could easily be won over by entreaties; what his daughter begged for, she also obtained. The traveller was detained and offered marriage with the king's daughter. The traveller did not hesitate long, kissed the king's hand, presented a ring to the maiden, and she a handkerchief to him, and thus they were betrothed. Methinks they did not wait for publication of banns. Erelong they were wedded; the wedding feast and festival were very prolonged, but came to an end in due course. One morning after all this the bridegroom was looking in somewhat melancholy fashion down on the country through a window in the tower. His young wife asked him what ailed him? He told her that he was longing for a hunt, and she told him to take three servants and go while the dew was still on the grass. Her husband would not take a single servant, but mounting his gilded horse and calling his gilded hound, went down into the country to hunt. The hound soon found scent, and put up a stag with gilded horns. The stag began to run straight for a tower, the hound after him, and the hunter after the hound, and he overtook the stag in the gate of the court-yard, and was going to cut off its head. He had drawn his sword, when a damsel cried through the window: 'Don't kill my stag, but come upstairs: let us play at draughts for a wager. If you win, take the stag; if I win, you shall give me the hound.' He was as ready for this as an old woman for a scolding match, went up into the tower, and on to the balcony, staked the hound against the stag, and they began to play. The hunter was on the point of beating her, when some damsels began to sing: 'A king, a king, I've gained a king!' He looked round, she altered the position of the draughtsmen, beat him and took the hound. Again they began to play a second time, she staking the hound and he his horse. She cheated him the second time also. The third time they began to play, she wagered the horse, and he himself. When the game was nearly over, and he was already on the point of beating her, the damsels began to sing this time too, just as they had done the first and second times. He looked round, she cheated and beat him, took a cord, bound him, and put him in a dungeon.

The brother, who went by the upper road, came to the lake, forded it, and came out all golden—himself, his horse, and his hound. He went for a night's lodging to the king's tower; the servants came out and welcomed him. His father-in-law asked him whether he was tired, and whether he had had any success in hunting; but the king's daughter paid special attention to him, frequently kissing and embracing him. He couldn't wonder enough how it was that everybody recognised him; finally, he felt satisfied that it was his brother, who was very like him, that had been there and got married. The king's daughter could not wonder enough, and it was very distressing to her, that her newly-married husband was so soon tired of her, for the more affectionate she was to him, the more did he repulse her. When the morrow came, he got ready to go out to look for his brother. The king, his daughter, and all the courtiers, begged him to take a rest. 'Why,' said they to him, 'you only returned yesterday from hunting, and do you want to go again so soon?' All was in vain; he refused to take the thirty servants whom they offered him, but went down into the country by himself. When he was in the midst of the country, his hound put up a stag, and he after them on his horse, and drove it up to a tower; he raised his sword to kill the stag, but a damsel cried through a window: 'Don't meddle with my stag, but come upstairs that we may have a game at draughts, then let the one that wins take off the stakes, either you my hound, or I yours.' When he went into the basement, in it was a hound and a horse—the hounds and horses recognised each other—and he felt sure that his brother had fallen into prison there. They began the game at draughts, and when the damsel saw that he was going to beat her, some damsels began to sing behind them: 'A king! a king! I've gained a king!' He took no notice, but kept his eye on the draughtsmen; then the damsel, like a she-devil, began to make eyes and wink at the young man. He gave her a flip with his coat behind the ears: 'Play now!' and thus beat her. The second game they both staked a horse. She couldn't cheat him; he took both the hound and the horse from her. The third and last time they played, he staking himself and she herself; and after giving her a slap in her face for her winking and making of eyes, he won the third game. He took possession of her, brought his brother out of the dungeon, and they went to the town.

Now the brother, who had been in prison, began to think within himself: 'He was yesterday with my wife, and who knows whether she does not prefer him to me?' He drew his sword to kill him, but the draught-player defended him.

He darted before his brother into the courtyard, and as he stepped on to the passage from the tower, his wife threw her arms round his neck and began to scold him affectionately for having driven her from him overnight, and conversed so coldly with her. Then he repented of having so foolishly suspected his brother, who had, moreover, released him from prison, and of having wanted to kill him; but his brother was a considerate person and forgave him. They kissed each other and were reconciled. He retained his wife and her kingdom with her, and his brother took the draught-player and her kingdom with her. And thus they attained to greater fortune than they could ever have even hoped for.

SERBIAN STORIES FROM CARNIOLA.

IN these we come to a very singular mythological being, *Kurent*, who has not, as yet, found a place in the writings of Slavonic mythologists. With respect to Kurent, Professor Krek writes as follows: 'The question as to the nature of the Slovinish Kurent is very difficult, especially as the tradition about him is, in my judgment, very corrupt. So far as I know, no one has hitherto discussed it scientifically, and what I am now writing to you is my own subjective opinion, rapidly formed. The name itself does not appear to be indigenous, but I think it is of Romance, perhaps of mediæval Latin origin, though I am not yet able to say what its signification is. In a mythological point of view, there is to be observed in the stories about Kurent a certain mixture of heathen-Slavonic and Christian elements; but I think the basis is entirely indigenous. If I mistake not, Kurent is essentially of Dionysiac signification, which is indicated by the fact that the Slovinish stories connect him closely with the vine-stock, and with wine in general, just as is the case with the Greek Dionysos. It is noteworthy that the Little Russians have the word "Kurent" in the sense of a merry wedding tune (Zhelechovskij, i. 391), and that the Slovinish tradition frequently puts Kurent in the place of "Pust," so that both represent the same mythological idea. With regard to "Pust," there is no doubt that, with his orgiastic system, he is just like the Greek Dionysos, although his name is recent, and rests upon alien conceptions; indeed, here the fact is of more decisive import than the name. The name is not connected with the old Slavonic "pust," *desertus*, but with "pust" in the old Slavonic "mesopust," in Bohemian "masopust," which are identical with the Greek ἀπόκρεως, in Latin "carnisprivium." Of what original names "Kurént" and "Pust" have occupied the place, it will now never be possible to determine. It is just in mythological matters, that all manner of old traditions are unsatisfactory, as everybody knows who has busied himself at all closely with this subject. Much that is Christian has similarly become mingled with the original pagan conceptions in the case of Kurent also, and it is not easy to separate them from later accretions. I think that the Slovintzes honoured Kurent with a special solemnity or festival at the same time that the other Slavonians celebrated the regeneration of winter, nature, and the birth of the solar deity. This mythological phenomenon has its analogy in the myths of other Ario-European nations, a matter so generally known that there is no need of dilating upon it now. What I wish to draw attention to is this: that the Slovinish "Kurent," as also his representative "Pust" is of Dionysiac signification, and I don't know to what to compare him more properly than to the Greek Dionysos. Circumspection is especially necessary in mythological matters, but I venture to affirm that my opinion will hold its ground before severe criticism. I purpose treating at greater length of this matter at a later time, but I do not think I shall find it necessary to retract any portion of my opinion.'

Mr. Morfill informs me, moreover, that *Kurenta grati* is given by Zhelikovskij in the sense 'to play the Kurent,' *i.e.*, the air so called.

XLVII.—THE ORIGIN OF MAN.

IN the beginning there was nothing but God, and God slept and dreamed. For ages and ages did this dream last. But it was fated that he should wake up. Having roused himself from sleep, he looked round about him, and every glance transformed itself into a star. God was amazed, and began to travel, to see what he had created with his eyes. He travelled and travelled, but nowhere was there either end or limit. As he travelled, he arrived at our earth also; but he was already weary; sweat clung to his brow. On the earth fell a drop of sweat: the drop became alive, and here you have the first man. He is God's kin, but he was not created for pleasure: he was produced from sweat; already in the beginning it was fated for him to toil and sweat.

XLVIII.—GOD'S COCK.

THE earth was waste: nowhere was there aught but stone. God was sorry for this, and sent his cock to make the earth fruitful, as he knew how to do. The cock came down into a cave in the rock, and fetched out an egg of wondrous power and purpose. The egg chipped, and seven rivers trickled out of it. The rivers irrigated the neighbourhood, and soon all was green: there were all manner of flowers and fruits; the land, without man's labour, produced wheat, the trees not only apples and figs, but also the whitest and sweetest bread. In this paradise men lived without care, working, not from need, but for amusement and merriment. Round the paradise were lofty mountains, so that there was no violence to fear, nor devilish storm to dread. But further: that men, otherwise their own masters, and free, might not, from ignorance, suffer damage, God's cock hovered high in the sky, and crowed to them every day, when to get up, when to take their meals, and what to do, and when to do it. The nation was happy, only God's cock annoyed them by his continual crowing. Men began to murmur, and pray God to deliver them from the restless creature: 'Let us now settle for ourselves,' said they, 'when to eat, to work, and to rise.' God hearkened to them; the cock descended from the sky, but crowed to them just once more: 'Woe is me! Beware of the lake!' Men rejoiced, and said that it was never better; no one any more interfered with their freedom. After ancient custom, they ate, worked, and rose, all in the best order, as the cock had taught them. But, little by little, individuals began to think that it was unsuitable for a free people to obey the cock's crowing so slavishly, and began to live after their own fashion, observing no manner of order. Through this arose illnesses, and all kinds of distress; men looked again longingly to the sky, but God's cock was gone for ever. They wished, at any rate, to pay regard to his last words. But they did not know how to fathom their meaning. The cock had warned them to dread the lake, but why? for they hadn't it in their valley; there flowed quietly, in their own channel, the seven rivers which had burst out of the egg. Men therefore conjectured that there was a dangerous lake somewhere on the other side of the mountains, and sent a man every day to the top of a hill to see whether he espied aught. But there was danger from no quarter; the man went in vain, and people calmed themselves again. Their pride became greater and greater; the women made brooms from the wheat-ears, and the men straw mattrasses. They would not go any more to the tree to gather bread, but set it on fire from below, that it might fall, and that they might collect it without trouble. When they had eaten their fill, they lay down by the rivers, conversed, and spoke all manner of blasphemies. One cast his eyes on the water, wagged his head, and jabbered: 'Eh! brothers! A wondrous wonder! I should like to know, at any rate, why the water is exactly so much, neither more nor less.' 'This, too,' another answered, 'was a craze of the cock's; it is disgraceful enough for us to be listening to orders to beware of a lake, which never was, and never will be. If my opinion is followed, the watcher will go to-day for the last time. As regards the rivers, I think it would be better if there were more water.' His neighbour at first agreed, but thought, again, that there was water in abundance; if more, there would be too much. A corpulent fellow put in energetically that undoubtedly both were right; it would, therefore, be the most sensible thing to break the egg up, and drive just as much water as was wanted into each man's land, and there was certainly no need of a watchman to look out for the lake. Scarcely had these sentiments been delivered, when an outcry arose in the valley; all rushed to the egg to break it to pieces; all men deplored nothing but this, that the disgraceful look-out could not be put a stop to before the morrow. The people stood round the egg, the corpulent man took up a stone, and banged it against the egg. It split up with a clap of thunder, and so much water burst out of it that almost the whole human race perished. The paradise was filled with water, and became one great lake. God's cock warned truly, but in vain, for the lawless people did not understand him. The flood now reached the highest mountains, just to the place where the watchman was standing, who was the only survivor from the destruction of mankind. Seeing the increasing waters, he began to flee.

XLIX.—KURENT THE PRESERVER.

MANKIND perished by the flood, and there was only one who survived, and this was Kranyatz. Kranyatz fled higher and higher, till the water flooded the last mountain. The poor wretch saw how the pines and shrubs were covered; one vine, and one only, was still dry. To it he fled, and quickly seized hold of it, not from necessity, but from excessive terror; but how could it help him, being so slender and weak? Kurent observed this, for the vine was his stick, when he walked through the wide world. It was agreeable to him that man should be thought to seek help from him. It is true that Kurent was a great joker; but he was also of a kindly nature, and was always glad to deliver anyone from distress. Hearing Kranyatz lamenting, he straightened the vine, his stick, and lengthened it more and more, till it became higher than the clouds. After nine years the flood ceased, and the earth became dry again. But Kranyatz preserved himself by hanging on the vine, and nourishing himself by its grapes and wine. When all became dry, he got down, and thanked Kurent as his preserver. But this didn't please Kurent. 'It was the vine that rescued you,' said he to Kranyatz; 'thank the vine, and make a covenant with it, and bind yourself and your posterity, under a curse, that you will always speak its praises and love its wine more than any other food and drink.' Very willingly did the grateful Kranyatz make the engagement for both himself and his posterity, and to this day his descendants still keep faith, according to his promise, loving wine above all things, and joyfully commemorating Kurent, their ancient benefactor.

L.—KURENT AND MAN.

KURENT and man contended which should rule the earth. Neither Kurent would yield to man nor man to Kurent, for he (man) was so gigantic—he wouldn't even have noticed it, if nine of the people of the present day had danced up and

17

down his nostrils. 'Come,' said Kurent, 'let us see which is the stronger; whether it is I or you that is to rule the earth. Yonder is a broad sea; the one that springs across it best shall have both the earth and all that is on the other side of the sea, and that is, in faith, a hundred times more valuable than this wilderness.' Man agreed. Kurent took off his coat and jumped across the sea, so that just one foot was wetted when he sprang on to dry land. Now he began to jeer at the man; but the man held his tongue, didn't get out of temper, neither did he take off his coat, but stepped without effort and quite easily over the sea, as over a brook, and came on to dry land without even wetting a foot. 'I'm the stronger,' said man to Kurent; 'see how my foot is dry and yours is wet.' 'The first time you have overcome me,' answered Kurent; 'yours are the plains, yours is the sea, and what is beyond the sea; but that isn't all the earth, there is also some beneath us and above us; come, then, let us see a second time which is the stronger.' Kurent stood on a hollow rock, and stamped on it with his foot, so that it burst with a noise like thunder, and split in pieces. The rock broke up, and a cavern was seen where dragons were brooding. Now the man also stamped, and the earth quaked and broke up right to the bottom, just where pure gold flowed like a broad river, and the dragons fell down and were drowned in the river. 'This trial, too, is yours,' said Kurent; 'but I don't acknowledge you emperor till you overpower me in a third fierce contest. Yonder is a very lofty mountain. It rises above the clouds; it reaches to the celestial table, where the cock sits and watches God's provisions. Now, then, take you an arrow and shoot, and so will I; the one which shoots highest is the stronger, and his is the earth, and all that is beneath and above it.' Kurent shot, and his arrow wasn't back for eight days; then the man shot, and his arrow flew for nine days, and when, on the tenth day, it fell, the celestial cock that guarded God's provisions fell also, spitted upon it. 'You are emperor,' said cunning Kurent. 'I make obeisance to you, as befits a subject.' But the man was good-natured, and made a covenant of adoptive brotherhood with Kurent, and went off to enjoy his imperial dignity. Kurent, too, went off, but he was annoyed that the man had put him to shame; where he could not prevail by strength, he determined to succeed by craft. 'You are a hero, man,' he would say, 'I am witness thereto; but beware of me, if you are a hero also in simplicity; I go to bring you a gift, that I have devised entirely by myself.'

He said and squeezed the vine, his stick, and pure red wine burst out of it. 'Here's a gift for you; now, then, where are you?' He found the man on the earth the other side of the sea, where he was enjoying a bowl of sweet stirabout. 'What are you doing, my lord?' said Kurent. 'I've mixed a bowl of stirabout from white wheat and red fruit, and, see, here I am eating it and drinking water.' 'My poor lord! you are emperor of the world and drinking water! hand me a cup, that I may present you with better drink, which I, your humble servant, have prepared for you myself.' The man was deceived, took the cup with red wine, and drank some of it. 'Thank you, adopted brother; you are very kind, but your drink is naught.' Kurent was disgusted, went off again, and thought and thought how to cheat the man. Again he squeezed his stick, again red wine burst forth from it, but Kurent did not allow it to remain pure, but the rascal mixed hellebore with it, which Vilas and prophetesses pluck by moonlight to nourish themselves with. A second time he went in search of the man, and found him at the bottom of the earth, where the pure gold was flowing like a broad river. 'What are you doing, my lord?' asked Kurent. 'I am getting myself a golden shirt, and I am tired and very thirsty; but there's no water here, and it's a long way to the world—seven years' journey.' 'I am at your service,' said Kurent; 'here's a cup of wine for you; better never saw the red sun.' The man was deceived, took it, and drank it up. 'Thank you, Kurent; you are good, and your drink is good, too.' Kurent was going to pour him out a fresh cupful, but the man would not allow it, for his nature was still sober and sensible. Kurent was disgusted, and went off to see whether he could not devise something better. For the third time he squeezed his stick; wine burst out more strongly, but this time it did not remain pure nor without sin. The rascal applied an arrow, opened a vein and let some black blood flow into the wine. Again he went in search of the man, and found him on the high mountain at God's table, where he was feasting on roast meat, which had not been roasted for him, but for God himself. 'What are you doing, my lord?' asked Kurent in amazement and joy, when he saw that the man was sinning abominably. 'Here I am, sitting and eating roast meat; but take yourself off, for I am afraid of God, lest he should come up and smite me.' 'Never fear!' was Kurent's advice; 'how do you like God's roast meat?' 'It's nice, but it's heavy. I can scarcely swallow it.' 'I am at your service,' said Kurent; 'here is wine for you, the like of which isn't on earth or in heaven, but only with me.' The third time the man was deceived, but cruelly. 'Thank you, Kurent,' he said; 'you are good, but your drink is better; draw me some more, as becomes a faithful servant.' Kurent did so, and the man's eye became dim and his mind became dim, and he thought no more of God, but remained at table. Suddenly God returned, and seeing the man dozing and eating roast meat at his table, became angry, and smote him down the mountain with his mighty hand, where he lay, half dead, for many years, all bruised and hurt. When he got well again his strength had diminished; he could neither step across the sea, nor go down to the bottom of the earth, nor uphill to the celestial table. Thus Kurent ruled the world and man, and mankind have been weak and dwarfed from that time forth.

LI.—THE HUNDRED-LEAVED ROSE.

THE man contended with Kurent for the earth. Unable to decide their dispute by agreement, they seized each other, and struggled together up and down the earth for full seven years; but neither could Kurent overcome the man, nor the man Kurent. At that time they kicked the earth about and broke it up, so that it became such as it now is: where there was formerly nothing but wide plains, they dug out ravines with their heels, and piled up mountains and hills. When they were wearied with fighting, they both fell down like dead corpses, and lay for a hundred and a hundred years; and the mighty Dobrin hastened to the earth, bound both the man and Kurent, and ruled the world. But the two woke up, and, looking about them, observed Dobrin's cords, and wondered who had thrown spider's webs over them. Raising themselves, they broke their bonds as mere spiders' webs, seized Dobrin, bound him with golden fetters, and handed him over to a fiery dragon, to plait the lady-dragon's hair and wash her white hands. Then said Kurent to the man: 'See, by quarrelling we got tired out, and fell asleep, and a good-for-nothing came to us and ruled the world. We have handed him over to the fiery dragon, but if we contend as before, a stronger than Dobrin will come to us, and will conquer both me and you, and we shall suffer like silly Dobrin. But let us give up disputing; you are a hero, and I think I am, too; the hills and abysses are our witnesses, when they crashed under our heels. Hear, therefore, and follow my advice. I have a garden, and in my garden is a mysterious plant, the hundred-leaved rose. By the root it is attached to the bottom of the earth, imprisoning a terrible creature—the living fire. In vain does the creature endeavour to release and free itself from its bonds, the roots. But woe to us, if you pull up the hundred-leaved rose out of the earth! The creature 'living-fire' would force its way through, and the earth, and all that is in it, would become nothing but a mighty desert where the water has dried up. Such is the root of the hundred-leaved rose. But don't seize hold of its top, either. It is in your power to pull it off, it is neither too strong nor lofty, but it conceals within it wondrous powers—lightning and thunder. They would knock to pieces both you and the earth, and all that is beneath it and above it; the hundred-leaved rose would alone remain; but a hundred and a hundred of God's years would elapse before a new earth grew up around it, and a living race was again produced. Such is the garden of the hundred-leaved rose. But it also possesses extraordinary petals. I have often sat a day at a time under them, and the petals would comfort me, and sing songs sweeter than even the slender throat of a Vila singing ever uttered. But from the petals there is no danger; pluck them, and next morning they will sprout forth handsomer than ever. But up to the present time I have not injured them, but have noticed in the night, how they fell and raised themselves again; and I easily understood how the stars and the moon go round, for all came up in the sky just like the petals of the hundred-leaved rose. Come, then; let us ask the wondrous plant, and then make peace together. The first petal is yours, the second mine, the third belongs to neither of us, and so on till we pluck all the petals: let him who pulls off the last petal be ruler on the earth, but not for ever, for that would be a disgrace to a hero, but for one of God's hours, a hundred terrestrial years; and when the hour passes, let that one rule again to whom that luck does not fall the first time, whether it be I or you, so that we may arrange to succeed each other in a friendly manner without dispute and dangerous discord. But the beginning is difficult; let us have no suspicion, either I as to you, or you as to me, but let all be of goodwill, and without trickery; let us ask the hundred-leaved rose, with whom there is no unrighteousness. The man agreed to what Kurent said; one hero trusted the other. They went off to the garden, and asked the hundred-leaved rose. The man pulled a petal, Kurent pulled one, and the third petal remained unowned. 'I am yours,' 'you are mine,' 'each is his own;' 'I am yours,' 'you are mine,' 'each is his own;' so said both heroes, as they pulled the mysterious petals. But it was not the will of the hundred-leaved rose that one autocrat should rule the earth. There were still three petals, the first belonging to the man, the second to Kurent, and the third to neither, and this was the only one remaining on the hundred-leaved rose. Kurent and the man saw that it was not destined for either to rule or to humble himself; they parted in grief, and roamed through the wide world, each afraid of the other, so that they did not venture even to go to sleep at night. An hour of God, a hundred terrestrial years, elapsed, and then both heroes met again. For the second time they consulted the hundred-leaved rose, and it arranged it so, that Kurent was to humble himself, and the man, who pulled off the last petal, was to rule. The hero humbled himself to him, but the man did not know how to rule, but allowed himself to be deluded, and lay down on a plain to rest and sleep. Thus he lay for a whole hour of God, a hundred terrestrial years, and the wild beasts came up and made game of him: foxes littered in his ear, and predaceous kites nested in his thick hair. The man was a great simpleton, but also a mighty hero, as tall, as a plain, the end of which you cannot see, is long, and as shaggy as a wooded mountain. But the hour of God had elapsed, and Kurent came to the sleeper, and woke him up in no agreeable fashion. The man saw that he had slept through his term of rule, and that it was his, according to the agreement, to serve during an hour of God, a hundred terrestrial years. Kurent began to rule, but he didn't go to sleep, but made use of his rule, and exercised his power to the full. He invited the man to dinner, and treated him in a courteous and friendly manner, that he might soon forget his servitude. Kurent kept this in view, and drew him a cup of wine straight from his own vineyard. The simpleton was tricked, and drank it up; but it tasted sour to him, so he grumbled: 'Bad drink at a bad host's!' Kurent did not get angry at this, but drew him a second cup of old red wine: 'Drink, and don't find fault with what is God's.' The second time the man was tricked and drank it up. It did not taste sour to him, but he said: 'Wondrous drink at a wondrous host's!' Kurent drew him a third cup, of wonderful wine, which the first plant, the first planted, yielded, of the first autumn in the first created year. The third time the man was tricked, but for ever. After drinking it up, he threw his arms round Kurent's neck, and cried out: 'Oh, good drink at a good host's! Treat me with this wine, and rule both my body and soul, not only for one hour of God, but from henceforth for evermore.' Kurent was delighted, and plied the man with sweet wine, and the man drank, and cried without ceasing, that he had no need of freedom so long as there was wine to be had with Kurent. Kurent laughed at him, seeing how the man's powers had decayed through wine, and that nobody could any more contend with him for the sovereignty of the earth.

CROATIAN STORIES.

THE Croats are believed to take their name from their former abode in the ancient Chrobatia, north of the Carpathian Mountains, whose name retains the same root, CRB(orP)T. Among them we meet with a wonderful hero, 'Marko' (No. 52), the account of whose *buzdovan*, or mace, the southern representative of Thor's hammer, may be compared with 'Little Rolling-pea's *bulava* (No. 22), and that of Ivan Popyalof' (Ralston, p. 66). Marko appears to have been a very unprincipled hero, with very slight ideas of honesty and fair-play. He is represented as gaining his vast strength from a superhuman source—a Vila, of whom more anon. In No. 53, we are carried into cloudland, and meet with representatives of the Clashing Rocks' (Symplegades), through which the good ship *Argo* had to pass before she could make her way into the Black Sea, and which, till their reappearance in this story, seem to have dropped altogether out of folklore. From this story, and also from several incidents in No. 52, we perceive that the Vilas of the South Slavonians are not denizens of the earth, the waters, or the woods, but of the clouds, and thus a journey has to be made into cloudland to find the daughter of their king.* No. 54 will remind us of Aladdin and his

* It must also be noticed that the hero is represented as catching the Storm-mare, just as Bellerophon does the horse Pegasus by the fountain Peirene.

wonderful ring and lamp, although animals play a part in it unknown to the Oriental tale. No. 55 introduces us to the singular relations supposed to exist between human beings and wolves, and No. 56 exhibits a curious mixture of destiny and ingenuity.

LII.—KRALJEVITCH MARKO.

THERE was once upon a time a mother who gave birth to Kraljevitch Marko. She reared him, and placed him in a position to become a hero. When Marko was growing up he was obliged to feed swine, but he was then weakly, and so dwarfish a lad that his comrades were able to beat him, and wanted him to be a sort of servant for them and tend their swine. But he was not willing to do this, so they beat him and lugged him by the hair, so that he was obliged to run away from them. He got away, and went into the fields, and there roamed about, thinking: 'They would be beating me all day, now one, now another of them; but as it is, when I go to them in the evening, they will only beat me once.' As he roamed about, he came up to a baby. He saw that it was a handsome one, and that it was lying in the sun. He made it a cool shade with branches, and went a little way off and sat down. As he thus sat, up came a Vila, and said to herself: 'Gracious God! who has done this? Let him ask me for anything in the world; I will give it him.' He heard this, approached, and said: 'Sister, I have done this for you.' 'You have done it, little brother? Come! what do you ask of me in return, that I may reward you for being so good as to make a cool shade for my baby?' 'Ah, dear sister! what I should ask you, you could not give me.' 'Well, what is such a mighty matter? only tell me.' He was thinking of this, that his comrades might not beat him at the pasture; therefore he said that he should wish that they should not beat him. She replied: 'Well, if that is what you wish for, come and suck my breast.' He obeyed her, went and sucked. When he had finished sucking, the Vila said to him: 'Well, go now and heave yon stone, and try whether you can heave it up.' The stone was twelve hundredweight. He went to heave it, but could not stir it from its place. Then the Vila said to him: 'Come and suck again; when you have done sucking, go and heave it. He went to suck, and when he had finished, went to heave it, but only lifted it a little. Then he went again to suck, with such effect that he could already cast it a little way. He went to suck once more. Then he was already able to cast it to a great height and over hills, so that it was no more to be found. Once more she bade him come to suck. He sucked his fill, and then she said to him: 'Go now whithersoever you will; no one will beat you any more—no, not your comrades.' He went merrily to the herdsmen, and they called to him: 'Where have you been that we are obliged to tend your swine?' and rushed upon him to beat him. He only waited for them. When they came up to him, he seized one, knocked them down, and the one who was in his hands was quite squashed, with such force had he taken hold of him. The other shepherds, who saw what he did, ran to the home of those whom he had knocked down, saying: 'Marko has knocked down your son, and so-and-so's, and so-and-so's.' They all went to his mother: 'What manner of son is this that you have reared up?—a brigand, who kills our children!' She was terrified out of her wits, thinking what her son had done. She began to revile him: 'Sonny, never did my eye see that you did anything; wherefore do you thus to me, that other people come to revile me because of your doings? Go! I shall be glad if my eye never sees you more. Why do you put me to shame?' 'Well, then, good! if so you say, I will go into the world.' 'Only go that I may never see you.' 'Well, then, good! go I will.'

He went. Now, he thought to himself: 'What shall I do? I am a hero, but I have not what a hero requires.' Then he went to a smith, at whose smithy were five-and-twenty smiths. 'God help you, smith!' 'God help you, Kraljevitch Marko! why have you come to me?' 'I have come to you that you may forge me a sword weighing twelve hundredweight; then you shall also forge me a mace, if you make the sword well; but you must know that it must be stronger than your anvil. If it cuts it through, you shall receive payment; otherwise, not. Have you understood me?' 'Yes.' 'Well, then make it now.' All five-and-twenty smiths went immediately and forged the sword. When it was ready, Marko came. 'Well, smith, have you got it ready?' 'Yes, Marko.' 'Now come, let me see.' Marko struck, but the sword broke into two pieces, and not the anvil. 'Ah! friend smith, you've not done it well; you get no pay.' He went on to another smith. 'God help you, smith!' 'God help you, Kraljevitch Marko! What work do you want done?' 'I have come to you to make me a sword weighing twelve hundredweight, and to make it stronger than your anvil, because, if it cuts through your anvil, you will receive payment; if not, you will get nothing. Have you understood me?' 'Yes.' 'Then make it.' Then up came the thirty smiths, worked at the sword, and worked until they had finished forging it. Marko came: 'Well, smith, is the sword ready?' 'It is, Marko.' 'Show it me that I may see it.' Marko took it, struck, cut through the anvil, and cut right into the block. 'Well, smith, you've made it well. Now that you've made me a sword, make me also a sheath for the sword, and also a club, that is, a mace, weighing twelve hundredweight, then I will pay you all at once. But when I throw the mace, it must not break; if it breaks, then you get no payment.' He made him a mace also, but did not make it well. When Marko threw it, he let it fall upon himself, and the mace broke. Then said Marko: 'You have made me the sword well, but not the mace. Reach out your hand that I may pay you for the sword.' The smith reached out his hand, and Marko cut it off with the sword, saying: 'There's your payment, smith, for the sword, that you may no more make such swords for any hero.' Then he went to a third smith, with whom thirty-eight smiths were at work, and said: 'God help you, smith!' 'God requite you, Marko! why have you come to me?' 'I have come to you to make me a club, that is, a mace, weighing twelve hundredweight; I tell you the truth, if I throw it up on high, and it breaks when it falls, you get no payment.' All thirty-eight smiths worked till they forged it. Marko came: 'Well, is the mace ready?' 'It is, Marko.' 'Show it, that I may see it.' When he gave it him, he threw it so high into the air that it was three days and three nights in the sky. When it came down, Marko presented his back; it fell upon him, and cast him to the ground, and blood flowed from his nose and teeth, but the mace remained sound. But Marko sprang up quickly, and said to the smith: 'Ah! dear smith! you've made it well for me; reach out your hand that I may pay you.' He reached out his hand to him, and he cut his hand off with his sword. 'Let this be your payment, smith, that you may no more make such staves for any hero.'

Then he went off to his mother and said to her: 'Mother, you see in me a hero; if you revile me, I shall go about the world.' Then his mother began to scold him: 'Why are you like this? Why don't you live like other people? You have oxen; go, then, on to the green hill and plough the fallows and pastures, and thereby support your old mother.' Marko obeyed her, took the oxen, and went. But he didn't go on to the green hill, to plough the fallows and pastures, but he went and ploughed the emperor's highroads. When the Turks saw this, they went to Marko—three hundred Turks, all chosen warriors—and said to him: 'Why, Marko, do you plough the emperor's highroads? you have the fallows and pastures!' Then at him, to cut him down. When Marko saw this, he hadn't with him either his sword or his mace, so seized his plough and felled all three hundred Turks. Then said he: 'Ah! gracious God! a wondrous hero!' Then he took the Turks' gold from them, left his plough, unyoked the oxen, and turned them loose on the green hill: 'Go, little oxen, on to the green hill, and feed and graze from pine to pine, like the cuckoo; Marko has not managed to plough with you, and now never will he more.' And home he went singing: 'Here, mother, you have gold enough, live upon it, and I will go into the world, that your eye may see me no more.'

He took his mace and sword, went and came to an inn, where some Turks were drinking red wine and conversing. 'We should be glad to make the acquaintance of Kraljevitch Marko and see him. We have heard that he is a celebrated hero. His brother Andro is in Stambol here. He is a hero, but they say that *he* is a still greater hero.' 'In whose service is Andro Kraljevitch?' 'In that of a pasha; he will soon come riding past here.' 'Good; I will wait for him.' Up came Andro Kraljevitch, riding with the pasha. Marko called out to him: 'Eh, adopted brother, Kraljevitch Andro!' 'Thanks, unknown hero, perhaps you are Kraljevitch Marko?' 'Quite true, I am Kraljevitch Marko.' 'Good; let us go into the inn to drink a cup of wine, that love and the fortune of heroes may thus unite us. Now we are not afraid of going into combat against any empire.' So they went on the way to an inn. Kraljevitch Marko said: 'Prithee, sing me a song, Andro.' 'Dear brother, I dare not. The Vila of the cloud would shoot me.' 'Don't be afraid; I am here.' Andro obeyed, and sang so that all the branches began to fall. All at once a spear flew against Andro and struck him down. Marko looked about to see whence it came, and espied a Vila in the cloud; he seized his mace and threw it at the Vila, so that it at once struck her to the ground. The Vila began to shriek: 'Let me go, Marko! I will bring Andro back to life, and will give you a wondrous horse, so that you will be able to fly in the air.' Marko agreed, and she took certain grasses, and brought Andro back to life. Marko obtained the wondrous horse, and both rode off to an inn and drank red wine. But in the inn there was a wicked harlot. She became enamoured of Andro, but he would not even look at her. She therefore put sweet honey into his wine, that he might drink the wine. Marko went out for a short time, and the wicked woman murdered Andro. But when Marko came in he seized the wicked woman, and spitted her on his sword: 'Take that, wretch, for murdering my brother Andro.'

He went on into the world. He roamed hither and thither, and when he met with any hero, he tried the fortune of combat with him, as in his encounter with black Arapin. Arapin built a tower beside the level sea. When he had built it handsomely and raised it high, he said thus to it: 'Handsomely, my tower, handsomely have I built thee, and high have I raised thee, for I have no father nor mother, no brother nor sister, nor even my beloved, to walk about in thee. But I have a love, the daughter of the emperor Soliman. I will write him the leaf of a white book, and send up to him by a black Tatar; for if he will not give her to me, let him meet me in single combat.' He wrote the leaf of a white book and sent it by a black Tatar. When Soliman read over the leaf of the white book, he shed tears abundantly, and his empress Solimanitza came to him and questioned him: 'Why do you weep, emperor Soliman? Ofttimes have letters come for you, and you have not shed abundant tears; what distress is tormenting you?' He told her this, that black Arapin had written to him, that, if he did not give him his daughter, he must meet him in single combat; and how could he meet him in single combat? She advised him to write the leaf of a white book to Kraljevitch Marko to come, promising to give him three loads of money. He wrote the leaf of a white book and sent it by a black Tatar. When Kraljevitch Marko read over the leaf of the book, he began to laugh greatly: 'Yes, i' faith, emperor Soliman! what will your money do for me, if black Arapin severs my head from my shoulders?' And he said not whether he would go or not go. The emperor Soliman was anxiously expecting the Tatar, who brought to him the words, that Marko neither said that he would come, nor that he would not come. Thereupon the emperor was sorrowful, for he had no such man who would deliver his daughter. There arrived a second letter from black Arapin, that he must give him his daughter; if he did not give her, he must meet him in single combat. As he read it, he shed abundant tears. Thereupon his only daughter came to him and asked him: 'Why do you weep, emperor Soliman? Letters have ofttimes arrived for you, and you have not shed abundant tears.' He replied to her: 'Dear daughter! You see that black Arapin writes to me, that, if I do not give you to him, I must meet him in single combat; and how shall I, poor man that I am, meet him?' 'You know, dear father, that there is one hero, Kraljevitch Marko. Write to him, that you will give him nine loads of money, if he will come and meet him in single combat.' The emperor Soliman wrote to Kraljevitch Marko the leaf of a white book, and sent it to him by a black Tatar. When he read over the leaf of the white book he laughed greatly:

'I' faith, emperor Soliman! what will your money be to me, if black Arapin severs my head from my shoulders?' Thereupon he did not say whether he would come or not come. Sorrowful thereat, the emperor did not know what to do. Then came a third letter from black Arapin, that he was coming, and that he must prepare, would he, nould he, to give him his daughter, and that all inns and shops must be shut for fear of him. Thereupon the emperor Soliman shed abundant tears as he read it. His daughter came to him: 'Why do you weep, emperor Soliman? Letters have ofttimes arrived for you, and you have not shed abundant tears. What distress is assailing you?' 'You see, dear daughter, that black Arapin writes to me, that if I don't give you to him, I must meet him in single combat! But how shall I, poor man, meet him?' 'Write, dear father, to Kraljevitch Marko to come, and offer him twelve loads of money, and a shirt which is neither spun nor woven nor bleached, but made of nothing but pure gold, and a serpent that holds a tray in its mouth, and on the tray a golden casket, and in the casket a precious stone, by aid of which you can sup at midnight just as well as at mid-day.' He wrote the leaf of a white book and sent it to Kraljevitch Marko by a black Tatar, and offered him all that his daughter told him. When Marko read the leaf of the white book, he laughed greatly, and said: 'I' faith, emperor Soliman! what will your money do for me, if black Arapin severs my head from my shoulders?' And then, too, he did not say that he would come or not come. Thereupon came the leaf of a white book from black Arapin, that Arapin had now got ready three hundred heroes, all in silver armour, and all chosen warriors. Then said Kraljevitch Marko to his piebald horse: 'Eh! piebald horse, my pearl! you know well that you must be faithful to me, for, if not, I shall cut off your feet at the knees, and that you must bear yourself valiantly.' And the piebald horse replied that he must saddle and mount with speed to go soon, and that black Arapin was already near. Marko saddled and mounted him, and went to the city where the emperor Soliman reigned.

Now, when he had ascertained by which road Arapin's men were coming, he presented himself to a young innkeeper, and said, knocking at the door: 'Open, and bring some wine.' But he excused himself, saying that he dared not draw any, for all inns and shops were obliged to be shut for fear of black Arapin. But the hero said to him: 'You must bring some for me, or I shall cleave your head to the shoulders.' The innkeeper saw that it could not be otherwise, and was obliged to bring him a cup of wine. Marko drank half, and gave half to his piebald horse. Then he brought two cups, one for Marko, and one for the horse. Meanwhile, Marko went into the garden to look about him. When he got there, he saw by the side of a brook a damsel in sorrow, and wondered what ailed her that she wept so piteously, saying: 'Ah! my rivulet! I would rather abide in you, than lie behind black Arapin's back.' When Marko saw that it was Soliman's daughter, he said: 'What ails you, damsel, that you weep so piteously?' She replied to him: 'Go hence, unknown hero! As to what you ask me, you cannot aid me.' 'Now, only tell me; maybe I shall aid you.' 'Black Arapin will come, and will take me away from my father and mother; but I had a man, who could have set me free, but he will not. I offered him twelve loads of money, and a shirt, which is neither spun nor bleached, but is made of pure gold; and a serpent, that holds in its mouth a tray, and on the tray a golden casket, and in the casket a precious stone, by aid of which he could sup at midnight, as well as at mid-day; but he won't. The sun has not seen him, neither has the moon thrown its light upon him, nor has he seen his mother more, nor has a bird sung to him.' Marko answered her: 'Don't chatter, don't chatter; but go and say that I have arrived. I am Marko; and let him dress and furnish you handsomely, and give you all that is requisite for Arapin, and all that he shall desire.' Then she ran to her father, and told him all that Marko said. Meanwhile, while Marko was conversing with the damsel, Arapin arrived, saw an inn open, and a horse in front of it standing tethered at the entrance. He said: 'Who is this, that is not afraid of my terror?' And thereupon he said that he would soon teach him to be afraid of him. After this, he shouted an order to the bedelija; the bedelija (such is the [Turkish] name for a horse) would not stir. 'Well, I'll go thither; I won't make quarrels; maybe I shall obtain possession of the damsel without any disturbance.' And, in fact, thither he went, obtained possession of the damsel, and all that he needed was given him. Then he went again to the inn, and saw the horse again standing there. Again he was about to go to the innkeeper to slay him; but he shouted to the horse, the horse wouldn't stir. Said Arapin: 'Well, I won't make quarrels, now that I have obtained the damsel without any quarrel.' When Arapin proceeded on his way, Marko came out of the garden, and his piebald horse said to him: 'Where have you been so long, that Arapin might easily have killed me?' 'Now don't fear, my piebald; we shall soon kill him, please God, not he you.' Then he called for one more cup of wine for himself, and one for his piebald. When they had finished drinking, they started on their way, and in pursuit of Arapin. Arapin had already told his chief officer to look round to see whether any dark fog came out behind them. He looked round, but saw nothing. But when he afterwards looked round a second time, he espied a dark fog, and said to Arapin: 'Yes, my lord, a dark foul fog is coming behind us.' Scarcely had he said this, when Marko attacked, and began to slaughter, his rearguard. Arapin said to him: 'Don't be silly, Marko; why are you playing the fool with us? I don't know whether you are jesting, or playing the fool.' 'I am neither jesting nor playing the fool, but am in earnest.' 'Do, then, what you can; throw what you have.' 'I won't; but throw you your mace.' Marko's piebald threw himself down, and Arapin's mace went over Marko's head. Then Marko threw his mace, and felled Arapin to the ground, and the piebald leapt to Arapin, and said to Marko: 'Come, see that you cut off Arapin's head.' When the piebald leapt, Marko, too, struck with his sword, and cut off Arapin's head, and the piebald quickly leapt backwards thirty paces. Then he left Arapin's carcase on the ground, gave the head to the damsel, and said: 'Kiss him, now that he is dead, though you wouldn't when he was living.' They went home, and the emperor caused a great entertainment to be prepared, and all Marko's friends, and his father and mother, to be invited, and Marko obtained his promised reward.

So, too, he tried the fortune of combat with Musa Urbanusa.* He had three hearts. Marko fought with him for three nights and three white days without cessation, so that red foam already issued from Marko, while not even white foam came from Musa Urbanusa. Then Kraljevitch Marko shouted: 'Eh! sister Vila!' The Vila replied: 'I cannot help you, because the baby has fallen asleep in my arms; but don't you know your secret weapon?' Then said Kraljevitch Marko: 'Look, Musa Urbanusa, whether the sun is now rising or setting.' Musa looked at the sun, and Marko drew his knife, and ripped Musa up. Musa seized hold of him so powerfully that he barely dug his way out from under Musa, whom he had ripped up. There he

* Musa, the Albanian, more properly Arbanasian.

lay, and Marko pushed himself sideways, and when he had extricated himself, went to look what there was in this man that was so strong. He saw that Musa had three hearts, one was beating, the second was beginning to beat a little, and the third did not yet know aught about it. On the third he saw a snake lying, and the snake said to Marko: 'Thank God that I didn't know of it; you wouldn't have done what you have done. But open your mouth, Marko, that I may enter into you, that you, too, may be as strong as he was.' Marko became angry, and cut the snake to pieces, saying: 'I don't need such a foul creature as you are.'

Then he proceeded on his way, and went about till fire-arms were invented. He went up to a shepherd, who was shooting birds. Then Marko asked him: 'What's this that you are doing?' 'Eh! you see, I'm shooting birds; and I could shoot you, also.' 'And how would you kill me with this thing? Heroes have not killed me; could you do so?' Then he reached his hand to him, and said: 'Shoot into my hand here.' He shot, and shot through his hand. Then said Marko: 'It is not worth my while to live any longer in the world; now any cuckoo could slay me; I had rather quit it.' He went into a cavern, and lives there still at the present day. Into this cavern a man was compelled to go, who was let down by a rope in a chest. When he arrived within, the Vila immediately stepped up to him, and said: 'Christian soul, why come you here?' He told her why and how. But Marko heard that somebody was conversing, and immediately asked the Vila who it was that had come in. She told him that a soul from that world had come to see what was in the cavern. Marko immediately said that he must come to him, that he might see how strong people in the world still were, and he must give him his hand. But she gave him a red-hot iron, and Marko took it, and squeezed it in his hands so that water spirted out of it, and said: 'Ah, ah! I could still live in the world if no one would talk about me for three days.' He also commissioned him to tell the lords that he should come there. He gave him a letter, too, and sealed it with his own hand, and allowed him to go up. He shook the rope, and got into the chest. Then they pulled him up, and he gave the letter to the lords; but, for fear of Marko's coming, the lords did not make the letter public for people to know how Marko had gone into the cavern. The footprints of his horse are still recognised.

LIII.—THE DAUGHTER OF THE KING OF THE VILAS.

THERE was a mother, who was expecting. As she once upon a time came out of church from mass, her pains fell upon her. Whither should she go? She concealed herself under a bridge, and became the happy mother of a son. The three Royenitzes also came thither. They are hags, who determine by what death every child is to pass from this world. One said: 'Let us kill him at once.' The second said: 'Not so; but when he grows up, then let us kill him, that his mother's sorrow for him may be greater.' But the third said: 'Let us not do so; but if he does not take the daughter of the king of the Vilas to wife, then let us kill him.' And so it was settled.

When he had grown up, he said to his mother: 'Mamma, I should like to marry.' 'Ah, my son, you say that you would like to marry; but there is no one to be married to you.' He asked her: 'Why not?' She told him: 'Yes; the Suyenitzes have pronounced your fate, that if you do not take the daughter of the king of the Vilas to wife, they will put you to death.' He then said: 'Well, I'll go in search of her; but first I'll go to ask a certain old smith; maybe he'll be able to tell me where she is.' The smith said:

'My son, it will be difficult for you to find out; but go to the mother of the moon; if she can't tell you, I don't know who will be better able to tell you than she.' He also gave him three pairs of iron shoes, and sent him off to the mother of the moon. 'Only, when you come to her, take her by the arm, then she will ask you at once what you want, and tell her without delay.' He went off, and just as he was on the point of wearing out the shoes, he came to the moon's mother, and took her by the arm. She asked him immediately what he wanted. He said: 'I want to find the daughter of the king of the Vilas.' She said: 'Well, my son, I don't know; but maybe my son knows. Wait till he comes home, and then you can ask him. But he mustn't find you; he would tear you to pieces at once. When he comes home, he will notice that you are here. I will conceal you, and when he asks for the third time where the Christian soul is, then say to him: "Here I am!" and he won't be able to do anything to you.' The old woman hid him under a trough. The moon came home, and asked: 'Mamma, you have a Christian soul here.' And when he asked for the third time where the Christian soul was, he announced himself: 'Here I am.' And then he could do nothing to him, otherwise he would have crushed him to powder. He asked him what he wanted. He said: 'I want to find the daughter of the king of the Vilas.' The moon: 'I don't know, but if the sun's mother doesn't know, I don't know who else does.' And he showed him the way by which he must go.

He put on the second pair of shoes, and when he was just on the point of wearing them out, he came to the sun's mother, and took her by the arm. She said to him at once: 'What do you want?' He said to her that, if she knew where the Vilas' castles were, he wanted to obtain the daughter of the king of the Vilas. She then said to him: 'Ah, my son, I don't know; but if my son doesn't know, I don't know who else does. Wait a little till he comes home.' She, too, concealed him under a trough, and he announced himself the third time that the sun asked: 'Mother, you have a Christian soul here:' saying, 'Here I am.' Neither could the sun do anything to him, but asked him what he wanted. He replied that he was in search of the Vilas' castles, and the daughter of the king of the Vilas. Then the sun said to him: 'Ah, I don't know; but if the storm-mare (that is, the storm or wind) doesn't know, then I don't know who will know.' Then he showed him the road, and said: 'When you come to a meadow where the grass is up to your knees, there the storm-mare is. If you don't find her there, wait for her; she will come to feed. Don't go directly to her, but hide behind a tree or in a hole, and when she comes, take her at once by the bridle, otherwise it will not be good for you.'

He went off, and put on the third pair of shoes, then went and went, and arrived at the meadow. When he got there, the storm-mare was not there till dawn. He hid himself under a bridge, and when she came to the bridge to drink water, he seized her by the bridle, and she asked him what he wanted. He replied that he wanted to find the daughter of the king of the Vilas. She answered him: 'Mount on my back.' He mounted, and she then said to him: 'But you mustn't fall off.' She reared; he almost fell off, but kept himself on with his foot. She reared a second time, and then, too, he almost fell off. A third time she reared, and then, too, he almost fell off, only he kept himself on with his knee. Then she said to him: 'This will be harmful to me.' She went off with him like a bird, and sped and sped up to two steps. When she came near them, the steps split in twain from the gust, but speedily closed again, and tore off a piece of the mare's tail. Then the mare said to him: 'You see how you harmed me when you almost fell off.' Then they went on till they arrived at the Vilas' castles. Then she said: 'Don't get drunk or forget, so as not to come to me.' He said that he would come, and went off upwards. They received and entertained him, and he asked them at once to give him the king's daughter. They promised that they would give her to him. Then they feasted, and ate and drank till darkness came on. And when evening arrived, he said that he must go out on his own account, and would return directly. He went off to the storm-mare. They had brought her a hundred quintals of hay. He concealed himself in the mare's tail. They sought him, and couldn't find him; but nevertheless they almost found him at dawn; but a cock began to crow, and then they could do nothing to him. Afterwards he went indoors, and they gave him again to eat and drink, and asked him where he had been. He replied: 'I slept under a hedge; I fell down, and soon fell asleep on the spot.' They gave the mare a hundred quintals of hay and several measures of oats. They enjoyed themselves the whole day till evening. He went out again and hid himself in the mare's mane. They sought him all night long, but couldn't find him; but at dawn an old witch told them that he was in the mane. They would almost have found him there, but the cocks began to crow, and they couldn't kill him now. But afterwards they killed all the cocks in the whole village. He went again into the castle. They gave him what he wanted to eat and drink, and the mare, as usual, a hundred quintals of hay and several measures of oats, and said to him: 'You must not go out anywhere in the evening; we will prepare everything for you that you require.' When evening came, they were on friendly terms with him, but nevertheless dispersed. He went out, and went to the mare. Where did she bestow him? She hid him under her foot in her shoe, for she had a large foot. They went to seek him again. But during the day he took two eggs, and the mare hatched them by evening in her throat, and they had almost grown up by evening. When they sought him again, they couldn't find him. At dawn they consulted the old witch. She told them that he was under the mare's hoof. They wanted now to take him out, but the cockerels which the mare had hatched in her throat began to crow. They could do nothing to him, but they wrung the two cockerels' necks. Now he said that they must give him the king's daughter, that he might depart. But the king said that he wouldn't give her to him, because he had not slept where he had prepared a bed for him. He declared that he had been drunk and had gone out, had fallen down, and gone to sleep on the spot. But the king would not believe him. Now he begged him to bring his daughter to him, that he might at any rate give her a kiss. But beforehand the mare instructed him that, when she came to kiss him, he was to seize her and pull her on to her (the mare), and they would escape with her. And he was also to take a brush with which horses are cleaned, a comb with which horses are combed, and a glass of water, and make good preparations for himself. But when the king granted his request that his daughter should come for him to kiss her, she stood on his foot in the stirrup, and as she stood to give the kiss, off started the mare, and made her way through the gate, and on and on she went. The king saw this, called for his horse, and after them. They were already far on their way. All of a sudden the mare said: 'Look round to see whether anyone is coming behind us.' He looked round and said: 'There is; he is all but catching you by the tail.' The mare said: 'Throw the brush!' He threw the brush, and a forest placed itself behind them, so that he could scarcely make his way through; the poor king could scarcely get through for thorn bushes. And they had meanwhile got a long way forward. The king, however, forced his way through, and again after them with speed, till he was again on the point of catching them. Then the mare said: 'Look round to see whether anyone is coming behind us.' He looked round and saw that he was already near, and the mare was all but caught by the tail, and said: 'He is near, and you are all but caught by the tail.' The mare said: 'Throw the comb.' He threw it, and a great chain of mountains, one after the other, placed itself there; and on they went further, so that they had already gone a great space, and the king with difficulty made his way over the mountains, and again after them, so that he was again on the point of overtaking them. The mare told him to look round to see whether anyone was coming behind them. He said that there was, and that she was all but caught by the tail. The mare said: 'Throw the glass with water.' He threw it, and a great flood of water arose, so that the king could with difficulty get across. And they had already got a long way on. No sooner had the king got out of the water, when on he went with speed, with speed, again after them, and was already on the point of overtaking them, when the mare was already near the steps, and the steps opened from the gust of wind, and the mare sped through, and they closed again, and the king couldn't proceed further through the steps, and shouted loudly: 'Son-in-law, don't go any further; I cannot do so. Let not my daughter complain that I have given her nothing.' Then he somehow threw his girdle over the steps, for he had nought else to give her save that girdle. And the girdle was such that whatsoever its owner wanted, he obtained. Then the king returned, and they remained happy. He thanked the storm-mare courteously, and went home with speed, for he bade the girdle place them at his house. They prepared a grand banquet, for they had plenty, and I was at the banquet and feasted.

LIV.—THE WONDER-WORKING LOCK.

THERE was once upon a time a woman who had one son. This son maintained himself and his mother; he fed their one cow, and brought wood and carried it to the town for sale, and with the money bought bread to support his mother and himself. On one occasion he carried sticks to market, and bought bread and went homewards. As he went homewards with the bread, he went through a wood, came up to some shepherds, and saw that they were going to kill a puppy, and said to them: 'Don't kill it; the poor animal has done you no wrong; give it rather to me.' The shepherds said to him: 'What will you give us? Give us that loaf.' He gave them the loaf, took the dog, and carried it home. When he got home, his mother asked him: 'Have you brought any bread?' 'No, but I have bought a puppy with the bread.' She then said: 'Wherewith shall we support it, when we've nothing to eat ourselves?' 'Well, I'll go gather sticks, sell them, and buy bread.' He went a second time to gather sticks, took them and sold them, then bought bread, went through the wood, and saw where the shepherds were killing a kitten, and said to them: 'Don't kill the animal; it has done you no harm; rather give it to me?' They said to him: 'What will you give us?' He said: 'What should I give you, when I've got nothing?' The shepherds said: 'That loaf of bread.' He gave it them and carried the kitten home. The old woman was again anxiously expecting bread. When he got home his mother said to him: 'Do you bring me any bread?' 'No, but I've bought a kitten with the bread.' The old woman then said: 'You've nothing to eat yourself, much less the cat.' He then said: 'It, too, will be serviceable. I'll go gather sticks, sell them, and buy bread.' He went a third time, gathered and sold sticks, bought bread, and went homewards. Going through the wood, he saw the shepherds killing a snake, and said: 'Don't kill the snake, it has done you no harm; why should you kill it?' He begged for it, too, because he compassionated it; it was beautifully marked, and he fancied it. Then said the shepherds: 'What will you give us not to kill it?' He said: 'This little loaf of bread.' He gave it them, and they gave him the snake. He went home with the snake, and the snake said to him: 'Now feed me; when I grow up you shall carry me home.' When he got home his mother said to him: 'Why haven't you brought some bread? Why have you brought this?' He said: 'It, too, will be of service.' Then he went a fourth time to gather sticks, took them to market, sold them, bought four loaves of bread, and brought them home. Then they all ate their fill—the dog, the cat, the snake, his mother, and himself. He maintained the whole set of animals. The snake grew big; he now carried it home. It said to him: 'Do you hear? my mother will offer you gold and silver, but don't take any, but let her give you the lock which hangs behind the door. Whenever you want anything whatever, only knock on the lock; twelve young men will come, who will ask you: "What are your commands?" Only say what you wish for, and you will have it immediately.' When he carried it home, its parents asked him what he wanted for bringing their daughter home. He said according to his instructions: 'Nothing but that lock, which hangs behind the door.' They said to him: 'We can't give you that; and what good would you do yourself with the lock? Let us rather give you a quantity of money, as much as you can carry.' He then said: 'I don't wish for your money; only give me the lock.' When they long refused to give it him, he was about to depart. But they saw that he ought not to go away without payment, so gave him the lock. Now, when he had obtained the lock, and had gone a little distance from the house, he knocked on the lock, and immediately out came twelve young men, who asked him: 'What are your commands?' 'Only that you place me at home at once.' He immediately stood in front of his cottage, and when his mother saw him, she rejoiced: 'Oh, my son! you have come home; how miserable I have been because you were not at home!' 'Well, mamma, don't talk! we shall now live better than we have done hitherto; I have brought you such a thing, that we shall live with ease.' Then he gently knocked on the lock, and up darted the twelve young men: 'What are your commands?' 'Food and drink for me, my mother, the dog and the cat.' And so it was. This pleased the old woman, and she loved her son still more.

Now it came into his head that he should like to get married, and he said to his mother: 'Mamma, go you to our king, and ask him to give me his daughter to wife.' His mother jeered him: 'What is this nonsense that you are talking?' 'Well, go you to the king and tell him!' The old woman did not venture to go at once; but at last go she did, and told the king that her son wished to marry his daughter. The king said to her: 'Good! provided he performs for me what I shall command him; if he breaks up these hills by to-morrow morning, as far as my eyes can see, so that the best wheat shall grow, and I shall eat a cake from it to-morrow, then it is good; if that shall not be done, he will lose his head.' She went home weeping: 'My son, you have done an evil thing; the king has said to you, you must break up all these hills by to-morrow morning, as far as the king's eyes can see, so that the best wheat shall grow there, and the king shall eat a cake from it to-morrow; and if that be not done, you will lose your head.' 'Well, mamma, if that's all he said, then she will be mine.' 'Ah! my sonny! how can this be? You cannot do it.' 'Don't talk, mamma, but let us go to sleep; you will see whether all will be ready to-morrow or no.' They took their supper, and his mother went off to sleep. Then he knocked on the lock, and out sprang the twelve young men. 'What are your commands?' 'I ask that these hills be broken up, as far as the king's eyes can see, and the best wheat must grow there.' It was done. In the morning the old woman went to the king with the cake. The king rose up and saw that it was really accomplished, and the old woman was waiting with the cake. The king came out, and she said to him: 'Good-morning; I have brought it.' Then the king said: 'Good! he has done this; now tell him that by to-morrow he must clear all the woods, as far as he can see, and the best vineyards must be there, and he' (the king) 'must eat grapes and drink new wine to-morrow; and if he does not do this, he will lose his head.' She went again weeping home, and told her son all that the king had said to her. But he only smiled and said: 'Well, well, only go to sleep, you will see whether all will be ready to-morrow or no.' When they had supped, the old woman went off to sleep, and he knocked on the lock, and the twelve young men sprang out: 'What are your commands?' 'I command that these woods be all cleared, and that they produce the best grapes.' This, too, was done. In the morning the king rose up and saw that the change was really effected. The old woman, too, was really waiting for him with grapes and new wine. The king said to her: 'Well, good! tell your son that he must accomplish one thing more, and then he will win my daughter. If he shall have as much cattle, and such a castle as I have, he will win my daughter; if not, he will lose his head.' The old woman went home again, and told him what the king said. Then he knocked on the lock, and immediately out sprang the twelve young men: 'What are your commands?' He ordered that by the morrow a better castle must be built than the king had ever seen, and that he must have more cattle than the king, and there must be a covered way from his castle to the king's, and that a better garden must be formed, and in it all kinds of trees, and all sorts of birds to sing in it. This, too, came to pass. On the morrow he caused his six best horses to be harnessed, and went to fetch the king's daughter, to go to the wedding. Then the king said that there should be wedding festivities for five years. They were married, and the wedding festivities took place. Entrance was free to everyone. The festivities had already lasted three years, when the king's resources were exhausted. Then said the young man: 'Now I will entertain for three years.' The king of the sea came, too, to the festivities, and fancied the king's daughter, whom the other had married. Once upon a time he saw how he knocked upon the lock, and that which he wanted immediately presented itself. When they went to sleep, the king of the sea stole the lock, and knocked upon it; up sprang the twelve young men: 'What are your commands?' 'That this castle and this lady be placed on the black sea.' It was done. In the morning the young man and his mother were terrified out of their wits, because they were lying in a simple cottage. But he knew at once that he had lost the lock. Then he went to the king and prayed him to take charge of his mother, that he might go to look for his castle. Well, he went to look for it, with his dog and cat. He approached that sea, saw his castle, and said: 'Cat and dog, do you see our castle? But how shall we get into it?' They went to the sea and sat down. He was weary, and fell asleep as he sat. Then said the dog and the cat: 'Let us go for the lock.' The dog said: 'You can't swim; sit on my back; I will carry you.' They went and came up to the wall. Then said the dog: 'I can't climb up a wall.' The cat said to him:

'You hang on somehow behind me.' And thus they arrived at the corridor. Now said the cat: 'You, dog, stay outside; I'll go in by myself.' The king of the sea had just such a cat. The cat went to the door and mewed: 'Miau.' Then said the king of the sea: 'Let the cat in.' Then the cat went in and took the lock so neatly that the king of the sea didn't see it; he then went to the door and mewed: 'Miau.' Then said the king of the sea: 'Let the cat out.' The cat went out, and the dog asked it: 'Have you got it?' 'I have; only go.' They went over the wall and into the sea; and when they were already not far from their master, the dog wanted to have hold of the lock, to carry it up to his master, and said to the cat: 'Give me the lock; if you don't, I will throw you into the sea.' Then they squabbled, and the lock fell into the sea, and a fish swallowed it; but the cat seized the fish, and said: 'If you don't give up the lock I will kill you.' The fish said: 'Don't kill me; I'll give you the lock,' and immediately brought the lock up. They went to their master, and carried up the lock. When their master awoke and rose up, he said: 'In what condition have you come?' They said: 'Our master, we have brought the lock.' 'Where is it?' 'Here.' Then he took it and knocked upon it, and out sprang the twelve young men: 'What are your commands?' 'I command that my castle be placed where it was, as well as that king and my wife.' It was done. Then he went into the castle, and she immediately ran to him and they kissed each other. But he caused the king of the sea to be impaled on a spit in the midst of the sea. Thus he obtained his castle back again, and lived happily with his wife, but the king of the sea was destroyed.

LV.—THE SHE-WOLF.

THERE was an enchanted mill, so that no one could stay there, because a she-wolf always haunted it. A soldier went once into the mill to sleep. He made a fire in the parlour, went up into the garret above, bored a hole with an auger in the floor, and peeped down into the parlour. A she-wolf came in and looked about the mill to see whether she could find anything to eat. She found nothing, and then went to the fire, and said: 'Skin down! skin down! skin down!' She raised herself upon her hind-legs, and her skin fell down. She took the skin, and hung it on a peg, and out of the wolf came a damsel. The damsel went to the fire, and fell asleep there. He came down from the garret, took the skin, nailed it fast to the mill-wheel, then came into the mill, shouted over her, and said: 'Good-morning, damsel! how do you do?' She began to scream: 'Skin on me! skin on me! skin on me!' But the skin could not come down, for it was fast nailed. The pair married, and had two children. As soon as the elder son got to know that his mother was a wolf, he said to her: 'Mamma! mamma! I have heard that you are a wolf.' His mother replied: 'What nonsense you are talking! How can you say that I am a wolf?' The father of the two children went one day into the field to plough, and his son said: 'Papa, let me, too, go with you.' His father said: 'Come.' When they had come to the field, the son asked his father: 'Papa, is it true that our mother is a wolf?' His father said: 'It is.' The son inquired: 'And where is her skin?' His father said: 'There it is, on the mill-wheel.' No sooner had the son got home, than he said at once to his mother: 'Mamma! mamma! you are a wolf! I know where your skin is.' His mother asked him: 'Where is my skin?' He said: 'There, on the mill-wheel.' His mother said to him: 'Thank you, sonny, for rescuing me.' Then she went away, and was never heard of more.

LVI.—MILUTIN.

A CERTAIN man had two children—one a boy, and the other a girl. This man required his children to relate to him every morning what they had dreamed. Indeed, the girl related her dream, whatever she had dreamed, every morning, but the boy did not, for he dreamed every night what eventually happened to him; he dreamed that he killed a king, took to wife a count's daughter, and became king in the kingdom in which he killed the king. Exasperated at this, his father thought the reason why he did not tell his dream was because he was afraid, and drove him out along a road, and beat him so that he cried piteously. A count was driving past, and heard the child crying. He ordered his servant to go to the man, and tell him not to beat the child, but say how much he should give him to take it away himself. The man said, in reply, that he need only take it away from before his eyes. He immediately took it, and delivered it to the count, and the count took it away home. The count had one daughter, who took a great affection for the boy. It was also a custom with the count that the children were obliged to relate what they dreamed. But he would not reveal his dream to the count, and say what he had dreamed; and he had dreamed the very same dream that he had dreamed at his father's. Then the count became very angry, and caused a vault to be built in his garden, inside which he was to be thrown, and it was to be constructed of such masonry that nobody should be able to give him anything to eat, and that no light should by possibility enter it. But the count's daughter, who was very sorry for the boy, went out to the masons, and promised them a purse of money, only to construct it in such a manner that she would be able to give him food at night. This the masons did, in return for the good money. He was seven years inside, and unable to sit or lie.

Now came a time when king sent a staff to the count, and said he would attack him with an army, if he did not tell him on which side the staff opened. Now the damsel came at night, and brought the lad food, saying: 'Now, I have brought you food for the last time, because a king has sent us a staff, and my father must open it; if he does not open it, he will attack us with an army. We must perish under the open sky, but you in this vault.' He replied that she was not to frighten herself, 'but go, lie down, and soon jump up and say to your father: "My dear papa, I have dreamt of good luck for us." He will say: "What?" Reply to him: "I dreamt that I should tell you that, if you will open the staff, you need only fill a tub with water, and put the staff in it; the staff will turn with that side up on which it opens."' Even so it came to pass. Her father did so, sealed up the staff on that side, and sent it to the king. The king wrote back to him: 'You have certainly done it, but not with your own stupid head. But you have one hard by your house, of whom you know not; he has done this for you.' Then he wrote a letter again to the count, and said: 'I shall send you three horses all alike, and you must tell me how many years old each is.' And all alike they were. One was one year old, the second two, and the third three years old. Then the damsel took him food, and said to him: 'Now I am bringing you food for the last time; you will have to die here, and we in the open air, for the king has sent us three horses exactly alike, and we must tell him how old each is.' He replied that she must go and lie down, and say that she had dreamt thus: that he must prepare three heaps of oats of three different years, and let the horses go to the oats, and they would go of themselves each to his own heap; the one which was one year old would go to the one-year-old oats, the second to the second, and the third to the third heap. She told him this. And it came to pass just as she told him. Then he wrote in reply to the king, and the king to him: 'Certainly, you have done this, but not with your own stupid head; but you have another who does it for you, of whom you are not aware. But I shall send you one thing more. I shall send you, on a given day, at the hour when you will be at dinner, a war-mace, weighing three hundredweight; it will strike the spoon out of your mouth. You must throw it back to me just as I threw it to you.' Indeed, this, too, came to pass. The mace flew in, knocked his spoon out of his hands, and flew off with speed into the cellar, inside which it stuck so fast that a score of soldiers couldn't move, much less throw, it. Now the count assembled, and invited all people, but no one was able to do it. She took him food again, and said to him: 'You have set us free twice, but certainly the third time you will not be able to do so, and now you will die here, and all of us in the open air.' He then asked her what sort of work it was that had to be done. She told him, and he answered: 'Go home and lie down, then get up and say that you have dreamt that no one else but I can do it, so I tell you; but the count will not believe you, yet will think, since you have twice dreamed with success, that possibly now, too, it may be true.' And so it came to pass. The count caused him to be dug out. He saw how weak he was, and said: 'I am stronger than he, but I can't throw it; how, then, can he throw it?' He then said: 'Go to a certain king; he has nine hundred cows, and has them all registered when each was calved. Buy for me one cow, which is neither more nor less than nine years old, and whatever he says you are to pay for it, pay. If you pay one kreutzer less, I shall be two hundredweight lighter.' Well, he went thither, and inquired whether he had such a cow. The king answered that he had. Then he asked the price. The king replied: 'Nine thousand pieces of silver.' He paid them, drove it home, and had it slaughtered immediately. The young man then said that he must be three months by himself in a house, without anybody being allowed to go in to him. Now he took at once two pounds of beef, but did not eat the flesh, but only the soup. This lasted for three months. Well, the cook told the count that he would not eat the flesh, in order to serve his own interests. Then the count went himself to him, and asked him why he would not eat the flesh. He replied that something must be brought him to eat. Now he took a piece, threw it upon the wall, and said to the count: 'You see the flesh has fallen down, and the soup has stuck to the wall; and so it is with me: the soup abides with me, and the flesh goes down from me.' Then he went out to look at the mace. He was already able to move it. Then he went in for three months to eat. Then he was able, with his left hand, to throw it two hundred fathoms high into the air. He went in once more to eat for three months. Now he was exceedingly strong, and told the count to write freely to the king, that on such and such a day, at such and such an hour, the mace would arrive, and knock the spoon out of his mouth at dinner. In fact, so it was. He threw it a hundred and twenty-five hours walk into the other kingdom. Now the king saw that he had done this also. Then he wrote to him: 'Certainly you have done all that I told you, but not with your own stupid head, but he has done it for you, whom you caused to be walled up in a vault. But you must send him here to me, that I may see him.' But he wanted to slay him. Now, the count was unwilling to let him go, but, nevertheless, he was obliged to do so. 'But do you know what, count? Cause all your people to be summoned hither, and we will select as many as ever we can that resemble me.' There were only nine such, and he was himself the tenth. Now he told him to have exactly similar uniforms made for them all, so that, at any rate, no one would know one to be different from another, and to provide similar horses for all, and then he would go thither. Even so it came to pass. Then the ten went. But before they arrived at the town, he said to them: 'Indeed, you don't know why we are going thither; we are going to be put to death; but I tell you not to be in any wise afraid. This king will give you the word of command when we enter: "Milutin (such was the boy's name), dismount!" Then you must all dismount so that no one is behindhand, but all alike, and at once. Then he will say: "Milutin, go into the house!"—all go into the house. "Milutin, shut the door!"—all off to shut it. "Milutin, take your seat at table!"—all do it at once. "Milutin, go to bed!"—all off to bed at once.' Even so it was. Thus the king could in no wise recognise him, and did not venture to slaughter them, but ordered his servant to conceal himself under a bed, and listen which spoke most wisely, and put a mark upon him. Now they all lay down, and began to converse as to what would come out of this. Milutin then said: 'Doubtless, till now he has not recognised me, and will ride after me, and will overtake us; but never mind that, only kneel down and pray to God. Then notice well: if I first emit fire out of my mouth, kill yourselves; but if he emits it first, have no fear whatever; this signifies to you that human flesh will seethe in human blood.' The man under the bed heard this speech, and cut off a piece from the heel of his boot. Morning arrived, and Milutin told them that each must look well at his clothes: maybe there would be some mark on someone's uniform. But all at once he observed that just his boot-heel had been cut off, and said: 'All give me your boots, that I may cut off each of the heels just as I have mine cut off.' Now the king came to summon them: 'Milutin, come to breakfast!' and they all went at once. And the king saw that they all had a similar mark, and, therefore, did not know which to put to death. Then he reprimanded the servant. Now said the king: 'Milutin, go home!' and they all went homeward at once. But erelong the king recognised Milutin by his horse—for he had the horse from the count—and overtook him. They immediately knelt down, as he had previously bidden them, and he began first to fight on horseback, but nothing came of it. Then they both dismounted from their horses, and fought thus, each leaping against the other so that the earth quaked under them. Thus they fought terribly for some time. But all at once they observed that the king emitted fire out of his mouth, and then Milutin afterwards. Then the king spat pure fire out of his mouth at Milutin, and Milutin also spat fire. The two fought on in this frightful manner; but suddenly Milutin overcame the king, threw him down, cut off his head, and carried it home to the count. Now all was merriment, and Milutin married the count's daughter, took possession of the realm of the king whom he had slain, and there was a grand festival. That's the end.

ILLYRIAN-SLOVENISH STORIES.

I AM afraid that our delightful friend Oliver Goldsmith has pre-occupied the British mind with a certain amount of prejudice against the region,

> 'Where the rude Carinthian boor
> On strangers shuts th' inhospitable door.'

But if the said rude and inhospitable person had been addressed in a tongue 'understanded of the people,' his reception of the 'Traveller' might possibly have been very different. Be that as it may, the folk-lore tales of the Styrian and Carinthian Slavonians are full of interest, and in them we certainly find the fullest account of the Vilas, and even a Vila marriage with a human being, which ends in an unfortunate separation, like those in Irish legends between mermaids and men. No. 57 gives us a singular variant of 'Cinderella,' in which the circumstances are different down to the conclusion, which is similar to that of the Bulgarian version, No. 37. No. 58 carries us completely into wonderland, where several old acquaintances will meet us in new dresses and relations. In No. 57 we have a singular legend of a white snake, an animal connected with which there are also superstitions in the Scotch Highlands.

The backwardness of the Slovenes is mainly due to the

ferocity with which Protestantism was stamped out by Ferdinand II., who, as well as his father, Ferdinand I., wrote his name in blood in the annals of Bohemia. (See Morfill's 'Slavonic Literature,' pp. 176, 177.)

As regards the language, the dual is as fully developed as in Lusatian.

LVII.—THE FRIENDSHIP OF A VILA AND OF THE MONTHS.

A WICKED woman married a poor man, who had already a little daughter named Maritza. Afterwards God gave her a daughter of her own, whom she loved and cherished more than her own eyes. On her stepdaughter, who was a good and very handsome child, she could scarcely bear to cast a look; therefore she drove her about, teased and tormented her, in order as soon as possible to make an end of her; she threw her the poorest remnants of food and everything, just as she would have done to a dog. Indeed, she would have given her a snake's tail to eat, if she had had one at hand; and instead of a bed, she sent her to sleep in an old trough.

When her so-called mother saw that the girl, in spite of all this, was good and patient, and grew handsomer than her daughter, she thought and thought how to find a pretext to get rid of the orphan out of the house, and devised one.

One day she sent her daughter and stepdaughter to wash wool; to her own daughter she gave white wool, to her stepdaughter black, and said to her with sharp threats: 'If you don't wash the black wool as white as my daughter will hers, don't come home any more, or else I shall beat you out of the house.' The poor stepdaughter wept piteously, entreated her, and said that it was impossible for her to do this. But all in vain. Seeing that there was no mercy for her, she tied up the wool and went weeping after her half-sister. When they came to the water, they undid their bundles, and began to wash, when a beautiful fair damsel from somewhere joined and saluted them: 'Good luck, friends! do you want any help?' The stepmother's daughter said with a scornful laugh: 'I want no help; my wool will soon be white; but our stepdaughter's yonder will not be so in a hurry.' Thereupon the strange damsel stepped up to the sorrowful Maritza, saying: 'Come! let us see whether that wool will allow itself to be washed white.' Both began immediately to rinse and wash, and in a jiffy the black wool became as white as fresh-fallen snow. When they had finished washing, her fair friend vanished nobody knew whither. The stepmother, seeing the white wool, was amazed and angry, because she had no excuse for driving her stepdaughter away.

Some time after this came sharp cold and snow. The wicked stepmother was continually thinking how best to persecute her unfortunate stepdaughter, and now ordered her: 'Take a basket and go off to the mountain; there gather me ripe strawberries for the new year. If you don't bring me them, it will be better for you to stay on the mountain.' The orphan Maritza wept piteously, entreated her, and said: 'How shall poor I procure ripe strawberries in sharp winter cold?' But all in vain. She was obliged to take the basket and go.

As she was going all in tears over the mountain she met twelve young men, whom she saluted courteously. They received the salutation in a friendly manner, and asked her: 'Whither are you wading, dear girl, in the snow thus in tears?' She told them the whole story prettily. The young men said to her: 'We will help you if you will tell us which month of the whole year is the best?' Maritza said in reply: 'They are all good, but the month of March is the best, for it brings us most hope.' They were pleased with her answer, and said: 'Go into the first glen on the sunny side; there you will get as many strawberries as you wish.' And indeed she brought her stepmother a basketful of most excellent strawberries for the new year, and told her that the young men whom she had met on the mountain had shown them to her.

Some days later, when the weather had become milder, the mother said to her own daughter: 'Go now into the mountain for strawberries; maybe you will find those young men, and they will give you similar good fortune, for they have shown themselves so wonderfully kind to our greasy stepdaughter.' The daughter dressed herself grandly, took the basket, and skipped off merrily on to the mountain. When she got there, she did actually meet the twelve young men, to whom she said haughtily: 'Show me where the strawberry-plants grow, as you showed our stepdaughter.' The young men said: 'Good! provided you guess which month is the best of the whole year.' She answered quickly: 'They are all bad, and the month of March is the worst.' But at that speech the whole mountain clouded over in a jiffy, and a storm beat upon her so that she scarcely panted home alive. The young men were the twelve months.

Meanwhile the goodness and beauty of the ill-used stepdaughter was noised about in the district, and a young, rich and honourable lord arranged with her stepmother to come on such and such a day with his retinue to betroth the stepdaughter to be his wife. The stepmother, jealous of the orphan, did not tell her a single word of this, but thought to thrust her own daughter surreptitiously into this good fortune.

When the appointed evening came the infamous stepmother packed her stepdaughter off in good time to the trough to sleep, then cleared up the house, prepared supper, dressed out her daughter to the best of her ability, and placed her at table with some knitting in her hands. Thereupon up came the betrothal party; the stepmother welcomed them, conducted them into the house, and said to them: 'There is my dear stepdaughter.' But what good was it? For in the house they had a cock, who began with all his might, and without intermission, to crow: 'Kukuriku, pretty Maritza in trough! kukuriku, pretty Maritza in trough!' and so forth. When the betrothal party understood and comprehended the cock's crowing, they insisted that the real stepdaughter must come out of the trough, and when they saw her, they could not sufficiently express their admiration at her beauty and grace, and took her away with them that very evening, and the wicked stepmother and her daughter remained put to shame before all people. Maritza was happy with her husband and with all her house to a great age and an easy death, for a Vila and all the months were her friends.

LVIII.—THE FISHERMAN'S SON.

ONCE upon a time there was a lord on the Danube who had a fisherman to catch fish for him. This lord was preparing a great banquet, and ordered his fisherman to catch three hundredweight of fish in three days. On the first day the fisherman went early in the morning to catch the fish. But he could not obtain any. The second day he went again very early in the morning. He made the round of the water, but again took none. The third day came. The fisherman went to catch fish, and went on till mid-day, but could not net any. In the afternoon he determined to go home by the waterside, and carried himself as if he were very much out of sorts. Suddenly up sailed a striped boat. In the boat sat a gentleman clad in green. He questioned the fisherman saying: 'Man, why are you so sorrowful here by the water?' The fisherman said: 'How should I not be sorrowful? My lord ordered me to catch three hundredweight of fish in three days; to-day is the last day, and I have not obtained any.' Then said the gentleman: 'Promise me that which you don't know that you have, and you shall to-day catch plenty.' The fisherman thought to himself: 'What I don't know that I have, I shall easily do without, if I do promise him.' And the gentleman at the same time added: 'And I will wait twenty years. In twenty years you will be able to fulfil your promise.' 'Agreed,' said the fisherman. He cast his nets and drew them out full of fish. He cast them a second time, and it was just the same. He cast them once more. The gentleman said to him: 'Only send home for them to come with a waggon and four horses.' They came with four horses. They packed the fish in, so that they scarcely drew them with the four horses. But before they went home the gentleman asked the fisherman: 'But do you know what you have promised me?' The fisherman said: 'My lord, I do not. What I don't know that I have, I have promised you, be it what it may.' The gentleman smiled, and said: 'You don't know that your wife will be the mother of a son, and this son you have promised to me. When twenty years have elapsed, you must just bring him here.' Then the fisherman took the fish home. On the one hand he was glad, on the other very downcast. When he brought them home his lord began to grumble, saying: 'You're a thorough fool! Why did a messenger come to me to say that you could not obtain any? Now you have brought me such a quantity that I hardly know where to stow them.' The fisherman excused himself, and related to his lord the whole series of occurrences from beginning to end. Afterwards he put a question to his lord: 'God only knows how it will be now, since I have done such an evil thing, that I have promised him my son.' His lord said: 'What of that? Twenty years is a long time. By then all may be changed.'

It came to pass. The fisherman's wife became the mother of a boy. He grew up right handsome. When he became a little older they sent him to school. At school he learnt so well, that at sixteen he had learnt enough to be ordained a priest. But his father and mother said: 'Not a priest, for he is promised. Let us rather place him for four years more in the black school.' When he had completed the course of the black school, he came back to the Danube, with all before him in the future, as if he were about to succeed, and behind in the past, because he had already been successful. Then said he to his father: 'Father, now it is time for us to go.' The father: 'To go? whither?' The son: 'Whither you promised me.' The father: 'Who promised you any whither?' The son: 'What? don't you know to whom you promised me twenty years ago? Let us go to that piece of water, where you then went to catch fish.' The father became very sorrowful. The son then said: 'Don't be afraid. Only quickly coat over arm and follow me. Only you must do what I instruct you to do. If you obey me, no harm will happen to you and me.' On the way he also instructed his father as follows: 'When we come to that piece of water, the striped boat will sail up just as when you caught the fish. In it will sit the gentleman in green to whom you promised me. The gentleman will push the boat to the shore in shallow water. I shall step on it with one foot, and stand on dry land with the other. Then say: "My son, I commend you to God the Father, and the Son, and the Holy Ghost. May these three always be with you!" When you have uttered these holy words I shall spring into the boat.' Everything happened exactly as the son told his father and instructed him on the way. The striped boat sailed up on the water. In it was the gentleman dressed in green. The son stepped with one foot on the boat, and stood with the other on dry land. His father commended him to God the Father, and the Son, and the Holy Spirit. The son sprang on board the boat, and the gentleman pushed it from the shore. All at once all sank, the boat, the gentleman, and the son. The father was terribly frightened, and cried out at the top of his voice: 'Jesus, Maria! my son has gone down to hell!' He then crept home very sorrowful.

His son passed through the water into a town which is called Perdonkorten.* In this town all the population was enchanted. He walked and walked about the town, but nowhere was there anybody. Hunger took possession of him, but he could get nothing to eat. He bethought himself of going to catch some fish. He went to the water, caught some, lit a fire, cooked them, and ate his fill. He then went into the shade, laid himself down, and fell asleep. He dreamt that he was told to go to pass the night in a lordly castle, to seat himself at table, to light a taper on each side of him, and wait. He did according as he had dreamt. The clock struck midnight, when suddenly the door opened outside of itself. A huge snake glided into the house. It came up opposite the young man, and besought him: 'Kiss me.' He cursed it, and said: 'Take thyself off from me, Satan! Thou hast no power over me.' The snake retired through the door. Thereupon day broke. The young man walked and walked again about the town. He saw here and there carriages ready harnessed, but no human being. In the afternoon he went again to the water to catch fish. When he had eaten his fill, he went into the shade. He lay down, and soon fell asleep. Erelong he dreamt what would have happened, if he had kissed the snake. He woke up, and thought:

* German, 'Wundergarten.'

'This evening I will go back, and will kiss it if it comes. In fact, he went again into the same house, seated himself at table, lit two tapers, and waited. The clock struck twelve. The door opened. Through it glided a very much larger snake, with two heads. It came up the room opposite him, and besought him again: 'Kiss me!' Terror seized him, for it was much more horrible than the one he had seen the preceding night. Therefore he cursed it again: 'Take thyself off from me, Satan! Thou hast no power over me.' The snake again quitted the house. Afterwards day broke. He went again into the town, caught fish, and ate his fill. When he had eaten, he went into the shade, lay down, and fell asleep. Ere long he dreamt again: 'Thou wouldst, nevertheless, have only done rightly if thou hadst kissed the snake.' He woke up, and said: 'This evening I will kiss it, even if it appears still more terrible.' In the evening he went into the same house. He seated himself at table, lit two tapers, and waited. When the tower clock struck twelve, the door opened. A terrible snake glided in. It had three heads, and was still larger than the one he saw the preceding evening. It came puffing opposite him. It began to twine round him, and beseech him: 'Kiss me!' He pressed his lips to it, and kissed it.

As soon as he had kissed it, the snake turned into a beautiful maiden, as beautiful as a damsel could be. The snake was the enchanted daughter of the lord of the castle. After the kiss, all belonging to the castle, and the whole town, were disenchanted. Erelong the father and mother of the disenchanted daughter came into the room. They welcomed him with the greatest joy. The father said to him: 'Friend, I give you my kingdom and my daughter, if she pleases you.' He replied: 'Let us wait a bit, that we may make a little acquaintance with each other.' Thereupon they prepared a grand supper. They supped, and did not go to bed till late. In the morning they got up. The young man and the damsel went a walk in the town. The whole town rejoiced over him, and pointed at him, saying: 'That is our deliverer.'

Now the young man was content with all. Only he still felt sorry, when he bethought himself: 'Here am I in such good fortune, while my father on the Danube is thinking that I have fallen into the abyss of hell. If I could only just go to my father on the Danube, to tell him of my luck, I should then be completely content.' Thereupon the damsel said to him: 'I have something such that you could easily go to your father, if you would but be sure to come back.' He said: 'You know that I shall come. Nowhere have I had such good fortune as here.' Now they agreed that she would wait for him seven years, if he did not return before. The damsel gave him a certain ring, and said: 'Here is this ring, look through it, and think to yourself that you would like to be with your father by the Danube, and you will find yourself there. When you wish to come back to me, look again through the ring, and think to yourself that you would like to be with me, and you will find yourself here with me. But you must not show it to anybody, lest you lose it. If you lose it, it will be very difficult for you ever to come to us.' The young man looked through the ring, thought to himself that he would like to be with his father by the Danube, and in a moment there he was. His father and mother were very, very glad to see him safe and sound once more. They asked him all manner of questions. He related to them how he had darted through the water into an enchanted city, and what had been his hap afterwards. The whole household jumped for joy at hearing how fortunate he had been. Especially rejoiced was his mother, who walked continually on tiptoe for joy. Afterwards his father took him to his lord, for whom he still caught fish. There, again, the whole household rejoiced greatly over him. The lord had two daughters. Erelong he said to him: 'Stay with us. I will give you a portion of my kingdom and one daughter, if it pleases you.' He thought to himself: 'There there awaits me a whole kingdom, and a larger one than this. The lady, too, there, is handsomer than this one.' Nevertheless he said within himself: 'Suppose I stay here a day or two. I shall easily go back before the time is out. Seven years don't pass so quickly.'

It came to pass that he went a walk one day with the two daughters. On the road the silly fellow showed them the ring, and told them how he had come back into that country. They thought to themselves: 'Behold! if we could but take that ring from him, then he would be glad to stay with us.' They went a little farther on, and one of them said: 'Let us sit down a bit here in the shade.' They sat down on the grass under a tree. They had not sat there long when one of them said to him: 'Listen! listen! What have you got in your hair?' He: 'I don't know that I've anything.' She: 'You have something; you have indeed. Let me look at your head.' Now she began to examine and stroke his head till he fell fast asleep. The other, on seeing this, put her hand quickly into his pocket, and took out his ring. They rose up, and prolonged their walk. They walked and walked about the country, when he put his hand into his pocket, and found that the ring was no longer there. He said: 'I've lost my ring. What shall I do now?' They said: 'Let us go back. We will look for it. Maybe we shall find it.' They went back to the selfsame place where they had been sitting. They helped him to look for it carefully. They looked for it in vain, for one of them had gót it in her own pocket.

After this, he remained five years more in that house. When the fifth year had elapsed, he said: 'This won't do.

If I remain here, I shall never get to Perdonkorten. Now go I must. There will be two years for me, eventually, to get there.' Once upon a time he was benighted. He went through thickets, where there was no living soul. He espied a light on another hill. He said: 'Thither I must go. There will be people there.' He went thither. There was nobody at home but a woman. He asked whether they would take him in for the night. The woman said to him: 'I would willingly take you in for the night, but I do not advise you to stay here. My three brothers are three thieves. When night is over, they will come home, and will soon put you to death.' He said: 'Never fear! Only bring me a pint of wine, that I may drink and wait for them here at the table.' When night was over, up came the three brothers home. He sat in the house at the table, and busied himself with the wine. They asked him: 'Who are you?' He replied: 'I don't know who I am. I'm a poor fellow who roams hither and thither in the world, wheresoever I must.' They said: 'But to what family do you belong?' He said: 'That also I don't know. All through I am knocking about in the world. Nowhere am I at home.' They said: 'What is your name? How do you write yourself?' He had gone through the course of study at the black school; therefore he knew how they wrote their names, and that they had lost a brother. He therefore told them their surname, and the name of their lost brother. They said: 'You are indeed our own brother, whom we lost many years ago.' He said: 'It is easy to see that I am.' They asked him: 'But are you willing to take up our business?' He said: 'Why not, if your business is honest, and one can easily get one's living from it?' They said: 'From our handicraft a living is got right easily. At home we do nothing at all, and have always plenty to eat and plenty to drink.' He inquired: 'What have you gained to-day?' They replied: 'To-day we have gained more than we ever gained before. We have obtained shoes: whoever puts them on will fly two hundred miles in half an hour. We have obtained a mantle: whoever wraps himself in it, nobody sees him. We have obtained a hat: whoever puts it on his head, and throws it before him, hills open themselves to him, so that he follows it whithersoever he will.' He: 'But is this true?' They: 'It is.' He: 'Now, then, let's try this dress on me. We'll see how it will fit me.' He put on the shoes, wrapped himself in the mantle, clapped the hat on his head, and stepped a little way from them. He asked them: 'But don't you really see me?' They said: 'Nobody sees you.' Then he gave a jump, so that the earth quaked. They hurried after him, as it were, in the dark; but he escaped them, for nobody saw him.

He then flew to the place where the sun rises. He thought to himself: 'The sun gives light in all regions; he will therefore know the way to Perdonkorten.' When he came to the sun's house, he asked the servant: 'Is my lord the sun at home?' The servant: 'He is not; he is gone to give light on the earth. He will come home in the evening. You must wait for him if you want to speak with him. Only I tell you that when he comes home, there will be such a heat, that you will curl up like a rasher of bacon, if you don't hide yourself.' The traveller: 'If it is so, I will bury myself in the ground. When the sun comes home, come and call me.' He went, and did bury himself deep in the ground. When the sun came home and flew down, the servant came to call him. 'Now, then, my lord the sun is at home.' He got up and went to the sun. When he came into the house the sun asked him: 'What have you got to say?' He said: 'I have come to ask you the road to the city of Perdonkorten. You enlighten all lands; surely you know the way thither.' The sun: 'I don't know the way thither. It must be somewhere among hills and narrow dales, where I never go. The moon gives light more in hollow places; you must go where she rises.'

He went. He leaped, and was at once at the place where the moon rises. Neither was she at home. He asked her lady's maid: 'Whither has my lady moon gone that she is not at home?' The maid: 'She is gone to give light on the earth.' He: 'I will wait, then.' The maid: 'It is dangerous to wait. When she flies faintly shining home, such a frost will be caused that you will stiffen like an icicle.' He: 'I'll bury myself therefore in the ashes. When she returns home, come and call me.' Towards morning the moon came freezing home. He shivered in the ashes, but didn't stiffen. When the moon had put herself to rights, her maid went to call him, and said: 'Now come; the moon is at home.' He rose out of the ashes, shivered a little, and went to the moon. When he entered the house, the moon asked him: 'What do you want? What have you got to say?' He said: 'Nothing wrong, my lady moon—nothing wrong. I have come to ask you the road to the city of Perdonkorten. You throw light into all dark holes; therefore, you surely know which way to go thither.' The moon: 'I don't know that. It must be among such hills that I never get there. If you wish to learn it, you must go where the wind rises. He flies over all abysses, therefore he will surely be able to indicate you the way thither.'

In a jiffy he was there. The wind was just then at home. He asked him: 'My lord the wind, do you know the way to the city of Perdonkorten?' The wind: 'Of course I do. Anyhow, I'm going thither to-morrow morning at three. The king's daughter there is betrothed, and I am going to blow for them at the wedding, that it may not be too warm. But I shall go through such abysses and such rocks, that I don't know whether you will be able to follow me.' The traveller: 'My lord the wind, never fear. No rock will stop me. I have such a hat, that if I throw it, the ground opens and I go after it whithersoever I will.' The wind: 'Well, then, let us go.' They went at three. They came to a terrible rock. The wind roared, and made his way by a hole through the terrible rock. He could not follow him. Therefore he took off his hat and threw it against the rock. The rock opened. The wind glided on in front and he followed quickly behind.

When it was half-past four in the morning, they had made their way to the city of Perdonkorten. The wind went to blow at the wedding that it mightn't be too warm for them. *He* went into the church, seated himself on a bench, and waited for the wedding-party. At eleven music was heard, and fifty couples of wedding guests came into the church. One was more handsomely dressed than the rest. His reverence the chaplain proceeded to say mass for them. After mass he began to take the marriage service. *He* was sitting on a bench, but nobody saw him, because he had that mantle on. Suddenly he rose from the bench, and gave a thump on the chaplain's books, so that they fell with a bang on the floor. The chaplain said: 'One of you two must have such a sin upon him, that you are unfit to receive this sacrament.' Now the bride began to relate how someone had once come to deliver them. With this person a mutual engagement had been made that she would wait for him seven years, etc. The chaplain: 'How much time has elapsed?' She: 'Five years and a half.' The chaplain: 'Now you two must wait a year and a half more. If in that time nothing is heard of him, then you may marry.' The chaplain, moreover, asked her: 'Which would you rather have, this one or that other?' The lady: 'I should prefer the other, should he come. But I know that I shall never see him again.'

He heard these words, and they pleased him. Now they went home from the church. He who had thumped the books walked amidst the wedding-party, but nobody saw him, because he had the mantle on. The damsel's father thought it hard thus to send the wedding guests away home, therefore he gave them several cups of wine. The guests drank the wine, and *he* went up and down in the house, but nobody saw him. When all the wedding guests had taken themselves off home, he doffed his mantle, hung it on a peg, and they recognised him as their deliverer. The beautiful damsel met him in the middle of the house. She threw her arms round his neck, and said: 'Behold! to-day I should have been married to another hushand, if God had not protected me.'

Hereupon they soon prepared a marriage with this new bridegroom. They went to the wedding. The wedding passed off successfully. They got ready a right handsome wedding-feast for them. They had plenty of everything—plenty to drink, and plenty to eat. Moreover, they gave me wine to drink out of a sieve, and bread to eat out of a glass, and one on the back with a shovel. After that I took myself off.

LIX.—THE WHITE SNAKE.

ONCE upon a time snakes multiplied so prodigiously in the district of Osojani (Ossiach), that every place swarmed with them. The peasants in that district were in evil case. The snakes crept into the parlours, the churches, the dairies, and the beds. People had not even quiet at table, for the hungry snakes made their way into the dish. But the greatest terror was caused by a frightfully large white snake, which was several times seen attacking the cattle at Ososcica (Görlitz Alpe). The peasants did not know how to help themselves; they instituted processions, and went on pilgrimages, that God might please to remove that terrible scourge from them. But neither did that help them.

When the poor people were in the greatest distress, and knew not how to act to rid themselves of this plague, one day an unknown man came into the district, who promised to put an end to every one of the snakes, provided they could assure him that they had seen no great white snake. 'We have not seen one at all,' was the reply of some of the number that had collected round the stranger.

Then he caused a great pile to be constructed round a tall fir, and when he had climbed to the top of the fir, he ordered them to set the whole pile on fire on all sides, and afterwards to run quickly aside.

When the flame had risen on all sides against the tall fir, the unknown man took a bone pipe out of his pocket, and began to blow it so powerfully that everybody's ears tingled. Quickly up rushed and crowded from all quarters a vast number of snakes, lizards, and salamanders to the pile, and, driven by some strange force, all sprang into the fire and perished there. But all at once a mightier and shriller hiss was heard from Ososcica, so that all present were seized with fear and dread. The man on the fir, at hearing it, trembled with terror: 'Woe is me! there is no help for me!' so said he. 'I have heard a white snake hiss; why did you thus mislead me? But be so compassionate as not to forget every year to give alms to the poor on my behalf.'

Scarcely had the poor man uttered these words, when a terrible snake wound its way up with a great noise, like a furious torrent, over the sharp rocks, and plunged into the lake, so that the foam flew up. It soon swam to the other side of the lake, and, all exasperated, rushed to the burning pile, reared itself up against the fir, and pushed the poor man into the fire. The snake itself struggled and hissed terribly in the fire, but the strong fire soon overpowered it.

Thus perished, along with the whole lizard race, the monstrous snake which had done so much harm to the cattle. The peasants were again able without fear to carry on their occupations, and the shepherds at Ososcica to pasture their cattle without anxiety. The grateful people have not up to the present time forgotten the promise of their ancestors, and every year on that selfsame day distribute gifts of corn to the poor.

LX.—THE VILA.

ONE warm summer day a tall and handsome young man of Veprim was going over the hill Uczka, and found by the path on the grass a beautiful maiden, dressed in white, with a sun-kerchief, and was astounded on beholding the beauty of her countenance. Not wishing to awaken her, he tore off a large branch, and fixed it quietly in the ground, to form a shade for her. Erelong she woke up, saw the branch which had been planted, herself in the shade, and the young man standing by her. She asked him: 'Are you, young man, the person who set up this shade for me?' He replied: 'I am; for your appearance pleased me, and I was afraid that the sun would scorch you.' She said to him further: 'What do you want for this kindness?' The young man replied merrily: 'Allow me to behold your most beautiful countenance, and to take you to wife.' 'Good! I am content to take you for my husband,' said she; 'but you must know that I am a Vila. But you must never utter my name; if you speak my name Vila, I must quit you at once.' He promised that he would not, conducted her home, told his parents all that had happened, and how it had happened, only did not tell them that his bride was a Vila. She pleased them, and they willingly consented to the match. Erelong they were wedded. The two lived for some years in cheerful happiness; domestic prosperity continued in every shape and form, and she bore him a little daughter, beautiful as an angel.

Some years afterwards the young man one summer morning heard it thundering quite early. He got up, went to the window, saw that a terrible storm was brewing, and said to his wife: 'Wife, it is a pity and a great misfortune that we haven't cut our wheat; the hail will beat it all down.' She said to him: 'Never fear; it won't beat ours down.' After saying this she rose and went in front of the door. When she came back a terrible hailstorm began to fall. Her husband said reproachfully: 'I told you we should lose all our wheat.' She laughed at him, and said in reply: 'Go to the threshing-floor; you'll see that it hasn't beaten it down for *us*.' When the hail ceased, the husband did go to the threshing-floor, and there saw all the wheat nicely put together in sheaves, and, on returning, called out in utter astonishment: 'Ah, she is a Vila! she is a Vila!' But that moment she vanished. Her husband remained sad and sorrowful with his little daughter without his Vila wife.

The Vila mother still came back from time to time, visible only to her little daughter, helping her in all needs, as the most careful mother, until she grew up to a marriageable age. When the Vila's daughter came to the proper time of life, she married and was the ancestress of the present family of Polharski.—So the story.

THE END.

Elliot Stock, Paternoster Row, London.

www.ingramcontent.com/pod-product-compliance
Lightning Source LLC
Chambersburg PA
CBHW060517030726
47498CB00004B/983

9783744773416